All at Once

Alisa Clements

New York
Harvard Square Editions
www.harvardsquareeditions.org
2012

Published in the United States by
Harvard Square Editions

ISBN: 978-0-9833216-4-4

Front cover photographs © Alisa Clements

Harvard Square Editions web address:
www.HarvardSquareEditions.org

Printed in the United States of America

For Annie, Izan, Tao,

and my parents, without whom . . .

ESPEL VALLEY

FLORIAN

Soon after I returned, my parents begged me to accompany them to the Leveras' annual gathering. Ordinarily I would have found some excuse, but this time I agreed in order to humor my father, who had not long to live.

Our carriage rattled mercilessly on the rutted lanes, and I feared for my father's fragile bones. As we rode along the ridge, the sea glimmered through the trees, a reminder of the world beyond. I sighed. There was no denying that this island was a marvel of nature. A volcano had pushed it up through the ocean; its rolling hills were covered in abundant vegetation; its rivers teemed with fish. Our ancestors had been fortunate to find it uninhabited; their descendants were honest, hardworking folk, who enjoyed modest pleasures. Nothing much ever changed here; I thirsted for those other lands, vivid with curious sights and sounds, where the rhythms of life followed fantastic patterns. I had not come away from there willingly. Now, my world was reduced to the never-ending obligations of family life. How I yearned to escape again! But then my father coughed behind me, putting a stop to such unworthy thoughts.

By the time we arrived the sun had slipped below the

horizon. We were met at the door by old man Levera himself, who fussed over my parents and led them off down a corridor, leaving me to my own devices.

The affair was as dull as I had expected, but I contrived to maintain a pleasant demeanor. Thirty or so of us stood about, chattering as if our lives depended on it — until *she* came down the stairs and the room fell silent.

The babble started back up quickly enough. I watched her make her way through the crowd, straight over to the sofa where I had been trapped by the convoluted musings of an ancient chemistry professor. She sat down heavily, as if crossing the room had tired her, and floated a wan smile over to me. The professor vacated his seat, mumbling an apology. My new companion observed me with such interest that I was compelled to fix my gaze on the ceiling.

"You're Florian Marsden," she said at last.

I had to look at her. "And you are Zar."

"You're back, then?"

"For now."

"Well, that's all we have, isn't it?" She made a rueful face.

I would have rolled my eyes at that but could not be so unkind. At the same time I was oddly affected by her comment, as though she had offered me one of her internal organs on a platter — something intimate, best left concealed. I could not think of a philosophical answer. "Your eyes are very red!" I exclaimed instead. I thought the abrupt change of topic might seem endearing, like a child dashing about for no clear reason.

Zar and I had met many years before. Our brothers had been good friends, but as she was so much younger than I, and a girl besides, we had never had cause to converse. Still, it put us on a footing that permitted some degree of familiarity.

"Were you crying?" I pursued.

"No," she replied, "I was just in the sea."

"Really!" The exclamation erupted too forcefully,

embarrassing me. I looked away again, toward a nearby window, feigning a sudden interest in the view. By now the grass and trees had taken on a single murky color; the sky disclosed a few pale stars. The ocean was not far from the Leveras' house — I could hear its faint roar — but had she really been out there swimming at dusk? I imagined the waves smacking her bare skin, darkness gathering up those parts of her that protruded from the swells.

The image made me fearful: her daring repelled me. I felt almost limp in comparison. I knew then and there that a romance was out of the question, though Zar's features were pleasant and her figure quite shapely as well. As a girl she had been merely pretty; now the air of gravity she wore made her seem wise beyond her years. Perhaps we might at least be friends.

"Really," she answered, as if it had been a question. "My skin is still salty."

She held out her hand. Thick veins ran along the top; the nails were short and uneven.

"I cannot see any salt," I said, stupidly.

She extended her arm farther and flapped the hand in my face. "Taste," she said.

I could not help glancing out at the room to see if we were being observed. Only Genero, who had gone to the same school as we, seemed to be taking any notice. He was standing in the far corner with a drink, talking to an older couple. Although he was conversing animatedly, his gaze was fixed on us. I wondered why he did not look away when our eyes met; nor did he smile, or offer any form of acknowledgment.

Already I had hesitated too long — I did not want Zar to think me overly concerned with other people's opinions. I seized her hand and drew it to my mouth, turning it over at the last and flicking the palm with the tip of my tongue.

"Hm!" I said, nodding.

She withdrew her hand and laughed. "You couldn't *really* have tasted anything — that was much too quick!"

She was right. "Well, perhaps another time," I replied, hardly knowing what I was saying — out of the corner of my eye I saw Genero approaching.

"We might go swimming, if you like," she suggested.

"Certainly!" I answered, hoping she had not seen me flinch. Such boldness in a woman was usually a sign of moral dilapidation.

Genero was bearing down upon us. "Greetings!" he called out, more loudly than need be.

"Hello, Genero," I replied, with a warmth I did not feel.

"Genero!" Zar cried out in apparent delight. She leapt up and took his arm, saying, "Come, there are some people I want you to meet! I told them all about you!" Turning to me, she added, "Excuse us!" most pleasantly, and led Genero off.

I was a bit dazed. Were they sweethearts? Married? I had not seen a ring. Was she not a strumpet, then? Or was Genero only one of many suitors? I had been away too long to know the gossip — later I would ask my parents what stories circulated about her.

I was relieved that she had left — and disappointed. My heart beat quickly as though I were about to leap off a precipice. A tic started up in my left eyelid. I could not remain there on the couch.

On my way to the drinks table I was drawn into a chat with the formidable Silvia Neres and her mother, who wished to impress upon me their hopes that I would join the church choir. Fortunately the lights began to flicker, which meant that Mr. Levera's speech was about to begin and it was time to assemble in the main hall where the rows of hard wooden chairs awaited us.

Mr. Levera was a philosophical gentleman who bestowed his musings upon a select group of guests once a year. In truth, no one in attendance had come to hear his prattle — the prestige of an invitation was lure enough. The family inherited its distinction from Ebar Levera, one of the valley's first settlers, a charismatic preacher who had built houses, fed orphans, and tended the sick with unfailing dedication. The present-day Leveras kept up the tradition of charity, although they were rumored to be falling on hard times like everyone else. I had been dismayed to find, upon my return, that the barter arrangement by which our families had lived for centuries was no more: a new law obligated us to engage in commerce with the rest of the island. Most of the young people were in favor of the change: they thirsted for novelty and quantity and things only money could buy. We were coming to resemble the wider world, which was not all bad, yet during my years abroad I had gained a new appreciation for our singular community and its customs, and I was distressed to find its proud independence undermined.

As I gazed fondly at old man Levera, staunch upholder of altruism, declaiming from his little dais at the front of the room, something about him reminded me of Zar. His nose, it was — the tilt of it. Recalling the unlikely conversation I had had with that young lady made me wish to catch sight of her again. I scanned the crowd as discreetly as I could, dropping my handkerchief then bending to retrieve it so as to manage a glimpse of the people behind me.

As it happened, she was in the first row, so far to the left that all I could see was a patch of black hair and a streak of emerald silk. She sat next to her older sister Lenée on one side and Mrs. Levera on the other. Genero was directly behind them, no doubt so he could keep an eye on her without being observed in return. I imagined that if I were sitting that close I would know her to be conscious of me. She would pour herself into the space between us without moving a muscle and I would recoil, unable to withstand her explorations, unable to respond. All my traveling, I thought, to what end? All these years spent adapting to peculiar customs, learning to bend but not break, to hold my own center — yet in the presence of such a woman I become weak as a child.

Suddenly Zar turned and met my eye directly. I felt my thoughts laid bare, as if a bolt of lightning had struck the top of my head and ripped it off. She immediately turned back around.

For the remainder of the ceremony I sat staring straight ahead. When it was over I corralled my parents, making regretful excuses for us as I led them toward the door. Silvia Neres interposed her lustrous bulk; I swiftly dispatched her, then started to pry my mother away from Genero in order to get us that final step over the threshold, when I heard Zar's voice close to my ear, breathing my name.

She brushed by; she did not stop but only murmured, "I did mean it about the swimming." Then she vanished into the crowd.

Genero's attention snapped away from my mother immediately, so that with one last tug I got her outside; but before I could safely remove my father and myself Genero asked, in a rather unpleasant tone of voice, "What *did* she mean about the swimming?"

My father seemed puzzled, too, and I chose to address him rather than Genero. "Zar Levera," I explained. "She and I were discussing where it is safe to go swimming and where it is not."

Genero's expression suggested there must be more to the story; my father remained perplexed. "But you never go swimming," he said, crinkling his brow and beginning to pant a little.

"I do not *swim* often," I said, "but I do like to spend time at the seashore. Come, Father, you are getting tired. You should not be on your feet so long. Genero, good night. Father, come," and we left.

A week later, I was back. I had been reluctant to take Zar up on her invitation, but my personal code of honor requires me to face my fears. It had been a good while since I had been put to the test: living with my parents those first few weeks had not presented any challenges, although sometimes I half-feared I might die of boredom.

I had found out from circuitous inquiries that Zar Levera was considered an odd bird. People said she was "too clever," which seemed obscurely connected with the fact that she had not yet married. My mother found that a shame.

"Several young men have asked for her hand," she said, "but she's turned them all down. She is quick-witted, and no doubt a comely young lady, but there *is* something a bit unusual about her. I believe she doesn't have many friends."

I rang the Leveras' doorbell that afternoon, exactly one week after the gathering, and waited. I waited until I could be certain that nobody was home, and then I heaved a sigh of relief. It was the best possible outcome: I had proven my courage but it would have no awkward consequences.

Just then the door opened — it was Lenée, the sister. She was not surprised to see me. Before I had a chance to state my purpose she led me up a set of stairs, pointed along one hallway, and disappeared down another.

I went the way she had shown. A door stood ajar, letting daylight seep into the corridor along with a noise I found disconcerting, a sort of rippling moan. Were these the quarters of an invalid? As I drew nearer I realized the sound was too continuous to be a human voice — a mechanical contraption, perhaps? I reached the door and stood there listening, but could make no sense of it.

I peered in. Zar was standing at the open window with her back to me. Stretched across the window frame, from top to bottom, were a number of pieces of string.

"Come in," she said, without turning around.

"What is that?" I asked, walking up to the strings, which I now recognized as the source of the humming. Upon closer inspection I could see they were strands of sinew or something akin. The wooden support on which they were strung fit neatly inside the window frame and seemed designed to pivot.

"That's so I can angle it to catch the wind coming from different directions," she said.

"The wind is making that sound?"

"Lovely, isn't it? I saw one onee on a hilltop. Larger, of course. So I thought I'd try it here. I just finished it yesterday." She looked away. "That is, I suppose it's finished, although . . . well, never mind." She stared out at the ragged clouds scudding along the horizon.

"Is this your room?" I asked.

"I suppose," she answered abstractedly.

Was she trying to be philosophical again? Mysterious? I experienced some irritation but decided to proceed with my inquiry. I could not say I understood the point of her contraption but it had given me an idea.

"So you can do anything you want in here?"

That made her laugh and look at me. "Of course."

"Then why not place a second one of these in that other window? You could set them at different angles, then they would sing to each other."

She stared at me as though I had just appeared out of thin air. "That's it!" she exclaimed. "I wasn't happy with this one: I wanted to contrast the sounds made by different currents of wind as if they were separate voices and couldn't think how. That's the solution, of course."

"You could even put thicker strings in one window and thinner ones in the other," I suggested. "Or make it easy to change them around, and try out various combinations."

Zar beamed at me. She said, "I have more wood downstairs and I have more of these strings; the only thing we don't have here in the house are nails."

I smiled, reaching into the leather bag I always carry.

After fumbling in it a moment, I brought out five nails, all more or less rusty and not absolutely straight, but serviceable. "I find these in the road now and then," I explained. "The bent ones can be knocked straight with a hammer."

"It'll take more than five nails to do it," she said.

"I know," I replied, "but at least we could start."

"A good idea in principle. But weren't we going to go swimming? Isn't that why you came?"

"Well, yes . . . "

"Then," she said brightly, "we can start on *that* right away. Swimming. Since it came up first. We could always build the thing tomorrow. That is, *I* can. Of course, if you want to help, the work would certainly go much faster, but you might be busy . . . "

"I would like to help."

"Let's go for a swim now, then." She preceded me into the corridor, down the steps, and out the front door.

ZAR

Shortly after we met again, Florian and I went for a swim at Leaper's Point. The waves were colossal and sent up towering plumes of spray whenever they crashed; you could lean into the wind that blew off the ocean and it would almost hold you up.

That day, I realized Florian was a Companion, a kindred soul. I hadn't recognized him as such when we were children; when we met again at my parents' party I noticed only that his presence was warm and somehow comforting. I suppose I must've had an inkling of something deeper — why else would I have suggested we go swimming? He says I turned around during my father's speech and looked right at him but I don't remember that; at the time I was concentrating primarily on keeping up a barrier between Genero and myself.

Leaper's Point was the perfect place for us to become reacquainted. First, we rolled in the waves and laughed a great deal. Next, we explored inland a little ways, following a vague trail that came back out on the edge of a cliff. We collected pebbles and shells and odd bits of branch and a feather, wrapped them in a leaf, and threw the bundle into the ocean. We made another bundle and wanted to burn it to see what the things inside would look like afterward, but we couldn't manage to start a fire with two sticks. That is, we gave up trying.

Then we spent some time imitating all the sounds we could hear: rustling leaves, snapping twigs, breaking waves, each other's breathing. We played a kind of hide and seek, trying to find each other with our eyes closed.

As we made our way back to our starting point I was practically floating along beside my new Companion. My clothes were stiff with salt, my skin reddened by the sun; I had not felt so alive in a very long time. I had been so terribly solitary! We said our farewells after making plans to work on the wind harp the next day.

That night I took supper in my room. An entity had been hovering around me ever since I got home and I needed to be alone in order to find out what it was. As I ate, the thing grew denser, until I could almost see it across the table from me.

This was not my first otherworldly visitor but it was the most formidable so far — impossibly vast, as if it spanned years and continents and were just barely able to fold itself into my small quarters. Try as I might, I could not decipher a message or a reason for its presence, so in the end I ignored it as best I could and went about putting away my dishes and getting ready for bed.

When at last I lay down and cleared my mind in preparation for sleep, the presence, which had continued to increase in density, now compressed itself further and slid into the small inner vacuum I had created.

Images began to form behind my eyelids. At first just edges and half-shapes, coming into view and sinking back down — flotsam carried along by a dark current. If I looked at these forms directly they vanished, then I had to empty my mind again.

Suddenly a picture formed that did not melt away: it was Florian, wearing an expression of mingled terror and delight. He looked just as he had earlier in the day at Leaper's Point when, clinging to a bit of rock, he'd had to struggle mightily against the tide drawing him toward the open sea. Right next to that figure a second one took shape: Florian as well, but not as I'd ever beheld him: here he was glowering, jaw clenched, eyes downcast. Then another, and another, until a whole array of these images of Florian lay across my inner field of vision: the boy I recalled from my childhood, the robust young man with whom I'd frolicked in the waves, a grizzled elder. In several of them he appeared in odd garments, the likes of which I'd never seen before, and in landscapes filled with hosts of fantastic creatures roaming amongst gigantic blocks of stone.

Presently the likenesses began to blur and coalesce into a single shape, which turned out to be a baby. It was sleeping, one hand splayed open on its belly, the other clutching a brown blanket.

A sudden jerk modified my perspective: now I was standing right beside the child instead of watching it through a sort of spyglass. The rest of the surroundings came into view: a bare, whitewashed room, a curved window letting in a spray of light. There was a faint trickling sound in the background, as of a brook.

I started to remember where I was. What I had taken for the sound of running water, I now realized, was the muted babble of the party down the hall. I had only stepped away from it for a minute to check on my baby. How could I have lost my bearings like that, even momentarily? It was troubling — I would have to speak to Florian about it later.

As I gazed down at our son, worry gave way to the joy

that always suffused me in his presence. He was sleeping deeply but this did not hamper our communication: we exchanged greetings, delicate as two small pools of sunlight overlapping. Then we began to frisk and chase about, our weightless spirit bodies swooping round the room. Time and again he eluded me, swifter and more nimble in the chase; laughing, I sought a way to corner him. Might I become more agile if I closed my eyes?

The very instant I did so, a shocking explosion took place inside my head. Yanked brutally out of my senses, I understood nothing except the desperate need to retain a shred of self — then it was over and I lay gasping as if I'd washed up on a beach. Which turned out to be my bed.

Someone was knocking insistently at the door to my room. Dazed, I could not respond. As the knocking did not cease, I struggled to recover my voice. "What? Who is it?" I called.

The knocking only grew louder. Now I was irritated. I got up quickly and flung open the door. Genero stood there, looking sheepish.

"Hello!" he said.

"Genero, what *is* it? You woke me!"

"I'm sorry," he muttered. "Is it late? I was just passing by . . ." He kept his eyes fixed on mine while attempting to cram a large sheaf of papers into his back pocket; finally he gave up and produced the crumpled sheets apologetically. "As a matter of fact," he continued, a little out of breath, "I happen to have my collected works of poetry with me, and I guessed that you might enjoy leafing through them. Or perhaps you would allow me to read them to you? Poetic import is often best conveyed through the author's own rendition. . . ."

He trailed off, taken aback by my expression of disbelief. Then he turned cheerful, struck by a happy thought. His eyeballs darted back and forth. "Of course," he said almost slyly, "now that you're up . . . we could have some wine! If you happen to have any on hand. Or not? Maybe you'd just like to hear a few of the poems?"

I frowned. "Could you leave them with me?"

"Well, if you're certain . . ."

"You may read them to me some other time. I didn't know you were a poet, Genero."

"Most of them are about you."

"Delightful." I plucked the papers from his hand. "Thank you."

"Thank *you*. All right, then, I wish you a pleasant remainder of the night." He raised an upturned palm to the skies. "May slumber soft wreath your fair brow." The hand dropped heavily, slapping against his thigh. "So sorry to have been a nuisance," he said, moving slowly from the door.

"Goodbye, Genero." I watched him amble off, then I shut the door and returned to my bed.

The room felt more spacious: the presence had gone away. It had delivered the visions, accomplished its purpose. I cast my mind back to the images of Florian, the visit with the baby. With a mental lurch so abrupt it made my stomach heave, I knew: Florian was to be my life-mate, the father of my son.

I recoiled, as if threatened by a blow, and cried aloud: "But I don't want to settle down and have a child!" For years I had arduously defended myself from this fate. My interests and projects were so numerous and varied that I never had enough time for all of them, and any task I put aside, however briefly, nagged me like a jealous spouse until it regained my full attention. With a flesh-and-blood spouse hovering about, how much more cramped I would feel! Solitude was my most precious possession. Yet the oracle had spoken; there was no room for argument.

To be truthful, a part of me did want to be a mother. The man involved would pose the greater problem: he would expect much more than I could give. I saw a lot of work ahead: Florian would have to understand my terms. I had already observed that he was slow in some respects, slow to get to his feet or finish a thought; he'd asked me to explain some things I'd never before paused to consider. He had trouble getting around himself, as though he were an awkward piece of furniture. Earlier that day, I'd been tempted to startle him once or twice, to see if I could knock him free of his idea of who he was — but I knew that would only make him shrink back. If I lived with him, I would have to curb my impatience — not stir him up, just wait until the sludge settled and what was clear and fine about him drifted to the top. It would be difficult: I wasn't used to being patient with people.

Then again, once we were forced into close quarters, his torpor might prove beneficial. It would prevent him from trailing me too closely. And, too, he *was* a Companion. It was the only thing that made the union at all conceivable. This bond of kinship would hold fast whatever differences might arise between us.

Nevertheless — my mind still oscillating between favorable and unfavorable aspects — even Companions are not necessarily people one wants around one all the time. And it was difficult to imagine loving the man in any but a sisterly fashion: I felt no passion for him and didn't think I ever would. That would cause him to suffer — for this I was terribly sorry. I liked him so much! He was such fun to be with! It would have to work out. I would love him as best I could. It would be all right — it would have to.

I gave a big sigh, added a few more for good measure, and soon fell asleep.

FLORIAN

I spent most of that summer with Zar. Things got quickly out of control. I only mean that I had to throw off all caution, as far as other people's opinions were concerned. I did not care that they gossiped, and that wisecracks were made about wedding cake when we went to the baker's — with respect to the matter of a man and a lady keeping company, people's imaginations tend to be limited. I only wished that Zar herself would think along those lines, but by then I had realized that that sort of thing did not interest her in the least.

In a way, this was a relief: it freed me from the discomfort that had always suffused my dealings with unmarried women. They could be so predatory, these young ladies, so calculating, weighing my every word and gesture on invisible scales. To them I was no more than a cluster of attributes that might hamper or help them on the road to fulfillment. Being with Zar, on the other hand, was like trailing a wild animal, a large feline perhaps, whose attention alit on me only occasionally. Even though we often talked and laughed, she was on the whole so absorbed in her pursuits that a comrade could only, after a while, prove a hindrance. I struggled with this, trying to convince her that I demanded nothing. But always, after spending a day together, coasting along on a wave of hilarity that delivered us breathless and spent to her door, there would come a point when she wished me to leave. She would not say this outright, which made it all the more hurtful.

Over the course of a few weeks I had, in fact, begun to burn with a white-hot flame for Zar Levera. The power she exuded did not repel me any longer: now that we were allies, I felt protected by it. We were superbly matched as far as interests and perceptions were concerned and often exclaimed at our good fortune in having found each other; I knew she liked me very much. She just did not like me *enough*. I wanted to believe she was merely timid, but had she harbored any secret appetite for me, I should have known it somehow. I had to keep reminding myself of that. I refused to become another Genero.

That summer I had come to look more kindly on Genero. I soon realized he was not Zar's suitor: she had rebuffed him a number of times. Yet he was drawn to her, "inexorably, rollingly, illingly," as he put it in one of his interminable poems. She read a few of them aloud to me, first shuffling and clearing her throat as he would have done, then holding the paper mere inches from her nose — Genero was shortsighted — and letting the words tumble out in the thin voice that so closely mimicked his. It was cruel. Genero was in point of fact likeable and had interesting things to say when Zar was not with us, but in her presence he turned into a simpleton. I hated to witness that. I did not want to be anything like him.

In spite of what was lacking between Zar and myself, I found solace in the deep bond we shared — if it was not deep enough, it was that she had not learned to trust me as yet. "Give it time," I told myself. I frequently checked an impulsive word or gesture so as not to arouse her suspicions. Of course she might have guessed at my condition, but at least I kept from her its true extent: how ravaged I had become, how consumed and corroded I was beneath my stalwart exterior — thinking of her, watching her, wanting her.

One afternoon the two of us rode out to Canna. It was late August, the air still and hot, in the fields a prickle of crickets, thousands of them chirping in the long grasses. We made our way into the forest, refreshed by the shade and a swift-flowing river. Sitting with our feet in the water, we talked for a bit of the reflections dappling its surface, then lapsed into an easy silence. After a while I suggested we move on; to my great astonishment, Zar calmly removed her blouse and put it into her bag before standing up.

"I hope you don't mind," she said, starting off ahead of me along the riverbank.

I picked up my shoes and followed her. I was unspeakably aroused. It was clear that she thought nothing of her nudity and deemed me enlightened enough not to take it as a provocation; if she had had any idea how incendiary it truly was, she would never have done it.

I could see scratches forming on her bare back as we plunged through some thorny thickets. My shirt was off too, but I hardly felt anything of the vegetation I fought off as I struggled to keep up with her. I was completely numb above the waist; even my brain was hardly working at all. But what would happen when we got back out onto the path? I felt a thrill of terror, as though I were looking down from the edge of a precipice. People already talked about us. "Maybe I *should* marry her," I thought. "Then they will not have anything to gossip about."

I realized with a shock that I meant it. Until then, I had taken Zar's fierce independence for granted. But somehow, watching her weave through the light-dappled leaves, I began to imagine that lissome body belonging to me. I pictured the bare back writhing ecstatically under my hands as I rode into oblivion. I had been forgetting that she was in fact a woman:

she would have to say yes; eventually she would break down and say yes.

All of a sudden I felt immeasurably tall, secure, and very, very satisfied. I was completely confident. "She will say yes" — I could relax, it was only a matter of time. Slowing my pace, I watched her disappear through the trees ahead. After a while I could no longer even hear her. The forest was very still.

I took a deep breath and looked around. Nature returned my gaze, mysterious and benign. The trees seemed to approve of my standing as still as they. Why had I been chasing along so desperately? The heart's desire stays out of reach so long as one pursues it; I was supposed to have learned this lesson already.

I heard her footsteps growing louder in the bracken and there she was, standing in front of me with her beautiful breasts and the beautiful alive expression on her face.

"Where *were* you?" she asked, with curiosity rather than annoyance. "I thought you were right behind me, and then I just now turned around . . ."

I was stung. She did not know when I was near her and when I was not? This was a woman who could discern the fragrance of a blossom a hundred yards away; I'd wager she could pick a speck of salt from a handful of flour. Why would she pretend to have been unaware of my absence? Had she also pretended to ignore my eyes on her skin, had she deliberately tantalized me, was she playing that game? The surge of power I had felt before returned. She underestimated her opponent: *I* was playing to win.

Understanding her ordinary feminine wiles, I felt exceedingly tender toward her. She needed to be protected against people like me who could see past her façade. She was not a goddess — just a woman who'd fallen into that trap women do, of treating their men as though they were children.

"I was just . . . here," I said.

"Oh," she answered, glancing around. "Yes," she added. She put down her bag and settled herself on the ground, prepared to relax and drink in the surroundings.

"No," I countered. I took her hand, something I had never done before, and pulled her back up. Before turning away, I told her:

"You have nice breasts."

This time I was the one to lead the way, trampling and breaking off twigs and holding aside branches to make her passage as smooth as possible.

ZAR

Seven days after our marriage I began to seriously regret what I had done.

I had agreed to the wedding in a spirit of play. Florian, on the other hand, was dead serious about it; he had insisted that our union be formalized, though he couldn't explain why. The ceremony was elaborately staged in the traditional manner; many of the guests looked uncomfortable, as if they were witnessing something they probably shouldn't.

Not everything went as expected, including the entertainment we had planned. An acrobat was to burst into the hall and lend a note of mirth — so we hoped — to this solemn occasion. When the time came, however, he was intercepted by somebody's father, a cantankerous man who decried the performer's "outlandish appearance." The older man sputtered in drunken outrage, waving his fists in the air. The incident was riveting, but the acrobat had to withdraw and the general mood was one of consternation rather than amusement.

Later I saw this scene as a presage: nothing really came, ever, of the many plans Florian and I made. I had wanted our union to be as fruitful as possible: I already knew we would conceive a child, but I hoped we'd produce much more than that together. Although I'd heard it said that marriage could destroy the finer feelings between two people, I thought it nonsense. How could Florian stop being my dearest friend? The extraordinary fondness I felt for him could, when necessary, be converted into desire or something approximate, and it was possible that over time I might grow to enjoy our intimacy. I supposed this would happen in conjunction with a systematic study of certain ancient exercises for the development of vital energies, in which only committed couples may engage.

As it happened, a week after we were married I realized how mistaken I'd been about the entire venture. There was no need to wait to see what the future held: it was already plain. The slight but critical misalignment between us, whose significance I had blithely downplayed, would always be present. The passage of time could but widen the gulf, and Florian and I would one day find ourselves peering across it, scarcely able to make each other out any longer.

For the first few days I was starry-eyed: after all, I loved the man. The prospect of motherhood no longer unsettled me — I even had some fits of weeping, so badly did I miss the child I'd glimpsed but could not yet hold in my arms. I knew only patience was needed, as everything was already in place: I had an agreeable husband, amorous but circumspect, and a charming baby soon to come. All seemed satisfactory. Perhaps it was for the best that this illusion was shattered as swiftly and brutally as it was.

Florian had spent that day away from home.

We lived on the rim of Espel Valley, with a generous view of the sea. The house was a little too dark because of the trees pressing in on three sides — I couldn't bring myself to have them uprooted — but in all other respects it was ideal. Just the right size, made up of all the right shapes, it was soft, and changed with the weather. I loved the wilderness that surrounded us, too, the tranquility. There was no visible sign of human life apart from the road that brushed up against our land, a mile or so from the house. On the far side of it lived the Dermotts, a peaceable elderly couple; Florian's parents' property lay some ten miles beyond that. Florian had gone to his parents' house that morning: a meeting was being held to discuss the future of the farm, now that his father was no longer fit to run it.

Florian was gone all day. I'd been thinking of taking care of certain errands but had a strong feeling I should stay home. Sure enough, in the early afternoon there came a knock at the door; I opened it cautiously then flung it wide when I beheld the shining countenance of my beloved cousin Paol. Visits from him were all the more precious for being so rare — he was almost always off traveling somewhere. We knew each other very, very well: he had been my first real Companion. I had often spoken to Florian about him and I hoped he would stay until Florian got home so we could all have supper together.

After we had embraced, I invited him in. He hesitated on the doorsill a moment; once inside, his movements seemed constrained, as if he were afraid of knocking something over. I thought it best to lead him out to the garden. Before long, we had invented a new game, a sort of cross between tag and hide-and-seek, with absurd rules that caused a great amount of hilarity. Finally, out of breath, we draped ourselves over some boulders and talked for a long time. When we went back inside I made tea; we drank it in silence, watching through the bay window as dusk settled over the valley.

Florian came home. When he entered the room and saw us reclining there, Paol propped up on one elbow, my head on Paol's knee, he produced a strained smile. He looked haggard. Had he been forced into a larger role in the farm business than he wished to assume? It was likely. I would ask him about it in a moment, but first I had to introduce the two men.

"Florian!" I sat up happily. "This is Paol!" I knew they

would enjoy each other immensely. Besides, making a new friend would no doubt cheer Florian up and take his mind off the farm for a while. I rose and pulled Paol forward as though I were presenting Florian with a very precious gift.

"Paol . . . ," Florian said in a strange voice. He squinted at Paol's outstretched hand but did not grasp it. I was shocked.

Paol raised his eyebrows. He said theatrically: "I *think* I'd best be going now."

Florian regarded him with distaste.

"Florian!" I was incredulous. "This is my cousin Paol, whom I've told you so much about! Don't you remember: the fort — "

"The fort," Florian cut me off, "and the morning glories."

"You told him about the morning glories!" Paol exclaimed.

"Yes, well," Florian said. "If you will excuse me . . . " He disappeared into our bedroom and shut the door.

Paol and I widened our eyes at each other then frowned simultaneously.

"Ah, little sister," he said softly. "I suppose you know what you've gotten yourself into."

"No . . . "

"You're about to find out."

I didn't like the sound of that but it seemed useless to question him; he'd said I would see for myself and I trusted his keen intelligence. I leaned against him and he took me in his arms, wordlessly reassuring me of his abiding love, his faith that I could vanquish any obstacles.

The bedroom door flew open. Florian glared at us. Paol detached himself from me.

"I'll walk you partway," I said.

The night was clear; it was good to be out in the open. I went with Paol as far as the gate, then he convinced me to turn back. We hugged again. Over his shoulder I could make out Florian's silhouette at the window, unmoving.

"I'll see you in the future," Paol said. That could mean in six months' time, two years . . . he himself had no way of knowing.

"And how I look forward to that," I replied.

We bumped foreheads lightly, then I stood there watching him dwindle down the path into the darkness.

I didn't want to leave the wide night sky behind; I felt reluctant to let myself be swallowed up by the cluster of trees, the little house. I would go fetch Florian and bring him out for a stroll over the ridge to the ocean — it would surely lift his spirits.

As I walked back I mused that it would take some time to persuade him to accompany me. We would have to have a tiresome discussion first: it was plain to see that he was jealous of my cousin. This was absolute nonsense, and I would warn him never to treat any of my friends in that fashion again — it had made me very angry indeed. If Paol hadn't been so understanding, I would have been mortified by my husband's uncouth display.

Engrossed in these thoughts, I reached the front steps then stopped short, alarmed: an acrid miasma hung in the air. I held my breath and pushed upon the door. The fumes were in the house, too, but my attention was diverted by the evidence of some great upheaval: the sofa had been overturned, a picture knocked askew on the wall; everything that had been on the table lay scattered on the floor.

I knew Florian was up in the study — a sixth sense usually kept me apprised of his whereabouts. As I climbed the stairs, the fog grew stronger, nearly suffocating me as I pushed open the door to the study. I recognized it then: it was the stench of despair.

The lights were off. Florian was huddled in a corner of the room, crying almost silently, his head in his hands. In response to my entrance his misery changed to a vicious resentment that seared into me like a hot blade. To counter the attack I pictured a current of clear sweet energy entering the top of my head and pouring back out through my heart. This did not diminish his rage but deflected it, so that it flowed around and not through me.

"Go away," he said, very quietly, through clenched teeth.

"I don't want to," I answered.

He was up in a flash. His face twisted in agony; a bruise bloomed at his temple. Arms flailing wildly, he advanced on me. "Go away!" he screamed. "Get out!"

I contemplated honoring his request, but incredulity kept me rooted to the spot. He stared at me with loathing. I took a step backward to pacify him. Nothing had prepared me for this.

In one motion he jerked away and brought the side of his head crashing against the wall. "Get out, get out!" he snarled, and he hit his head again, this time right where the bruise was.

"No!" I cried, hurrying to him. I enfolded him in my arms; he sagged for an instant then stiffened.

"Let me go!" He struggled, not hard enough to break free. "Let me go — and go away! Please, why can't you understand? Leave! Now!"

It was clear he was trapped in a nightmare. Despite his entreaties, instinct told me to stay, to ride it out with him. I sensed that my unwanted presence might help purge the mysterious poison. I tightened my grip and hung on for as long as he let me.

Finally he twisted out of my hold, turned, and spat in my face. That nearly did send me away but I thought I'd wait and hear the explanations then and there instead of at a later date. They were not long in coming.

"You are my *wife*! I hope you realize that! That means something, you know? How can I bear it, knowing that anytime I leave the house some shameless scoundrel may creep in to cavort with you here on our sofa!"

I was horrified at his presumptuousness. I made a valiant effort to surmount my anger and speak calmly.

"Florian," I said. "My cousin Paol did not *creep* in. He's someone I love dearly and that's no secret — I've told you so several times."

"Loving someone dearly does not have to involve sucking their sausage, does it?"

"What?" Florian was rather prim, as a rule; I'd never heard him use such language.

"Well, was that not what you were doing?"

"No, Florian, it was not! And even if it had been . . . !"

" 'Even if it had been'? Then what?"

I was furious. "Then . . . then that would be fine, too!"

"Oh it would, would it?"

"Florian, you *know* what my philosophy is on all this!"

"Philosophy be damned — you're my *wife!*"

The truth of it stunned me into silence. Only now could I clearly discern the unbridgeable chasm between us.

He seemed to think my lack of rebuttal meant acquiescence. "No male guests allowed in the house when I'm not home!" he shouted suddenly.

"You must be mad!"

"I am entirely serious!"

The argument that followed lasted into the early hours of the morning and when it was over we retired to separate rooms.

That night something changed. The rift caused permanent transformations at the most profound levels of my being, destroying and reconfiguring the terrain of my innermost self: from then on a part of me was profoundly repelled by Florian. Eventually it got so that I could not even bear to have his hands on me. I was already pregnant at the time and couldn't tolerate much of anything next to my skin

— clothes, sheets — so that provided an easy excuse. Later I ran out of excuses. This physical repulsion was only the surface manifestation of a deep current of alienation, and though the next few years brought us at times closer, at times further apart, we never were able to fulfill the possibilities I'd imagined for us.

FLORIAN

"**W**hy did you marry her, then?"

I was sitting at my parents' kitchen table. I usually tried to avoid personal conversations with my mother, but this time her concern had worn through my defenses and I had wept hard and breathlessly as she stood with one awkward hand on my shoulder.

"Well . . ." I shrugged off her hand; she moved away. "I love her."

My mother began clearing the dishes from the table and taking them over to the sink. For some reason the sight of our son's little enamel cup and the spoon he had used threatened to bring on the tears again.

"But why didn't you wait a bit longer and get to know her better? I never understood why you wanted to rush into it in that fashion."

She took away the spoon and cup and began wiping the table clean. I had no answer; I could not confess to the intoxicating lust for power, for possession, which had given me no peace until I had led Zar to the altar. My mother sighed, went to shake out the damp cloth in the sink, and came back to sit across from me.

A breeze drifted through the window — Ara's thin voice floated in on it now and then, mixed with motes of dust dancing in the sunshine and the smell of new-mown hay. He was outside playing horses with his good friend Nooks, a farmhand who had been with our family for decades. I was glad Ara had left the kitchen before my collapse.

"I have always suspected that she pressured you into it," my mother said. As I opened my mouth to protest, she continued: "I've heard that the girl was desperate to get married to someone, anyone, when you came along."

"Hogwash!" I exploded. "She could have had anyone she wanted! You told me yourself she turned away any number of fools!"

"And you were the last fool left," my mother replied sharply. "Did you know how strongly her parents were leaning on her to get out of the house? They were having a hard enough time making ends meet, and she was practically taking the food out of the mouths of the younger children. She could've married, or gone out and taken up some suitable occupation to help with her expenses, but all she did was roam the woods or lock herself up in her room all day. She only came down to join the family at mealtimes." My mother grimaced. "Well, I can't pretend to know what was going on in her head, but her parents certainly are thankful that you came along. They didn't know how they were going to get rid of her."

I was stung. "They never seemed that poverty-stricken to me. They have that big party every year, for one thing."

"People have ways of disguising their circumstances. Indeed, they weren't downright starving, but there were other things. Their youngest boy was away at school and they could barely pay for it, all on account of an ungrateful girl who'd gotten her schooling and could have been making her own way in the world." She paused. "You mean she never discussed any of this with you?"

"No," I said. I could not explain. Zar and I tended to speak very little about things most people discussed as a matter of course. I always feared she would despise me if I tipped too far toward the ordinary; besides which, our union was founded on the premise that we understood each other more deeply than words would permit. I was good at *appearing* to understand, at least. I believed her when she told me I had extrasensory abilities — the only problem, she said, was that I was not conscious of them. But she was encouraging: awareness would come in time. She had all these plans for getting us to the point where we would do something she called AutomaTravel. I was more than willing even though I didn't know exactly what it was — I pictured the two of us climbing into some kind of fantastic miniature interplanetary conveyance. They would slam the doors on us, there would be a roar and a sheet of fire, and we would shoot off so fast that in less than a second we would be no more than a dot on the horizon. I was unclear as to what would happen to that dot, but I guessed I did not need to know. Probably something you could not explain in words. It sounded exciting, anyway — but it never did happen. Not long after we were married Zar completely lost interest in helping me develop my talents — or in doing anything at all with me, as a matter of fact. I did not understand. Nothing fundamental had changed in our relationship: how could it? We were like brother and sister — forever, probably even after we died, she had explained. Her certainty in this regard was tied in with some visions she had had early on of Ara and me. One night we were giving a party; the baby was sleeping in the nursery and after Zar went to check on him she came back reeling with shock, saying she had experienced that moment before. I was not sure how the eternal sibling theory related to those premonitory visions, but they had at least convinced her that the two of us were meant to be together. Who could contradict that, especially since it had come to pass? And yet, if our being together was predestined, why had it become so unsatisfactory to her? My wife shrugged off my questions and assured me nothing had changed; to insist would have been the reaction of the common man, so I did not.

My mother cleared her throat. "I'll go and see about Ara," she said. "He could probably use a bath."

"All right, Grandma," I answered. She went out and I returned to my thoughts. I never did understand why Zar was so upset by ordinary differences of opinion. She cherished philosophical ideals of freedom yet could not stand being contradicted. I tried to tell her that all marriages involve some degree of conflict, but she did not believe they should have to.

Jealousy was the first issue on which we took opposite stands. To Zar, jealousy was an annoyance like a severe cold: unpleasant, but one had to suffer through it. She said it was a usual enough feeling but didn't actually make any sense and one had to keep it under control. That was the kind of pronouncement I only appeared to understand. To me, jealousy was as indomitable as any other force of nature and when it rose up and took over, I did not think, I obeyed. Usually I exploded like a fireball — I could never contain it. Nor did I see why I should have to. If Zar's affection was deflected toward others, how could the two of us undertake the delicate exploration of our most intimate mysteries? According to one of her books, *Inner Friend, Outer Friend*, success in such endeavors was reserved for those who were able to train their attention exclusively on their partner and themselves. Zar claimed you could undertake these practices and lead an ordinary life as well, but the book called for asceticism. I piled most of our furniture away in a back room to demonstrate my eagerness for AutomaTravel; alas, it was already too late. Our first disagreement, concerning that unsavory cousin of hers, seemed to definitively set Zar against me — or rather, further apart from me. I thought there must have been more to it than that: married couples were always quarreling, then making up. Why did she have to hold a grudge? She said she did not, but she never treated me the same way after that.

Even so, we occasionally had some good times, as we had used to in the old days: we would embark on modest projects or set out for unknown destinations, and after finishing the task or returning from the excursion we would enjoy a few more hours of peaceable companionship. We had some tender nights under the stars or in the cocoon of our home, though these became steadily fewer and stopped altogether shortly after she was with child.

The months before Ara was born were the most difficult for me. Zar decided she had to spend as much time as she could by herself. It was as if I were falling down an interminable chute in the total darkness of incomprehension. Zar had a way of fitting a large distance into a small space: she would recoil from my touch only slightly, but I felt as if I had been hurled across the room. During her pregnancy she did not let me lay a finger on her. It was strange, what was happening to her: watching closely, as she had taught me to do, I saw her gradually cave in, like a hillside, in slow motion. Everything on the outside was slowly being torn down and pulled in to nourish the growing life. She was absorbed in herself — it really did not have much to do with me.

After repeated bouts of shouting and entreaties, which were met by freezing silence from her side, I gave up and left her alone. I would go instead into the woods and find a place where I could rant and rave without any witnesses. Then I would ride on to some suitably desolate spot — a part of the coastline, a hillside perch — trying to avoid places Zar and I had gone together. I would set my wrung-out self down and slowly let a sort of peace seep in. At those times I let my defenses down completely and was so raw that whatever I saw or heard I also felt: a creaking bough could set off a twinge in my heart; the monotonous chirping of crickets would cause my teeth to ache.

Sometimes, instead of staying by myself, I would call on Dommy and Carl. We had grown up together, part of a whole clan of boys from different families who had reached manhood around the same time. Eventually, fate had led us all down separate paths; Dommy and Carl were the only ones I still visited. They were not much given to talking about problems, but they could sense my distress and find clever ways to distract me from it for a few hours. In the end, though, I always had to return to the oppressive gloom of our small house, through which I roamed uneasily, my spirit restless and empty.

At last, however, an auspicious event brought new hope and cheer into our home: our son was born.

I was just at this point in my reminiscences when my mother came back into the kitchen pulling Ara behind her. All I could see of him was the arm she was tugging at: he seemed to be pushing against the doorjamb with his other hand, trying to prevent his feet from crossing the threshold. He was two and a half years old.

"Let go and he will come in," I told my mother. She released his hand.

"I will not!" Ara shouted, from just beyond the door.

I grinned. "Stay out, then!" I called back.

My mother shook her head. "If you keep letting him have his own way in everything, he'll turn out just like his mother." She stood there waiting for an answer, her hands on her hips.

Ara's head appeared behind her at thigh level then dropped suddenly to the ground. He reached forward and began laboriously dragging his body into the room. When he had pulled in everything but his feet, he stopped. Then he lay still, apparently satisfied.

My mother turned around and peered out the door.

"Where . . . ?" she said, then looked down and saw him. Ara closed his eyes and pretended to be sleeping.

"What in heaven's name are you doing down there?" she

asked. "Now your clothes will be as dirty as the rest of you! Florian, the child is a disgrace. He agreed to take a bath, but only if I would promise not to get his feet wet. Now how am I supposed to do that? I told him I would cut them off for him before he got into the tub. Then he became very naughty and tried to run away. Luckily Nooks caught him for me; I don't stand a chance, because of my bad knee. I don't know what you're going to do with that child."

"Nothing," I said. "Ara, come here."

He opened his eyes to check my mood and intentions; reassured, he got up, ran over to me, and clambered onto my lap. He was indeed filthy. His eyes shone out from a mask of dirt and dust. Some of his hair stuck up in wisps; the rest was matted to his scalp. Although his arms and legs were bare he appeared to be wearing brown gloves that reached to his elbows and knee-high brown boots.

"What were you doing?" I asked.

"My horse fell in some quicksand," he said. "It almost drowned, but then it got saved."

"I pulled him out," my mother said. "He had Nooks dig a hole in the yard and put water into it and he was in there on his hands and knees for God knows how long. I don't know why that man doesn't have more sense than to encourage this foolishness."

"A bath is certainly in order," I replied. To Ara I said: "If you want your feet to stay dry, you can stand on your head in the tub."

Ara was good at standing on his head. He liked the idea and slipped off my lap, ready to go; I reckoned he would change his mind once the bathtub started to fill up. My mother made a disapproving face.

"Will the two of you be staying for supper?" she asked.

"No," I said, quickly inventing an excuse. "Dommy and Carl invited us over."

I had not known where we would go when we left home

in the morning; I just knew I had to get away and wanted Ara with me for comfort.

"There are some clean clothes of his in your old room," my mother said.

Ara and I went off to the bathroom and discovered that if I ran a very shallow bath for him he could easily lie in it with his head *and* feet sticking out of the water. Afterward he ran around the bathroom, squeaky clean except for his mud-boots, which now only reached to the tops of his ankles and left dark prints all over the floor.

By the time we had wiped everything up, the afternoon light was golden and the air tinged with coolness. We rode away on Starling, the roan mare, as my mother stood at the door and waved. I held the reins in one hand and Ara before me in the saddle with the other. He waved back and kept his eyes on his grandmother as long as he could — he loved her, though he did not always understand her.

A pleasant journey across the valley with Ara's wiry little body warm against mine: he sang and called out the names of things and so did I. It occurred to me that I was more like a grandfather to him: these past few years had aged me unduly. At home especially I felt like an ancient, creeping around the house trying not to make a sound so Zar would not know where I was. Not that I had anything to hide, but for some reason I simply did not want her to be able to track me. I had the feeling she could do so despite my best efforts, which then caused me to worry that I was turning into a paranoiac.

We had settled into the routine of a couple married twenty years, sometimes taking breakfast together, sometimes not. The atmosphere was neither hostile nor warm. There was not much left for us to talk about . . . except Ara. Ara was the ray of light. He made it bearable. We were united in the joy of bringing him up — not to say that it was easy.

Materially, we were all right. The farm was prospering, though I felt uncomfortable about lining my pockets with profits skimmed off the workers' backs. The whole business of money was still strange to people of my generation, who had seen the commerce of our isolated community shift from an exchange system to a money-based one. We questioned the premise of assigning numerical value to goods and labor, contesting it even as we struggled to live by its rules. Young folks growing up now, on the other hand, cared more about the cash than about how it got into their hands. Zar and I were trying to educate Ara to be conscious of every aspect of every situation he found himself in, wanting him to be as clear-sighted as possible — despite the fact that his natural lucidity presented us with a real challenge sometimes.

I hugged my boy a little harder until he squirmed.

We reached Dommy and Carl's at dusk. A chill wind had picked up. The windows glowed invitingly; as I tied Starling to the post I was filled with pleasurable anticipation at the prospect of a long comfortable visit, gossiping and joking with the two men. I would sink into my favorite armchair with my feet up on the cherry-wood table, a glass of sweet wine in my hand, as Carl lit the fire — according to him, Dommy did not know how. We would joke and discuss nothing much at great length while Ara tumbled about, occasionally drawing us into his games.

He had already gone into the house by the time I finished tying up Starling, and when I got to the door I was surprised not to hear the laughter and exclamations that usually greeted our arrival. The house was silent.

"Ara?" I called.

No answer. I went down the hall and peered into the drawing room.

There he was, in a big chair that almost swallowed him up, staring solemnly at a young woman seated on the other side of the room. She was the prettiest woman I had seen in a long time. Her hair was blond and untidy, her face milky like clouds on a night of full moon. Everything about her was soft, from her expression to the curves beneath the cotton dress, but there was no weakness there, the softness that of a newborn foal getting to its feet a few minutes after birth. My knees buckled — I felt like a grandfather once more.

"Hello," she said pleasantly.

"Good evening," I replied. "You have already met Ara. My name is Florian. Excuse us for intruding like this. And you are . . . ?"

"Emily — a cousin of Dominic's. Carl and Dommy went out to get some wine, but they were supposed to have been back by now. I'm glad you're here — it was starting to get boring." She smiled at Ara. "I like *him*. Does he talk? Can he do anything besides sit?"

Ara continued his impersonation of a rock.

"No," I said. "He is incapable of sound or movement."

At this, Ara jumped down from the chair making wild guttural noises. He did a crazy whirlwind dance in the middle of the room and ran out. Emily looked at me inquiringly.

"He will be fine," I said. "I think he has never seen anyone like you in his life."

I did not feel like playing games with this young woman, despite the immediate and powerful attraction. I was all-over weary, unwilling to relinquish the relaxation I had expected the evening to bring. I decided to simply enjoy her presence as I would that of a fragrant bouquet — it need not detract from the comfort of the armchair, the fire, the good-natured bantering of Dommy and Carl or the wine they would bring with them when they came. I wanted to pull this girl to me like a pillow and curl up there on the rug. My spirit was sore — she would soothe it. She would do everything in her power to please me, demanding nothing in return.

"What do you mean, he's never seen anyone like me in his life?"

"Anyone so beautiful," I said. "Emily, I am tired."

"I can see that," she replied. "Why don't we sit by the

fire? Dommy started it before they went out."

"*Dommy* started it?" We laughed.

She rose from the couch, taking up two cushions and throwing one to me, then went and sat on the hearthrug. She placed the cushion behind her and lay back. "Come tell me why you're tired," she said.

Ara traipsed in and out of the room several times while I was explaining it all to her; he looked at us with interest but did not want to be included. He would stay a few minutes then amble out again, conscious of our gaze upon him, muttering to himself or swinging his arms like an ape. Each time Emily would turn back to me, demure but curious, and press me for more details. We were so wrapped up in what I was saying that we even let the fire die out; when Ara next came in, he asked us why it was so dark in there. Emily turned up the oil lamps and went to the kitchen, returning with some food and drink that she shared out as she listened to me. After we ate, Ara dozed on my leg. Finally Dommy and Carl returned, stumbling and laughing.

"What's going on here?" Carl roared, and they both fell out laughing again. On their way home they had stopped in at a party and polished off a good bit of their wine; they had a long story about one particular guest who had said and done various preposterous things while they were there.

The rest of the evening passed in a blur. We had a lively time. I took care not to drink too much so as not to make everything still hazier; in truth, I was vividly aware only of Emily. Her presence imbued me with a great sense of relief. She was very friendly but never once indicated, by gesture or implication, any physical attraction to me. When we said good night she gave no sign of wanting to meet again. I was already passionately in love.

"She'll be staying with us for a week," Dommy said on the doorstep.

I knew that she was his only cousin; that she lived in

Erinor and was a seamstress, unmarried. I hoisted sleeping Ara up over my shoulder and shook her hand.

"It was nice meeting you." I could not think how to say what I really felt. On an impulse, I added: "See you tomorrow."

She looked surprised, pleasantly so. "That'll be fine," she said.

All the way home I felt incredibly light, vaporous. Even coming through the dark trees into the dark house did not dampen my spirits the way it usually did. I went about putting Ara to bed and getting ready myself without any concern as to how much noise I was making in the process.

ZAR

The long days, the long nights. I had trouble sleeping. I had let myself fall deeply, so deeply; now I was coming back to consciousness like someone mistakenly buried alive without a casket, breathing in crumbled earth and coughing it out, a damp weight pushing on me from all sides. This is why I was having trouble sleeping: because I was waking up. I could only see darkness, but at least I could see! The will to fight myself out rose up in me with a panic. Where had I been? How had I got there? I remembered burrowing feverishly. So it wasn't true that I had simply fallen — I had willed myself there? I hadn't known what I would find. I didn't know what I had found. The previous few years melted behind me, became a single moment. In this moment Ara was growing up, Florian, too, and I was . . . I was . . . that was the mystery. I remembered well enough what had occupied my time, but it didn't seem to have *brought* me anywhere.

Of course Ara was bigger, and that was something, but his life wasn't mine. He was so clearly an old soul with a mission — I could help him along only because he was still hampered by his child's body and reasoning, but as soon as he could he would be off, gone from me. His curiosity was boundless; he liked to do a lot of roaming. My hardest task was restraining him or bringing him back when he'd been out too long or too far. He hated me for it — he wasn't yet wise enough to forgive. Other than that we got on splendidly, and the deep recognition between us never changed.

Aside from providing guidance to Ara, my chief occupation was furthering my studies, which I had to do on my own since no partners had presented themselves — Florian, unfortunately, was not suitable. The gap between us was impossible to narrow and I found myself increasingly unable to present only a half-face to him, the part he found acceptable; I felt I was betraying myself and preferred to avoid him entirely. He got a lot of good out of that, though he never would admit to it: he learned to think for himself and not, as he had practiced during his travels, like everyone else, nor, as he had tried so long to do, like me. In his solitude he seemed to develop a finer feeling for things, a more confident step. He was becoming better friends with himself; I could see it in his face. I was only sorry he continued to be so shaken by our estrangement, but when I wasn't directly in his presence I thought of him very little. I was working my way through the *Universal Treatise of Ancient Wisdom,* which involved learning Sanskrit and some delicate gymnastics.

The image I retain from those years is a diorama: our little house huddled in its trees, Ara straining against the fence, Florian saddling a horse, and myself locked in the study with the soles of my feet pressed to the top of my head. That was the tableau from which I slowly began to extricate myself. It took weeks, months. I left off my exercise regimen and instead followed whatever impulse arose. I began feeling tenderly toward Florian again, so knotted up and terrified of me; I made tiny overtures to which he responded gingerly. I stayed closer to Ara, accompanying him on his rambles and observing silently as he performed his incomprehensible rituals. I could tell he liked having me there though he appeared to pay me no mind.

A restlessness gathered momentum inside me, a strange craving, I didn't know for what. I began dropping by the Dermotts' regularly; it started with a few tablespoons of sugar that I needed in a hurry and turned into an almost-daily chat over a pot of tea. I found the older couple not as dull as I'd assumed; though slow-moving they were observant, and Lucy Dermott's irreverent comments often made me laugh. They accepted my company without questioning why I had kept aloof for so long. If they thought me odd it didn't bother them. Sometimes I brought Ara with me — I was pleased that they treated him as a person, not a little child.

It was during one of these visits, when I was trying to describe the strange urge I had been feeling, that Lucy startled me by suggesting:

"You would make a good teacher."

I was momentarily taken aback. I had been looking for an answer on a different plane, trying to puzzle out philosophically what was necessary for a human being to achieve in this life and what was not.

"You would," she insisted. "You're very curious, and you're good at sharing your curiosity."

"But what could I teach? I don't know how to *do* anything, really."

"People already know how to do too many things," she said. She shifted in her chair, settling herself more comfortably. Lucy was a squat woman who had never suffered the handicap of good looks; she made no effort to disguise her intelligence. She always put me in mind of a friendly toad, never more so than when sitting in that particular armchair, which appeared to give her a broad hump and a pair of haunches.

"What they need to learn," she continued, "is how *not* to do anything. Anything with their hands, at least. You could teach them how to see better, how to listen for things, how to feel a little more. I've watched you with Ara. All children need that kind of training but too few of them get it. It would make them better at whatever it is they *do* want to do."

"I don't know," I said. "Whom exactly would I teach? I know what the school is like. I can't imagine they would let me teach seeing and feeling there."

"There's a new school, too," Lucy answered. "Did you know about that?"

I didn't. I didn't know that much about our community; I knew who most people were but always encountered them when I was on my way somewhere and never stopped long enough to inquire about more than the state of their health. The other couples our age already had larger families, and while Ara occasionally played with some of the children, Florian and I kept our interactions with the parents to a minimum. I couldn't remember hearing anything about a new school.

"Where is it?"

"It's in Tucan" — the next valley over. "They teach all sorts of things there. I think they would like you."

I could feel gooseflesh stealing over me. Anytime something of powerful significance is mentioned, even if I've no idea what that significance is, all the little hairs on my body stand up. I can't explain the phenomenon; all I know is that it's a reliable indicator, an exhortation to pay close attention.

The conversation turned to other matters, but as Ara and I were leaving, a while later, I remembered what Lucy had said about the school and was instantly covered in gooseflesh again.

"Thank you for giving me the idea about teaching," I said. "What is the name of the school?"

"It's called Red Pepper," Lucy said. "An unusual name, but it's certainly fitting — from what I've heard, the children there are a pretty spirited bunch. Well, you'll see for yourself." Lucy seemed certain I would visit the school on the strength of her suggestion; suddenly I knew she was right.

She continued: "When you get there, ask for Miss Wolcott. She'll show you around. And tell her I want to know when she's going to get rid of that terrible man who keeps breathing down her neck all the time — her mother's been complaining to me."

I laughed. "I'll be sure to ask her."

On the way back to our house I considered the idea of teaching. It was new but already seemed familiar. From that, the gooseflesh, and Lucy Dermott's contagious enthusiasm, I knew that the Red Pepper school would play an important role in my life. It gave me a lovely warm feeling to imagine myself ensconced in a quirky pod: the children would be bright-eyed, the teachers friendly and open. There would be a common goal, everyone focused on the process of self-realization.

By the time Ara and I got home, I was thrilled. I wished Florian were there so I could tell him about it, but he was out as usual. He worked long hours at the farm, and I knew he occasionally went riding by himself or visited friends; he never spoke of whatever else he may have been doing. During my long slumber I had been glad not to have to know anything about him — now my curiosity was returning, but he wasn't matching the pace of my thaw. After the initial shock of seeing me emerge from isolation, he had struggled with his lust, his loneliness, and his injured pride; the pride had triumphed and Florian retreated to a safe distance. Whereas I now would've liked to know where he went and what he did when he wasn't working, he didn't volunteer the information and I felt too shy to ask. We stayed on safe ground, mostly discussing Ara; sometimes he would talk about his father's farm and the pressure the family was under to turn the farmland over to the government.

I had started smelling a woman on him when he came in sometimes. This emanation was an insubstantial aura rather than an actual scent — it took me a while to realize what it was. I knew he snuggled himself in its cloak, thinking it invisible to me. I detained him every night now for an after-dinner chat; as soon as the conversation ground to a halt he would retire gratefully to his room. There he would revel in the residue that clung to him, imagine it back into flesh and have his way with it. With her, whoever she was.

I had no wish to find or confront her: I was not jealous in the least — which is why I was surprised to find this development so troubling. I still felt no desire for Florian and was relieved that he had found a source of comfort. I only wished he had the decency to confide in me, as his friend, as the mother of his child — to talk to me about the joy she brought into his life. If I'd been anybody else, any other human living under the same roof, he would've told me straightaway. The rejection hurt terribly. I was ashamed to have made any advances and retreated some distance back into my own shell. But I continued to miss the wholesome camaraderie we'd had in the early days; I wished he could unbend a little and allow me to be good company, instead of perpetually hurrying out to chase down the Mystery Woman.

I heard Florian's step on the path. I was glad. Now I could tell him about Red Pepper and the gooseflesh, and get him to help me think of things we had learned raising Ara that could be included in a lesson plan.

When the door opened, Ara dropped the book he had been leafing through and ran to greet his father. Florian swung the child around by the ankles then gently laid him on the floor where he remained immobile, watching the room spin, a beatific expression on his face.

Florian then turned away and took off his coat and boots. Knowing I was looking at him he made his face impassive. The woman smell wasn't on him, only the faint scent of horses, earth, and open air.

"Daddy, you were at the farm?" Ara asked.

"Yes, I was," Florian answered.

He moved past me with a brief apologetic smile as though we were strangers in the narrow corridor of a crowded railway carriage. My eagerness to speak with him evaporated — he wouldn't want to discuss anything with me. I went up to my room and sat there glumly, listening to the two cheerful voices accompanied by sounds of cutlery and scraping chairs in the kitchen below. I was no longer excited about the Red Pepper school. It was ridiculous to have imagined I could teach: I felt heavy and despondent; what enthusiasm did I have to impart? Doomed to isolation, I would stay locked inside this little dark house, inside the mute awkwardness of my peculiar personality, forever. I began to cry.

After a while I heard Florian go out again. Ara ran upstairs to look in on me: seeing my tear-swollen face he raised his eyebrows inquiringly. I could give him no explanation and he went away, leaving me even more bereft. Bleak solitude stretched endlessly ahead: had I risen from one living entombment only to be trapped in another? I could not withstand it — this time it would kill me. I must save myself somehow, though I felt powerless to do so. If only something or someone would come to my aid! There was no more solace to be gained from my private studies: the ineffable void only became the more ineffable the deeper one penetrated into it. Florian had placed himself out of my reach, and though I could always draw strength from Ara, it was unfair to him and would not sustain me. No disincarnate entities had visited me in a long time. The chaotic busy world of ordinary people, which I had always shunned, was the only door I hadn't tried. An answer might lie behind it. In the morning I would ride over to Red Pepper. Even if I couldn't teach, there might be something else I could do to help them. Lucy had said they would like me; she wasn't one to say such things lightly. That gave me hope. It was the only one I had at the moment.

I went to find Ara, helped him to undress, and brought him to bed with me. He seemed fine, just tired. He sank into a leaden sleep; I followed him.

Early the next morning I rose in a mood of grim determination and began getting myself ready. Florian had not come home — it was the first time he had stayed out all night. I woke Ara; after breakfast we set out for Tucan.

Autumn had stretched itself over the countryside, idly picking clean the skeletons of the trees. A few ravens spiraled up in the bitter wind, protesting hoarsely at our passage. Ara was still sleepy; he said nothing.

When we reached the outskirts of Tucan I began looking for someone to ask directions of, but the streets were bare. We stopped at a small shop, empty except for its proprietress, a woman muffled in a shawl. She knew of the school and explained how to get there.

It wasn't far: after another five minutes' ride we turned off the country road onto a dirt track that led through a pasture and ended at the front door of a long, low, whitewashed building. Children's voices rang out occasionally from behind the misty windowpanes. A thread of wood smoke wound its way out of the chimney; Ara sniffed the air with pleasure. We dismounted, gave the horse some oats and stroked her, then went to pull the bell-cord.

A thickset, ruddy-faced man opened the door; he was out of breath. Wiping the sweat off his brow with a large handkerchief, he tried to shush the shrill cries of a pair of tiny children tugging at his pant-legs.

"Is Miss Wolcott here, please?" I asked.

"She is. She's just finishing up a lesson with her group; can you wait a bit?"

"Certainly. May we come in?"

"But of course!" He bent down to shake Ara's hand.

"James Sonnet," he said.

"Ara Marsden," Ara responded.

Mr. Sonnet straightened up and grasped my cold hand in his big warm one.

"I'm Zar Levera," I said.

"Pleased to meet you. Kindly follow me." He led us into a small, overfilled room. Books, baskets, papers, pieces of wood, rag dolls, butterfly nets, lengths of rope, and swatches of colorful cloth were among the objects heaped onto every surface. Mr. Sonnet cleared off a chair.

"Perhaps you would like to come with us?" he asked Ara. The two small children squealed delightedly. Ara looked at me.

"Well, I don't know . . . ," I began. Seeing the familiar flush starting to darken his face I asked Mr. Sonnet: "What do you have planned?"

"It's almost time for refreshments — my helpers and I were putting the final touches to the preparations. Would you enjoy helping, Ara?"

"Yes!" Ara cried, going over to take the man's hand.

I was astonished. I had never seen him approach a stranger so readily. And yet, I always trusted Ara's instincts. His immediate reactions to people were founded on an intuition less clouded by experience than mine.

"I'll see you in a while," I said. They left in a hurry.

I sat on the dilapidated chair and looked around. I felt I knew the room already; I couldn't think why until I realized it was the kind of familiarity that is linked not with the past but with the future. It had been many years since I had experienced such a strong precognitive intimation -- my last visions had been those of Florian and Ara, long before Ara was born. I'd since been waiting for another sign, additional intelligence from the Beyond, and the longer I'd waited the more fearful I'd become that this avenue of insight had been closed off to me permanently. Now it seemed I'd been told, and told again, that the Red Pepper school had an especial significance as yet unknown to me.

A loud sound startled me out of my thoughts, a sustained tone that filled the air completely. It cut off abruptly; there was complete silence in the building then an eruption of dozens of voices; chairs were pushed back and small feet clattered on wooden floors. The door opened and Miss Wolcott — I presumed it was Miss Wolcott — came in. She was an unusually handsome young woman, though with something strangely fluid about her features.

"Miss Wolcott?" I said.

"Please call me Emily," she answered.

"I'm Zar — Zar Levera." We shook hands, then she sat on the edge of the table near me. I noticed that her face seemed a little shaken under its pleasant smile. It reminded me of a milk pudding that hadn't quite set. Perhaps she'd had a trying class — I remembered the kids at Red Pepper were supposed to be "spirited," and I wondered if she'd been teaching here long. "My friend Mrs. Dermott gave me your name."

"Oh, Lucy Dermott! Such a wonderful woman!" Emily said. "She's a friend of my mother's."

"She said you might have something for me to do here at the school."

"Oh!" Emily seemed shocked, then recovered herself. "Quite possibly! Of course, such a matter is not for me to decide — I'm just one of the teachers — but it's true that we've been shorthanded for a while and could use some help. What did you have in mind?"

I didn't understand her initial dismay, but I assumed she simply hadn't been expecting an inquiry of that nature. Probably she had thought I was a prospective parent come to ask about fees and things of that nature. I explained my predicament to her as well as I could: my lack of work experience coupled with a strong desire to share what I knew. She listened thoughtfully, chewing on a stub of pencil. I liked her. She was neither arrogant nor subservient. Her interest in me seemed genuine, and she offered a few surprisingly insightful questions, drawing me out. When I finished, she said:

"I think you would like it here. Red Pepper methods are certainly nontraditional, at least as far as local traditions are concerned. Our primary mission is to help children develop all of their faculties. Whereas a satisfactory level of accomplishment in the academic subjects is encouraged, this usually comes about naturally as the children's perceptions expand. I could give you the standard speech about our educational philosophy, but I expect that taking a tour of the school would be the best introduction by far."

The door opened: it was Ara, dropped off by Mr. Sonnet, who waved and disappeared again. Ara seemed to have had a very good time. He came toward us slowly then stopped short, looking at Emily with great interest.

"Ara, this is Miss Wolcott."

"I know," Ara said.

"When James told me that you were here to see me, he introduced Ara," Emily said quickly. "A charming young man, indeed!"

"I forgot to tell you!" I had suddenly remembered Lucy's message. I went on in sepulchral tones, as if transmitting otherworldly knowledge: "You must get rid of that unsuitable man who has been keeping you company!"

Emily seemed more disconcerted than amused. I realized my attempt at humor had fallen short and resumed my normal voice. "Lucy told me to tell you that."

"Oh, she did!" Emily half-laughed.

"Why — has someone been pestering you lately? Or is the fellow not in fact as terrible as all that?"

"There is no one, really," she said.

"Oh?" I paused. "It's the same for me, I suppose," I said, surprising myself. Something about the woman prompted me to confide in her. "It's possible to have a companion who isn't there *really,* if you know what I mean."

"I can imagine," she answered. At that moment I caught a whiff of Florian's characteristic scent, as though a stray air current had coaxed it from a hidden pocket. I supposed that meant he was thinking of me. I wondered what he was doing right now.

"Mommy, I want to go home," Ara said, coming over to me and pushing his face into my thigh.

"But honey, we were just going to take a tour of the school with Miss Wolcott! What's the matter? Didn't you have fun?"

He didn't answer. I touched his forehead: it was hot.

"I think perhaps he had too *much* fun," I told Emily. I felt overtired myself. Pleasant though our conversation had been, I was not used to interacting with strangers — it was a strain. In any event the groundwork had been laid; there was no need to rush into things.

"Perhaps we could come back in a few days," I said. "You might talk to the director or whomever is in charge, and meanwhile I'll give some serious thought to outlining a course of study. I have a better sense now of the school's philosophy, and there will be time to delve a bit more deeply later on."

"By all means," she replied warmly, getting to her feet. "I did enjoy making your acquaintance. I hope you *will* come back."

I stood up as well.

"Goodbye, Mrs. Levera. Goodbye Ara," she said.

"Goodbye," he mumbled, without looking at her. His listlessness worried me; I was eager to get home as fast as possible, give him some tea, and have him rest.

"Goodbye Emily. I enjoyed meeting you as well." I really had. She was not a Companion, I was fairly certain of that, but maybe she could be a friend. I had no close female friends; the idea excited me. It would be an ordinary, lighthearted friendship: we would talk about books and opinions, go for walks, have dinner at each other's homes. Florian would realize that I was not completely dependent on him for companionship: it would be a relief; he might relax a little more. The fact that another person valued me, sought me out, might make him sit up and take notice. I could even allow him to become a bit jealous. Emily would be faithful to me — she would come over for dinner and we would go off again just the two of us, laughing, to finish the evening at her place.

Suddenly I felt suffocated, almost nauseous. It was all too much, overwhelming. I was eager to get away from there. Emily had led us back to the front door, and once we were outside I gathered Ara up onto the horse. He did not seem at all well.

We got home quickly. I gave Ara some ginger tea and put him to bed. Florian returned a few hours after we did, showered, changed out of his farm clothes, and went out again.

That night my head roiled with new possibilities and it took me a long time to fall asleep. Then I had a sort of nightmare: I dreamt I was up to my knees in quicksand and Emily was watching me with a compassionate air. Even as I continued to sink, this evidence of sympathy greatly reduced my fear.

FLORIAN

"You must bring your lover by to meet me," Zar said one evening. I was stunned. But then, it should not have been a surprise. I had always wondered exactly how much she knew or suspected, with those uncommonly developed antennae of hers. But as she never brought up the matter, I did not either — it was easier that way.

After a while I had not even bothered with pretense. I would stay out for several nights in a row, coming home only briefly for fresh clothes and to spend a bit of time with Ara. I supposed Zar did not give a fig about that side of things; she had humiliated and pushed me away until I had finally stopped trying. If she did care, she hid it well, and if she was hurt it served her right. Let her put her lofty ideals about jealousy into practice! At least her philosophy made me feel less guilty about what I was doing. Anyway, we did not talk about it because we hardly talked about anything meaningful; it would have been vulgar to choose *that* as a reason to resume a dialogue.

I was relieved when she issued the invitation. I had half been expecting some kind of confrontation and imagined it would take a more disagreeable form, even though Zar had not seemed angry. In fact, these last few months had brought about a startling change in her: she seemed more present than she had been for the past few years. Downright friendly, even, as if trying to make up for having frozen me out so thoroughly and for so long. There had been times, before, when I would have done anything to wring a drop of warmth from her — my inability to achieve this caused a pain so sharp that I would have preferred to die. Once, I even stopped eating, in order to put an end to the agony of it all, but instead my senses sharpened and I felt five times more alive; my despair was miraculously skimmed off, exposing something like a small root, naked but indestructible, I had not known was there. And then, gradually, I stopped caring so much. Part of me still wanted nothing more than to throw myself on Zar and lose myself in the beauty of her unspeakable wisdom. To have her stroke my head and hum softly, as she did with Ara, would have erased the years of anguish, would have made me whole again. But by now I had become a bundle of scar tissue and could not soften toward her, would not: my defenses packed in and held upright the growing fragile sprout of my new strength.

Emily helped me forget what was left of my terrible longing. It stayed there, forgotten. I buried myself in her. I could not get enough of her spreading sweetness; she was vast and cool, cheerful and uncomplicated. With Emily I could be myself — there were no hidden dangers. Not that she was simple: she knew a lot and carried it well. She understood my awkwardness and stubborn ways, and accepted me as I was. Through what miracle did this luck fall to me? The best-looking woman within a hundred miles! I was given the evil eye at the post office, the general store, and the farmers' market in three different valleys. I was considered odd already and the fact that I, a married man, had conquered such a desirable unwed maiden did not enhance my reputation. Of course Zar must have heard about it. I decided to act nonchalant.

"What do you have in mind?" I asked. "A cup of tea? Dinner? Or merely a quick inspection at the door?"

Zar rolled her eyes. "Are you serious about her?"

I had to blush. I said yes.

"It's a matter of principle: you shouldn't have to skulk about like that."

"Skulking! You see me go out, don't you?" I was indignant.

"That's just it: you have a perfectly good house, with plenty of room in it . . . "

"What are you saying?" I asked.

"Honestly, Florian, don't make yourself out to be a simpleton. It wastes time."

I swallowed that one: she was right. I slowly began to realize that she was serious. That she would make a point of championing that beloved philosophy of hers. Could she actually stand to stay in the house while Emily and I made merry in one of its rooms? It was preposterous; she was going too far.

Then I thought of how the journeying back and forth from Emily's place had been wearing me down. She lived with an elderly aunt who could not be permitted to see me come and go — I had sustained a number of scratches from the rosebushes beneath her window and lost a great deal of sleep in the past weeks. How convenient it would be to have my lover here instead! I looked at Zar. It was just possible. It really was possible. This woman was a genius. I felt a rush of love for her that frightened me: I had been able to suppress those for a long time now. But perhaps she was bluffing.

"Are you saying I should bring her here to sleep over?"

"Why not?"

We could stay in the back room — it was set off from the rest of the house by a corridor; noise would not travel. I liked that room: we kept it bare, except for a straw pallet; it had a nice window. The early morning light would fall on sleeping Emily. I hadn't had a chance to see that yet, although I had set myself the task of studying Emily's naked body in as many different settings as possible. Because I always had to leave her before dawn I had never seen her contours slip out of the shadows, edged with silver, then blossom in the full light of day. I was obsessed with Emily's body.

"Oh, Zar," I said, and sighed. I felt grateful toward her — humble, as I had back when she treated me as her pupil. I said: "I will ask if she wants to spend a night sometime this week. Maybe I can help make dinner."

"Hmm," Zar said. "Does this lady have a name?"

"Her name is Emily. Dommy Wolcott's cousin."

Zar opened her eyes wide. "Oh really?" she said. "What does she do?"

"She teaches at a school in Tucan." Emily had gotten the job shortly after I had met her. She taught the children how to card and dye wool, spin, weave, and sew. Some of our happiest times were spent in the forest gathering armfuls of butterwort and indigo to make the large batches of dye she needed.

Zar had a strange smile on her face. "Well, speak to her and see what she says." She turned and left the room.

I felt giddy, as though I had just robbed a bank and were gazing at the stacks of banknotes waiting to be spent.

Emily came over the following Wednesday afternoon. I had gone directly from the farm to meet her at Red Pepper. As we approached the house my nerves were raw, but she was calm as ever.

"Afraid of what?" she had asked as I lay beside her gnawing my fingernails, the night after telling her of the invitation, which she had promptly accepted. "The woman wants us to know each other. It makes sense, after all. If we don't get along, that'll be too bad. That's the worst that can happen as far as I can see."

Emily always could see far. That knowledge reassured me. Still, I wanted to argue: it seemed like there *must* be a significant problem, something to prevent such a meeting taking place, but when I opened my mouth nothing came out: there was nothing to oppose.

As we walked together toward my front door, however, I was seized by a terror that made me desperate to flee, and I had to fight myself to stay on the path. Under any other circumstance, with Emily only inches away, I would have plunged my panic into her arms — to have to refrain from that was an additional torment.

As it turned out, I need not have worried. It made me look like an imbecile. There I was, straining to appear unflustered, as the two women greeted each other with a perfectly ordinary degree of politeness.

The evening went very well. Ara, of course, was a helpful presence. I had worried that he might be indiscreet, perhaps refer to some intimacy he had witnessed between Emily and myself, but he was pretending he was meeting us all for the first time.

I relaxed somewhat when the women went into the kitchen, leaving me with Ara.

"What do you think of all of this?" I asked him.

"Do I know you?" he answered.

I had to think about that one. "Are you knowing me right now?"

"Yes."

"So then you know me."

He was not convinced. "I don't know you. I never saw you before tonight."

The game had possibilities but I needed to concentrate on what was happening in the kitchen. I diverted Ara's attention to something he could play by himself and sat listening. I was too far away to distinguish words: I could perceive only a rhythm with ample but not overlong spaces between the sounds. The lower voice was Zar's; the overall tone of the conversation was calm yet lively. They were probably not talking about me.

In a little while I went into the kitchen and offered to help. Zar was busy snapping beans into a bowl; Emily was rolling out some kind of dough and soon had me forming it into patties. They laughed at my clumsiness and I did not let on that it smarted. I told myself I might as well enjoy being in the presence of the two people I admired most in the world, and tried to slow my pounding heart.

They conducted themselves admirably, of course. Nobody even came close to scratching anybody else's eyes out. We improvised a meal out of an unlikely combination of ingredients: the preparations were suspenseful, the outcome surprisingly delicious. Emily, being the most socially graceful, was always able to steer the conversation away from any potential unpleasantness, and the three of us talked easily; for the most part I took my cues from them.

In the later part of the evening I did take some initiative, suggesting we play a parlor game that used to be Zar's favorite. It consisted in building up a story: we took turns adding one word at a time. Each player would further or thwart the gist suggested by the previous players' choices, while trying to maintain some thread of logic. It was challenging, the results unpredictable. We were laughing for a long time after Zar read it out loud.

It had been ages since I had spent time with Zar in this manner. It was good; *she* was good, very good. At one point I felt some pangs in my stomach, so strongly that I could not dissimulate them. I believed that they were due to the conflicting emotions I harbored but blamed the ale I had drunk. The two women suggested mint tea as a palliative, so mint had to be picked — in the dark — and brewed and so forth, with more jollity and jesting throughout; by the time I finally got to drink the damn thing the pains had disappeared anyway.

When it came time to say good night, Zar left us in the living room.

"See you in the morning," she said.

"See you!" Emily answered cheerfully. Her hand was already on my shoulder. Earlier in the evening I had let it rest there briefly but had then felt compelled to shrug it off.

I took her to the back room, which I had tidied up earlier in the day. Ironically, we fell asleep forthwith, perhaps because we had both had a slight excess of drink with dinner — Zar did not partake. I remember only that I flung myself down on the bed and hugged Emily gratefully to me.

Next thing I knew the room was awash in sunlight; it must have been approaching midmorning. Groggy, I scrambled to my feet and peered at the clock on the dresser. "Damn!" was the first word I uttered, pulling on my pants. I was already over an hour late for the meeting with the conservation representative who was coming to talk with us about our farmland.

I took a moment to gaze fondly down at Emily, who blinked back at me from within the blankets.

"Do you want to come with me? If so, you will have to hurry." I did not want to wait, but courtesy required me to offer.

"No." She stretched and curled up again. "I want to sleep a little longer. I already told them I wouldn't be coming in today."

I was glad to be able to leave right away. I was dressed, needing only to put on my boots, which I had left by the front door. I got on my hands and knees to give my lover a kiss then went straight through the house and out. My head cleared as I rode over to the farm; I felt refreshed, washed, new, incredulous, grateful, blessed.

EMILY

"Hello Emily" — they pass and talk through me. Neither one is dangerous on their own. A little pitiful even; I love them the more for it.

The man is hopeless, of course. He has been charging at me relentlessly, he never seems to tire. I tolerate him because I've been lonely. He's gentle, yes, and handsome; he has a playful manner. He could easily be someone's Everything but unfortunately that someone is not me.

The woman is a different story. I have loved her since I first saw her. She is a leaping flame. Very dark. But transparent. Bubbles trapped in it. She is sharp, that one. Swift cuts. I love her so much I could explode; I do not stop exploding.

When all this started, I had no idea. It was just a dalliance with the man. He did not want to talk about his wife and I certainly did not either. He was so wild about me that he did his very best to please me — and his very best is actually quite good.

That part of it is all shriveled and cracked now. The woman's dark star eclipses anything that has to do with the man and with anything else.

ZAR

She came into my bed. She might've had an instinct that took her straight to where I was; more likely she tried every door until she found mine.

I had heard Florian rush out and was lying there listening to the sounds coming through the open window, birdcalls like strings of bubbles underwater, the dry staccato of crickets. Then came a noise I didn't expect, close by. Someone breathing. Knowing it was she, I lay still and waited.

"Don't scream," came her voice from just behind my ear.

"You couldn't make me." It was a statement of fact but I think she took it as a challenge.

Now the weight of her knee came onto the bed, warm against my shin through the blanket. She paused, then brought the rest of herself up and sat with her back against the wall and her knees crooked over mine, not touching them. I still wasn't looking. Every social instinct I had cried out for me to do something, say something, but I was more curious to know what would happen if I didn't. She didn't do or say anything either.

I had never met anyone like her. Our natures were

different. Hers had a narrowness I was sure very few could detect, and she knew I had perceived it. She was immensely attractive: I felt the magnetic pull, but it made me slightly nauseous as well, as if I were inhaling vapors of ammonia. On the whole, to have her on the bed with me was reassuring only *because* she neither moved nor spoke. That established kinship between us.

I probed to see what she was doing on an energetic plane. She was not in fact pushing as hard as I would've expected, but she had woven etheric cords between her body and mine, and had already knotted the ends in deep. At least I knew she wouldn't try to hurt me, given the burning tender passion that radiated from her end of the cords. I swiftly severed them: her body slumped sideways on the bed.

"You're very strong," she said. Her voice was muffled. After a pause: "Can I touch you?"

She lowered herself so that we lay face to face, though I could only see one bright eye past the mound of blanket between us.

"No," I said.

We stayed staring at each other for a long time. Her gaze traveled occasionally over my face. The one eyeball seemed curiously lubricated. It slid around as if unattached to the socket. The iris was gray, the pupil intelligent, voracious. Whenever I looked all the way into it, I felt in danger of fainting, and would retreat to its surface, to the minute convex image of myself reflected there.

I found myself quite enjoying this unusual interaction, when suddenly her eye glazed and became still. That could only mean she had entered a more absolute state of perception. Intrigued, I unfocused my own eyes and went after her.

She was opening herself to me: she wanted me to explore her, just like that, without moving or touching or even looking; she wanted me to penetrate every hidden chamber so she wouldn't have to be so alone in there. It was purely selfish: she was eager to give herself away, like a dog turning on its back to have its belly rubbed. All she saw of me was what would fulfill her need.

I refused to do it. I couldn't help knowing more than I wanted to already, from what had passed between us there in silence: I'd been suffused with the swirl of ambition, loneliness, confidence, and fragility that was her essence. But there were some dark pockets I recoiled from, horrible things; I was under no obligation to accompany her there — I didn't know her, nor she me.

"Is Florian not enough?" I asked abruptly, though I knew. Her eye slowly refocused.

"Florian?" she wondered, as if she'd never heard the name in her life.

"My husband? I thought you were acquainted?" I was picking up the thread of the previous night's game, in which Ara had so readily joined us. When Florian introduced us, Emily and I feigned we'd never met. I hadn't yet been back to the school, and the occasion to converse with Florian about it hadn't arisen. Pointless though it was, the pretense established a complicity that made the evening more pleasurable. I believe it heightened our sense that we were acting, she and I, acting out the roles of Wife and Mistress, which helped us to interpret them in ways that flaunted convention. Florian, in his ignorance of our complicity, could not help but seem a little foolish to us.

"I like Florian," she said.

"He more than likes you," I answered.

"Well . . . ," she said. I hadn't realized she was as unattached as that. It made me glad.

She had raised herself slightly so I could see her whole face; now her eyes ran boldly over the outlines of my body under the blanket. Her curiosity was innocent and unashamed. She stared as if by staring hard enough she could pierce the blanket. A vibration started up deep within me, somewhere in my midriff. It spread like wildfire in dry grass, outward in all directions, until I was ablaze; the hairs on my arms stood on end. I didn't know what she had done. Suddenly I ached for her.

I reminded myself that she only wanted me for her own purposes. Apparently she had esoteric skills and used them tactically. I could tell she had never had any training: she operated out of instinctive wisdom without the sense of ethics that training usually imparts. Evidently she had no compunction about manipulating people. No wonder she had Florian wrapped around her little finger.

Quickly, I created an etheric shield like a transparent bubble around myself. Normally I would've used my hands to draw its contours in the air; it sped the process up — but I didn't want her to know what I was doing. I was excited to have encountered an opponent who could function on these planes; I respected her, but I would have to teach her a thing or two. That would be easier if she remained, for a time, unaware of my techniques.

Once I sealed the bubble, the fierce pounding within me turned to a dull throb. I registered a corresponding dejection in her face.

"You'll have to make do with Florian," I said.

It was cruel, impossible, but she would think that I meant it. I wasn't prepared, however, for her answer:

"No. You are mine."

Absurd. Yet her tone held a subtle violence; she believed what she had said. The principle was unacceptable; besides, I hadn't fought myself out of Florian's stranglehold at such great cost only to subject myself to another's. The woman was decidedly deranged but possessed, as lunatics so often do, a measure of uncommon lucidity that enticed me. Her ability to meet me on some of the most rarefied levels of awareness made her a source of very possible delight. What if she was right — what if I were, in fact, hers? She might be just insane enough to be channeling some genuine insight.

With these thoughts, my protective bubble began to thin. The lattice of its invisible fabric stretched: pores formed, then gaping diamonds. I was letting too much through. The pulsation began gathering intensity again.

"I think you'd better go," I said.

Emily rubbed her face with one hand, very thoroughly, pushing the cheek flesh up into the eye socket and down over the jaw, massaging the brow, coming down roughly over the nose and mouth. Then she opened her eyes and looked at me: her expression was clear, untroubled.

"We have all the time in the world," she said.

She slipped off the bed, crossed the room, and went out the door. I smiled and stretched out.

EMILY

I am part of the household. We are putting on an addition to the back room so there will be a washroom and another area to cook and eat in and a door to the outside. The man throwing himself into it, ordering special painted tiles. The woman acting the role of a housewife: "Be careful with that hammer, darling!" I'm in the middle, not expected to do a thing, I'm a pet; they house and feed me. They're not doing it for me, though. It's for us.

She won't let me touch her. Or rather, she does — in every way but skin to skin. That contact she won't allow. No rubbing up through clothing either. Damn her.

My taste for the man has fallen away. He'll know that when I let him. Not just yet: he's too happy right now.

It is really *my* house — they are the furniture. I pass in and out of their lives as I've passed in and out of so many. I spend little time with them on the whole. Nights, mostly. Convoluted velvet nights.

<u>SALVADOR</u>

JOSEPHINE

The sun smothers me like a thick coating of grease, wedges itself into the little creases of my neck and arms, works its way into my ears and under my clothes. I wade through the heat that swims up from the cobblestones, pausing to rest now and then in patches of shade cast by diminutive balconies. No trees on the streets, though bushes and saplings sprout from cornices of abandoned churches and through the ornate façades of ruined colonial houses. At this time of day anyone with half a brain in their head must make it a point to stay inside: there's almost no one around except for some tourists getting the most out of their sightseeing dollar. Wiping the sweat from their eyes, they meander dutifully between shops offering gemstones, postcards, handmade lace, percussion instruments, and *capoeira* gear.

I'm scanning the storefronts, too, trying to find an Internet café so I can send off a message to Ralphy, my best friend in San Francisco. I need to let her know what an incredible idiot I am — a discovery I just made today.

I got here yesterday evening, intending to get a good night's sleep before starting in on the field research. I timed my arrival for just after Carnival — sorry to miss the big party, but fares were a whole lot cheaper. The plan was to take two weeks to research and write my chapter on Afro-Brazilian spiritual symbolism, then go back home to edit it. What I didn't know — until this morning — was that I actually picked the worst possible time to come: all the *terreiros*, the houses of worship where *candomblé* is practiced, are officially closed between Carnival and Easter. I simply can't believe I missed that fact in my preliminary research. So when I showed up at the tourist info center bright and early this morning to sign up for a tour and found out the terreiros were closed, I almost broke down and cried. Since firsthand observation of the religious ceremonies is essential to my work. I'll just have to stay put until the terreiros open up again. This trip is going to wind up costing me more than anticipated, and I hope Ralphy will accept to look after my cat and handle my finances a bit longer than we had agreed on.

The discouraging thing is that I think I've already seen about all I want to of this city. The part I'm in now, bristling with churches and tourist traps, is known as the Pelourinho. Named, my guidebook informs me, after the pillory that used to stand here as a means to discipline rebellious slaves, the neighborhood retains a subtle aura of anguish. The Portuguese architecture is quaint, and the crafts on display are kind of interesting, but that's about it. The rest of the city, what I've seen of it on the way from the airport at least, is a cheerless sprawl: six-lane highways snaking past twenty-four-hour supermarkets and huddles of high-rise tenements giving way to sidewalks clotted with grimy merchandise downtown. Nothing to convince me that I'm in Brazil, although glimpses of exuberant vegetation suggest a tropical latitude, and the people come in more different shades of brown than I've ever seen in one place before, even New York City.

A bus lumbers by, engulfing me in a cloud of black smoke. I realize my search for the Internet café isn't very methodical; maybe I'm dawdling because I have no idea what I'll do with myself after I send the e-mail. I can't sit inside the hotel — I'd suffocate — and I'm not eager to perch in a café or on a park bench or trail around a museum; I've done enough of that in Europe already. Maybe I'll just go looking for the library my guidebook mentions: not too exciting either, but there might be a small chance of finding something that could pad out my thesis.

There's only one thing I really *want* to do, not today but soon, and that's go to the ocean. I've always liked the ocean. At home I sometimes pack up a picnic, put my cat in her carrying case, and drive out to Stinson Beach. I spend hours watching the waves roll in, letting their hollow roar wash through me, while the cat hunkers down in the sand with her ears back and sniffs the salt air. Here in Salvador, it seems like the sea is almost always visible from wherever you happen to be, but they say the water's heavily polluted until you get farther up the coast. That's where I'd like to go. Take a bus up there or somewhere beyond and spend a day. Maybe I could even find a place to rent, some dingy but clean bungalow with a sea breeze rippling the thin curtains. The hotel I'm staying at now, near the Pelourinho, is horrible. The building is dark and cramped, jammed between an adult film theater and a pawnshop on a narrow side street; the only window in my room gives onto a corridor. This morning at breakfast a fellow guest told me I'd been crazy to go strolling around the neighborhood at night. She was Austrian, the first person I've had a real conversation with since I got here, but she barely spoke English and the only other language I know is Spanish, so our interaction was limited. She's been here for a few weeks and kindly tried to impart some of the wisdom she's acquired: she told me to stay away from the men and the misery. At least I think that's what she said — her Spanish wasn't so good.

Pondering this advice, I almost walk right past a sandwich board that says INTERNET — AQUI. I push open the door and find myself in a small room where ceiling fans creak above five computers, all of them occupied. A few people are waiting and I take my place at the end of the line, propping myself against the wall.

Ten minutes later the line has only moved ahead by one; I resort to my guidebook, checking to see whether there are any events of interest scheduled to take place at this time of year. There aren't. I turn to the back of the book and start studying the list of useful phrases — "Where is the drycleaner's, please?" — when suddenly the lights go out, the computer screens darken, the fans slowly wind down. Since I hardly speak any Portuguese I improvise a kind of sign language to ask the woman next to me: Should I wait? Will the power come back on? She assures me it will, but no one seems able to say how long it might take.

I hesitate on the threshold before stepping back into the scalding sun, then set off for the library.

By the time evening comes, I'm thoroughly depressed. The library turned out to be a bust: I know enough Portuguese to decipher the titles of books but nowhere near enough to read through the ones that interest me. Why didn't I wait to learn the language before coming? I curse my recklessness, my blithe assurance that a reasonable command of Spanish would get me by. There went my only hope of getting anything accomplished while waiting for the terreiros to reopen. Now what? I don't know a soul in this city. The Austrian woman left. The only people who've tried to make my acquaintance were a trio of unappetizing men; when I tried to evade them they pretended not to understand and kept whining and pawing until I very firmly said the word "Polícia." Then they peeled themselves off with hate-filled eyes — "frigid bitch!" — and slid away. No one else has approached me, except, in passing, to try to sell me things. I'm not used to being so completely alone — I almost wish I'd brought my cat. The isolation, on top of the unfamiliar climate, food, language, and people, might well prove too much for me.

I know it's too early to tell, but I suspect coming here may have been the biggest mistake I've ever made. Everything is too loud for me here, turned way too far up: the sun is outrageous, the faces in the street so striking I can barely look at them, and then there's the music. Music, in one form or another, overwhelms me at every turn: drunks at a bar sing off-key and pound on tabletops; hippie kids float past with tambourines and flutes; a rhythm clangs on a lamppost, backed up by frantic tapping on a matchbox; syncopated clapping breaks through the wall of my hotel room at three in the morning; rolling thunder issues from small boys with drums larger than they. Too much. Too loud. I find myself moving through all of this within an invisible bubble of silence, initiating contact with people only if I really need something; I prefer short conversations, as they give me a better chance of keeping up.

At home I'm accustomed to speaking freely, copiously: it's my job, as professor at a small community college, to do so. When I'm in my apartment I speak to my cat and my plants, and when I go out with friends it's never the meal or the movie that matters but what we talk about. I used to discuss everything with my husband, but it's been three months now since he left, the wound is closing up, and I've been working on reconfiguring my life. It was definitely inappropriate to demand a leave of absence on such short notice, but I endured the disapproval and cleaned out my desk meditatively. I thought I could do anything, be anyone, no longer defined by my role as The Wife. Unprepared, however, to step *too* far out into the unknown, I decided on this trip to Salvador as a way to connect adventure with some degree of academic achievement. As soon as the idea occurred to me, I got busy: applied for a visa, found a hotel on the 'Net, and made a reservation for two weeks. Ralphy drove me to the airport, though I could've taken a taxi. It was nice of her. And here I am, wondering, "What the hell?"

Next day I venture forth to try once more to send that e-mail. This time I'm feeling kind of desperate about getting through. The night was bad: my room has one large overhead fluorescent light; it's that or pitch-blackness. The window has to remain closed, otherwise anyone walking down the corridor can peep in at me. Between the heat, the mosquitoes, and the muffled noise from the street, I could hardly sleep. This morning I'm on edge; I need to get in touch with Ralphy, with home base, with somebody who knows who I am.

As I walk up to the Internet café I see that the door is open but it looks dark inside. I put my head in: a man is sitting in the gloom.

"I see you here yesterday," he says in English.

"Oh?" I say, surprised. "Tell me, is the power still off?"

"Power?"

I gesture toward the computers and the light fixtures, tap my left wrist with my right index finger in the universal sign for "time," then upturn the palms of my hands. He upturns the palms of *his* hands and shrugs.

"Is there another Internet place near here?" I ask. He just looks at me. I point outside. "*Internete*?"

"If you want, you use Internet in the house. You go, free." He speaks haltingly, as if withdrawing the words one at a time from a disused memory bank.

"So why are you waiting here?"

"Here it has a very good es-canner. We es-canner break, and I need produce three hundred propagandas tonight."

"By tonight?"

"Yes. But you, you use computer at the house. E-mail, no problem. I give you address. Two, three, nine— "

"Hold on a minute. Where is it?"

"Near! Not far. I show you on paper. You go up stairs.

Say Rumo send you." He writes the address down and sketches a little map.

"Thank you very much," I say. "Good luck with the scanner."

"Bye-bye," he says. "*Adios.*"

The address is 239 Rua do Travesso. I almost turn back several times. I don't *really* want to show up at someone's house and ask to use the Internet. It would've been impolite to turn the guy down, but he's not going to care if I don't make it there; I'm sure I'll never see him again. There must be other Internet cafés. On the other hand, following this lead would force me to interact with some regular Brazilian folks, see how they live. And it's a fact that if the power hadn't gone out yesterday I probably wouldn't have talked to that guy today. Meaningful Coincidence? All right; I'll take the challenge.

The place turns out to be an old building in the middle of the historic district, on a cobblestone street of youth hostels and art galleries and musty looking restaurants. Up the worn wooden stairs to the second floor, I knock on the big green door. There's a rustling noise inside, then silence. A bird calls briefly beyond the stairwell window. It's almost ten o'clock, the day is sunny, the heat just gathering.

Without warning, the apartment door swings open onto a dark room. Tall, shuttered windows along one wall let light leak in around their edges, enough so I can discern the shapes of about a dozen people stretched out on the floor. The person who let me in retreats before I can make out their features and lies down a few feet away.

I close the door softly and stand there, uncertain, in the near-total darkness. The room is uncomfortably stuffy, hotter than outside. There's a sound all around me, a low soft rushing noise that seems at once unfamiliar and intimate; then I realize it's the sound of breathing, all the people in the room breathing, their in and out breaths overlapping in one seamless flow. What on earth . . . ? And the sound is getting louder, subtly but steadily — there's something indecent about it. I'm dismayed at the mistake I've made in coming here and would leave right away, but I don't want to cause another interruption. Instead I sit down, hoping that whatever it is will be over quickly.

Gradually the voices become more substantial, the breathing shifts into humming: no melody, just an agglomeration of tones hovering in the same range. They get slowly louder, so slowly that it's impossible to identify any transition point. Will they just *keep* getting louder? How far can this go? I feel around in my pocket for any bits of Kleenex I could surreptitiously insert into my ears — blocking them with my fingers seems somehow impolite, if anyone *is* watching me. The humming picks up volume like a snow-slide gathering momentum and threatening to turn into an avalanche; luckily I manage to locate a small wad of tissue and tear two small pieces from it. But just before putting them into my ears I pause for a moment, stop thinking about how bizarre the whole thing is, stop being afraid it's going to get out of control, and just focus on the noise itself. And once I do I find I can't stop listening.

My hand goes slack in my pocket, my jaw drops slightly. The more I try to concentrate on the sound, the more elusive it becomes. The many elements that make up the whole are in constant flux, blending, falling away, or overpowering one another. The only thing my ear can really latch onto is the *loudness* of the overall sound mass, the infinitesimal gradations from one volume level to the next.

Little by little, the closed-mouth intonations become more urgent; the humming turns into chanted vowels that break off into jagged shrieks. Now people are screaming outright. This is the frenzy I'd been afraid of but I'm no longer cringing, I'm listening in fascination, and watching, too, as some of the figures writhe on the ground, others get to their knees, to their feet, gesticulate madly, throw their whole weight behind the torrents of sound.

The excitement is contagious, electrifying. I decide to give it a go. As far as I can tell no one is taking any notice of me — even if they were, they wouldn't be able to pick out my voice from the surrounding din.

One tentative shout is all I can manage at first: unsatisfying, but it loosens things up. All the accumulated fears that have been eating up my insides like poison twist into a big long cord that rushes from my gut through my mouth and explodes on contact with air: a huge relief. The eruption leaves me hollow, almost weightless — my body merely a vehicle for sound. I scream again, and again, barely able to hear myself in the welter of voices. Absorbed as I am, I don't perceive right away that the collective volume level has begun to drop. My voice is now the loudest of all; I quickly lower it to match the rest. It becomes clear to me that we're supposed to bring down the volume gradually, just as it went up.

Never before have I participated in anything remotely like this, although I do enjoy World Music and some CDs that my friends find outlandish. Not that this noise is really anything I'd call music, but I don't know what else to liken it to. There's definitely some art involved; at least, it takes an ensemble effort to achieve the desired progressions.

Once the overall volume has dropped down to almost nothing, I realize I have to manipulate the muscles of my mouth very subtly in order to pull off the transition from Very Quiet to Quieter Still. By now my eyes have adjusted to the darkness. I glance around the room and notice, pressed into one of the corners, someone with headphones on holding out a boom microphone. Well, that explains something: these people aren't nuts, they're just producing some kind of an audio recording! That's a relief: although I don't understand what's going on, I can at least give it a label. While I'm busy thinking these things, I forget to pay attention to the tones I'm making, but my voice carries on without me.

We're making only the softest of sounds now, until the room is so quiet only the sound of my own breathing reaches my ears. And finally I breathe silently, feeling the slow heave of my chest, its rhythm interpenetrating with the faster thump of my heart.

We stay still for a long time. I've ended up slumped at the base of a wall. Slowly, I become aware of a bird outside; a passing truck rattles the windowpanes. Too soon, someone opens one of the shutters; people gather themselves up slowly, with a kind of hushed reverence, then, in short bursts of speech and laughter, the room fills with cheerful conversation.

I'm dazed; can't analyze what's just happened or think about much of anything except the good feeling that comes into my limbs when I stand up and shake them out as the others are doing. Now I can see that the people in the room are of all sizes, shapes, and colors — they could've been hand-picked for an ad campaign promoting diversity. No one seems to notice me. I feel bereft: for the duration of that strange experience I'd had a sense of belonging; now I remember the unfriendly streets, the dismal hotel room awaiting me. Reluctantly, I start to move toward the door, when a smiling woman approaches me. Bronze skin, silver hair; I can't tell her age. She says something enthusiastic in Portuguese.

"*No hablo,*" I answer. "*Por favor . . .*" I make the pacifying gesture that is supposed to mean "slow."

"Oh. Where are you from?" she asks in British-flavored English.

"I'm American. And you?"

"From Guyana, originally. But I've lived here most of my life. So you're on holiday?"

"No," I say. "I've come to do some research — I'll be here a few weeks."

"Oh," she says. "Will you be staying with us?"

This takes me by surprise. "I'm staying in a hotel, at least for now. Why? Who's 'us'?"

Now it's her turn to be surprised: she raises her eyebrows. "The group," she answers. "Isn't that why you're here? I thought you said you wanted to do some research about us?"

"No, no, my research is about something else. I only came because your friend sent me . . . I think he said his name was Rumi. He said I might be able to send an e-mail from your computer. He certainly didn't tell me to expect any of this!" We both laugh. "What's your group, anyway?"

"Short answer: it's a theater group, an anarchist theater group. We perform mostly on the streets, on buses, on the beaches, sometimes in theaters and schools and things, but our performances are more successful when they're unexpected. Have you ever heard of the Theater of the Oppressed?" I shake my head. "We use many of their techniques. This exercise we just finished, though, was invented by one of your compatriots, a woman named Pauline Oliveros."

She interrupts herself to greet a pair of young men who pass us on their way out; the three of them exchange a couple of exuberant sentences in Portuguese — I can't understand a thing. She turns back to me with a smile.

"So tell me then, what is your research on?"

"Short answer: Afro-Brazilian symbolism," I say, feeling a bit embarrassed. When I mentioned it at the college or to my friends, the topic always sounded perfectly legitimate — mysterious, too, as though someone *should* be sent out to investigate and report back. Now, though, it sounds strange to me: I'm so completely foreign here — what can I possibly hope to find out?

The woman doesn't react negatively though; on the contrary. "Terrific!" she says. "We make use of candomblé elements and concepts quite a bit in our work."

"In plays, you mean?"

"Not exactly. We have another project under way that's only peripherally related to the theater. We're conducting quite a bit of research ourselves, as a matter of fact — perhaps if you have any spare time while you're in Salvador you could take a look at what we're doing. You might even find it relevant to your own work."

"Okay." The prospect cheers me. I have no idea what it's about, of course, but it would be something to fill my time with, something potentially interesting. I don't want to tell the woman that I actually have nothing whatsoever to do over the next few weeks, because then I'd have to explain my embarrassing miscalculation. Instead, I say: "So, you have a computer?"

"Yes of course," she answers. "Let me take you there. What's your name, by the way? I'm Veronica — they call me Vero for short." She pronounces it "vair-oo."

"Josephine."

"Nice to meet you. Come," she says, taking my hand and setting off across the room. It's so crowded that I have to follow along, my hand locked in hers. How odd to have a stranger take hold of me like that, as though it were a perfectly natural thing to do! Could she be gay? The thought makes me pull back involuntarily, tugging against her grip. Nothing against lesbians or bisexuals, but the very idea of intimacy with anyone at this point makes me cringe.

Vero turns around to see what the matter is; I force a smile and she smiles back, a little puzzled, then faces forward again. Maybe she's not especially into women and this is just a demonstration of the Brazilian warmth I've heard so much about. I make a mental note to ask Ralphy, whose dissertation included a chapter on cross-cultural body language and gender — she co-teaches Women's Studies with her partner and is forever commenting on the postures and gestures of women in different situations.

"Here," says Veronica.

We've navigated through the crowd and entered a small windowless room whose center space is almost entirely taken up by two desks, one with a computer on it. The walls are lined with bookcases crammed full; precarious piles of books on the topmost shelves reach nearly to the ceiling, which is covered with posters — I assume because there's no wall space. I can't read all of them but it's standard "alternative" fare: AIDS action, pro-choice, anti-capitalism, Free Mumia, Buy Nothing Day, etc. It reminds me of the student center at the college; the resemblance makes me feel a little more at home.

Veronica has turned on the computer and is waiting for it to boot up.

"What exactly makes your theater group 'anarchist'?" I ask. "Is it very chaotic? I don't really know what anarchy is," I admit.

I surprise myself by asking these questions. My guess is that along with the tension I released earlier through the screaming, I must've lost some of my habitual shyness. You'd think that standing up in front of a classroom all these years would've cured me of it, but in that context I always have a clear outline of what to say and do. It's one-on-one interactions with strangers that are difficult for me, the improvisation necessary: I can rarely achieve the same sense of control that I have when addressing a group.

"It's *anarchism*, not anarchy. Most people think the term means lawlessness and destruction — that's just propaganda. The truth is that there are all sorts of anarchists, just like there are all sorts of anything else. Some do advocate direct action, which is a catchphrase for capturing the public's attention through violent methods. But the ultimate goal of the anarchist isn't to destroy the present order: that's merely one step in the process of establishing a more equitable system. The idea is to structure the global society so that every human can have all their needs met, in a context of respect for the freedom and well-being of every creature on earth."

"But . . . " I frown.

"I know," she says. "It's a long discussion. If you're interested, as I said, stick around. But now, I believe you wanted the Internet . . ." She motions toward the computer screen, where the familiar icons stand at the ready. "I must get back to the group. Take as long as you like."

"Of course," I say, meaning I'm sorry if I've delayed her. As she leaves I sit down in front of the computer and start clicking around.

Maybe an hour later, I'm done. I've sent e-mails to Ralphy, my mom, and Jorge, my ex-husband. That last one took the most time: it was only something stupid about the insurance but it had to be worded just right, the tone detached but not hostile. My message to Ralphy on the other hand allowed me to unburden myself — I may even have gotten a little carried away.

After shutting off the computer I sit blankly for a minute, looking around the room. What should I do next? I definitely don't want to participate in any more oddball exercises right now, even though I do perceive a pleasant aftereffect from the vocal workout. The idea of being outside again, strolling through the bright day, actually seems appealing. I'm satisfied with my unexpected adventure. I don't really buy into the political stuff, it seems more naïve than anything, but the experience has been interesting and Veronica seems very nice and I'll definitely plan to return for a visit.

I find my way back to the big room. The people are now sitting on chairs, immobile, their eyes open. I have to walk by them to get to the door — creepy. Veronica detaches herself from the group and follows me out onto the landing.

"Thank you so much," I whisper earnestly.

She smiles warmly and whispers back, in that melodic

British accent: "You're welcome. Anytime. Come back anytime."

"When are you going to be talking about candomblé stuff?"

"Well, let's see. Tomorrow at nine there will be a meeting you could come to. I'm not sure exactly how much *talking* will be going on, but it should interest you, anyway."

"Nine p.m.?"

"Yes. So long!" She shuts the door before I even have time to turn around, but I don't take it amiss. I like her. I like the fact that she's friendly but not effusive. She's dedicated to her agenda, obviously very busy, yet open to incorporating new elements — me, at least. She might even be interested in my work: I am, if I may say so, a genuinely accomplished scholar. Although I'm insecure about my choice of research topic and sometimes have doubts about the academic system in general, there's nothing else I'm interested in or better at. That's reassuring in a way: I don't question my choice of career, as I've seen so many of my colleagues do, because in point of fact there *is* no other option for me. Along the way I've enjoyed modest success and been commended for having put together a few banal ideas in such a fashion as to produce a clever and startling conclusion. I've also built up a comprehensive compilation of images of ritual objects, which I can download to any computer; maybe Veronica would like to see them. We could discuss things and go places and have some fun together: a normal, intellectually oriented, low-key friendship would hit the spot right now. Even if she *is* a lesbian, she clearly has too much taste to press the fact on me. I imagine serving Veronica tea in the dingy seaside bungalow, curtains blowing in the wind. It will remind me of the times I used to house-sit for my aunt in Monterey and would bring Ralphy up there for a weekend. Veronica is a person I feel I could really talk to. Wow — great.

The rest of the day passes agreeably enough. I select

postcards then write them in a café overlooking the bay; I discover a large second-hand bookshop and spend at least an hour browsing; I sit for a long time on the stoop of a boarded-up building, watching the stream of people flow by. My thoughts succeed one another in a dreamy tumble as the day deepens into dusk. For dinner I eat fried fish at La Bamba, a little restaurant down the street from my hotel.

The night in my room is not as bad as the one before. I bought a battery-operated pocket fan that I prop up on the pillow: it puts the mosquitoes off a little and allows me to lie there in relative comfort, staring into the dark until I drift off.

In the morning I go out for coffee and toast at the counter of a nearby bakery. Several other customers are having breakfast, including a man who is either seriously drunk or socially disabled. He keeps an eye on me the whole time I'm there, but waits until I'm on my way out to accost me; then he leans into me, attempting a sultry stare through half-lidded eyes while sputtering broken English into my ear. His name is Napoleon; he has a place nearby we can go to; he likes reggae music. Although he comes on like a jackhammer, he evaporates quickly in the face of my impenetrable armor.

Proud of my efficiency, I'm striding down the sidewalk like an Amazon, when a boy catches up to me and points at my purse. I misinterpret his gesture as a plea for alms and grip the purse more tightly; noticing that it's open, I zip it shut. The boy seems satisfied, walks away. I realize he was only trying to warn me to be more careful, and I am ashamed of my mistrust; it makes me want to run after him and offer him some money. What an absurd idea — but it appeals to me precisely for that reason. I unzip the purse again and reach for my wallet: gone.

It had to be Napoleon: nobody else came close enough to me to have been able to pull that off. I'd thought he was just a garden-variety lech rubbing up against me, but maybe he wasn't even as drunk as he acted. In any event, he made off with the wallet, which contained my money, travelers' checks, credit cards, and various picture IDs. Yes, it was idiotic to have been walking around with all of that, but it never crossed my mind that I might get mugged in broad daylight. He took my camera, too. Thank God, my passport is still in my purse.

I retrace my steps until I find one of those tourist police officers who are posted every few blocks in the Pelourinho. I explain what happened — she appears sympathetic, but not surprised.

"Come, please," she says, and leads me to headquarters, a few streets over. It's an old building, like all the others in the neighborhood; dim passageways and staircases connect large airy rooms with French windows. The policewoman leaves me in a cubicle partitioned off from one of the rooms: three chairs are lined up on one side of a substantial desk, bare except for a blotter pad and a telephone. The overhead fluorescent light is on. I feel nervous, though it's all perfectly straightforward, what needs to be done.

In a little while two men come in who look like they could be brothers — they have the same chin. Neither of them seems pleased to see me. They take the two free chairs and carry them over to the other side of the desk. After sitting down they ignore me and start up a discussion that seems not exactly urgent but of great fascination to them both, centering perhaps on some tricky philosophical question. One of them keeps absentmindedly banging a desk drawer open and shut, which is annoying, to say the least.

Eventually they turn their chairs to face me and the drawer-banging one asks me in Portuguese what it is I want.

"I am American," I say, hoping this will prompt them to speak English. It doesn't.

"*Americana*," Banger says.

"*Norte-Americana*," the other corrects stiffly.

Then they both stare at me, like, "Yes, and . . . ?" I stumble through my story in half-Spanish, half-Portuguese, resorting to gestures to convey some of the details.

Only when I've finished, sweating, does Stiff deign to roll out his serviceable English. He asks me a lot of questions, most of which, as far as I can tell, have no bearing on the facts of the case I've stated. Whether I'm married, when I got divorced, whether my ex-husband is supporting me, why I would want to stay in a strange city alone without a man. It comes out that I have visited 239 Rua do Travesso yesterday. The brothers perk up. They stand and straighten their suits and bring their chairs back over to my side of the desk. I stand up, too.

"You come with us," says Stiff.

"Where?" I ask.

He looks at me with exaggerated surprise. "We will collect your stolen property from this address, 239 Travesso Street."

"What? No, it couldn't be them!"

"These people are bandits."

"But it's impossible, because I was with them yesterday, and I still had my wallet this morning!"

"You *think* you had your wallet this morning," Stiff says somberly. Then he walks out of the cubicle, leaving me with Banger. Banger looks me over, takes hold of my wrist — I don't quite have the nerve to try to free myself — and leads me out and down a long gallery. We meet up with Stiff outside.

The three of us walk over to Travesso Street. I've tried again to protest, but Stiff doesn't favor me with a response. With a little luck, Vero will be there and can translate for me and straighten everything out. I feel strange walking between the two policemen, as if I were on the wrong side of the law. Passersby gaze at us curiously.

Once we reach the building, we troop up the stairs and Banger pounds on the green door with unnecessary force, not stopping until it opens. A man with longish hair looks out at us.

"Ah, Senhor Pereira," he says, nodding at Banger, whose fist is still raised.

"Senhor da Selva," Banger answers, with the most frightening smile I've ever seen in real life. He then begins to speak to the man, gesturing toward me a couple of times. Senhor da Selva predictably denies all knowledge of the incident: first bewildered, then indignant, he regards me with contempt. He and Banger argue back and forth.

"Wait, no!" I try to interrupt, but Stiff tugs on my sleeve and glares at me.

Banger yanks Mr. da Selva out onto the landing and pins him to the wall with one hand, motioning with the other for Stiff and me to enter the apartment. Banger slips in after us, slamming the door behind him. Now it's Mr. da Selva's turn to pound. The sound of his outraged knocking and shouting fades as we advance into the apartment.

The big room is empty today, and bright: all the windows are open, the chairs stacked to one side; a mop and bucket stand in the corner. Cautiously, Banger proceeds down a hallway. I follow him; Stiff brings up the rear. We come to an open door on one side of the corridor. Banger holds up his hand for Stiff and me to wait, peeks around the door frame, then steps over the threshold and waves us in: it's the little library I sent the e-mail from.

Banger surveys the room with disgust. He slips a boot-toe in the lower corner of one of the bookshelves, tugs, and steps back. The whole bookcase shudders and two of the tall stacks of books on its very top come crashing down. Inspired, he turns and shoves the computer right off the desk. It makes a loud crunching sound as it hits the floor, spitting glass. I can still hear the muffled thuds of poor Mr. da Selva's fists against the door.

"Ha, ha!" Banger laughs. Stiff hasn't blinked an eye. My own response is to freeze. I know if I protest at all, Banger will turn on me and Stiff will prevent me from leaving. I'm terrified, remembering stories I've heard about renegade cops. My best hope is to be meek and cooperative. If I get out of here I can complain to the American Consulate or something, but escape is my first priority.

The pounding in the background has stopped. Banger is emitting a strange low growl, and twitching — like a man starting to morph into a werewolf in a horror movie. His skin seems to be fighting to stay in one piece: some terrible pressure is building inside him. I half expect steam to start coming out of his ears at any moment.

I'm staring at him, slack-jawed, all social graces forgotten, when a sudden motion causes me to glance at the doorway. Vero's head appears there, behind Stiff's back. Her gaze travels quickly around the room, taking everything in, settling on Banger. I turn back around so as not to give her away. I can sense her thinking furiously, deciding on a plan of action.

She steps into the room. Stiff lets her pass, probably because she's a woman. Banger, the momentum of his metamorphosis interrupted, gives her an evil look, flexing his fingers. Vero goes right up to Banger, slips between his rigid arms, and lays her cheek against his chest. Then she reaches around and gives him a good, strong hug.

All of us are blown away, but Banger most of all. The crazy energy that was churning inside him evaporates instantaneously. He sags like a big bag of jelly — good thing Vero's arms are around him, keeping him from hitting the floor. She reaches out with one foot and snags a chair leg, pulls it over so that the seat is more or less underneath him, and lets him down gently.

Just then, loud running footsteps resound in the hall and Mr. da Selva bursts into the room followed by two other people. One of them is holding up a video camera, the sight of which makes Banger pull himself together enough to curl his lips into a snarl. He stands up and takes a step toward the camera. Vero's kept a hand on his arm this whole time — I'm amazed he hasn't at least batted it away.

Meanwhile, a lot of Portuguese is being shouted back and forth. Even Stiff is getting into it. I catch some of what's being said and imagine the rest: it seems the theater people are outraged but trying to keep their emotions under control, insisting on a dialogue, whereas the policemen only have a party line and want no discussion of it.

Suddenly a truce seems to have been reached. They all stop jabbering and look at me.

Veronica puts her hands on her hips and asks: "So. Did you tell them we stole your wallet?"

"No! I didn't! It's a complete misunderstanding!"

"Not really," she says. "But it's not your fault. They don't need much of an excuse." She speaks with the policemen: again, a feverish argument breaks out. Banger and Stiff finally stalk out of the room; the other four remain, glowering.

"Are they going to pay for the damages?" I ask Vero. A wry smile crosses her face.

"No. They've had it in for us for a long time. They usually just threaten us with citations for violating building codes. The building inspector is on their team, of course; they'd create problems for us no matter where we lived. We're just lucky they let us get away with not making monthly payoffs."

"But I really didn't accuse you," I say. "There's no way you could have done it, anyway." I feel I've made a faux pas, without knowing how. I try to rectify it: "You were nowhere *near* my wallet at the time it was stolen."

She squints one eye: a wince? "I've told you, it really hasn't much to do with you at all," she replies. "They want to make trouble for us; you came along, provided an excuse. I hope they didn't give *you* too much of a hard time . . . ?"

"Not really, no," I say.

Mr. da Selva is transferring the plastic and glass shards of the erstwhile computer into a wastebasket. The others are busy picking up books.

"Bruno!" Vero calls. Mr. da Selva looks over at us. His face is tired, but kindly; the net of laugh and frown lines cast over it suggests intelligence and a good sense of humor. He addresses me in English with a rich Brazilian accent:

"Your name is . . . ?"

"Josephine," I say. On an impulse: "Jo."

"But why did you want to bring these policemen to us, Jo?"

"Bruno! You *know* what happened!" Vero interjects angrily.

Bruno smiles. "I was joking," he says.

I manage a small smile. "So, what will you do without a computer?" I ask. "Was that your only one?"

"It was. We will manage to get another at some point." His English is perfect, though his accent causes some of the letters to melt into others. He brushes the last crumbs of glass onto a paper that he drops into the wastebasket, and then he stands up.

"We have to laugh, of course," Vero says. "This was precisely the kick in the arse we needed — to get a move on, step up our work. We've been lazy. The time is now, and we're not ready. Excuse me." She leaves the room abruptly.

Bruno introduces me to Doce, a guy, and Paula, the woman with the video camera. They've given up on putting the books back up on top and are stacking them on the floor instead.

"Veronica is my wife," Bruno says to me out of the blue. "Did she tell you about our work?"

"You're a theater group, right?"

"Yes, but our focus, right now, is on a system that makes the Internet obsolete. We call it the Outernet. It will allow us to connect with each other when there *are* no computers available. The system is already in place, but the problem is the access. Veronica is right: we need to push harder. We are certain that at some moment in the future the entire Internet will go down, but we do not know when. At that point it will be essential to be able to access the Outernet at will."

"So . . . it's basically a kind of, what? Cell phone network?"

"No, it uses no machines at all."

"Telepathy?"

"In a way, but it is more than a communication device. It allows also for storage, retrieval, and transmission of great quantities of information."

"Wow." I can't think of an intelligent remark. The sound of his voice distracted me a bit from what he was saying: it's so sonorous and resonant, with undertones that tickle the inside of my ear.

"And you? What are you interested in?"

"Me . . . I'm studying African cultures transplanted to other countries. That's it in a nutshell. I'm working on writing a book."

"What is the book about, exactly?"

He said "exactly," so I guess I'll go into detail. "Well, I already did a thesis on the metamorphosis of several key African mythological tales after they were brought over to Cuba, Haiti, and Brazil. After that, I wanted to focus on comparing the parallel evolution of religion in the different countries, so I thought I should start with one place and examine it in depth. That's why I came here to research candomblé."

"Why?"

I don't know what it is he hasn't understood. "You mean why here?" He must know that Salvador is candomblé city and has the greatest concentration of people of African descent in all of Brazil.

"No. Why . . . the interest?"

"Oh. Well, the truth is I'm not sure. My grandmother was from Haiti originally and told me some stories when I was growing up, but I didn't really become interested in anything involving my African origins until I was in my twenties — then, somehow . . . I don't know. Anyway, I can't explain it, but I think I have a responsibility to help transmit some forms of knowledge that are being threatened with extinction."

"Why would they go extinct if they are vital and powerful?"

That's the best question anyone's asked me in a while. "On the surface it appears that newer generations just lose interest, distance themselves from the old ways," I reply. "I think, though, that that's the result of a deliberate campaign; not a campaign exactly, more like a brainwashing program . . . It's hard for me to explain it without sounding like a conspiracy freak. It has to do with TV, advertising, school curriculums, a generalized sort of . . . oh, I don't know . . . mentality. A mentality that doesn't put worth in things like really learning from old people or from dreams." I'm conscious of the rambling, superficial quality of my explanation, and try to bring it up a notch. "When dreams, for instance, are seen as merely the jumbled results of a physiological sanitation process, it prevents people from looking for what the dreams have to teach them. Then a whole body of knowledge concerning oneiric interpretation falls into disuse and is eventually forgotten."

Suddenly I'm embarrassed — I didn't expect to find myself blabbing on like this, like I was in front of my class. I got so involved with threading one thought into the next that I was barely aware of my surroundings while I was talking; at the same time, if Bruno's face hadn't displayed genuine interest I wouldn't have gone on as long as I did. I pause, wondering how he'll respond. Maybe some of the words I used aren't even in his vocabulary; maybe he didn't understand half of what I said.

"You appear to have thought about all this quite a lot," is what he comes up with. My excitement dissipates instantly. What a vacuous thing to say! But maybe that's unfair; maybe the issues I brought up simply aren't compelling to him. He's studying me with a kind of affectionate bemusement; he's actually quite handsome, though not my type. An interesting man.

"Have you any proof of this brainwashing hypothesis?" he asks, taking me by surprise. I had been almost certain that the import of my little speech had slid past him.

"Proof? Not exactly . . . what do you mean?"

"Being a scholar. You must collect evidence to support your theories, no?"

"Yes, of course, but this particular angle . . . I haven't . . . it's only what I've observed . . . kind of obvious, really."

"Does the deliberate suppression of cultural traditions have any relationship to the ways in which those traditions are modified in the countries you are studying?"

"Yes, of course."

"I can think of some texts we have here that would help you make your case. Some books about propaganda and social manipulation, a lot of material from recently declassified files. Some videos, too. There is also quite a lot I could indicate to you on the Internet, but of course at the moment I cannot show you here . . . " He glances wistfully at the wastebasket.

"Look, let me tell you again how sorry I am that I caused all of this. I can't even believe it."

"As Veronica said, it was not your fault. They detest us. We are a thorn in their flesh that they would have ripped out long ago if not for our ties to certain people and groups. One connection in particular has been helpful in protecting us, but the police are hungry, and now and then they cannot help themselves. As long as the Chief of Police does not find out, the underlings get away with it."

"Why don't you go to the Chief of Police then?"

"It does not work that way. Sometime I will map it out for you. Okay?"

"Okay. I would like that."

"And you can map out the migration pattern of African religions for me. Your version of it. You did not really tell me very much."

"That's true." I pause, distracted by Paula and Doce's laughing attempts to create the highest possible pile of books without its falling over. Images of Banger unleashing his fury replay in my mind's eye. "How come that policeman let her videotape him?" I ask Bruno.

"He is an idiot. It excites him to be on camera, to know that someone, anyone, is going to look at him." Bruno makes a face, then smiles briefly. "Well, should we have some lunch now?"

He turns to Doce and Paula and they exchange a few words, whereupon we all go down the hall to the kitchen. It's roomy and has a couch I sink down on gratefully. The others pull out various foodstuffs and start to prepare a meal; I realize I'm exhausted, glad my halfhearted offer of help was turned down.

Vero comes in, moving briskly. "Takes a lot out of you, doesn't it?" she says. She breaks off a banana from a bunch, tosses it over to me. "Hostility engenders stress. Here. This will help. And this." She separates a few collard leaves from the ones Doce is about to dice, rinses them off, then hands them to me.

"Like this? Raw?" I ask. The leaves look tough.

"It's the best way," she says. I eat the banana first, chew dutifully on the greens. Not a very exciting taste, but also not as bitter as I'd expected. Surprisingly sweet, in fact. I ask for water when I'm finished.

Vero hesitates before filling a glass from the water filter and bringing it to me. "Really, you shouldn't drink from half an hour before to half an hour after a meal," she says.

"That wasn't exactly a meal," I say. "Why not?"

"The liquid rinses off the lining of your stomach, interferes with the digestive juices," she answers. "Drinking with meals is one of those bad habits passed along by our ancestors, but that's all it is, a habit."

I'd never thought of it as a habit — I just take it for granted. The idea of having to go thirsty while eating food scares me a little. "So you study nutrition here, too?" I ask.

"We didn't set out to. But we found that it was necessary. It has so much to do with how well we do our work: a healthy diet not only makes us more productive, it keeps us in a better mood, which makes us even more productive, which puts us in an even better mood, and so on."

It sounds a bit weird the way she says it, mechanistic, like some sort of fascist health program.

"But mostly, it's very helpful for the Outernet work," she continues. "The electrolytes in our brains need to be balanced ever so precisely for all the right circuits to be completed."

"Circuits?"

"Our internal machinery. We have to keep it running as smoothly as possible. It's one of the greatest challenges of this project, in fact: it can be incredibly difficult to reprogram your habits. We're all struggling with that to some degree; the beauty of it is that the struggle itself teaches us about facets of existence we would normally ignore, but that we need to become familiar with in order to pursue our work."

"Hunh," I say. I'm not sure I understand what she's talking about.

Meanwhile, Bruno and the others have been transferring bowls of food from the counters to the big wooden table at one side of the room.

"Come eat!" says Paula, smiling, shy about trying out her English on me. I stand up; Vero slides off the arm of the couch where she's been sitting, onto the seat. She lies on her back with her knees hooked over the couch's arm and her feet dangling down. She answers my inquiring look:

"I'm not eating right now. You go ahead."

Lunch consists of rice and beans, a garlicky salad composed of different kinds of chopped-up greens, and an orange vegetable. Really good, despite being under-salted. I drink water with the meal and so does Doce. We talk about customs in our respective countries; Vero joins in from the couch. Doce and Paula seem to understand English fairly well but aren't comfortable speaking it, and often they all lapse into Portuguese. Sometimes I try to follow; sometimes I just let it wash over me. It gives me a chance to simply observe them. Paula is elfin, a punk tomboy type, full of piercings and defiance and the radiance of youth; she might actually be a teenager. I like her. Doce must be her boyfriend — he just seems bland to me. Nice, but bland. And Bruno: there's something solid about him, reassuring, but also a restlessness just below the surface. I'd guess he's five or ten years older than I am.

I eat a lot during the meal, and quickly. By the end I feel bloated and uncomfortable.

"Let's go lie down," Vero proposes. Everybody laughs, because she's been lying down this whole time.

"Are you all right?" I ask. They laugh again.

"Let's just say I'm conserving energy," she replies.

"But you didn't eat," I point out. "Didn't you say that eating the right kinds of things was important for keeping your energy up? Or something like that?"

She smiles. "True. But at the times when our bodies don't need the nutrition, it's more taxing for them to have to process unnecessary matter."

I offer to help with the dishes and clearing up but the

others refuse firmly.

"Why don't you go lie down with Veronica," Bruno suggests. "She needs the company."

I don't know what that one's about and certainly don't want to ask. The heaviness in my stomach, however, makes lying down a seductive idea. Perhaps just for fifteen minutes or so, I tell myself.

Veronica gets to her feet and takes hold of my hand once again, leading me out of the kitchen through the back door. We go up a narrow staircase and emerge in a rooftop garden whose concrete floor is crowded with hundreds of potted plants. Some of the trees and bushes are taller than I; plants also hang from a latticework of tubing, their cascading foliage forming thick furry curtains. The effect is that of walking through a rain forest, or so I imagine. Vero brings me along a narrow path to the outside edge: we lean over the railing and look at the street below. After the moist, filtered light of the miniature jungle, the bright sun is like a bludgeon on the back of my neck. There's a nice breeze, though.

"This whole top floor is ours. It used to be just an open space, but we built a structure in the middle."

"Where?" I can't see anything but plants.

"In the middle. The garden goes all the way around, and there's a house in the center. Just a room, really. When our daughter is in town, that's where she sleeps, and we often have other people passing through and staying with us for a while, helping out with the project in exchange for room and board. When I first saw you I assumed that's what you were here for. I thought perhaps you'd made arrangements with one of the others and I hadn't heard about it yet."

"Where's your daughter now?"

"She's traveling in Bolivia — she won't be back for another few weeks."

"How old is she?"

"Twenty-two. Let's go inside."

We pass back through the vegetation and reach what looks like a hut made of ridged reddish bricks, a single room with big windows on three sides and a door on the fourth. Vero enters, invites me in. It's still and shadowy inside, reminding me of a church.

She circles the room, pushing open the wooden shutters to let in air and light. The walls are painted blue, a restful medium blue. Furniture has been kept to a minimum: a low table with a lamp and a jug of water on it, two mats on the floor, one at the base of each of the side walls. A chair in one corner is heaped with clothes. Narrow shelves hold books and an assortment of objects: rocks, shells, feathers, stones, little bundles, items I can't identify.

"Bruno collects things," Vero says, following my gaze. "Myself, I prefer open space. This is a compromise." She sits on one of the mats then stretches out with a big sigh. I sit on the other with my back against the wall.

"Aren't you going to lie down?" she asks.

I take off my shoes. Then I stretch out — a little awkwardly, because she's watching me. The cover on the thin mattress is a rough dark blue cotton with a faint musty smell. I lie on my back and look at the ceiling's striations of shining tin and shadow. There's a gap between the roof and the tops of the walls — sunlight comes in more strongly on one side. I can hear the barest breeze whispering in the leaves outside and, if I try hard, Vero's breathing.

I wonder what she's thinking — I can't imagine. I've never met anyone quite like her before, so self-possessed, yet not arrogant in the least. She seems to have accepted me immediately, without question or fuss. Lying here with her reminds me of sharing a room with my sister — although my sister certainly did not accept me without question or fuss.

My thoughts drift to tonight's meeting. Will it involve the Outernet? Probably. Will I actually get to see what the Outernet is? They say the machinery is internal — but what does that mean? I've heard of groups of people attempting to achieve higher levels of consciousness together, but I never conceived that it would be possible, in a trance state, to send and receive huge amounts of complex data as one does on the Internet. And I think I understood the guy to say that this Outernet thing is supposed to replace the Internet or be even better than it. But what does it have to do with candomblé? Veronica suggested that their work might have some relevance to my research.

Remembering my reason for being here gives me a twinge of anxiety. I have to get something done soon, somehow! Yet a curious feeling of well-being pervades me, a kind of disconnection from ordinary life — suspension in a timeless zone. I may be in shock from the morning's violent events, I caution myself, and I try to remember whether the legs of shock victims are supposed to be raised above the heart or lowered. I bend my knees to be on the safe side. Am I a little numb, or is that my imagination? It's just that I'm not feeling the strain I usually do from meeting new people, and considering I'm lounging around with someone I met only yesterday, that's pretty odd. Maybe they put something in my water, I think idly. I don't really believe it, but the thought makes me want to determine exactly how different I'm feeling: I turn my attention inward.

Something is definitely strange. More alert now, I notice a distinct tingling, like tiny bubbles just under the surface of my skin: a physical sensation that always lets me know there's a focused beam of psychic radiation somewhere in my vicinity. My innate psychic abilities have always been fairly strong, but over the years I've managed to suppress them, or at least suppress my awareness of them. Originally that took some effort; now it's become a habit — reflexive, like scratching your nose when it itches. It just makes it easier to get by. But now and then something slips past the filter — usually, I realize, at rare times like this when I'm not talking or *doing* anything.

Closer attention to the tingling reveals that the sensation is affecting only one side of my body, the side nearest to Veronica. Is she sending something out at me? If she is, I'll put an end to it. I won't even try to figure out what she might be doing — I really don't like messing with these kinds of phenomena too much.

"What are you conserving energy for?" I ask in a casual tone. Involving her in a conversation would be the quickest way to divert her attention from any psychic endeavors, but I keep my voice low in case all this is in my head and she's actually sleeping.

"For tonight," she answers immediately. "Meetings can be quite draining."

"*That* draining!"

"Yes. But don't worry. It won't be for you, I don't think."

"How come the others aren't fasting and resting?"

"We all have different roles to play. You could compare it to a rocket launch: they're the ones who handle the million technical preparations, but I'm the astronaut who actually gets blasted out into space. Not that you can really break it down like that, but to give you an idea. The goal is for everyone to be astronauts eventually, but in this phase of the experiment I'm the main guinea pig."

I'm satisfied that she's been sufficiently distracted, if she actually *was* trying something. I can't locate the tingly feeling anymore, but then that might be because I distracted *myself*, so I decide to relax and see if I can locate it again. I shift into a more comfortable position and close my eyes, but my investigation is forgotten as stray thoughts turn into dream fragments and I fall into a deep sleep.

When I wake up the air and light have changed: it must be late afternoon. Veronica is snoring peacefully. I sense another presence in the room and turn my head: Bruno. Smiling at me, he lets himself down on the floor beside Vero, strokes her hair. She keeps on snoring.

"I do not want to wake her up, to make her move over," he says. "Maybe I will just lie on the ground. Downstairs they are making too much noise, the telephone is always ringing, it is just too crazy." The colloquial American expression sounds fantastic delivered in such a flavorful accent.

I sit up immediately and pull my shoes to me, intending to relinquish the mat, but he says: "Please! No!" And then: "Do you think you can move over only a little bit? I am not so very fat."

"Of course!" I reply. Quickly, I scrunch up facing the wall. Bruno lies down, not touching me; he sighs with relief once he's fully relaxed and doesn't stir again.

It seems like ages since I last lay next to a man, although it was only really a few months ago. I'm completely tense — it's all I can do to keep my respiration rate steady so as not to betray my agitation.

Minutes pass. I realize I'm braced for something, but nothing happens. Ever so slowly I begin to relax, to breathe normally, to shift my position when it becomes uncomfortable. I notice my face is held in a grimace and let it soften. I don't know if he's sleeping — that would've been rather quick; in any case I don't feel anything at all emanating from him besides 98.6 degrees. This intrigues me: how can he be so neutral?

I send out an exploratory tentacle. It's strictly against my principles: deliberately intruding into people's thoughts is even more distasteful to me than tuning in to them involuntarily. Now I'm trespassing into the level of consciousness that people usually keep private. Strange: I can detect nothing. I venture deeper: still nothing.

I pause to think. The only possible explanation is that Bruno must have created an energetic shield around himself — because if it's not a shield then he must be some kind of E.T., and I'm not prepared to believe *that*. So the shield must be what I'm pushing into; no wonder it feels so empty.

I regulate my mind, sort of the way you'd set a camera's aperture and focus, then try not to think of anything. This should allow me to mesh with the shield, which will allow me to figure out what it's made of and give me a better understanding of the person behind it. A shield really isn't the best defense: it's good at deflecting things that come hurtling at it, but not so effective when it comes to the type of slow, crafty prying I'm attempting right now.

After a few minutes, I've picked up the information I need. The barricade is composed primarily of fear, suggesting that the person inside it was hurt to such a degree that he will never "let anyone in" except under the most strictly controlled circumstances. A wave of empathic sorrow washes over me, and something gives way. A tiny breach has opened; without thinking, I slide through it.

Now Bruno's essence billows around me: an exquisite softness, at the same time innocent and wild; this could be the secret heart of a young animal, perhaps a small boy. His hopes and fears, peculiarities and secrets, appear as translucent blobs suspended in the softness, but I don't examine them. It's time to pull out: I got what I came for, I found him. And now I know that his shield is very old. He may not even be aware it's there. He's certainly not aware that I've been traipsing around inside him, thank heavens for that.

I reel in my feeler and subside, aware once more of the blue room, the delicate light, the even breathing of my hosts. Despite the sour aftertaste of guilt at having trespassed, it's a comfort not to be lying next to a total stranger anymore. Having struck through to his innermost self, I'm reminded that at that deepest level our human personalities, like our bodies, are made up of only slightly differing proportions of the same basic elements. Yet Bruno seems more familiar to me than can be accounted for by universal truths — thinking back, I realize he's had this aura from the first. My interactions with him have been very different from the ones I've had with Vero: she accepted me without much curiosity, whereas he pressed me for details about my work, as though talking to a close friend after a long separation. At lunch he was asking me questions about lifestyles and customs in the United States as though I'd been a tourist there and not a resident: it was a little odd.

"Jo." Bruno's voice startles me.

"Yes?"

"I was thinking about your research. How can you do a comparative study of African and African-based religions without involving all the other world religions?"

"Well, I know what you mean," I say, inwardly delighted by the fact that he's been ruminating on this. "But it would be an impossibly huge task."

"What if you had some help?"

"But it's not really necessary, is it?"

"It depends, what is your objective. What it is that *you* really want to know. You say you are in the business of transmitting information, but there must be more to it than that, something else you want for yourself, something you want to discover."

I have to think for a minute — how to formulate it? "The main question I have, I don't think can be answered," I say. "I'd like to know if religious symbols have power in and of themselves, or if they're just representations. Or again, whether they have a function something like that of a placebo, and it's the mind's belief in them that has the real power. If I knew that, I would have a better idea of what it really *means* when the symbology undergoes changes over time. Same goes for myths and rituals. Without that piece of information my work feels a little empty to me."

"Maybe it is not as useful as it could be, true," Bruno says. He understands! "That is why you might need to incorporate the ritual elements of *all* cultures into your study. To examine universality, if there is such a thing. You seem to be interested in the relationship between form and content itself, not just in the particular expressions of the African forms."

"You're right." But I'm not confident I'd be able to take on a subject of such magnitude, and find myself discouraged, once again, by the inadequacy of my project. I don't try to hide the dejection that comes into my face. Though I'm staring up at the ceiling, I know Bruno is looking at me.

"Of course," he says, "you must start somewhere. It would be impossible to bite into the whole thing at once. Examining the African traditions is an excellent point of departure, especially if that is where your heart leads you. And you know, some people say this part of Brazil has preserved more African customs intact than the regions where those customs originated."

I don't feel like talking about it anymore. "I guess you're right," I say, sitting up. "Well, I'd better be going now."

"Oh really? Why?"

"I need to get back to the hotel; I have a few things to do. I guess I'll be coming back tonight for the meeting — Vero invited me."

"Good! If you want to come before it starts, you do not have to wait until nine o'clock. Come when you like. Me, I think I will try to sleep for a little while now."

I make my way back through the artificial forest to the staircase. The back door to the apartment is locked: I knock and wait, then give up, deciding to take the stairs all the way down — there must be a street exit.

Once outside, it takes me a few seconds to get my bearings and figure out which way leads back to the hotel. As I walk, thoughts of my new acquaintances are replaced by tedious considerations relating to this morning's theft: foremost is the need to call the credit card companies. I hope the clerk at the hotel lets me put those calls on my tab. What really depresses me, though, is the idea of returning to the police station to complete some kind of report. It's not a matter of principle: if they caught the thief there'd be at least a chance of getting some of my cards back, like my driver's license. I hate the idea of seeing Stiff and Banger again, though; maybe I'll just forget about it.

The streets are dusky. Eyes gleam from doorways, music slips out here and there. Warm yellow light pours from the windows of handicraft shops and restaurants. I keep my thumb hooked through the shoulder strap of my bag.

Making the calls from the hotel turns out to be no problem: they just put it on my bill. But now I have to stay on here until the replacement credit cards and travelers' checks arrive — then I'll be able to find a better guesthouse or something. This place is so depressing, I'd be willing to bet that every minute I spend here shortens my life by an hour. I still have a little Brazilian money in my pocket, probably enough for bus fare: maybe tomorrow I can take that trip up the coast and see what it's like.

I go to my room and stand for a few minutes under the shower's meager trickle. Afterward, lying on the narrow bed, my skin agreeably damp and cool, I start thinking back to Bruno, to that tender hidden part of his. Somehow, from a distance, it doesn't seem so wrong to sort through the perceptions gathered in my brief reconnoitering excursion, to connect the dots.

A picture forms. Bruno is one of those boys who never grew up. It's inescapable: the strongest impression I have is of a child. I can imagine us going around together as if he were my son, accompanying me on my errands. And the enthusiasm he displayed in regard to my research was almost childlike — how remarkable that he should have become so genuinely engaged, not in any effort to chat me up or impress me. I like how his mind works.

I summon up the feeling of being surrounded by his essence and soak in the little pool of memory for a few minutes. So refreshing. Despite the fan buzzing at my head, the dubious lumpy mattress and the weighty stillness of this closed-in room, I find I'm pleased with my new life and the doors that have suddenly opened up in it. To keep a sense of balance, I turn my mind deliberately back to the theft and the ugly scene with the cops, but these thoughts don't puncture my elation. In fact, a gleeful vindictiveness rises in me as I recall the policemen's wanton brutality: a thirst for retribution, justice. I must act somehow to help prevent incidents like the one that took place this morning. Maybe it wasn't sheer coincidence that I was there as a witness. What shall I do, write a denunciatory article? Something. I'll ask for Stiff and Banger's badge numbers when I'm at the station tomorrow. Meanwhile, I'll go back to thinking about Bruno for a while. It's comforting. And comforting, too, to think of Veronica, whose cool determination I admire so much. What a great couple. I'd be curious to meet their daughter.

Night must have arrived. I get up, switch on the fluorescent light, and look through my suitcase. I decide that casual clothing is probably best and choose the gray pants and the green T-shirt with the picture of the tortoise.

The clock in the lobby says 7:15. I'll get something to eat on the way; I think I have enough money left. I stop in a by-the-kilo restaurant that's surprisingly decent: a good selection of vegetable dishes and a low-key atmosphere.

Back in the street, I ask someone for the time. Only 8:30 — the meeting won't start for another half-hour. Should I walk around a bit longer or get there early? I'll go up now. I can always read a book or something while I wait.

Doce opens the door. The front room looks much as it did in the morning, with the stacked chairs and the mop in the corner, only the ceiling seems lower somehow. It's dark. There's no sign that anyone else is around.

"Bruno *e* Vero . . ." Doce points upward, then makes the

sleep sign, tilting his head onto one palm and briefly shutting his eyes. I nod and indicate that I'll wait in the library.

The desk that had the computer on it is gone; there's an armchair in its place. I spend the next hour or so picking books off the shelves and leafing through them; I'm not really in the mood to read. Just as I start getting seriously restless, Vero appears.

"Oh, hullo!" she says, looking pleased. "I heard you'd arrived. Sorry — I guess we're running on Brazilian time, but we'll be starting soon. Are you all right? Do you want to keep reading? Bruno and I are in the kitchen, and a couple of other people, too. Would you like a glass of water?"

"Hi! Yes, no, yes please — I'll come with you." We laugh, and I follow her out.

The kitchen seems more like a stage now, lit with incandescent bulbs that cast stark shadows. Bruno is sitting at the table across from two men and a woman. Paula is on the couch, sorting through some papers.

"Jo!" Bruno slides over on the bench. "Come have a seat!" He addresses the others in Portuguese as I walk over, explaining that I came to Brazil to do some research for a book and am interested in learning about the Outernet. At least that seems to be the gist of it — he uses a number of words I don't understand.

The men stand up to shake my hand, offering their names, which I instantly forget. The woman, a spiky-haired blonde with wide teeth, observes me with a friendly expression as I sit down. The wood is warm from Bruno's body.

"Jo, this is Velma — Velma, Jo," he says. "Velma is a theater director visiting us from Sweden. She studies the physiological effects of sound; her plays are based on sound instead of text. We have been discussing some ideas she has that could be helpful to us."

"Nice to meet you," says Velma. Her English is very

correct; she enunciates carefully, isolating each word in a tiny pocket of space.

"Likewise." We smile and nod at each other. "When did you get here?"

"Only this morning."

"You must be tired." More smiling and nodding. The others launch into animated Portuguese. "So . . . how do you fit into this Outernet thing?" I ask her.

"How much do you know about it?"

"Hardly anything. I get the idea that it's some sort of virtual space where people can communicate with each other. But I don't understand how you can access it without any external apparatus. Through some kind of hypnosis?"

Velma hesitates. "I suppose this could be one way to induce a favorable state of consciousness. My own work has more to do with the effects of sound frequencies on brain waves. Have you heard of this?"

I shake my head. I've never been a science person.

"By listening to particular tones, we can cause our brain waves to synchronize with them, making changes in our awareness."

"How does it work?" I'm certain I won't understand her explanation but don't want to let our conversation stall. The three men have started punctuating their speech with animal noises; at my side, Bruno breaks into a deep growl that makes the bench vibrate. One of the others counters with a deafening bray. They fall out laughing.

Velma leans toward me to make herself heard. "If a person listens to a certain tone with one ear, and to a tone pitched just a fraction higher with the other, the combination creates a third tone, and that—"

"Wait a minute!" I interrupt.

"Yes?"

"If you were going to use a technique like that to access the Outernet, you'd need *some* kind of machine or instrument to produce the sounds, so there would in fact be *some* kind of external hardware involved, right?"

Velma starts to reply but is drowned out by the men, who have abruptly intoned a Tibetan-sounding chant. Their resonant baritones mingle in an impossibly drawn-out syllable, until one by one they run out of breath and wind down, laughing and gasping for air.

Velma waits for them to subside, then pursues. "It is possible to create tones with the voice, but this is something a person can do only for a limited time: it makes friction on the vocal apparatus. Also, it attracts a lot of attention. My research focuses more on the sounds produced by the middle ear."

"Middle ear?" I picture an esoteric organ, like some kind of third eye on the top of the head.

"That is the name for a membrane inside the ear. Its function is to bring the air-pressure waves from the outside down to a manageable level. But on closer look we see that this membrane actually has the ability to *generate* sound, which is then perceived as external." She pauses. "This means, in theory, you can make soundtracks inside yourself."

"So your middle ear could make some tones — and then what? You'd space out? What would happen?"

"The implications of my research, as it applies to the Outernet project, are still under investigation."

"Oh. Well. Very interesting."

She smiles, then stands up and goes over to talk to Veronica, who's joined Paula on the couch.

Bruno is in the middle of chuckling at something one of his pals has said but notices my look and returns it inquiringly.

"Bruno," I say. "What happens once you're tuned in to the Outernet? Is it like 1990s science fiction? Great icebergs of data floating in space? I mean, how exactly does it work?"

"It is beyond words," he answers. Seeing my expression,

he quickly adds: "Really. Because it is different for every person. To tell you the truth, very few of us have spent any length of time there. Once you are logged on, you will see your own version of it."

"Logged on? I'm going to log on?"

"If you can find your way there."

I have the feeling these people are being deliberately mysterious: are they truly unable to be more specific, or are they concealing information? Perhaps I'm too much of a newcomer? Still, they've invited me here: I might as well ask questions. "Can I send a message to a friend on the Outernet like I can on the Internet?"

"In a certain manner, yes. The only difference is that with the Outernet your friend may not be aware of having received it."

"What — no inbox?"

"They may not know they have an inbox."

"So you can't use it to make an appointment with someone for twelve o'clock the next day?"

"Only if that person is also tuned in."

"It's like online chat?"

"You could say that."

It doesn't sound too useful to me; maybe it's one of those discoveries that everyone is impressed by just because it's new. I'll try to keep an open mind, though. "Well, it sounds interesting. I'd definitely like to give it a go. But I thought Veronica said that right now she's the only one of you going up, or out, or wherever?"

"She is the only one who has succeeded in logging on for a prolonged period; the rest of us have not achieved consistent results. We do assist her, when she is there, by handling the external details of the environment to make it more . . . more comfortable for her. Keep her from banging her head and that sort of thing."

"Banging her head! Is it like an epileptic seizure?"

"More like possession, which you must know something about."

"Oh." Yes, I've read the texts, seen some films. I hadn't quite bargained on signing up to be possessed.

Bruno continues: "It does not always take that form. Most people enter a state more like a coma — it depends on the individual. Do not worry. You try it out, and if you do not like it, that will be the worst of the consequences — you will never have to do it again."

"Why wouldn't I like it?"

"People are different," he replies. "But so far, everyone who has made it there once has done all they could to go back again. And again, and again." He stares off into space, seemingly lost in the memories he's evoked. He stays like that a few moments; the others, noticing, seem to know what he's thinking of, and similar faraway looks come onto their faces. There's a hush.

The silence is broken by a low rattling sound coming from Vero. All eyes swivel toward her. The strange grinding moan stops abruptly and she sits up, shoulders hunched, chin on chest, trembling. She starts to mewl like a lost kitten. Paula and Velma get off the couch and sit at her feet; Bruno nudges me and we both rise and go stand in front of her.

The tremors gather strength, culminating in one great spasm that convulses Vero's whole body. Then she stands up, rather unsteadily, looking right through Bruno. She pats the air as though searching for something, and begins to shuffle her feet. Velma quickly returns to the table, reaches underneath, and pulls a drum from an embroidered bag. Resuming her seat on the floor, she begins to tap out a simple rhythm. Vero's searching motions slowly come into synch with the beat. She's dancing: a kind of dance I've only ever seen in documentary films. Close up like this, what strikes me most is the peculiar quality of the movements: they're very plain — a half-turn, a sweep of the arm — but the way they're linked, the fluid force that animates them is what's so remarkable, so distinctly *not* of human origin. Even when she stops dancing, the force stays humming around her — you can perceive it by the effects it produces, like the wind. The entire surface of Veronica's skin is rippled by minute waves in shifting moiré patterns, like some state-of-the-art special effect. Although she herself is no longer in motion, these vibratory designs seem to be responding to the beat of the drum. I have to wonder whether that's what's actually happening, or whether the fluid in my eyes might be pulsating with the drum sounds, causing rhythmic alterations of my vision. In any case, as I'm wondering this, Velma stops playing and the whole phenomenon evaporates.

Vero opens her mouth and begins to speak Portuguese in a deep, nasal voice. She motions for Paula to get up and places her hands on the girl's shoulders, muttering something while looking in her eyes. I can't catch any of the words: it's all too low and fast. When Vero is done speaking, Paula takes her hand and kisses it.

Vero then addresses Velma, then Bruno at greater length, and finally me. Her features haven't changed, yet the face looking into mine is completely different. She holds me with a serious and compassionate gaze, speaking urgently of work and the past and something complicated and important that needs to be done, the sooner the better. Although most of her words escape me, I somehow understand that sharing this moment with her has far greater significance than anything she might possibly be saying.

Then she starts snapping her fingers all around my body, drawing something down from my periphery after every few snaps and flinging it away with a flick of the fingers. I saw her do this to Bruno at the end of her conversation with him. Each time she snaps her fingers it feels like a little hole is created in my — my what? The sensation isn't located in my physical body but just beyond. And when she makes the yanking-out motion, it seems to lighten the atmosphere around me, as if the pull of gravity has been reduced a notch. My rational mind has to weigh in, of course, to acknowledge that all of this could be pure suggestion, and that I might merely be imagining the feelings.

When she's finished, she turns away from me and stands silent; then her whole body starts to go slack. Bruno and Paula rush forward to support her and help her back to the couch. They sit her down. Bruno drapes a white cloth over her head and holds it there for a minute. When he removes it, Vero's eyes are closed; she's frowning and breathing hard. Paula brings her a glass of water, which she drinks without opening her eyes: the frown smoothes out and her breath slows. After giving back the glass, she remains immobile, hands clasped on her lap. We break out of our poses: Bruno and Paula settle on the couch on either side of her, and Velma and I return to the table. The two other men are still there, goggle-eyed, apparently riveted to their bench.

"Is it over?" I ask.

"No, we are just making a pause," Velma says.

"What happened?"

Velma answers: "Sometimes when Vero logs on, there appears a friend of hers, a helper-spirit, to clear the path. Now that part is over, and she is entering into a chamber of the Outernet."

Several questions come to mind, although I don't want to be a pest. "How many chambers are there?" I can't help asking.

"Ssh!" Velma says, laying a hand lightly on my arm, her gaze fixed on Vero. Vero's eyes are open again. She appears relaxed and says a few words to Bruno, who beckons to us. This time the men also go over; the four of us arrange ourselves in front of the couch.

Vero is alert and seems almost the same as before the "possession," but not quite. Something's different. She looks around and at us, but I have the impression she's gazing simultaneously at a second picture, not quite on the same plane as the kitchen.

Paula has a folder and a pad of paper. She consults a couple of documents in the folder and prompts Bruno, who asks Vero a series of questions. Then Paula writes down Vero's answers. Sometimes Vero takes a long time to answer, so long that I space out, losing myself in my own thoughts, reviewing the e-mails I wrote yesterday, hoping my cat is adjusting to life in Ralphy's apartment. Then the sound of Vero's voice startles me back into the room once more. I can't follow much of the dialogue but adopt an attentive expression, wondering how long this is going to go on; I've started to feel very sleepy.

Suddenly Bruno turns to me: "Do you have any questions for her?"

"What do you mean? Like what sort of question?"

"Anything you might be curious about. With the Internet, when you want information about something, you put a keyword into a search engine. It is basically the same principle on the Outernet, but instead of receiving a list of relevant sources of information you get only one answer, a summary of all existing information on the subject. And this answer is expressed in the format most suited to your particular needs."

"How does the Outernet — or whatever — know what my particular needs are?"

"Good question. Do you want to ask that?"

"Okay."

Bruno puts the question to Veronica. Again a long silence. This time I don't space out but watch her face with fascination: her eyes move in tiny, precise increments, tracking something invisible to me. Finally, she delivers the answer to Bruno in Portuguese; when she's done, he translates for me.

"They said for you to look at your skin: look at the skin of your arm."

I obey, and he continues: "You know that the air, this air that surrounds us, is a necessary element for the skin to exist. Realizing this, you can see that the boundaries of your body extend far beyond your skin. In the same way, your mind is only a kunnel. You contain—"

"Excuse me?" I interrupt. "Kunnel?"

"The seed?" replies Bruno, looking puzzled. "I thought 'kunnel' was another word for seed?"

"Oh! You mean 'kernel.' "

"Yes!" He smiles, and proceeds. "The *kernel* is contained by the fruit, and also contains it. There is no bond more intimate. Your needs are known to the Outernet community because that community *is* you. How do *you* know when you are thirsty? That is how *they* know when you are thirsty. Understanding *why* is not crucial — getting something to drink is. Follow this answer wherever it leads."

Bruno falls silent. I can't make much sense of it.

"That's all?" I ask.

My question surprises him. "So much!" he exclaims. Then he does a funny kind of sign language thing, blinking slowly as he nods and makes a gesture of appeasement with one hand. This reads to me as: "Don't worry, we can go over it again later." For some reason his gaze travels over my chest, stomach, and lap, before he turns back to Vero and engages her in conversation.

I'm left with the surprisingly potent after-impression of the look he swept over me: its path seems etched into my flesh. Warmth radiates from each invisible trace and penetrates deep inside my body. Now why on earth did *that* happen? Clearly, it must be a physical anomaly — perhaps I'm ovulating, or just overtired or overstimulated. I decide to ignore the phenomenon although that's difficult: fluids have started to seep from me, my heart is beating too fast, my skin tingling. I try to fight off the symptoms but can't detach myself enough to get a grip on them. Then I begin to worry that this physiological tumult will make me behave oddly; I want to get away but can't face the formalities of leave-taking, the probable questions, entreaties to stay a while longer.

The others are now collecting and putting away items used in the ritual; the energy has dropped from the room. Veronica appears, holding a pitcher of water and a glass.

"Would you like some?" Her eyes are clear; she's back to her normal self.

I accept gratefully. My parched lip sticks to the rim; I drink and drink and somehow it quiets the riotous jangling of my nerves. Handing back the glass, I'm surprised at how much calmer I feel.

"More?" she asks, as if she knows how vital it is. I have a sudden sense that we share a special understanding, the same impression I'd received earlier when the spirit was speaking through her. Without knowing why, I see us as co-conspirators, the other people in the room merely backdrop to our plot.

"Those are quite some waves of heat you're giving off," she comments, as I drain a second glass.

I almost choke on my last mouthful of water. "Oh, really?" Let's hope she doesn't understand me well enough to realize her husband is the one responsible for that! I'd like to move away from her, yet I want her company. Actually, since I have no control over my body temperature, I wish she could just stop being aware of it.

If you formulate a wish for something in a certain way, you can sometimes manage to swing the course of events in your preferred direction — another one of those childhood talents I set aside along with the telepathy. All of that seemed dangerous, more than I could handle: I found it hard enough to cope with the demands of *ordinary* life. The ethical questions raised by reading minds, the grave responsibilities implicit in glimpsing the future, the unfair advantage of being able to make a person think or feel what I wanted them to — all these made me reject my own gifts. Part of me did think it a shame to let them go to waste, but I comforted myself with the knowledge that it was like having a buried treasure somewhere that I could dig up if I really, really needed to. Now today, for some reason, I've found myself tapping this resource on the slightest of pretexts. First I let myself peek into Bruno's inner sanctum, and now I've executed a series of deft mental manipulations that I don't actually understand, though I'm certain they took effect and Veronica can't sense my heat anymore. Well. I *am* surprising myself. I'd better get out of here before any more surprises pop up.

"Vero," I say. "I'm going back to my hotel."

"Good night, then," she answers. "Come again soon!" Once again I'm grateful for her matter-of-factness, her sincere but undemanding friendliness. She adds: "Will you be all right walking back?"

"Sure," I reply without hesitation. "Of course." But then I'm *not* so sure. At the very least I should steel myself against the pallid fluorescence of the nocturnal streets, the bleary faces on the prowl.

"I don't know," Vero says, examining me. "Bruno!" she calls. He comes over to us. She speaks to him in Portuguese.

"Okay — you ready to go?" he asks me, and heads off toward the hallway.

"What?"

"I asked him to walk you there," Vero says.

"Oh, but he doesn't have to! I mean really! I'll be fine!" A note of desperation comes into my voice. The man's proximity may rekindle the blaze I could barely withstand; in a one-on-one situation, I may not be able to dissemble.

"You probably *would* be fine, but we don't want to take any chances — don't want to lose the newest member of our crew! Tonight is a full moon and there are characters who're bound to be acting up out there. Besides, it's not far."

Bruno has returned, presumably to find out what's holding me up. Hearing this last sentence, he groans. "What do you mean, not far?" he asks, looking distressed. "All the way over the hill and across the square!"

Dismayed, I blush. "You really don't have to come with me, you know. Seriously. I'm not scared at all."

His grimace of disbelief relaxes into a smile. Vero gives him a shove and shakes her head.

"He's just having you on," she says. "He doesn't mind going with you one bit. Only that he always has to act the opposite of what's expected of him."

Having me on! That's about as funny as giving someone whiplash. I frown and rub the back of my neck: I hate being played for a fool. "Thanks anyway," I say, smiling tightly. Turning on my heel, I walk quickly away, down the hallway, and out the door. I'm sure they're looking at each other in surprise. Whatever.

The breeze outside is cool and nice. Moonlight floods the streets, lending a strange cast to the atmosphere. Not too many people: a clutch of bedraggled tourists, a few prostitutes bulging out of their tiny costumes, a man unconscious on a doorstep. Irritation dissipates as I get into stride, energized by the fresh air. I'm on the alert, though I keep my head down.

Having arrived at the hotel without incident, I cross the lobby and mount the stairs. The dingy surroundings don't bother me as much — not more palatable, just irrelevant. I'm impatient, wishing the morning had already arrived and I were refreshed and ready to set out again. The important thing now is to get some sleep.

I awaken in a sweat, the stale air lying heavy upon me. Faint gray light from the courtyard leaks in around the window frame. As I push open the window in hopes of a breeze, a shape springs back from the other side.

I shut the window again in a casual manner. My heart pounds; my pulse throbs in my throat. Now I'm aware of a thin biting whine, more a feeling than a sound, perhaps only the tautness of my nerves. The walls seem thin, almost transparent. As silently as possible, I step into the bathroom and wash in the little shower cubicle, wondering how well my splashing sounds can be heard outside, whether they're being translated into images. I hurry to get dressed, collect a few things, and leave. There's no one outside my room anymore.

I walk away from the hotel fast and take a few turns at random before realizing I don't know where to go. I'm not sure what time it is, but it must be too early for much of anything except a coffee somewhere and then finding a place to sit outside. Right or left? To the left the street slopes downward, a little wedge of blue sea at its far end. To the right it winds around a corner. I head toward the bay.

The air is already thick with gathering heat. People are heading briskly to work or school, hair still damp from the shower, skirts and pants as yet uncreased. Families that slept in doorways are folding up bedding, packing away their possessions. No coffee shops or bakeries open yet.

The street empties into a wide, windswept square. I cross over to stand at the railing on the other side, beyond which the ground drops away and the sea stretches out into a silvery haze. I try to picture the coast of Angola beyond the shimmer, sending out a mental hello to anyone who might be standing there staring in my direction. Then I sit down on a nearby bench, drink from the bottle of water I have with me, and chew on a half granola bar I find wedged in my guidebook. Instead of planning out the day, I figure I'll run through some of my practices — haven't done any since I got here.

I start with an invocation my grandmother taught me, savoring its images: "Ancestors, you who have preserved the mystery of featherless flight, you are welcome in this house, please call today." It reminds me that my home is wherever I happen to be, and settles me more firmly in the unfamiliar city, beneath the open sky. The prayer calls for a recitation of the names of friends and family — comforting, to think of all those, alive and dead, who've helped make me who I am.

I move on to the Four Directions chant, facing each of the points of the compass in turn. I hope that to passersby I appear to be simply admiring different views of the landscape; my chanting is more of a mumble. I address the four directions, identifying their qualities within myself; it's a Native American-influenced ritual, whereas the first one was of Yoruban derivation. Then I perform the self-blessing, acknowledging the different parts of my body and offering up the wish that they may continue their magical work. I don't know what culture that ritual is from, but I'm glad somebody invented it: it feels good.

I finish up with the Taoist practice of circulating an "inner smile" among my organs. As always I'm amazed at how vivid — and pleasant — the sensation of smiling can be when it's merely imagined.

All these things make sense to me; whatever other effects they may have, they invariably leave me feeling much lighter. I know I fall smack into the "spiritual materialist" category, picking up bits from one tradition or another, practicing or discarding them for days, months, or years.

In the avenue behind me the traffic rumbles and squeals. Shoes rasp along the sidewalk. The first street vendors are hawking their wares to the thickening crowd. A young couple ambles over to lean on the railing and peer into the distance.

Thoughts intrude, turning down the volume on the sensory input: I must have been here for more than an hour. I'm kind of antsy: I know I should go deal with the police — get it over with.

As I walk up the front steps of the police station, I remind myself that I have nothing to be nervous about. The tourist industry is the lifeblood of this city, and I'm a respectable United States academic with a valid passport and no crimes to my name.

A guard sits at a desk just inside the entrance. The first time I was here, the police lady led me right past him, but I can't very well breeze through on my own. I'm not actually sure he's awake: he's a very large specimen, his eyes so sunken into the flesh of his face that it's impossible to tell if they're open or closed. His hands are hidden from view; now and then one shoulder jerks up. It's probably better to disturb him if he's sleeping than risk having him wake up as I sneak in.

"*Olá, senhor,*" I venture. A little more loudly: "*Senhor!*"

His shoulder jerks again. I think I see a glint amid his eyelashes. Since there's no other reaction forthcoming, I decide to proceed as if I had his consent. No sooner have I strolled into the central hallway, however, than a resonant croak erupts from behind me:

"Brep!"

I don't turn around. I've just spotted Stiff exiting from a door on one side of the hall and crossing over to another. I hail him in order to legitimize my presence in the narrow eyes of the guard, who has just said something else I can't fathom. Stiff doesn't seem to hear me, so I hasten toward the door he's disappeared through, just as the guard emits a third, louder sound. I find myself looking into a small office, in which Stiff is talking with another policeman. When he notices me he interrupts the conversation, waves the man away.

"Yes, miss," he says to me, by way of greeting. "It is better if you do not press charges against the people of 239 Travesso Street."

"What!" I splutter. "But I had no intention of pressing charges!"

He surveys me critically. "Then we cancel the matter?" he asks.

"Yes, of course! I only came to make a formal declaration of the theft of my possessions. I noticed you didn't write down anything I told you yesterday."

"For what reason do you wish to make a declaration, miss?"

"Well, I thought it might help me get my things back."

"What exactly was stolen?"

"A wallet and a camera."

"Show me your passport."

He takes it, copies down the number and my name.

"The truth is, miss" — he gives me back the passport, along with the first smile I've seen on him, a sad one — "there is no chance to locate your possessions. Hundreds of suspects exist. If you have determination, you will look at four hundred, five hundred photographs; you will inspect a dozen lineups of twenty men each."

"I would have to do that?"

"Yes. And even then, you will never get back your possessions. The bandits always sell these things immediately."

"Oh."

"Well, miss. I hope the rest of your stay is comfortable, and do not hesitate to contact us if you have a need."

"But those people, at 239 Rua do Travesso . . . you . . . they . . . "

"I hope you do not think to contact them again. Perhaps you do not realize this group is a radical Maoist cell associated with terrorist activities in Germany in the late nineteen seventies. They are not innocent hippies, miss. They are an arm of a dangerous worldwide organization. It is not advisable to get involved. In the best of cases, you receive a stray bullet. A possibility. I am sorry. Have a good day."

He shows me the door with his index finger. Startled by the blunt dismissal, I sidle over and grip the door frame, fighting against the powerful sensation of being popped out of the room like a cork.

"No matter what organization they are a part of" — my voice cracks a bit, taking away some of my self-confidence — "I didn't find they deserved the treatment you gave them."

"Certainly, because you do not know what crimes *they* have committed . . . but I repeat: do not continue your association with them. For your safety I could give you a legal order to leave this country, but I know that is not necessary. I know you understand the matter is serious."

"Yes," I say, eager now to get out. "Well, thanks anyway; goodbye."

"Goodbye, miss. I hope I will not see you again!" He flashes the sad smile, perhaps to temper the rudeness of his statement, then turns away. I retreat down the hallway, past the guard, and out.

The experience has left me shaken and I decide to walk fast to try and dissipate the nervous energy prickling inside me. I'm heading in the direction of 239 Rua do Travesso but become more and more afraid that a police officer could be tailing me. I wind up taking a long detour, a decision I then regret because it does nothing but make me seem even more suspicious if I *am* being followed. By the time I arrive at Rua do Travesso, I'm sweating.

This time it's Vero who opens the door. Her face seems smaller. All of a sudden I hear someone coming up the stairway behind me and I practically shove Vero back inside in my hurry to get in and close the door.

"What's wrong?" she asks. The footsteps pass on the landing and start up the next set of stairs. "Someone you know?"

"No," I answer.

"Come sit down!" She's off in the direction of the kitchen. "You must tell me what this is all about. I can offer you tea — have you had breakfast?"

I'm relieved to be here. No one else is in the kitchen; the

space is filled with light coming through the high-set windows. Vero gets out a second mug and pours tea from a pot on the counter.

"The police didn't want me to come see you," I tell her.

"Oh, really," she says, handing me my tea. "Honey?"

"Yes, please."

"Well, I'm glad you did anyway. Are you worried?"

"No; well, yes. I tend to be, in general."

"It's good you already realize that. That's some preparatory work out of the way. One thing we already know about the Outernet is that in order to log on it's helpful to be free of fear. We're trying to learn how to dismantle as much of our fear as possible."

"Why not all of it?"

"Too ambitious. We don't have unlimited time." She blows on her tea to cool it, then raises her head abruptly and addresses me with surprising vehemence. "Who *are* you, anyway?" She's staring at me with a puzzled frown. I'm taken aback, but pleased. Everyone usually seems to take my existence for granted, myself included. I'm not quite sure how to answer, though.

"How do you mean?"

"I mean, you confuse me. In some ways you're so open, so present, I feel I know the essential about you and don't need any more information. On the other hand, you're traveling inside a sort of armored car I can't really break into."

"An armored car!" I repeat, shocked. I hadn't known it was so obvious.

"Yes: the rigid compartmentalization of academia, that way of thinking; what you've told us so far about your life. It's certainly normal to snuggle oneself into a niche — but what's *not* normal is to remain as curious as you seem to be, curious enough to step out of line. It's not so much that you came all the way to Brazil that surprises me, as it is your willingness to participate in our activities. Including just

126

hanging out upstairs."

I wonder what she's getting at. "Well, and why not?" I ask.

"That's exactly the attitude. It's lovely. So what's holding you back?"

I feel defensive, without knowing why. "Back from what? I'm just the same as anyone else. I've got tendencies one way and tendencies the other, and I muddle along with that."

"I'm sorry," she says, reacting not to my words but to my tone. "But," she pursues, "why *muddle*? You're so close: superimposed but just a fraction off: the edges don't quite meet. *So* close."

"From what point of view?" I ask shortly.

She widens her eyes. "I don't know. Mine, I suppose."

"And you, now," I say, "your edges are all met up? That must be a nice feeling."

"It's not that my life is that wonderful, believe me."

"Why not? You live in a really interesting place, you're working full tilt on a really interesting project, with great people, you have a family — what's missing?"

"Come on, Josephine. I'm human. What's missing? Money is missing, for one. Food, utilities, dentists, everything is expensive in this 'really interesting' city. Not expensive to someone with U.S. dollars to spend, perhaps, but to us. We can never pay all the bills at once — it's a constant scramble. The work is good but it's hard; sometimes I just get so tired. And it always seems like we won't get enough done in time. My family — well, my marriage, as such, disintegrated long ago, only Bruno refuses to give up on it. Our daughter is fraying herself a path through the labyrinth of hallucinogens, hard drugs, and mysticism — we can only pray she makes it to the other side. And as for myself, sometimes I wonder."

She pauses, but I have no idea what to say.

"Sometimes," she resumes, "I think it would be better for me to give all this up. I could make decent money, not good money but decent money, as a seamstress — I used to have a shop. Or teaching English: there's always a demand. I could breathe easier and find a nice little place to rent outside the city, somewhere my daughter might want to spend time: she's always enjoyed trees and plants and open sky. It would be healthier for her. It would be healthier for me. And I might have time to do a few of the things that I like to do, that I want to do, but never get a chance to around here."

"Like what?"

"Like sewing. Besides working for other people, altering clothes and so forth, I used to make costumes. Fantastic ones, out of burlap and lace and velvet and canvas and feathers and plastic — I used everything. The last project I had was making the costumes for a production we put on; they were glued and nailed together as well as sewn. I was inspired by some photos of costumes Picasso created for a Dada play and I made these three-dimensional collages on wearable frames. Now I have some new ideas, but never the means or the time to realize them. So there's that. Growing vegetables is another thing — we do what we can up on the roof raising herbs and greens and tomatoes, but I'd love to have a real garden and spend time in it. Lots of things."

We stay silent for a moment. Then I ask: "So why don't you? Choose that other life. And does it even have to be a choice? You can't have a job and live outside the city and still do the Outernet work and the theater stuff?"

"The Outernet work is a full-time job already. It really is. You haven't seen that part yet, but we do a lot of outreach, a lot of networking; we're constantly having meetings as well as individual consultations with many, many people. And being in the center of the city makes strategic sense. Relocating at this point would cause a delay we can't well afford. Look at it this way: the goal of our work is to help ensure that the human family survives at all; costume design, gardening, all that is secondary. The aspect of the Outernet we're researching most urgently is the one that will allow global communication if the time comes when the usual means aren't accessible, so that as many people as possible can participate in making decisions about the planet's future."

Decisions about the planet's future? I remember the Maoist thing — it makes me uneasy. I don't have the patience to wait and watch for clues: I want to know. "Are you affiliated with any political party?" I ask.

"Not exactly. We call ourselves anarchists because it puts a lot of the right ideas into people's minds — or if they're the wrong ones, then we have an easy starting point for discussion. But there is no 'party,' so to speak: only a number of groups and individuals who have created a worldwide network of connections . . . helped enormously, of course, by the Internet. Now we need to wean ourselves from that technological dependence. But to answer your question, since we haven't any hierarchy, any chain of command, we don't constitute a political organization as such. No one person can tell another what to do — just make suggestions. Decision making is in the hands of all, since the outcomes affect everyone. And the material goods at our disposal are distributed among all. The concept of financial profit is irrelevant, but everything one does benefits oneself in one way or another."

"How is that different from communism?"

"Communism is not unreasonable, in its effort to dismantle systems built on economic disparity. Its problem is that it transfers power from one set of hands into another and preserves a meritocracy. It also tends to centralize and separate off its various operating parts. There are many irreconcilable differences between our viewpoints."

"So how does your vision accommodate the reality of innumerable individuals all wanting something different and all of them convinced the show should go the way *they* want it to?"

"Consensus. No matter how difficult it is to achieve. So

many things seem impossible to us, not because they are intrinsically so, but because we've received the lifelong conditioning we have. If you can start even one generation going under a different set of governing principles, the thing will propagate itself effortlessly."

"But how can you ever make the transition?"

"That's one question," she says, "we are working on."

I take a sip of my tea, which is almost cold. Well, if she is in fact a Maoist, she doesn't want to come out with it. Or maybe she's not one herself but has close ties to some Maoist militants, in keeping with her all-inclusive philosophy. I realize it's hard for me to completely discount Stiff's warning. Hmm. I guess I won't worry about it unless I have to.

"So, what are you up to today?" I ask. "I have some questions about what happened last night, but I know you weren't expecting me now, and I'm sure you've got a lot to do. I could leave again — I need to go to the Internet café at some point. Or I could stay and read or something, or if I can help you in any way . . ."

"You picked a good time to show up," Vero answers. "I'll actually be going out in a moment, but I'm glad we had a chance for a chat and a cup of tea. We'll have plenty of time to talk more later on. Do feel free to stick around. Bruno is upstairs; he'd be glad to see you. Other people may come in and out. You can make yourself comfortable down here — wherever you'd like. I'll be back, oh, probably midafternoon."

She's sorting through papers on the table, putting some of them in a folder she then places in her handbag. "I have an appointment with an executive from the water company: it's my last effort to resolve the dispute before having to call in a solicitor. They were charging us for twice the amount of water we were using, and then cut us off when we wouldn't pay the bill. We managed to get them to turn the water back on, but they refused to recognize their mistake and are threatening to shut it off again. After I'm finished with them I have to meet a friend, and then I need to go to the market and bring back some groceries."

As she's about to leave the room she stops, looks at me, and smiles with a kind of pleased affection. Something occurs to her; she drops the smile, says "Wait," and goes to pull open a drawer under the kitchen counter. She rummages around and extracts a key on a green ribbon.

"Here," she says, handing it to me. "Come and go as you like."

I'm pleased. "Thanks!" I say.

Then she's gone. I sit and watch as the space she took up folds itself back out. A subdued blanket of noise presses in from the street — two of the three windows are open. Traffic, voices in conversation, barking: they all wash together. The apartment itself is silent except for vibrations at the very edge of sound, like the ones in the floorboards caused by an occasional passing truck. A shaft of sunlight slices through a half-filled water glass, producing a delicately warbling crescent on the tabletop.

It's so peaceful to be in a hospitable environment, alone, but I think I should go up and at least greet Bruno. It might seem odd if I don't. I climb the stairs to the roof.

When I emerge into the fresh air my first thought is that it's raining, though sunlight infuses the canopy of plants. Then I realize that an artificial mist is being sprayed out of the grid of pipes overhead. I make my way to the little house. The door is ajar; I push it open a bit wider.

Bruno, in faded blue shorts, is crouching over something in a far corner of the room. His back is to me; at the squeak of the door hinge, he looks over his shoulder and grins. "Welcome," he says.

"What are you doing?" I ask, stepping into the room.

"I am trying to make the nail lie balanced on the blade of this saw," he answers. The saw's back edge rests on the floor.

"You don't have enough light there," I say, noticing that

his shadow is falling over the saw. "Why don't you move a bit?" He does, and I take up a position on the other side of the blade, watching his unsuccessful attempts to place the nail just so and detach his fingers from it without making it fall.

"Let me try," I say, on an impulse. The challenge absorbs me: the exact point of equilibrium is so minute. Once I've succeeded in finding it, both of us watch, transfixed — could it still fall? — the nail poised there across the blade.

"Changes your perspective, doesn't it?" Bruno asks. He's right: I've been concentrating so intently on the tiny area that when I look away everything in the room seems heightened somehow. It's like trying on the eyeglasses of someone whose vision is only slightly worse than yours.

"My turn," he says.

This time he pulls off the balancing act; I clap, then stand up, ill at ease now that there's no diversion. I'm reluctant to leave the room, as if being here with Bruno were an opportunity I shouldn't let slip by, but I can't think how to take advantage of it.

"Well, I guess I'll go back downstairs," I say. "I just came up to say hello. Vero let me in, but she left. She said I could hang out downstairs. What are *you* going to do?"

"I will have breakfast, I think, and then sleep. I was up all night reading. I will come down with you now."

First, though, he decides to take me on an extensive tour of the garden, showing me this plant and that in a sequence determined by common attributes such as leaf shape, nutritional value, and so forth. We zigzag among the rows of pots, crossing from one side of the roof to the other, doubling back, squatting down to examine a specimen, or peering up — me on the tips of my toes — to make out some attribute of a hanging plant. The pipes aren't misting anymore; scatterings of water drops are left on the leaves. The foliage overhead provides shade that is by no means cool, but is pleasant even so.

I enjoy following Bruno around and listening to him. Although I have no special interest in plant biology and don't actually pay much attention to what he's so carefully explaining, the sound of his voice is soothing. The faint smell of his sweat is strangely sweet, like a child's, with just the tiniest acrid note, and something else mixed in it, too, a scent that seems familiar. At first I think it's oranges, but that's not it. I become so focused on identifying it that I tune out his words completely, though I throw in an "oh" or "really" at random intervals. All the while, I'm attempting to maneuver discreetly so that my nose remains as close as possible to one or the other of his armpits. More often than not, a sudden shift in wind direction fills my distended nostrils with the scent of damp earth or sap from a snapped stem.

Despite my efforts I can't put a name to the smell; all I can be sure of is that it intensifies whenever our bodies come into contact, through the momentary pressure of his hand on my arm to emphasize a point, or the solid warmth of his body leaning against me as he tries to pluck a leaf or push a branch out of my way. Each time, the after-impression of his touch stays on my skin: a fibrillating patch that takes a few minutes to subside. Strange, but not unpleasant. Does Bruno experience any such effect? He seems oblivious, entirely given over to the wondrous properties of the plant realm and the desire to share his knowledge with me. He's doesn't talk continuously: often he falls into silent contemplation of whatever it is he's been showing me, thoughtfully turning over a twig or loosening some dirt with his fingers.

Without warning a delicious arousal steals over me once more. The sensation isn't sparked off by a touch or, as was the case yesterday, by a glance; it doesn't radiate inward from the surface but spreads slowly from deep inside, so slowly that I have time to observe it with detachment — until it grows more excruciating than pleasurable. Panicked, I fight to keep my vital signs under control.

Bruno notices but makes no comment, continuing his

lecture instead. "Like this flower here," he says, reaching across me, his arm brushing against my chest. He plucks a startling looking flower from a vine. "This is a passion flower."

The flower has a rich purple convoluted center with a miniature cream-colored space-pod rising out of it, an aureole of long white petals, and a sprinkling of tendrils.

"All of this is passion fruit," he says, waving toward the trellis covered with robust, dark-green leaves. A few purple and white flowers peek out here and there. "The whole plant has sedative properties — it falls into the category of nervines — although the leaves, flowers, and fruit each have a slightly different action upon the body."

It's hard to focus on what he is saying. My breath is labored; sweat beads up on my forehead faster than I can wipe it off.

Bruno picks a few leaves from the vine and puts them in the pocket of his shorts. "We will go downstairs and make you some tea from these," he says. "I think it is a good idea."

I manage an embarrassed half-laugh, but his acknowledgment of my condition relieves me of the strain of trying to act normal. As soon as I give that up, I start to tremble. "I don't know what it is," I say. My chattering teeth chop up the words. Waves of hot and cold run over me.

Bruno watches me with concern. "Here, this will be more rapid," he says. He plucks a passion flower off, then grasps my wrist and leads me to the low wall at the edge of the rooftop. Gently, he tugs downward on my hand until I'm sitting on the floor with my back against the wall, then goes over to a spigot a few feet away. There's a bucket under it and a small clear plastic cup upside down over the tap.

Bruno removes the cup and fills it with water. He puts it on the sunny ledge and floats the flower on the surface, then stands there with his eyes closed for a minute. My curiosity distracts me a bit from the physical discomfort. Bruno opens his eyes, takes the flower out of the cup, and gives me the water.

"Three or four drops should do," he says. Fishing in his pocket, he extracts one of the leaves and folds it to form a sort of scoop, which he hands me. Despite my shivering I'm able to get some water in the crease of the leaf and bring it to my mouth.

Instant clarity. My nerves stop buzzing. It's as if I'd been a marionette jerked about by some amphetamine-crazed puppeteer and the strings had all been cut at once. My whole body is both numb and achy; I feel as if I've been through an actual wringer. But the stillness in my mind and flesh is an enormous relief.

"Thanks," I say. "How could that do that?"

"It is the quickest form of flower essence," he answers. "Usually, to make flower essences you must follow many instructions about using pure water, not contaminating the vessels, leaving the petals in for a certain time, etc. But we have found that when necessary, a lightning-quick infusion allows the energetic imprint of the petals to be captured by the water and produces a good result, even if it is not as complete as it could be."

"Well, it was great," I say. "Thank you so much."

"You are welcome. We will make the tea from the leaves anyway. Have you ever had an attack like that before?"

"No." Then I feel bad about lying. "Not really," I amend. "I did have a kind of one . . ." I trail off. He must think I'm trying to remember back across a distance of years. "It was last night," I finish.

"Really!" He looks at me with interest. "At what point?"

"I'm not exactly sure." It's only a half-lie. I don't remember what time it happened, but I remember why, which is more relevant. Should I tell him that a look from him was responsible for setting off volcanic rumblings I could barely keep under control? Perhaps it wasn't really the look, but something I ate, after all. Or the water I brushed my teeth with at the hotel. I'm glad I only had four drops of that tap water just now. It dawns on me that I'm taking a long time to answer his question, which I now realize I've forgotten. Or maybe I already answered it. Oh yes, that's right. Clearly, I'm a bit dazed.

Bruno's expression is still worried. "Will you lie down while I prepare the tea? I will bring it up for you," Bruno says.

I don't want to cause extra work for him. The fact is, though, that my legs feel hollow and the idea of going downstairs doesn't appeal to me at all.

I follow him back into the room and sink down on one of the beds; he leaves again right away. It feels so damn good to simply lie there — I soak it in. My mind skims over thoughts and images, returning in between to the agreeable softness of the mat under my body.

I'm not sure if I dozed off or not, but here's Bruno with a mug. The tea is cool enough for me to be able to take several gulps.

"Go ahead, finish it," he says, sitting on the edge of the mattress. I drink it all and lie back down. Probably best to sleep the whole thing off.

"Do you mind if I lie next to you?" Bruno asks.

My rapidly growing drowsiness prevents me from caring too much. "That's fine," I mumble, moving over.

He lies down, but this time, instead of keeping his body apart, he scoots up close and puts an arm around me. Of course I'm more alert now, waiting to see what else he might do. He does nothing. We're so close that I can tell he doesn't have an erection. This reassures me. I realize I can relax into his friendly embrace and rest deeply. I give a big sigh and fall fast asleep.

When I come to it's with difficulty, but something seems to be forcing me awake. Once I've managed to open and properly focus my eyes I see Vero standing by the door watching us with a curious expression on her face. Bruno seems to be asleep. Our positions have shifted while we slept: now he's facing away from me and I'm snuggled up against his back with my arm flung across him. I stare back at Vero, a mixture of shame and dread rising in me.

ESPEL VALLEY

FLORIAN

For a while I thought everything was, miraculously, turning out fine. Better than fine: it was Paradise. For the first time in my life, I enjoyed perfect good fortune. My residence was in a wild and beautiful location, yet not so remote from civilization as to be inconvenient. I was able to provide my family with good, plentiful food and all other necessities of a comfortable existence, thanks to my work on the farm. It required handling tools and plants and animals, solving sums and problems, having discussions with workers and transactions with the outside world — tradesmen and showmen and people wanting you to pay for things you'd always had for free. There was a movement to take our farm away from us and turn it into conservation land, but it was no more than a shabby ploy and I enjoyed outwitting the government men who occasionally sidled up to the barn, wheedling and threatening us in turn. The work was demanding, and I enjoyed it.

My private life, too, was more than satisfying. My wife happened to be the woman I respected most in the world — and then there was my mistress, a playful and inventive partner. Implausibly, the three of us coexisted in a harmonious fashion. My son, little Ara, accepted the other woman as a stepmother; our household was remarkably free of strife. For a man of modest ambition such as myself, the elements of a successful life were all in place. And I was happy, truly happy — waking up and falling asleep happy.

In the early days with Zar I had been happy, too, but there had always been a gap between us. I blamed myself at first, thinking that I overwhelmed her with my awe, and for a while I tried to concentrate on her flaws and frailties. But even so, I was slightly anxious every time we interacted. Later, things between us got downright hostile and stayed that way for a long time, but recently we had resumed cordial relations.

My greatest difficulty after Emily came to live with us was adapting my mind to the situation. It was a daily struggle for me to believe that I, Florian Marsden, was living harmoniously with two wives! Zar and I did not actually engage in intimacy any longer, yet of course we had had our share in the past, which is usually enough to cause jealousy. But no: Zar seemed truly at peace with the arrangement. In fact, she and Emily spent more and more time together, especially once Zar started teaching at Red Pepper as well. I had to admit that what she had tried to explain to me in the past was true: the existence of one bond did not detract from the other; on the contrary, they were mutually enhancing. I was grateful to Zar and began liking her better again. I even caught myself wishing that she, too, had a lover, someone to make *her* feel good, since the two of us were not easy with each other in that way anymore. There was a wound between us that was still raw although I never did understand what had caused it, and I thought it would take a lot of time and perhaps something else before we might be able to reach out and touch from either side of it. I was not driven to plumb the depths of this mystery, however: why be bothered, when I could find certain comfort in the arms of my mistress? When Emily was around, that is to say. Indeed, this was my only complaint: Emily was never present enough. At first I was simply grateful whenever she *was* there, but over time I also became resentful when she was not. But not at first. At first everything was blissful.

A few months after Emily moved in, we decided to go on a belated *ménage-à-trois* honeymoon excursion to the mountains. It was a recess between terms at Red Pepper, so we would be able to bring Ara and stay away several days. The weather was agreeable: early spring, real warmth seeping in at last. Always a chill at night though, still.

We set off at dawn and rode all day except for a few brief stops. It was tedious for us as well as for the horses, but we wanted to put as much distance as we could between ourselves and home. We followed the coast, sometimes high on the cliffs above the water, sometimes down along the shore.

Midafternoon we headed inland. The terrain was mountainous and only scrubby trees held out; villages here were few and far between, their clumps of sullen houses battered by the constant wind. The very barrenness of the landscape delighted us, it was so foreign; even the inhabitants looked different from the people back home, with shorter bodies, elongated faces, and a listless cast to their shoulders. It was much cooler up here, too — we noted this as the road began to wind amongst the foothills, but we were not prepared for the dramatic drop in temperature that came with nightfall. It was early still when darkness closed in around us: clouds had thickened on the slopes and we were riding straight into them. We had passed two or three inns along the way, but after night set in we did not come across any more establishments of that nature. There were hardly even any houses left, just the steadily climbing road and the wind's doleful whistle in the leafless trees. When Ara started to shiver uncontrollably we knew we would be forced to beg for shelter at the next dwelling we encountered.

And then we saw it, set back from the road by a front yard hacked out of the wild surrounding brush: a sizeable house, two stories high, with a wide veranda running round it. A few windows glowed yellow. As we came to a halt, the front door opened and a hunched figure appeared.

"Granddad!" Ara cried out, starting off up the narrow dirt path that led to the steps. The rest of us exchanged alarmed looks and hurried after him: Ara's grandparents, my mother and the Leveras, were back home in Espel Valley. By the time we caught up with our boy he was on the porch, standing before a very old man with great quantities of whiskers and wrinkles on his face. The man's eyes were bright. He was smiling.

"Good night, sir," Emily said.

"Please!" the old man answered, in a voice part whisper, part croak. "Just call me Granddad."

"Granddad!" Ara exclaimed again.

Granddad beamed. "I love young'uns," he said, shaking his head fondly. "I had a fine time with my grandson when he was that age. Why don't you all come on in?" His speech was slightly furred.

He shuffled backward, pushing the door wider as he did so. We filed past him into a large parlor, sparsely furnished. An appetizing smell hung in the air.

"Would you-all like something to eat?" He ushered us into the adjacent dining room and disappeared through a swinging door into the kitchen.

The dinner table was small, barely longer than it was wide, with a place set at either end. We brought over four of the chairs that stood along the wall and crowded ourselves into them. Someone was rattling pots in the kitchen; we sat and rested, grateful to be out of the frigid night air.

Pretty soon Granddad began a series of trips back and forth from the kitchen with glasses of water, napkins, plates, cutlery, and condiments.

"Who's the other plate for?" Ara asked him at one point. He had apparently been wondering why the table had been set for two when we arrived.

Granddad did not seem surprised by the question. "Oh — that's for Grandma. She'll be here in a minute."

"So it's just the two of you living out here, then?" asked Zar.

"Yes, it is. It used to be there was a lot more people living in this old house: my son and his family, and of course my mother was with us for a long time. But now it's just Grandma and me."

He was passing around behind us, ladling food onto our plates. When he was done he sat down and picked up his fork.

"Enjoy!" he said, waving expansively over the table.

We hesitated.

"What about Grandma?" Ara asked. The food was steaming on her plate.

"Oh, don't worry about her. She'll do fine. She just eats slowly, is all." He took a bite of mashed potato. The rest of us followed suit, all except Ara, who was squinting at Grandma's empty chair, pushed back a bit from the table.

"Ara." I nudged him. "Eat something." He only crinkled up his face, squeezing his eyes shut then opening them wide to gaze at the chair as though hypnotized. I became impatient and spoke sharply. "Ara! Mind!"

Dutifully he looked down at his plate and began to poke at the food.

"Mary and I moved up here on the ridge way back in '37. The road you came up on wasn't a real road then — at least, it didn't connect up with the county road at all. It just meandered all around the estate." Granddad interrupted himself. "More water?" he asked, taking up the pitcher and topping up our glasses, including Grandma's, which was half-empty. "We fell in love back in North Valley and got hitched and then her uncle willed her this here piece of land. Well, I built this house with my own hands and Mary helped, too. We've always done everything together . . . and we're just as much in love today as we ever were." He raised his water glass and gestured slightly with it toward the empty chair, a roguish twinkle in his rheumy eye.

I did not think the others could see Grandma any more than I could. We took it in stride though, and ate the good plain food while the old man, who clearly enjoyed an audience, held forth about days gone by. He expressed no curiosity whatsoever about us, our origins, our occupations; he seemed to take our presence for granted. When the meal was over he proposed showing us to our rooms.

"Actually," he said, "I won't go up with you. I've been up there once already today, tidying up, and my hip's been giving me some trouble. I sleep down here. But you'll find fresh towels in the bathroom — you can light the lamp at the top of the stairs; just snuff it when you're ready to turn in. There are four rooms — the young man is used to sleeping alone?" He looked at Ara.

"No, he hasn't really ever— " Zar started to say, but Ara interrupted:

"I want to!"

Granddad smiled.

"Are you saying you'd like each of us to sleep in a separate room?" Emily asked him politely.

"Why yes, I think that would be the most proper, don't you?"

It was an odd stipulation, but it would have been unseemly to argue with our host. Perhaps he could not abide the idea of strangers copulating in the hallowed family sanctum; once we were upstairs, however, I was certain we could do as we pleased — the bad hip would likely prevent him from coming to check on us. With effusive thanks and good nights we retreated up the spiral staircase.

146

Upstairs, a hallway with two bedrooms on either side of it led to a small bathroom. The first room we looked into was somber despite its floral chintz — Zar chose that one. Ara took the one that was decorated in a more youthful style; he climbed on the high bed to see how well it bounced. Emily and I had the remaining two rooms, separated by the hallway; each had an additional door giving onto the porch, a narrow affair that ran all the way round the house.

Zar went into the bathroom with Ara while Emily and I embraced in Emily's room, then I retreated to my room and Zar and Ara left the bathroom and I heard Emily go in and waited my turn. Then I performed my ablutions and when I came out there was silence from the other three rooms and no lights under their doors. I turned down the hallway lamp.

The room I had chosen must have been the master bedroom: it had a double bed, a large wardrobe, a dresser with a mirror. I pulled back the bedspread, put my nose to the sheets: they smelled freshly laundered. I went over to the door that gave onto the porch. There was a cobweb over the latch; a small brown spider scuttled to safety on the wall as I destroyed its home. I let myself out, followed the porch around to the back wall of the house, and leaned over the railing. The chill air was refreshing after the musty warmth of the house. A garden lay below: withered stalks in the furrowed earth. Beyond it was a lawn of high grass with objects jutting out here and there, edges brushed by the faint moonshine. I had no idea what they were. A dense mass of bush and trees hemmed in the lawn, blending into the night sky. What possessed people to come forge a life in a wilderness such as this? It sounded as if Granddad had had to struggle mightily in order to maintain his homestead up here — what had made it worth it to him? His enduring love for his wife seemed to provide all the justification for existence he needed.

Suddenly I missed Emily: the comfort of her soft body, her yielding, knowing eyes. I looked toward her room: the glass pane in the upper part of the door was dark. I went over and tried the handle. It did not give. I knocked softly: nothing. I passed back through my room and crossed over to Emily's other door. It opened easily — but the twin bed inside was empty. I was utterly disoriented for a second, so unprepared was I for that.

I slipped into the dark room, walked hesitantly over to the bed, and sat down. Where could she be? I tried to tell myself she might be nestled in with Ara, loath to leave him alone in this strange house. But I knew she was not with him: she was with Zar. This late at night? Perhaps they were talking and I simply had not heard them as I passed through the hallway.

I could make out the outlines of a door in the wall. A closet? I knew Zar's room was on the other side of that wall. It was hard to tell whether this was a closet door or not. I stepped up to it and placed my ear against the wood. I decided to open it and if it turned out not to be a closet I would say "Oh — I thought it was a closet." Already I was not thinking too clearly. Small tremors ran through me, as if I were falling ill.

Abruptly I opened the door. It did indeed lead to the adjacent room. A bit of moonlight fell across the high bed upon which Zar and Emily were kneeling, facing each other — naked! Despite the cold! They did not bother to look at me. Emily's hand was on Zar's thigh.

I could not comprehend it. I stepped back instinctively, shutting the door as if against an icy draft.

I sat on the bed, my head reeling. I never knew! How long had this . . . ? How could it be? What should I do? Could I wrest myself free from the horror that had started up deep inside me? This last seemed a question of immediate survival: the pain was overwhelming. Everything I thought was mine had been destroyed in one blow. I knew I would never be able to face either of those women again, lest my agony erupt as murderous rage. I would ride out of here before daybreak; where I would go was of no importance. Our life together was ruined; we would divide up our possessions . . . "Although you know what? Damn it all to hell!" I fumed. "They can have everything. The house and everything in it. Ara. He must have known all along. But when . . . ? During the day, of course. When I was on the farm. And at Red Pepper."

The betrayal filled me with nausea and an unbearable sense of impotence. I wanted to pick up the flimsy bed and ram it through the door I had just shut; showers of splinters would have suited my mood perfectly. But harming Granddad's house or any of his possessions was out of the question. There was no way to feel better, so I did what I could to avoid disintegrating completely. Instinct told me to concentrate on something else, anything: I made myself stiff as a board, tensing every muscle against the pain that kept mounting, threatening to annihilate me.

Then the door opened. I did not move at all, not even my eyes, but I could see that it was Emily, fully clothed. She came over and sat on the bed beside me, trying to fish out my gaze; she put a hand on my back and allowed me a soft caress. Though I could not respond, her touch loosened a swell of emotions in me: violent disgust, fear, shame, self-pity, yearning. I fought to keep all of this from pushing its way to the surface, but sure enough I burst into sobs.

She tried to comfort me and in a little while I did stop crying but still could not move. Eventually she gave up and stretched out on the bed.

After what seemed like hours of intricate debate with myself, I lay down beside her. She stirred, mumbled sleepily, and put an arm around me. All I craved was a little comfort, in light of the fact that my whole world had just fallen apart. I no longer had the strength to be furious — I only felt defeated, hopeless. And it had been my habit to turn to Emily for solace. One last time . . .

I freed my left hand, which was wedged between us — slowly, so as not to waken her. With the lightest of touches I undid each button I could reach on the front of her dress. My face was near her collarbone. I watched my hand as it slid beneath one side of the open dress and closed over the firm, familiar breast. This filled me with a pleasant sensation: a welcome contrast to what I'd just been through! I sighed and instinctively started to angle my head to bring my mouth nearer to her breast.

My lips were almost on her skin when her hand came up, interposing itself. I froze. Emily had never refused me before. Now she turned away and curled up facing the wall. The horror was compounded.

I got up and walked carefully out of the room, crossed the hallway, and with equal care let myself into my own room and lowered myself onto the bed. I was caught between a desperate wish to sink into unconsciousness, and the determination to stay awake so I could saddle up as soon as dawn broke. My thoughts kept swimming into one another. Part of me insisted: "But what is wrong? Zar accepts your relationship with Emily, Emily accepts yours with Zar, so you should be able to accept this, too!" It did not matter, I told that voice. It did not matter if it was logical or not: I simply could not stomach it.

I kept my eyes fixed on the ceiling until it became a little paler. Then I picked up my bag, stopped in the bathroom, and made my way downstairs. All I had to do was cross the parlor and open the front door, but the floor creaked louder than I expected and to my dismay a light flared up behind me and I heard Granddad's strange hoarse voice.

"Who's there?" He was shuffling toward me.

"Damn it," I muttered, and quickly went to meet him. "Granddad," I said. "It is just me. I am just leaving now. Thank you so much, Granddad, for your hospitality. God bless you."

I was hoping he would let me off the hook with that. I knew I looked like a madman, I had seen myself in the bathroom mirror: tear-swollen eyes and my entire face fallen in like a bad cake. Surely Granddad would have pity on me and let me go, without inquiring into my condition. In fact, he seemed oblivious to it, and cheerily suggested:

"Well, how 'bout some coffee before you set out?"

"No, Granddad, thank you; I never drink coffee."

"Well how 'bout just this once you drink some? Keep an old man company just a little while longer? I get up around this time myself — Grandma sleeps late. I like to greet the dawn — old native custom, heh heh. And I do love to share the majesty with a fellow soul."

There was nothing I wanted less right now. I was afraid that Zar or Emily might wake up and come downstairs, but I was too weak to struggle against the old man's will. I let him maneuver me into the kitchen and onto a chair.

He poked around in the stove and lit it; he uncovered a pitcher of water, poured a potful, and set it to boil. I wished he would not make so much noise in his preparations; luckily his voice was low as he talked. For some reason he was giving me the benefit of his long-accrued wisdom concerning marital matters. I was numb and could hardly follow his prattle; I told myself I would stay an extra half-hour, no more.

Granddad went on and on about respect and so forth while I mentally counted the minutes, until he said something that caught my attention.

"And it don't stop when one of you dies, no sir. 'Until death do us part' is man's law, but not God's. If she's alive, it don't matter if she's curly-haired or freckle-faced, bony or plump, and if she's dead it don't matter if she's dead. Once that love's taken root it's for good, and you could kick and scream and try to run, but there's nowhere you can go that it's not right there with you."

I knew what he said was true. It made me aware that

deep inside me, beneath the smoldering wreckage of my beliefs and expectations, lay an indestructible kernel of love for both women. The realization made me suddenly, irrationally happy, and though the feeling vanished after a second it was enough to shift my whole mood just a fraction. I was less convinced of the absoluteness of my loss, even though it was impossible to imagine it being otherwise. The state of high tension I had been in for the past few hours released its grip ever so slightly, making space for an overwhelming weariness to push in and expand. Then I was glad for the coffee that burnt my mouth and kept me focused on the pain.

As Granddad droned on I managed to gulp down the full cup of scalding liquid, then got up and went to the door. The old man had made his way onto the subject of the equation of truth and beauty and seemed barely distracted from his train of thought as he saw me out. Although he interrupted his monologue to wish me well, I felt certain he would continue talking once he had shut the door on me — explaining it all, perhaps, to Grandma.

ZAR

I t worked better than I had planned — so well, in fact, that I almost regretted it. That night at the old codger's house I allowed Emily to touch me for the first time, not because I felt any differently toward her, but in order to make Florian jealous, to get my revenge.

During the first months of our trifurcated situation I had artfully disguised my growing anger. The arrangement was in many respects satisfactory: Emily was a stimulating companion for me as well as for Florian — in very different ways, of course. I was happy to be in the presence of a mind that could follow my meanings instantly, and we put our mutual understanding to good use at the school, where we devised a class called "Weaving: Thought and Sensation." I enjoyed Emily's company, but I did not feel close to her on some essential level. It was like being good friends with someone from a different galaxy.

Putting up with her infatuation was at times tiresome, but we never spoke of it. Once I'd taken the appropriate precautions I didn't feel anything for her, physically, and that's all there was to it. Our relationship was fruitful enough otherwise.

What was bothersome was the manner in which Florian treated me during this period. It took visible effort for him to speak to me directly, as if he couldn't exactly make out where I was. When he did address me he was courteous, often with a note of concern in his voice. It made me want to retch.

Every evening around a certain time he would metamorphose into a pop-eyed lapdog, sitting by the door waiting for his mistress. Unfortunately, the loyal little dog was often obliged to retreat, forlorn, to his plush quarters at the back of the house. He was always irritable with me on such an evening if we happened to cross paths, and the following morning as well. On the whole, he didn't have much use for me anymore, except on the rare occasions when the two of us went away or did something together and he got swept up and ended up forgetting, for a while, about Emily. Emily was certainly impressive, but not *that* impressive; the poor man had again fallen into the trap of making another person the sole focus of his existence. It's true that he did also spend a great deal of time working — his other primary interest. But I found he was growing disturbingly cool toward Ara, not out of any conscious attitude but simply because he was so riveted by Emily. More and more, he failed to understand the thoughts Ara was trying to convey, treating his son more as an idea of a child than as the person he actually was. If I brought up the topic, however, Florian would become irritable, and insinuate that I was critical of him only because I was secretly jealous of Emily. This irked me greatly, as it was intended to.

Florian could not have known of Emily's infatuation with me, but he must have sensed that something was not right. I didn't quite like to see how casually she treated him at times. It was clear that she gave him just enough to keep him going, but no more. In any case, the whole affair began to get a little tawdry for my taste. I soon tired of the role of gracious wife, but in Florian's view it was an excellent fit. His small-mindedness angered me. If he had wished we could have tried again, laid aside the grievances, and met in naked honesty — but there was no penetrating his veneer of forced friendliness. Most infuriatingly, there were times when I could see that Florian was *not* completely unaware of his effect on me, but took a vicious pleasure in treating me like a respectable matron.

I grew incensed and decided to indulge myself. I would strike back at him for his condescending behavior. Hitherto, I'd always retreated or isolated myself when enraged; this time my anger drove against its usual restraints. Since I hadn't been able to dampen it through any of the means I'd tried, I would give in to it, let it set my course — I felt dangerous.

The plan was simple but required some preparation. I began by encouraging Emily, ever so slightly. It was enough. Every crumb I tossed she pounced on and devoured, her appetite made still more ravenous. Not that I allowed her to lay a finger on me yet; I only let her know, through minute reductions to the distance I maintained between us, that something in my attitude was changing. I had few qualms about manipulating her thus, as manipulation was her own usual mode of operation.

It all succeeded perfectly, except for a slight miscalculation that resulted in her reaching a full pitch of feverishness when there were still five more days to go before our excursion to the mountains. I was relieved that Florian didn't seem to notice anything amiss.

This trip, I had decided, this family outing, was to be the setting for my surrender to Emily's desire. Unfamiliar surroundings would lend dramatic flair to the scenario, heighten the shock. It was a matter of shattering Florian's complacency as thoroughly as possible. I hadn't given much thought to what might come after I delivered the blow. All I knew was I'd been stung and wanted to sting back, hard.

And so it happened that on the first night of our journey we sheltered at the house of a funny old man, and while

Florian was getting ready for bed, I tapped on the door that connected my room to Emily's and invited her in.

She was astounded, of course, but acted nonchalant. She said she would be right there, and stayed in her room an extra few minutes. I could feel her straining toward me, champing at the bit her pride imposed; I could hear her pacing. I remained where I was on my side of the wall, close to the door, so that when she finally slid in she bumped up against me in the near-darkness: she'd assumed I'd be waiting in bed.

I steadied her, then took away my hand and looked her well in the eye — as well as the moonlight permitted. I saw she was nervous, as if I were threatening to despoil her instead of offering the gift of myself. I found that curious.

"Yes — you understood me right," I said with a small laugh.

I moved slowly away from her toward the bed, starting to undress as I went. Once I was completely naked I knelt on top of the coverlet. The room was chilly but the moon's faint incandescence clung to my skin and warmed it. Emily watched me. I stayed there kneeling, motionless, looking straight ahead past the end of the bed at the window, a rectangle of black just a shade lighter than the surrounding walls. I was impatient. "Let's get it over with," I thought.

I watched in my peripheral vision as she approached then stopped close to the bed, methodically removing her clothing and dropping it on the floor. She came and knelt facing me, right in close. In one swift motion she stretched her spine and curved herself over me; I couldn't help but draw back a little. It was like being enfolded in the wings of a vulture.

She reacted to my retreat, subsiding like a wave that failed to break.

Now she held her face an inch from mine: we stared into each other's eyes. Uncertain, she sought a sign of refusal or encouragement, and chose to interpret my lack of response as acceptance. She laid a hand on my knee.

Just then the connecting door opened. Out of the corner of my eye I saw Florian's shape in the doorway, transfixed. He stood there no more than three seconds then slammed the door.

Emily's attention returned to me and she slid the one hand up my thigh while reaching the other around to the small of my back; she pressed as much as she could of herself against me. But it was all too quick: Florian's intrusion had been brief but violent, stunning me as a sharp slap would have. I needed to recover from it.

I drew back once again. Emily stopped what she was doing, lifted her head from my neck, and looked at me.

"Wait," I said. "I think you'd better go see about Florian."

This seemed to confuse her thoroughly for a moment: Florian had been the furthest thing from her mind. Displeasure flashed across her face but she bent her head submissively, climbed down from the bed, dressed, and went back into her room, shutting the door behind her.

I stood up and stretched my stiff limbs, then got between the cold sheets and pulled the quilt up to my chin. I was glad to be lying down. I felt a deep sense of relief that Emily was out of the room and my goal had been accomplished. It didn't matter exactly what would happen next — the shaking-up of things would lead to improvements, I was somehow sure of that. Anything had to be better than the hackneyed roles we'd allowed to imprison us: Florian as the happy king, lord of all he surveyed, Emily as royal concubine, myself as wise sister to them both.

I didn't know whether I'd go any further with Emily. I doubted she would, in fact, possess the self-restraint, the talent to coax me from my shell, to warm me from the inside out. I'd been curious, but now my primary purpose had been achieved — Florian would have drawn the obvious conclusions, and it was not absolutely necessary to enact them. We would see.

I turned my attention to the unfamiliar room. Soberly furnished and decorated, it seemed to narrow at the top, to taper in. Though my eyes had adjusted to the darkness I couldn't make out much more than that, but I could feel remnants of someone's presence clinging to the walls — the previous occupant, a woman. Not Granddad's mother, as I'd first thought, but his wife. It was Grandma who had lain where I now lay, who'd swept her gaze countless times across the bent-in walls, the window, the massive wardrobe. She had closed her eyes and then opened them and the room had still been there. Her days had brought her little joy, confined to this house, to the company of an exuberant but tiresome husband.

The vision struck my head like a heavy object and I didn't want to think about it anymore. I decided to fall asleep and induced a trance state in myself in order to do so.

Emily returned at daybreak. She got into bed with me but did no more than fit herself against my back. The soft warm pressure was soothing, and I soon fell asleep again.

It must've been several hours later that the door opened and Ara came into the room — the sound woke me. I was overwhelmed, as always, by his beauty, by the brightness of his face. His personality was so strong that it stood out about a foot on all sides of his body, but his independence didn't make him tough. In fact, he was probably the kindest person I knew. I always wanted to hug him.

"Come here," I said, moving over to make room for him; Emily stirred behind me.

Ara drew nearer. "Where's Father?" he asked.

"I don't know," I replied. "He isn't in his room?"

"No."

"He must've gone downstairs already." I turned to Emily

and questioned her with my eyes. She looked away with a slightly sullen expression; I took this to mean that she'd found Florian, or left him, in pitiful condition. "Come in here where it's warm, honey," I said, and Ara clambered up onto the bed.

The three of us stayed there for a half-hour or so. Florian slipped from my mind as I concentrated on Ara and the dreams he'd had: some of them involved the girl whose room he'd slept in. As usual he'd remained conscious of the fact that he was dreaming, which made his adventures particularly interesting.

Once we were all dressed, we went downstairs and found that Florian had departed long before. Granddad didn't have much to say about him, merely that they'd had coffee together.

"But Father doesn't drink coffee," protested Ara.

The old man smiled vaguely in response and continued his disconnected musings as he fixed more coffee and served us oatmeal porridge — it was rather tiresome to have to listen to him. We liked him and were very thankful for his hospitality, but glad to get away when we were finally able to do so.

Florian had left us two of the horses and all of the supplies. We agreed, without much discussion, to turn around and go home; neither Emily nor I was in the mood for a pleasure trip now. As we trotted along we spoke first of one thing and another but soon fell silent. I wondered if Florian would be there when we got back. I remembered his reaction to Paol's visit and hoped, mostly for Ara's sake, that he hadn't done anything dramatic. However despondent the man might feel, I knew he'd recover eventually, whereas Ara didn't have sufficient experience to know that.

It was just getting dark as we reached home. We dismounted and took our things inside. There were signs that Florian had passed through, nothing out of the ordinary: apparently he'd bathed, changed his clothes, and gone out

159

again. The air in the house did have a strange, prickly quality to it, but that was all I could detect.

Emily and I set about unpacking, made a meal, then took turns telling Ara stories. It wasn't until a few hours later that Florian returned. Emily was putting Ara to bed; I was sitting on the living room floor laying out Tarot cards. I'd just placed the Tower card in the "Recent Past" position when my husband walked through the door.

One look at his face and I put down the deck. He was wearing an expression I had never seen on him before. Its utter blankness was chilling — I actually shivered.

He glanced at me with little interest and sat down in the big chair facing me. He seemed a thousand leagues distant.

I knew that this wasn't only about Emily and me. "Florian," I said. "What happened?"

"The farm," he answered dully. "It's gone."

"What do you mean, 'gone'? How can it be gone?"

"It has to close down by the end of the summer. The government men came today. I was in a meeting with them just now. We did not think they would be able to push the conservation project through but they did. There is no recourse."

I sat there absorbing the news, evaluating the possible consequences of this development. Materially, we could manage. The house and land were ours, and with Emily's and my salaries from Red Pepper we could get by until Florian found something else. If, that is, he would be staying with us. I understood now why he seemed so thoroughly empty: in less than twenty-four hours he had been stripped of everything that defined him. I wanted to reach out, to try to comfort him, but his terrible blankness made that impossible.

I looked back at the last card I had laid down, in which two figures plunged from a collapsing tower: a sign of fundamental change, the destruction of a way of life built upon unsound foundations. Picking up the deck again, I turned over the next card, the Five of Cups, and placed it in the "Near Future" position. Its depiction of a person mourning over three spilled cups, unmindful of the two still standing, suggested that one turn from loss and focus on what remains. Well, then.

Next I turned over the card that was to represent either oneself or the overall situation at hand. It was the Hierophant, a symbol of conventional morality, and a caution against submitting to it.

Just then, Florian asked in a flat voice: "Whom are you reading for?"

I glanced up in surprise. He wasn't looking at me or at the cards, only staring unseeingly out the window.

It was a good question. "I'm not sure," I answered. "For me, I suppose, or for us . . ." I wondered whether he wanted to know what the cards said, but there was no sign of further interest on his face — I wasn't sure why he had asked and decided to leave it alone. Returning my attention to the reading, I continued laying down cards: the Five of Swords, a picture of strife, for "How Others See You"; in the "Hopes and Fears" position, the Death card signified an absolute end and the start of something new; then, as "Final Outcome," a complete surprise: the Three of Cups. The scene pictured was of three friends toasting each other's health as part of a joyful celebration. I couldn't imagine in what context such rejoicing could take place, given the present circumstances.

That was the hard thing about reading Tarot: the cards were always accurate, but one often didn't know which aspect of a given situation they illustrated, or what the projected time frame was. In this case, for instance, did the card indicate a festive atmosphere that would prevail once our existing household had broken up and Ara, Emily, and I were free of the frictions Florian's presence imposed? Or was there to be an actual reconciliation between Florian, Emily, and myself? Despite the uncertainty, it was reassuring to know that lighter energies would come into play at some point in the future. I could've done another reading, tried for clarification, but I was reluctant to clutter up my mind with a multitude of possibilities.

I gathered the cards together and wrapped them carefully in the piece of raw silk I always kept them in. When I stood up Florian did too, surprising me. I intended to head to the kitchen for a glass of water but paused, waiting to see what he would do. Eyes downcast, he brushed by me and went into the hallway.

I remained motionless, listening to his heavy tread as he made his way upstairs and into the study. He locked the door from the inside. Dispirited, I went to the kitchen and drank water then made my way to my room. I, too, locked my door — the last thing I wanted right then was Emily slithering between my sheets. I wanted to sleep deeply and wake up with a clear head and plenty of energy to face my changed world.

EMILY

I t's much better with him out of the way. He keeps to himself now like a wounded animal. He pretends he wants nothing to do with us but I know all it would take would be a soft word from me, a touch. Not yet, at any rate. She is still playing games with me and I must work out how to outsmart her. I have a better chance if I don't waste time pacifying him. She drives me mad. The smallest taste and now I can't sleep for thinking about it. I don't even go anywhere else these days — just to work and back home. I'm becoming dull. But as soon as I manage to get where I want with her I'll feel free to set my sights elsewhere. Hopefully it won't be too much longer.

FLORIAN

I came back from the mountains riding hard, trying to think and not to think; at any rate, by the time I reached home I had a plan. Truth be told, I was not sure where exactly I would go but I knew I would pack some things and leave again. I had traveled before — there were people who would be delighted to see me again, places I wished to revisit, others I had always meant to explore but had not had the time. I began to feel almost glad at the prospect of a real adventure, even as I repeatedly thrust to the back of my mind the circumstances that had led me to contemplate such an undertaking. Then I realized that I could not pack up and head out forthwith: first I would have to ride over to the farm to find my brother. We would need to make arrangements to distribute my share of the workload while I was gone.

The house, after little more than twenty-four hours' absence, struck me as curiously unfamiliar. Now that I was preparing to part from it for an indefinite period of time I saw it afresh, as a stranger might. Humble, harmonious of planes and angles, it might almost have grown out of the soil along with the surrounding trees. The inside was more spacious than the outside suggested, a fact often remarked upon by visitors, yet as I entered I felt a weight press down on me. All the well-known, well-worn trappings of our communal life seemed to be sheathed in an invisible coating, hard as diamond, which repelled both my look and my touch. I no longer belonged there.

Hastily, I washed off the grime of the journey and threw on clean clothes then went back out, mounted Caravel and rode off to the farm.

When I came away from there several hours later I was a different person. I had learned that the farm was doomed, the land it sat on commandeered by the government for "conservation purposes." If the decision to turn the land into a nature preserve had been reached out of a genuine concern for the local wildlife, it would have been more bearable. What rankled was knowing that the real interests that lay at the heart of this arrangement had nothing whatsoever to do with the general good and everything to do with shifting a substantial amount of lucre from one pocket to another, while conferring prestige and an aura of moral rectitude upon a man who would be running for office in the coming elections. It was transparent but there was absolutely no recourse.

I think it was not even the imminent demise of the farm, my family's way of life for generations, that affected me so — it was the realization that under these circumstances it would be impossible for me to travel. A great deal of work had to be undertaken immediately: arrangements had to be made for the disposal or storage of equipment, livestock and grain; the remainder of the crops needed to be harvested and sold. I could not leave all of this to my brother and the others.

Up until that point I had been able to come to terms with Zar and Emily's betrayal only by imagining myself well away, swept up in a colorful whirl of new landscapes and acquaintances. The idea of having to stay on in their proximity filled me with dread, but I saw no palatable alternative. Seeking refuge at Dommy and Carl's or my mother's house would have meant a set of interactions and explanations of which I felt incapable; at home, at least, I would be able to isolate myself. The women would understand and keep away from me. I would simply exist, stolid and unthinking as a block of ice, until conditions changed and I could at last melt away.

Did I consider suicide? Only fleetingly. It would have caused too much havoc: I wanted to escape, not loom larger in everyone's life. And there was Ara. A temporary separation would not be too hard on either of us, I thought, but I would not consider leaving him for good.

Life as a glacier turned out to be surprisingly tolerable. After a few initial attempts at communication, the women left me alone. They must have explained the situation to Ara's satisfaction because he did not seem disturbed by it. He did not ask me any questions. Now and then he came and sat in the room with me for a while, wanting only to be near me but not given much to talk; he would bring a book or a game and occupy himself peacefully. Sometimes I would call him over to where I sat by the window and enfold him in an embrace. Then I would hold him in my lap and we would stare out across the wooded valley, watching the treetops ripple like water in the wind.

Most days I rose early and rode over to the farm. What had to be done there was difficult, but manageable. Whereas at first I had cursed the fate that prevented me from leaving, now I was glad for it: I sensed that I was molting, and this was best accomplished in a quiet place. Old layers of myself were sloughing off; the ones exposed had time to toughen up a bit, to learn the feel of wind and weather and become resistant to them. I was changing, that much was certain — into what, I knew not. Now I spent almost all my free time by myself, whereas in the previous months I had dedicated every available moment to Emily. It was true that I had been alone quite often prior to meeting her, but now solitude was a choice: a haven, not an exile.

I could hardly remember, at times, what had happened to precipitate this newfound independence — my life Before seemed like a dream, remote. The intense emotions I had felt first for Zar, then for Emily, then as a result of discovering their intimacy — all that was dulled by time, as though it were a chapter in a book, with little relevance to my present life. Perhaps I was aided by some unknown inner force that went about its work unbidden, like a robust immune system. If I tried, probing after the fashion of a child pushing with its tongue at a loose milk tooth, there was indeed a twinge — but that was usually enough to make me draw back. Something was there, unresolved, and one day I would tackle it, but first I had to gather strength. Instinct told me — I could not understand this with my rational mind — that the way to become stronger was to methodically dislodge all my supports, all that from which I had hitherto derived comfort and strength.

I had begun by abandoning the company of the two women; I went further and rid myself of so much as the hope of reuniting with them at a later date. Just as my past had become lifeless to me, so, too, did I begin to pick myself free of my ties to the future, of the expectations that, unquestioned, had heretofore provided the basis for my existence. I wanted to discard my old, acquired ideas and, in their absence, learn what I truly needed — I would proceed from there. The first step, identifying the bare essentials, kept me absorbed for months.

In the first days after coming down off Granddad's mountain I had no appetite whatsoever and instinctively avoided all food. I had experimented with fasting once, back when I was trying to worm my way out of life; it had produced the opposite effect and catapulted me into a more vibrant state of health. This time, I felt driven, not by an urge for self-destruction but for self-preservation. For three days I drank only water; I stayed at home for the duration of the fast. Symptoms of influenza appeared, as well as a rash that spread over most of my skin, but I supposed this was only my body's way of purging accumulated poisons. I slept and woke and slept, my mind growing progressively emptier. On the morning of the fourth day, though I was weak, my mind had a new clarity. It was as if I had had a hitherto undiagnosed vision deficiency and had just received my first pair of spectacles: I saw and understood certain things I had always missed before. I understood, without knowing how, that it was time to end the fast and that I must drink some kind of juice: apple, or perhaps beet. I realized that in order to make juice and otherwise take care of myself I would need to leave the study where I had been holed up and move into the quarters we had built at the back of the house. Emily would simply have to find some other place to sleep; there was plenty of room elsewhere in the house. I felt a stab imagining her in bed with Zar — that was probably where she spent her nights now anyway — but it passed quickly: I could not let that be of concern to me.

When I came down from the second floor for the first time in four days, it was early morning still; the sun had barely risen. I was relieved despite myself to find Emily asleep alone in the room we had previously shared. I woke her and explained, with no emotion in my manner, that she would need to remove all her belongings from that part of the house — I gave her an hour to do so. I would return to the study and wait till she was finished.

From Emily's expression you would have thought she had seen a ghost — but then, she always did look a bit stupid first thing in the morning. She scrambled to collect her wits and proffered an endearment. Her tone of voice was intended to be sweet; I found it cloying. Then she lifted the bedsheet in a gesture of invitation. With my newfound clarity of vision I could tell her warmth was feigned: it was not desire that made her speak and act as she did, but concern — for herself. Her discomfort intensified when I backed away in response: this move was unprecedented in all our interactions to date. With this one gesture I had demonstrated that she no longer had the power to yank me around like a child's toy; that the three days I had just spent in retreat were not an aberration; that I was in earnest and she had best get up out of that bed and collect all her things. I stood there a second or so, savoring the moment, then turned on my heel and went to the main kitchen to see if there was juice or fruit to make it with.

In the following weeks, food became my primary area of exploration. Initially I turned to books for instruction, but when I realized that the more convincing theories of nutrition contradicted one another, I decided to rely solely on my own body for guidance. I experimented with different quantities and types of food, taking notes. I examined the ways in which certain ones affected my energy and found that it depended quite a bit on whether I consumed them singly or in combination. For the most part, meals consisting of just one foodstuff left me far more invigorated than when I mixed several types, but there was no generalizing: some foods rendered me lethargic unless I ate them along with others. That consideration alone became the object of a prolonged, minutely detailed study.

Then I looked at the difference between eating early or late in the day, and at varying intervals. The research was exhaustive and it took a great deal of time to acquire and prepare the various ingredients, in addition to constructing a methodical approach. I brought my meals with me on the days I worked at the farm.

The project pleased me: it was intellectually stimulating, and the diet afforded me a greater sense of physical well-being than I had ever experienced before. I soon knew just what to eat in order to stay in top form.

The second phase of my research led me into uncharted realms — at least, I was unable to find any books on the subject. Now that I had outlined some general principles, I wanted to explore a subtler range of nuance. First I chose a foodstuff and varied its cooking time by a minute or two, or by only a few seconds — taking care to record the results in the proper scientific manner. Next I examined the difference between indoor and outdoor storage. I was slowly developing a theory that food, raw or cooked, absorbs light and other rays from its surroundings, and that these influence the human system.

Logic then led me to investigate the ways in which I myself might be altering the food as I selected and handled it: what effects might be produced by the mood I was in at the time, or by the manner in which I looked at or talked to the food or neglected to do so. These experiments were more difficult to draw conclusions from than the first set but were equally rewarding. For one thing, my perceptual faculties had been gradually, unconsciously honed in the process, so that I could now detect the most minute variations in my mood and energy. It was gratifying to be able to sense the difference between a mouthful of rice that had been steeped in sunshine before cooking and one that had absorbed a night's worth of moonlight.

I came to realize that my research would be even more interesting if I could experiment in this fashion with every step of the growing process — thus did my newfound hobby come to affect my attitude toward the farm. At first, upon learning that it was doomed, I had been relieved that I would soon be free of responsibilities, better able to travel and begin anew in foreign parts with my share of the proceeds from the sale of goods and livestock. Now, however, I began to look about for a suitable plot of land within a reasonable distance, where the whole operation could be started up again. My ideas on the matter were not completely formed, but I could conceive of approaching the enterprise in a whole new way. Instead of taking for granted that maximum production would be the ideal — maximum yield per acre sown, per hen or cow fertilized — the emphasis would be on quality, subtlety, variety. Though my experiments with food had been of the most varied nature I had consistently kept the portions small. I had grown lean but stronger, though I took no more exercise than before. Absorbing larger quantities only detracted from the energetic benefits of food, in a surprising but undeniable inverse correlation.

As soon as I had grasped this principle as it applied to nutrition, I began to realize that it applied to all areas of life — that in fact I had been applying it unconsciously from the time I locked the study door behind me on the first night of my new life. Without knowing why, I had detached myself from most of the possessions I formerly considered essential to a comfortable existence. I cleared all the furniture out of the rooms I'd occupied with Emily: table, chairs, shelves, bed — I needed none of these. I kept one blanket, which I used alternately to sleep in, sit on, or wrap around my shoulders when it got cold. I kept two shirts and two pairs of pants for daily use; the rest of my clothes I stored against the time when one or the other of the four items would deteriorate to the point of uselessness. To my surprise I found that, though it was no hardship to make do with those few clothes, it was more difficult to shed my concern over others' disapproval of my meager wardrobe. In fact, the greater the number of possessions I rid myself of, the more frequently I found myself bumping up against ideas and assumptions I had held for as long as I could remember, usually without being aware of them. Now they loomed large and awkward, like pieces of ugly furniture in an overcrowded room. I understood that discarding the rubbish and keeping only what was truly useful and good for me was, in this realm, too, the next order of business. With little left to distract me from the task, I rolled up my figurative sleeves and went to work.

SALVADOR

JOSEPHINE

An odd phenomenon indeed. I've been in Salvador ten days now, ten days that feel like a decade. How does such a perceptual distortion arise? Ever the academic, I've tried to figure out the explanation, find the smallest box it can comfortably fit in, shut the lid, and label it. "Number of events per hour" is the closest I've been able to come. In an e-mail to Ralphy, I speculated that my brain, accustomed to absorbing brand-new experiences at a given rate, say one every few months, is providing me with a completely skewed readout on elapsed time now that these experiences are occurring with greater frequency. The logic is reasonably coherent if not scientifically valid, and I felt quite satisfied with myself after sending the e-mail, until I realized I hadn't described the most important thing about all this: how it affects me. Given that an untold number of years have passed, subjectively, since I arrived here, I'm a very different person than I was before I came. To tell the truth, I'm not quite used to this new version of myself, but we get along okay.

Bruno and Vero have witnessed the change — commented on it, in fact, without seeming surprised. I know this has helped me take it in stride. Our friendship is partly responsible for my having come unstuck from my old self, and has tempered the attendant discomfort by providing me with a sense of belonging, even in this very foreign land. We seem to know each other extremely well already. Maybe that's because I've ended up spending the greater part of each day with one or both of them, but the familiarity seems deeper than the time together would account for. Like the fact that they're able to track subtle and gradual shifts in my thinking and personality — how do they do that? And I seem to have an uncanny knack for being able to guess what they're thinking: sometimes, in the moment just *before* one of them speaks, I hear a sort of pre-echo of what they're about to say, so soft that I tend not to pick it out of the noisier rattle of my own thoughts, but distinct enough that when the words are spoken aloud I know I'm hearing them for the second time.

In other ways, too, the pair seems inexplicably familiar. Maybe this is all some form of déjà vu, which supposedly isn't anything more than a kink in the brain's processing functions. Or maybe I picked up some kind of tropical parasite here that's affecting my perception. I should probably have a stool test done, just in case. Anyway, whatever the explanation, Bruno and Vero are without a doubt exceptional people, and I count myself lucky to have met them.

Veronica, now: she's incredible. I've decided to call her Veronica instead of Vero; I find it suits her better. She's the quintessential wise woman, combining extensive factual knowledge with great spiritual depth; it's clear to me now why she's the only one of the group so far to have succeeded in connecting to the Outernet with any regularity. I appreciate her unselfishness, too: though there are a million tasks and people constantly demanding her attention, she's chosen to devote quite a lot of time over the past few days to the question of how best to get me logged on to the Outernet. It's not just the time she gives but the gracious and unhurried way she gives it. I know she likes me, though there's an odd polite distance between us. For a while I thought it was because she was mad at me after that time she found me snuggled up with Bruno, but she knows that nothing happened — we've talked and she didn't seem troubled by it. She's definitely beyond anything like garden-variety jealousy. I like to think it's just a question of time before we get to know each other even better and melt the ice once and for all.

Bruno, on the other hand, I've felt comfortable with right from the start. It helps that I tend to forget he's a male, a potential partner in that complicated and exhausting Dance of the Genders. True, a couple of times I had intense sexual feelings in his presence, but I've come to believe those were just coincidence. In any case they haven't reoccurred — thank heavens for that — and we've fallen straight into a friendship as innocent and sweet as strawberry syrup. I'm less in awe of him than I am of Veronica, therefore more at ease. He doesn't have the same breadth of knowledge as she does, the same brilliance of mind; his intelligence is like a joyful spider darting about, laying down gossamer threads connecting one idea to another, resulting in webs of unorthodox architecture but surprising coherence. The nice thing is that my own thoughts always seem to reinforce and support his constructions: a comment of mine will often provide a missing strand between two points, allowing him to reach a conclusion he had fallen short of. Conversely, he has a talent for unraveling doubts or questions I have and reconfiguring them into new insights. It's a rich symbiosis.

As far as the Outernet is concerned, while Veronica has helped me plan a procedure for gaining access, Bruno is the one who's guided me through the steps of her plan, taking it as a starting point and offering ideas for modifying, discarding, or changing the order of the experiments as we go along. He's the one who suggested I make it a priority to visit the Museum of Afro-Brazilian Culture, which is why I'm here waiting on the steps for the museum to reopen — I hadn't known it closed between noon and two p.m. I'm not sure what exactly I'm supposed to get out of this excursion, but I have enough faith by now in Bruno's intuition to follow his advice without knowing where it will lead. The museum is a must-see stop on the tourist circuit anyway, and I knew I'd have to come by at some point, but I didn't feel any particular urgency about it. My attention this week has been consumed by the investigation of different techniques that may — *may* — enable me to enter into a trance state conducive to Outernet access; I've put aside any thought of my other research for the moment. It's actually imperative that I give my full attention to the Outernet issue, since all my endeavors in that field have so far met with spectacular failure, even in the preparatory exercises. Bruno and Veronica both advise me not to let that be the slightest bit discouraging, as a negative frame of mind will delay my progress even more. Remaining optimistic is in and of itself no easy task, but I'm managing fairly well overall. My main problem, as far as Bruno and I have been able to determine over the course of a particularly intensive brainstorming session in which I told him my whole life story, has to do with the attitudes I've built up toward my extrasensory perceptions. The combination of being exceptionally gifted in that domain — if it is a gift — and having worked so hard to suppress these abilities has produced an abiding state of internal conflict that has only now come to my attention. I'm finding that it's not enough for my intellect to tell the rest of me: "Okay, you can relax your grip, I now permit my second sight to develop freely" — the restraints I clamped on long ago aren't responsive to this kind of suggestion. As a matter of fact, the complexity of psychological defenses is so great that such a command is in danger of producing the opposite effect and *increasing* resistance. The only reason I have any hope at all is that some unusual incidents *have* taken place lately, at odd moments: there was that time I was able to get a glimpse of Bruno's "essence" just after I first got here, and the curious phenomenon of tuning in to Bruno and Veronica's thoughts before they're voiced. At least this tells me my faculties are still alive, if largely dormant; it's just that I'm not able to summon them at will, reliably — and that's what I'd have to do in order to unlock my own personal portal to the Outernet.

Having understood that I cannot simply *direct* this current to flow, I've been trying — with my friends' assistance — various circuitous approaches to the desired goal. In the past couple of days I've listened to a tape of shamanic drumming, learned some yoga asanas, been shown basic capoeira moves, tried Buddhist meditation and a form of deep breathing known as Rebirthing. The physical exercises only resulted in my limbs becoming hopelessly tangled up, while the contemplative instructions caused me to nod off and awaken without so much as a memory of my dreams.

Bruno's new theory is that what may be at play here is a certain principle of cosmic dynamics whereby the more effort is put in to a task, the more elusive the object of pursuit becomes. To illustrate this idea he asked me to imagine a fishing pole attached to my head with a carrot dangling from it about four feet in front of my face. No matter how hard I might run toward the carrot I will never reach it and will only become exhausted — less likely, as a result, to conceive of other solutions.

Hearing this, I let my frustration and despair erupt for the first time. "Then it's completely hopeless!" I exclaimed. Tears of rage came to my eyes. "Forget about it! I don't want the damn carrot anyway!" I crossed my arms and scowled, expecting a reprimand for letting negativity get the best of me.

Bruno didn't seem put off, however; in a gentle voice he said: "You know, Jo, maybe that is it right there."

"Right *where*?" I answered belligerently. "Are you saying that if I give up the chase the carrot is going to mysteriously detach itself from the rod and slip into my hand? I don't believe it. I'm seriously sick of all of this, and I don't want to do it anymore. I don't want you and Veronica to waste any more time on me either. You both have plenty of other things to do — why don't you just get back to your business and I'll get back to mine?"

"But Jo," he said, putting an arm around my shoulders, "this *is* our business. You know it is not a waste of time for any of us, and I do *not* think you should give up. This is partly selfish: I am certain that if you succeed in getting to the Outernet you will make such valuable contributions to our group. But it is probably true that you need a break, a chance to progress with your own work. Maybe you have anxiety, subconsciously, about not going forward with your research. Maybe if you get something done on that you will be more free to let yourself go on this end — who knows? It is worth trying, anyway."

That's when he suggested I visit the Museum of Afro-Brazilian Culture. I told him I thought I'd rather just hole up in my hotel room and organize my notes instead of gathering more material. After all, I've already visited any number of collections of African art in the States and Europe, and I doubt I'll be able to get anything really new or interesting out of this one — but he convinced me.

"I think it is the place to start," he said. "I do not know why. It will not take you so long, anyway — it is just three small rooms. And then you can go to your hotel and spend three weeks writing if you need to. But start there."

Like I said, ultimately, I take him on faith. I think it's just a psychological trick to distract me from the Outernet in order to bring me closer to it; that's probably why he insisted on my visiting this particular museum. The relevance to my research topic might help fool my mind, convince it that I really *am* focusing on something besides the Outernet. How can it work, though, since I *know* I'm not actually interested in anything else just now? I guess if it does work, I'll take time to puzzle it out.

I just wish the museum would open. It's a little past two

already and I've been sitting on the steps of this fine old building for a good forty-five minutes in the broiling sun. A thin band of shadow from the archway above has allowed my face and shoulders to escape incineration, but the rest of me is begging to be scraped up and deposited in a cool dark place. Maybe it would've been worth spending the money to buy a drink and loll under an umbrella at a nearby café. The only other patches of shade I can spot — doorways, awnings — are all already occupied.

The Terreiro de Jesus is a large square flanked by two impressive churches, its centerpiece a big fountain bedecked with sculpted garlands and grim-looking gnomes. There isn't anything else except some public phones and a couple of trees — no benches. The only spot of color in the sun-bleached expanse is the stack of brightly painted musical instruments guarded by their seller. I've seen them before — Bruno told me they're called *berimbaus*. Used mainly in the game of capoeira, they consist of a wooden bow with a wire and a gourd attached to it. Now and then the vendor picks one up and plays a few rhythms to attract the attention of passersby. The sounds of the stick striking the taut wire are harsh, but the simple rhythms are strangely absorbing. For some reason they make me feel as if a total stranger is telling me something I didn't know about myself.

The metallic rasp of a bolt startles me out of my thoughts, and the museum door swings inward. I stand up quickly, finding myself dizzy and momentarily confused. The guard who opened the door is giving me the once-over, while a gaggle of tourists shuffles towards me from the square.

I pay admission and enter the first room of the collection while a multilingual babble thickens in the hall behind me. The room is divided into small areas, each with a glass case or two and a sign: MASKS AND SCULPTURES, TEXTILES, MUSICAL INSTRUMENTS. I pause in front of a map with text charting the evolution of the slave trade, then drift between the exhibits.

Some beautiful things: reds and indigos in deep

conversation within a piece of Nigerian cloth; a small, sentient-looking bust of Obá, king of the Bantu; two finely carved heads with slitted, hinting eyes. On the whole, though, there's nothing extraordinary, nothing I can use, though perhaps I'll come back and study one or two of the king's masks in order to flesh out my existing description of African carving techniques.

The tour group has managed to fill the room almost completely by now. Their guide alternately smooths down her bangs and hoists herself up onto her toes to try to get the group's attention. I decide to move on to the next room.

This section is devoted to art produced in Brazil, whereas the first held only pieces of continental African origin. On the wall immediately to the right of the doorway is a series of old photographs of men and women, some wearing turbans and fancy clothes, some not. From the accompanying text I see that all of them are *mães de santo* and *pais de santo,* the spiritual heads of different candomblé houses. One woman in particular catches my eye. I don't know why: she's on the plain side, shown from the waist up, wearing eyeglasses and an ordinary looking dress. The photo, like many of the others, seems to have been taken sometime in the first half of the twentieth century. Somehow, this one stands out from all the rest, almost as if it were raised slightly off the wall.

I look back at the text in hopes of finding some explanation for this phenomenon, but the corresponding caption gives no more than the woman's name and the name of the terreiro she is associated with. Neither is familiar, yet as I read them I experience a wave of gooseflesh. What can that mean, I wonder, my mind suddenly as taut as all the little hairs on my body. I brace myself for illumination, a flash of insight, but nothing comes. The hairs droop back down and I become aware of other people waiting for me to step away from the text so that they, too, can read it.

"I'll write the information down," I tell myself. "It's a clue."

Taking out my notebook, I copy the names. The woman's is Mãe Iara Pereira dos Santos Silva; the name of the terreiro is Casa do Morro Pequeno. That, I can translate: House of the Small Hill. Then I cross over to the other side of the room.

The displays here are each labeled with the name of a different *orixá* — the divinities from the candomblé pantheon — and consist of photographs, text, ritual objects, and ceremonial costumes. I think, once again, how eager I am for the candomblé houses to resume their ceremonies: it's not just so that I can complete my research, but because I'm certain that the true meaning of the religion will come alive for me once I witness the rites being performed. Until then, there's an emptiness to any study of it I might make; the purely intellectual approach now seems inadequate, whereas I formerly embraced it as objective. While the objects before me are impressive, with a rich nest of vibrations humming just under their surfaces; while the photos capture moments of complete abandon or absorption and the text meticulously details practices and prayers — none of this really has much significance for me, I realize. It's depressing.

And then I emerge from my thoughts, my eyes focusing on the object I had, unknowingly, wandered over to. It's a small, silvery — what? It's roughly the size and shape of an old-fashioned hand mirror, but where the mirror should be there are only figures hammered in the metal. Two fish rise up and outward from either side of the handle; above those two more swim toward each other at a forty-five-degree angle; between their heads a star or starfish closes off the oblong shape. In the center of the whole thing is a flower with four broad petals.

No sooner have I identified these shapes than the object begins to fill my field of vision — or is it my vision that's narrowing, closing out everything else? It happens so quickly I have no time to be startled or scared or to react in any way. The center of the flower expands until I can no longer discern its outer edges: only a field of rippling silver is left, in my ears a dull roar. I've lost all consciousness of my body and my surroundings; there's no fear, nor any other emotion: I only know I must wait: something is about to be shown to me.

Seconds pass, or minutes, and brighter flashes start to break up the outer edges of the silver space. Gradually they acquire definition: a curl of light twists toward me then vanishes; a gleaming triangle emerges and cuts across from one side to the other. The shapes become denser, more detailed, webbed with a pattern of fine lines that resemble scales. And after a moment I realize that these are indeed the undulating skins of fish leaping or gliding past. As they shoot up and break the surface of the water billowing lazily above, they leave effervescent streaks, like comet tails.

I become aware of another presence sharing the space with me. It's as if it had been holding back, waiting for me to recognize my surroundings, to identify the fish and the water, before making itself known. And I understand its decision — I understand a lot, in these few minutes, though I'd be unable to say how exactly the pieces of information collect and connect in my mind. I understand that the fish and the water are as much a part of this presence, this entity, as a foot and a head are part of a body. The entity is vast as all the world's oceans put together, and yielding, as water is. Fertile, too, like earth, but softer and richer, it possesses all the qualities of spirit analogous to the material qualities of water. Receptivity, understanding, compassion — and strength. There's a side to this being that's anything but soft and sweet: hugely powerful, it contains the potential for savage, pitiless destruction on a massive scale.

The entity waits until I've had a chance to contemplate all of its qualities, then enfolds me into itself. It's not a physical embrace but carries a sense of affection. In that moment I merge with it and experience each of its attributes, this time as if they were mine: limitless love and compassion, indomitable violence. Where before I had been a spectator, removed, I now become saturated with these extreme emotions. The sweetness of loving so absolutely is sheer bliss; at the same time, white-hot fury threatens to rip me apart. The limit of my capacity to feel is strained, the breaking point close at hand. I begin to fear something might snap . . . but then it all begins to ebb away.

The intense sensations drain out of me. Shapes swim into focus, solidify: I find myself looking once more at the small silver implement, pretty and lifeless on its peg on the museum wall.

My mind can't process what has just happened. I'm sure of one thing only: that I need rest, urgently. I have to get out of this building.

When I step into the street the heat crashes on me like a ton of bricks. I realize the extent of my exhaustion: my legs are hollow, the soles of my feet tender, as though they'd been whipped. It takes a lot of concentration and a number of encouraging phrases mumbled to myself to get me the few blocks to Bruno and Veronica's.

Bruno opens the door and I practically fall into his arms. Luckily he's solidly built and not easily startled. He catches me and grips me with one arm — in the other hand he's got a wooden spoon clotted with dough. He must've been baking: dabs of white flour adorn his shirtfront; a dishtowel is tucked into his pants as a makeshift apron.

"What is the matter?" He pats me on the shoulder as best he can with the hand holding the spoon, smearing me with greasy dough in the process. Laughing through my tears of exhaustion, I push his hand away. I want to tell him everything but don't know where to start. Mostly I just want to lie down.

"Come into the kitchen with me," he says, "so I can put the cake in the oven. It is an experiment: no eggs, butter, or wheat, but I think it will taste nice. I am making it for the meeting tonight. You are welcome to attend, of course! I did not think we would see you for a few days at least. But what happened to you? Why do you look so upset?"

I follow him into the kitchen and start explaining while he turns on the oven and puts the cake in. Before I can get very far he says: "One minute, please," piles the dirty dishes in the sink, and wipes off the counter.

"There," he says. "Sorry, but now I can pay better attention. Let us go upstairs where it is more comfortable. But please, do not forget to remind me to come down and check on the cake in about forty-five minutes."

We go up to the little rooftop house. The sparsely furnished room is steeped in sunlight but pleasantly cool. Husks of sound drift in on the breeze: the tiny honking of cars from the street far below, a brief altercation. Soothed, I concentrate on relating the details of my adventure as accurately as I can; the nervous alarm that propelled me here quite disappears.

When I finish my story Bruno watches me solemnly for a few minutes before saying anything. I wait, knowing he's sorting and ordering his thoughts with care before offering them to me. I return his gaze, studying his open, friendly face, handsome in that way I never liked before because it's usually accompanied by arrogance or the other self-important attitudes of men used to being fawned over. It's only in the process of getting to know and appreciate Bruno that my aversion to his good looks has decreased. In fact, I've come to realize that if he weren't married to Veronica the two of us might have a chance to start something wonderful — but as it is, no way. I push the thought firmly out of my mind, as I do every time it creeps in, and concentrate instead on my gratitude for our high-octane friendship.

"Well," Bruno finally says, "it looks like you have been given some pretty clear directions."

"I figure I should find out more about that mãe de santo whose picture made such a strong impression on me, but I don't understand the fish and water thing. What — do you think I'm supposed to take a trip to the ocean?"

"That is probably a good idea, but I think it's more than that. The object that sent you off is called a *leque* — do you know what that is?"

I shake my head. "Can't remember. I think I might've read something . . ." I trail off.

"It's a sacred ritual tool — each of the orixás has one. That particular one belongs to Iemanja, whose name means 'mother of the fish' — she is the spirit associated with the ocean, motherhood, fertility."

"I know about her. She's the one people go down to the beach on New Year's Eve to make offerings to."

"Correct. We also celebrate her feast day here in Salvador on February second: she has a shrine in a part of town called Rio Vermelho. Starting in the very early morning, people line up to deposit flowers and presents for her in big baskets; in the afternoon the baskets are taken out on boats and put in the sea. All day long there is music and dancing and processions in the streets."

"That sounds nice."

"It is."

"So what does it have to do with me?"

"The fact that her leque unfolded into other dimensions for you indicates that she was calling you, to tell you something. If I were a candomblé adept I would say it meant without a doubt that she is one of your main orixás. I really do not know exactly how much you know about all of this, so stop me if it is unnecessary."

"No, please go on. Even if I've read things in books, it makes it much more real to hear you talk about it."

"All right. Well, according to candomblé thought, each of us has at least two divinities that have a strong influence on our destiny. Although the initiate pays tribute to all the orixás, the one or two that are *donos da cabeça* — rulers of the head — are the ones she or he must pay special attention to.

The appropriate offerings must be made, the days of the week consecrated to them must be observed, certain foods or colors should be avoided, and so on."

"So, if you were a candomblé devotee you'd say Iemanja is a mistress of my head, but since you're not . . . ?"

"I have a great respect for candomblé; I do believe in the orixás and this belief comes out of my personal experiences. At the same time, I know it is just one religious system out of the hundreds in existence all over the world. I do not understand enough about cosmic dynamics to be able to explain how they can all be right, though I think they all are to some degree. But there is also a large part of any religious system that I find arbitrary, that reflects only human imagination, not any fundamental structure of existence. That is why I never could get too involved in candomblé, why I never joined a terreiro: because I cannot completely believe in all the laws and prohibitions that must be observed in order to stay in the good graces of the 'saints,' as the orixás are often called. Is it really true that Ogum's special day is Tuesday and his color is deep blue? It may be — but then why are his colors black and green in Cuba, where the religion is called Santeria? And if I am really a child of Oxalá — whom I feel closest to — are bad things going to happen to me because I do not wear only white on Mondays and Fridays? Or is it that things would just go a little more smoothly if I did? I do not know. I could investigate scientifically, I suppose: try one way for a few months and then switch. But I do not have the time, or, more truthfully, the interest. My other work calls to me more, and so I must remain in doubt. Sometimes, when I feel the impulse, I make an offering to one or the other of the orixás, and I remain conscious of their influences in the world around me. And from what you tell me I believe Iemanja put out a call to you, but as far as what that means, I think only you yourself can determine. I do not think it is a bad idea to try to investigate that according to the conventions, for instance by consulting a mãe de santo. You have enough wisdom and intuition yourself to make a good judgment about the information you receive. Maybe the place to go is the terreiro of the mãe de santo who caught your attention — what was it, 'Happy Hill'?"

"House of the Small Hill," I correct.

"That is one I have not heard of before. But then, there are hundreds of terreiros spread around the city. We will find out where it is. We have some friends who must know; in fact, one of them will be coming to the meeting tonight. I will introduce you. His name is Doidinho."

"Does it mean something?"

"It is a nickname, really: the diminutive for *doido*, which means something like crazy, kooky. I think you will like each other. His English is not very good, but you will manage." He smiles at me for a moment. "And now, shall I leave you to rest? You seem better, but still exhausted. Now I understand why! I have often seen people coming out of trance after being possessed; usually they are completely emptied out. That is what you look like. In fact, Jo, that is probably exactly what happened to you."

"Possessed?" I laugh. "In a museum?"

"It can happen anywhere. If the orixá has something to tell you it will not wait around for the drumming and dancing and chanting and incense."

"Wow," I say. I sigh and stretch out on the mattress, staring up at the tin ceiling. Possessed. I never thought it would happen to me, and I certainly didn't imagine that it could happen in such an ordinary context. But Bruno's right. I *was* taken over: first by the vision, then by the actual entity merging with me. Just remembering the intensity of it makes me want to sleep for weeks. I shut my eyes.

"Do you want me to work on your back?" Bruno asks.

"God — I would love that." I roll over onto my stomach, close my eyes gratefully.

Bruno comes and sits down next to me. He doesn't touch

me, but as a prickling starts up on the nape of my neck, followed by steadily increasing warmth, I realize he's bringing his hand closer to my skin, ever so slowly. Although I remain immobile, my body feels as if it's straining upward to meet his hand. I become acutely aware of the few centimeters between our skins as he begins to move his fingers above the surface of my body, over my shoulder blades. At first I'm disappointed: my muscles had been anticipating a deep, thorough kneading. As I give up that expectation, however, I'm able to perceive what's actually happening: I can detect the minute movements of his fingers, not only in the space between us but within my own flesh. How can that be?

The question is fleeting: my mind slips into wordless currents of sensation and is carried off. Delicious ticklings start up in the outermost layer of my skin and scamper down to the very marrow of my spine. From there they spread in ripples of pleasure, radiating outward and suffusing my entire body with a deep nourishing warmth.

The door opens. I hear it from very far away, then Bruno speaks and a female voice replies. I have no interest in the exchange, nestled as I am into a thoroughly new and delightful realm of sensual satisfaction. What pulls me back is a sudden chill. Bruno's hands are no longer poised above me. Something's wrong.

I shiver, focus on the voices in the room. The female one is Veronica's.

"And your fucking cake is burning," she says in a tone I've never heard her use before, venomous and absolutely cold. I take note of the fact that she's addressed him in English — it can only be for my benefit. All the pleasant feelings rush out of my body as though a plug had been pulled.

Slam! Furious footsteps retreat; the room is still. Could Bruno have left, too? I open my eyes to find him sitting cross-legged on the floor beside me, considering me gravely.

"Wh— what's wrong?" I stammer. He leans over and gives me a brief kiss on the cheek then stands up. He seems remote, the kiss peremptory, as if it served only to mark a boundary.

"Well, my cake is burning, that is one thing. I must go down and turn the oven off; she certainly will not do it for me."

"But what was wrong with her? She was furious! Was it . . . us?"

"I am not sure what it was. We will work it out."

I've been rebuffed: he's dismissing my concern, telling me to mind my own business. His tone is meant to be reassuring but its impersonality constricts my chest. He adds, in the manner of a kindly physician:

"The main thing for you right now is to get some rest. I am sorry we were interrupted; maybe I can come back upstairs in a while. But for now, please, try to relax again, to get some sleep. You have been through a lot; you absolutely must recharge."

"But . . ." The door closes behind him. I can't imagine resting now; Veronica's intrusion shot me full of adrenaline and I'm buzzing like a fluorescent light on the fritz. Whatever would make her that mad? I don't want it to be what I think it is, so my mind keeps fishing for explanations that have nothing to do with me: she just found out Bruno made some really stupid mistake or forgot to do something he was supposed to . . . or . . . it could be that someone else made her mad; maybe it's a problem with their daughter, she might be strung out somewhere and Veronica thinks Bruno needs to wake up to the urgency of the situation . . . No, I have to stop pretending I don't know. What she was furious about was finding me with him again, with his hands on me, or at least over me: that's what it was. I can tell myself that it doesn't make sense, that she's very open-minded: she's told me she and Bruno haven't slept together for years; she's said she makes no claims on him. It doesn't matter. I can recognize jealousy when I see it. Well, shit. Now what? The answer, if there is one, is beyond me at this point.

Hopelessness reopens the floodgates of exhaustion and I lie back, overcome. In less than a minute I'm sound asleep.

Later, much later, a blurry sound at the edge of consciousness, a touch: someone is tapping firmly on my shoulder. It's hard to lift my eyelids; they're like heavy garage doors. But the tapping is insistent — I manage. The room is quite dark now, the person who woke me a darker silhouette. Bruno. Seeing that I'm awake, he rocks back on his haunches, waits.

"Mm." I try out my voice: it's raspy. My throat is dry. "What time is it?"

"Just after seven," he replies. "The meeting is about to start. Do you want to come?"

His tone is friendly as always, yet I'm disturbed by the absence of any reference to what happened with Veronica, any curiosity as to how I'm doing, whether I've recovered from the experience of being possessed. It's the same remoteness I sensed earlier: subtle, but jarring. Extremely painful, in fact.

I realize I'm angry, resentful that the warmth into which I had dissolved could vanish so swiftly. I curse myself for having allowed myself to be so open: now I want to nip back into my shell, pull up the hatch, batten down the shutters. I certainly *won't* be attending their meeting, not tonight and maybe not ever again. I'll have to see how I feel once I've had a few days on my own, but right now I think I don't care if I never see them again, not this well-meaning but insensitive lug of a guy here nor his sniperish wife, or whatever she might be to him. And yet — I shouldn't have to slink off like a dog because of someone's shoddy treatment of me: my ego wants to retaliate. It commands me to exit gracefully, to pretend I'm fine, not hurt in the least. I think I *will* go to their meeting after all — and then leave halfway through, as though it's too boring or inconsequential to waste my time on. And then I won't come back for a long time, if ever.

Having run through this sequence of thoughts in less than two seconds, I barely appear to hesitate before answering, "Sure, I'm coming." Maybe now he'll ask how I am, or volunteer something about his spat with Veronica — but no, he merely waits for me to stand up and follow him out the door. That seals it. The part of me that was still hopeful snaps shut. A familiar feeling.

Back downstairs, we're swallowed up by what appears to be a party in full swing. Bruno vanishes. People are crowded into the kitchen, standing around with drinks in their hands or munching on snacks. Bruno's cake is not in evidence although I detect the pungent odor of something charred. Paola and I exchange smiles; she ladles some orange liquid from a large punch bowl into a cup and hands it to me. I take a small swallow, nearly gag. Carrot juice. God. Do these people *have* to be so relentlessly wholesome? Turning away, I set the cup down discreetly on a countertop and scan the room for something I can actually drink; I'm desperately thirsty. Tap water would do as a last resort, but the guidebook says to stay away from it.

Then I notice a guy off by himself, near the pantry, pouring himself a little glass of beer from a brown bottle. I'm not a big beer drinker but that'll do nicely just now, I think, as I head toward him. I hope he doesn't polish off the bottle while I'm trying to elbow my way through the crowd.

"*Oi*," I greet him. I gesture toward the bottle, lifting my eyebrows. It's a bit ruder than I usually like to be, but I feel so disconnected from this situation that I don't really care. He doesn't seem to mind, though; he smiles, looks around for another glass, and ends up cocking his head to one side and wagging an index finger between his glass and the bottle, offering me a choice. I pick the glass, watching him while he fills it.

He's about forty, I'd guess, on the short side, with dreadlocks, a jutting forehead, and a wide smile. Personable. The problem is, I muse, sipping the thin but pleasantly cold beverage, I've got myself in a corner and haven't planned an exit strategy. The guy is about to open his mouth to start a conversation, and however grumpy I may be, I can't turn my back on him now he's poured me a beer. So I might as well take the initiative, make the opening move in such a manner as to ensure as short an interaction as possible.

"No *português*." I spread one hand, palm up, and make a rueful grimace.

"*Ingliss*?" he asks. "*Italiano*?"

"English."

"Oo-ut eez ee-ore naymee?" Well, I guess this can't go *too* far.

"My name is Josephine. What is your name?"

He starts drawing letters in the air between us, getting a little confused since he's making them backward for my benefit. D-o-i-d-i-n-h-o. "Doy-jee-nyo," he nods energetically, pointing at his own chest.

What do you know, it's Bruno's candomblé friend. Despite myself, I feel a surge of curiosity, an eagerness to talk to him. Suddenly the language barrier changes from welcome insulation to irritating obstacle. How on earth can we discuss candomblé? I might as well try my best. I interrupt his stammering attempts to find out what country I'm from, cutting to the chase: "Candomblé?"

His already cheerful face lights up even more, as if a thousand-watt floodlight had been trained on it.

"*Sim! Sim! Candomblé! Com certeza! Você gosta de candomblé?* You likee candomblé?"

"Yes, sim, I like candomblé." I smile back at him, wondering how to explain that I'm just interested, not a follower — but it's too complicated. Instead, I venture the name of the terreiro I want to know more about. I hope I'm pronouncing it reasonably correctly. "Casa do Morro Pequeno?"

"Casa do Morro Pequeno! Sim! Sim!" His head is pumping up and down with so much force I'm half afraid he'll give himself whiplash and have to be carted off to a hospital before he can tell me any more.

"*Onde?*" Where?

He replies in such a rapid stream of Portuguese there's no chance of my extracting any information from it. Noticing my blank stare, he stops midsentence. He points at me, then at himself, then back at me, while raising his eyebrows and nodding his head in a more controlled fashion. I take it he's asking whether I want to go to the terreiro with him. In order to confirm my interpretation, I imitate the three gestures — hand, head, and eyebrows — repeating, "Casa do Morro Pequeno?" In response, he exaggerates the nodding, drops the eyebrows and finger.

"Sim! Okay!" he exclaims.

So it's settled. Somehow we'll work out the details. But now the rest of the people in the kitchen are putting down their plates and cups and beginning to push toward the hallway. Doidinho and I acknowledge this to each other nonverbally, then he takes the glass from me and pours the remainder of the bottle into it, indicating that I should drink up. We tag along behind the crowd as it shuffles down the hall and empties out into the main room.

Veronica is to be the center of attention, it appears — like at the last meeting, though that one was more informal. This time she's wedged into a narrow red velveteen armchair on a sort of dais, and everyone else is sitting in a semicircle on the floor.

I take note of the resentment that surges up as soon as I see her, and try to compose my face into an expression that will hide my hostility without simulating friendliness. Tricky.

As it happens, she doesn't once glance my way, although it seems like she's making eye contact and smiling and waving at everybody else. I decide she must be ignoring me on purpose — fine. I remember that my plan is to leave soon anyway, putting on a small but public display of boredom. That makes me feel better.

The murmurs die down, the lights dim, all except one directly above Veronica's head. It's obviously meant to function as a spotlight but the placement is wrong: her eye sockets are thrown into deep shadow, giving her a ghoulish aspect. No words of introduction are offered: everyone must know what's supposed to happen, must either have seen Veronica's performances or heard about them. A few faces are familiar to me: Velma, Paula, Doce, the guy from the Internet café. Doidinho is sitting just behind me. Most of the people are staring at Veronica intently while others have closed their eyes, perhaps in hopes of entering a sympathetic trance state. Whereas I, too, was rapt the first time I witnessed the process, my ill humor now has me impatient, cynical. I note the jerk of her shoulders as she slumps in on herself, and wait for the moaning, the shaking, the dancing, pondering when exactly to make my exit. Definitely before she has a chance to come over and say anything to me. But the minutes pass and nothing spectral or spectacular is forthcoming. Veronica merely shifts in her chair and rolls her head on her neck as if to alleviate tension.

More time elapses. Whispers flicker through the crowd, people cross and uncross their legs, straighten or relax their shoulders, look at one another. The murmurs grow steadily louder as Veronica's inertia appears to congeal, trapping her in the chair like a bug in amber.

Here comes Bruno, head ducked to decrease attention to himself — a stagehand called on to fix a prop in the middle of a play. He bends down and says a few words in her ear; obtaining no response, he places two fingers on her neck, presumably to check her pulse, and then tips her chin back so he can see into her eyes. Suddenly her hand comes up to push away his; in one violent motion she stands up, uttering a harsh exclamation followed by a gesture of impatience. The crowd is transfixed once again.

Veronica turns abruptly: it's clear she's about to walk off her platform. Then she changes her mind, appears to become conscious of the audience; her posture softens, she shakes her head. *"Não posso."* The words crack the silence, two pebbles striking a pane of glass: "I cannot."

Her eyes scan the crowd, or seem to; they come to rest on me, hold my gaze. Her expression is neutral but the reason for her singling me out is unmistakable. "You," I read. "You did it. It's all your fault." A chill seizes me but I return her stare, matching her blank expression. Others are turning toward me curiously, looking from my face to hers and back again, trying to understand what's going on. Bruno is the one who puts a stop to it, stepping between us and breaking the eye contact. A few more soft words in her ear, a gentle arm around her shoulders, and he leads her off the platform and out of the room.

Now the crowd erupts into excited babble; people stand up, seeking out their friends. I notice an invisible barrier between myself and the others: despite the press of bodies, not one so much as brushes up against me; eyes seem purposely averted. Or is it just my imagination? I'm heading toward the front door when I feel a hand on my shoulder: Doidinho.

He widens his eyes and rolls them in what I take to be a succinct comment on the evening's events. It makes me smile. As we go down the stairs, he puts his arm through mine. "Oh, no," I think, immediately on guard, but once we've reached the street and are in the cool night air he releases me.

Reaching into his pocket, he fishes out a crumpled piece of paper, smoothes it, out and hands it over. Two stick figures grin up at me, one with a skirt, one *sans*. Floating behind them is a rudimentary house — at least I assume it's behind, since it's much smaller than they are. "Casa do Morro Pequeno" is printed unsteadily below the house. In larger writing, below the stick figures, it says "12:00," with a picture of a sun next to it, and *"amanhã."* "Tomorrow." The whole effort is touching and I'm kind of ashamed that I misrepresented my language skills so effectively at the start of our interaction: if he'd tried to set up a meeting verbally, I would've understood.

"Amanhã, okay!" I nod emphatically, then think of something. Where will we meet? *"Onde?"*

"Aqui!" He points to the pavement right in front of number 239. That's maybe not such a good idea.

I point up the hill. "Terreiro de Jesus?"

"Okay, okay!" He leans forward and pats me on the shoulder several times, smiling, then turns and scurries away, calling out, *"Tchau!"*

Strange man, I think. Harmless, but strange. Nevertheless, I'm satisfied that a plan is in place, glad I'll be striking out on my own for a bit — without Veronica or Bruno, that is. Glad, too, that Bruno didn't even introduce me to Doidinho — won't he be surprised when he finds out where I've been! That makes me realize I'm taking it for granted that I'll report back to him eventually. My anger seems to have cooled off — but I still think it's a good idea to make my absence felt.

Boy, that Veronica is kind of a nutcase. Wonder why she couldn't get her act together this evening. Was it really because of me? I'm starting to feel more sorry for her than upset. I would actually look forward to talking with her, straightening this thing out. After all, her function in the Outernet work is an important one, and if she can't do it anymore, they're in trouble. Maybe in a few days, day after tomorrow or so, I'll go back there.

Engrossed in these thoughts, I've reached my hotel; I go up to the airless room, fall onto the bed, and sleep until the middle of next morning.

Having missed the hotel breakfast, I head to the nearby bakery and order buttered toast and a cup of strong, too-sweet coffee with milk. The single plastic table is already occupied by a couple of teenagers downing hamburgers and Cokes, so I eat standing up.

By the time the kids leave, freeing up the seats, I'm almost finished, not sure whether it's worth sitting down. Then I notice a newspaper lying on one of the chairs. It's been a while since I've tuned in to news from the world at large — not that there aren't TVs and newsstands around, it's just that I've been going around like an ostrich with my head buried in this Outernet business. Time for a breath of fresh air, a look around.

I sit down, pull out the newspaper, and unfold it. There, on the front page, is a large color photograph of a man in a military uniform inspecting a row of heavily armed soldiers. I can't make much sense of the accompanying text, but something compels me to return to the picture. The man's profile is haughty, the nose lifted, the mouth unsmiling. All of a sudden it strikes me: I know that face. It's the cop from the police station, the one I'd nicknamed Banger. I never saw him after that day he destroyed Bruno and Veronica's computer, but here he is now, front-page news: he must be some kind of big cheese. The thought is disturbing.

I flip through the rest of the paper, reading headlines, scanning articles: same old, same old. Violence on a large or smaller scale, catastrophes, breakdowns. The president of the United States grins, his hand bearing down on the shoulder of a dignitary from another country. The wreckage of an airplane litters an urban area. Sports. TV listings. Horoscopes. I fold it all back up: Banger comes out on top again. Sad world. I check my watch, drain my cup. Time to go meet

Doidinho in the square.

The steps of the church are almost smoking, they're so hot. Lucky I brought the paper along: I spread it out and take a small, mean pleasure in sitting on Banger's face. What a crazy time of day to be out, going on twelve noon. The sunlight is hard, punishing the occupants of the square: the tourists, pushing their way across as fast as they're able, the berimbau seller, who's draped a bandanna over the top of his head, and a random assortment of foolish stragglers such as myself. Hard to believe I was here only yesterday, just over on the other side, waiting for the museum to open — unaware that my complacency was about to be so thoroughly shattered.

I sigh, look at my watch again: Doidinho is due in fifteen minutes if he's not on Bahian time, which I hope he isn't.

"Yo." The voice is unmistakably American, United-States-of-America American. It belongs to a woman who's just swept in to my field of vision and clambered purposefully up to the step I'm sitting on. She stands surveying the square with one hand shading her eyes, the folds of her long Indian-print skirt almost brushing my arm.

I don't react, alarmed that she might have pegged me as a compatriot. I consider pretending I can't speak English. Keeping my head perfectly still, as if I hadn't noticed her there beside me, I swivel my eyes to look down at her feet. They're bony, caked with dirt. The left one sports a silver ring on one toe, a Band-Aid around another, and a tattoo of a scarab; the right ankle is wrapped in macramé, probably made out of hemp. Wow. She's the real thing.

"Unreal, hunh?" she marvels, still surveying, then gathers up a fistful of skirt and sits down next to me. Ignoring her is no longer an option. I turn slightly, bestowing a quizzical look upon her.

She really is a classic case: the mousy face of the littlest girl in first grade, the one who was always left out or trodden upon, peers out from between curtains of hennaed hair. Her nose has a stud in it, silver rings pierce her lower lip, and her ears are punched through with half-inch holes. A bunch of things hang from chains around her neck: I identify a crystal, an ankh, a shark tooth or bear claw or something, and a miniature dream catcher. It's like she bought an identity wholesale from Hippie Heaven.

"You American, or what?" she asks.

I surrender. "Yeah," I say. "North American."

"What?" She squints at me. "You mean like Canadian?"

"NO," I answer, letting my exasperation show. I was always one of the ones responsible for snubbing or stomping on girls like this in first grade. "I mean, *like*, U. S. of A."

"Oh. That's what I thought." I could kill her. "Sucks, hunh," she adds.

"What sucks?"

"Belonging to the most imperialistic country in the whole wide world. Being responsible for maintaining injustice and oppression at home and financing dictatorships and stuff abroad. Messing up the environment and refusing to help clean it up. You know about all that stuff, right?"

Boy, is she annoying. "Uh, yeah. I've heard about it." I'm on the verge of terminating the conversation right here, but her one-dimensional denunciation irritates me too much. I add: "It's not like the United States is the only villain in the world, though."

"You got *that* right!" she exclaims. "It's the worst, but not the only one. Check out this scene, for instance." Her sweeping gesture indicates the whole of the square. "This architecture. Pure Portuguese. Those guys came over here, ripped out all the jungle, and built an exact replica of what they'd left back home. They killed off the natives and brought in slaves to work for them, and didn't even notice they were out of line."

"Kind of like what happened in the United States."

"That's what I'm saying! Those guys all think alike. The big bullies. And they do whatever they can to help each other out. Like how we supported the military dictatorship here in the seventies. Did you ever get anyone to tell you about that? *That* was a trip!"

As a matter of fact, Bruno and I had talked quite a bit about what life in Salvador was like during that period. I feel obligated, once again, to attack the girl's tendency toward oversimplification. "Some people say it's still a kind of dictatorship. The instigators were never punished; in many cases they just transferred power to whom they chose . . . although some things are freer, for sure . . ."

"Come on! It's way different! You don't have people getting disappeared or tortured for opposing the government. Listen, I've been living at the Hippie Village up in Arembepe, you know where that is?"

I've seen it in my guidebook: an official tourist attraction up the coast a ways. The houses in the photos looked like someone gave Dr. Seuss a bunch of palm fronds and put him to work. I nod.

"Some of those guys up there have been around since the sixties, and when you hear what *they* have to say about the dictatorship, you're glad you're here *now,* and not *then,* you know what I mean?"

"I guess," I say vaguely, and consult my watch again. Noon on the dot. No sign of Doidinho. I could get up and walk about a little bit, keeping an eye out for him. I'm truly not interested in discussing politics with this young lady. I don't owe her anything just because she thrust herself into my space.

"But they say it's happening again, you know?" she pursues. "The signs are there. You have to look behind the smokescreen. The ones who saw it happen before can tell. We might even see some real action before too long. How long are you gonna be in the country?"

I don't answer but stand up and stretch, delivering a stagy yawn. "I'd better go look for the person I'm supposed to meet," I say.

I hear a thwack, look down: she's smacked the newspaper I was sitting on with the flat of her hand. "*This* guy!" She picks up the paper and shakes it at me. "See?" She means Banger.

"Yes, I see. What about him?"

"There's an example right there of what I'm talking about. One of the nastiest characters around; got his start during the dictatorship and that's where he learned his techniques. Now here he is with a promotion, with more power to go around doing whatever he wants. It's scary."

"How do you know so much about him?"

"I know this guy, man. He used to be just a plain old cop — I've seen him in action. Me and some friends were just hanging out once, smoking a joint, but we should've left the apartment of the guy we bought the weed from, you know? But he was a nice guy, he wanted to play us this CD, so we were all sitting around listening to it, and then *blam*! This guy here" — she shakes the paper again — "kicks down the door and rushes in followed by a few other cops, all with their guns out. They take one look at what's going on, shove me and my girlfriend onto the floor, and then start to rough up the guys — our other friend, who's Brazilian, and the dealer guy. And I mean rough. This cop was the worst; he was having a great time. He shoved their heads in plastic bags and held them tight around their necks, practically killing them, so that when he finally let them breathe they'd confess, tell who the bigger supplier was. That was pure hell, man. My friend didn't know anything, so he couldn't confess anything. He almost got brain damage from that. At the end the cop was so disgusted he kicked him in the nose. Blood all over. And the dealer — he got it worse. Never saw him around again after that. Boy, were we glad to get out of there."

Her eyes are wide from remembering; she's hugging her knees. I'm appalled but not surprised to hear that about Banger. I almost start to tell her about my own encounter with him but don't want to prolong the conversation.

"That's awful." I shift my weight, go down one step, pause. "Well, so long," I say.

"Yeah, take care," she replies. "I mean it: watch out. If any trouble starts up, head over to the American Consulate. They'll help you out."

"Thanks." I launch myself onto the sidewalk where I almost collide with Doidinho, who was heading straight toward me. After an exchange of smiles and rudimentary greetings we set off at a brisk pace, leaving the Terreiro de Jesus.

As we turn down one street and then the next, tourist-oriented establishments disappear, replaced by cheap clothing stores. Each storefront is tended by two or three desperate salespeople clapping loudly, singing out terms of endearment to the passersby, sometimes reaching out to grab them by the sleeve. Freelance vendors also work the pavements hawking ballpoint pens, crocheted cell-phone cases, pirate DVDs, waggle-headed dashboard dogs, and Chinese umbrellas. It's lunchtime, so the narrow space left on the sidewalk is filled to capacity and there's no room for overflow into the road, what with cars and buses swerving dangerously close to the curbs.

After a few arduous blocks of this we're swept along with the crowd into a vast bus station. Doidinho hasn't tried to make conversation with me; he's just kept turning around to make sure I was following him. Now he guides me to one of the five or so platforms where the big buses discharge and reload. The bus we want is already here; we join the line of people boarding, then climb up and find seats.

The ride is long; traffic makes the going slow and at each stop more passengers get on than off. The city undulates out from the road in a series of hills crowded with small houses, many of them unfinished, their raw red bricks the color of the earth. Laundry lines stretch between windows; tall grass grows wild, pale green and luminous against the dusty red. A giant tree rears up, its swollen trunk topped by a snarl of branches: long ago, this area was blanketed in rain forest. We pass through dingy, semicommercial neighborhoods that feature a surprising number of full-service medical laboratories, and eventually turn onto a less congested thoroughfare that hugs the coastline. Now the sea is only a few yards to our right, impassive under the glaring sun. It doesn't actually look inviting, but it's a relief to have that wide vista open up, to scan the horizon. On the other side, heavily populated areas thin out to stretches with just a few restaurants and hotels, followed by more clumps of small shops and grimy apartment buildings.

After about forty-five minutes of this we turn back inland. The sprawl doesn't seem to end. The seat is hard and the view monotonous by now; I try to distract myself by observing my fellow passengers and coming up with adjectives for all the different skin colors on display, challenging myself by avoiding food analogies like chocolate, caramel, cinnamon, nut brown, etc. I decide that one woman's complexion has the luminosity of corn silk and another is the shade of a weathered wooden clothespin, while the old man sitting by my side reminds me of nothing so much as the dark purplish leaves of Japanese maple trees. The entertaining aspect of the game goes flat, however, as I reflect on what I've learned about the racial situation in this country. The myth I bought in to before arriving — an exported image in the same package as string bikinis and ace soccer players — is that this is a land where all the races interbreed and exist in harmony. What my friends here have spoken of, and what I've observed in the past ten days, in supermarkets, banks, and the "finer" sorts of stores; on billboards, TV, and magazines, is that the so-called harmony is only a familiar hierarchy in which the lighter-skinned folks hold the better, higher-paying jobs —

manager, teller, salesperson, driver — while the darker ones tend to be relegated to functions like cleaning staff and security.

I look down at my hand gripping the chrome armrest: wet sand? Probably half of the people in this bus, and in the city at large, are the same color as me, but even within that category they divide themselves into "black" and "white," designations that depend not only on skin color but on hair type, features, even income.

Doidinho plucks my sleeve. He's been sitting across the aisle from me; now he stands up, motioning for me to follow him to the front. The bus jerks to a halt and we step down onto a teeming sidewalk.

We start walking away from the main avenue. Small yards appear, trees, the lush green of palm fronds and banana leaves soothing after so much dusty reddish brick. The narrow streets are no longer paved but made of red earth, a deeper red than the bricks. We've been gradually heading downhill; now the ground levels off and we turn onto a wider road that forms a kind of boundary. Along one side of this road runs a huge gray conduit, about as wide as a person is tall, stretching off in both directions. A lithe silhouette walks along the top of it, a half-mile or so away, arms swinging out now and then for balance.

Pointing at the tube, I frown inquiringly at Doidinho.

"*Água,*" he replies.

A little farther on we pass a small group of women gathered by the side of the pipeline. They're washing clothes, using the trickle from a seam in the plastic to fill pails and basins. I wonder why they would pick such an inconvenient method, then realize they must not have running water at home.

We're passing houses now whose structures dissolve into collage: sheets of metal lashed with barbed wire to uneven, fissured planks; patched canvas nailed to pieces of signboard whose elegant lettering fades into illegibility; lattices of branches stuffed with hardened mud; rusty grates and fragments of old furniture. It's impossible to tell easily where the doors or windows are and what is meant as fencing; I can't very well stop and stare. But I slow my pace and scrutinize the jumbled façades as discreetly as I can. Between these constructions, narrow passageways offer glimpses of swept dirt courtyards, where flowering plants have been arranged in pots, and chairs placed in the shade of venerable trees.

Stillness reigns along this road except for occasional muffled voices or the crow of a rooster. Far above, a large black bird glides on the wind. Doidinho seems content to walk in silence, for which I'm grateful.

After a while he leads me onto one of the side roads, sloping upward once again, where the dwellings turn back into recognizable houses. We stop in front of a gate set into a high, blue-painted wall.

"Casa do Morro Pequeno!" Doidinho exclaims, gesturing toward the gate with a flourish. He rattles the chain, claps his hands in summons.

Seconds pass, a minute, then someone comes and unlocks the gate, pulling it inward. A young man, possibly a teenager, greets us with a searching look instead of a smile. His shirt and pants are white; the string of green and white beads around his neck indicates his affiliation with a particular orixá, but I don't know which one. He stands aside to let us pass then closes the gate.

Doidinho stops before a wooden barrel full of water standing by the wall. A cup floats on top; he scoops up some water, circles it above his head three times, then splashes the contents on the ground. He hands me the cup, and I perform the ritual without mishap under the young man's solemn gaze.

We head toward a cluster of low buildings placed on

three sides of an open area. The compound is surprisingly large. Trees shelter the buildings and thicken behind them; I can make out the edge of a fenced-in garden, a pond ringed by a low stone wall, a clothesline on which various items of clothing, all white, flap in the breeze. We pass a tortoise gnawing mango peels in the dust — it takes no notice of us. Everything is neat, well tended, and strangely silent. I remember once again that this is the time of year when activities in the terreiros are suspended, and anxiety stirs in the pit of my stomach: what exactly am I doing here? This visit has been made possible by Doidinho — whom I don't actually know — simply because I pronounced the terreiro's name and expressed an interest in it. Will the residents mind my crashing their downtime just because a photograph happened to catch my eye in the museum? I'm not even prepared with any questions — what can I possibly find out, especially with my limited ability to communicate? Perhaps I just need to relax and accept my role as a tourist — a label I dislike but cannot reasonably disown.

Stopping before a tiny, whitewashed house, our guide points to the door, then vanishes. It turns out to be a freestanding bathroom containing a toilet and a shower stall. Doidinho encourages me, in pantomime, to take a shower. He also removes something from his backpack and pushes it into my hands: a crumpled white T-shirt and skirt that seem to be more or less my size. I'm taken aback, but I enter the small, spotlessly clean room and lock the door. After the first shock of the cold water, it's pure pleasure to sluice off the grime and fatigue of the long, hot trip. No towel has been provided so I wipe myself off with the T-shirt I'd been wearing, then put on the white clothes.

Stepping out of the bathroom into the soft afternoon air, I feel like a new person — still full of curiosity but much calmer. Doidinho laughs at me, probably because I must look so much happier. He goes in to take his shower while I wait on the little stone bench outside. When he reappears, dressed in white as well, he, too, seems different. Not merely refreshed but better defined, as though he had acquired more personality somehow. Or perhaps it is I who am seeing him more clearly. Gratitude jolts me, so acute it's almost painful: the man has gone to so much trouble for me, asking nothing in return. I have a keen eye for ulterior motives and he's entirely devoid of them. He smiles, beckons, and we walk up to one of the long, low buildings.

The young man is waiting for us. He throws wide a heavy door and leads us down a corridor, then knocks on another door. After leaning in to listen for an answer, he pushes it open; Doidinho and I follow him in.

The room provides a pleasant contrast to the gloomy corridor: a window lets in the late-afternoon sun and the chortle of birds. There's something else in the air, too: a softness, almost tangible, as though we had entered a different atmosphere, a thicker and milder one. The impression is so odd that my body covers itself in gooseflesh.

Behind a table at the far end of the room sits a large woman, all in white except for many multicolored necklaces of beads. Her head is wrapped in a kind of turban; voluminous skirts cover her feet. She smiles warmly at us, nodding as if everything were now all right, everyone accounted for. Our escort takes up a position against a wall, standing; Doidinho and I sit in two chairs facing the mãe de santo — I'm sure that's what she is, though I'm a bit disappointed that she's not the one whose picture I saw in the museum.

Doidinho says a few words to her, after which she speaks to the young man, who then, to my surprise, addresses me in English.

"Dona Janaina says, what is your question." His speech is hesitant, almost as heavily accented as Doidinho's, but it reveals the fruit of careful attention paid in English class. It's a great relief to have a translator, but I have no idea what to answer. My question? They're all waiting: the woman's head is tilted, an expression of kindly interest on her face; Doidinho has shifted toward me in his seat; the young man is watching me intently, ready to seize my words the moment they leave my mouth and submit them to the alchemy of translation.

My question. My interest is so general, so vague. I know I came here because of the museum, hoping to find out why, out of all the pictures of mães de santo there, I felt so drawn to the one associated with this terreiro. Truth is, I think it must have been a clue, hinting at something I don't know about myself. As if I were a mystery I carried around, ever trying to solve it. Yes, I suppose what I actually want is just to know myself, to understand myself better.

The seconds are ticking by; I can't sit here ruminating on my psychological makeup with these three people waiting for me to say something purposeful. So I blurt out: "I want to know more about myself!"

My translator looks at me, confirms: "You want . . . to know . . . you?"

"Yes."

He relays this to the mãe de santo, whereupon both she and Doidinho nod sagely.

"Put your hands on the table, please," the young man requests.

I scoot my chair forward and place my hands on the table. Doidinho adjusts them so that the fingers, not the palms, are resting on the edge. I hadn't examined the items in front of me until now: ropes of beads form a centerpiece on the white cloth; shells and hunks of crystal of varying sizes are arranged within and around the beads. A glass of water and a flickering candle have been placed in two corners.

Dona Janaina leans forward and begins to gather up cowrie shells. Once she's got them all, she rattles them in her cupped hands, bows her head, closes her eyes, and begins to mutter. She shakes the shells over one part of the table then another and another, punctuating phrases of a litany I can't understand a word of. After a while, she lets the shells tumble into the center of the table and examines them. She picks most of them back up, rattles them, lets them fall, and repeats the process several more times. Finally she sits back, then begins to speak in Portuguese, looking at me, leaving room between sentences so the young man can translate. "The mistress of your head is Iemanjá," she begins.

My skeptical mind wonders if Bruno told Doidinho about my experience in the museum, and if he then told this woman.

"Omolú and Nana" — two orixás about whom I know nothing — "also play important roles in your life. These orixás ask you to care for them, making the correct offerings. When you do this, your life will be much easier; doors will open for you. You are an independent woman, but need help. Your intelligence is strong but your heart needs attention. You are suffering because your husband took his attentions from you."

I'm shocked that she should have guessed this last fact about my life — something I haven't told Bruno or Veronica or anyone in Salvador, something I've been trying desperately to forget — to no avail.

She continues: "In reality, you are living with only a shadow of your husband."

Upon hearing this I resume breathing normally, though my disappointment in her is crushing. I am *not* living with Jorge anymore: we've been divorced and living apart for three months. So she was just guessing, I should have known — or does she mean that the *memory* of him is the shadow? But she keeps talking, and the young man keeps translating, faster than I can react to it all.

"Your husband fell in love with another woman, and you had to accept this even though it destroyed you. That is now finished, and at the same time not finished. It is necessary to

211

repair your relationship with these two people. You took a trip together; after this, everything changed for the three of you: you, your husband, and the other woman. Do you ride horses? No? Are you sure, you never did? Strange."

Dona Janaina looks discomfited, but goes on. "Omolú has been protecting your emotions by keeping you isolated, maybe in a profession where you are distant from other people even when you are near them. Now you must learn to follow your heart, not your head, and especially you must learn the courage to act, not only react. But the most important lesson for your life right now is to discover what *you* need. Your actions must be based on that, not on the needs of other people." A pause. "There is no more."

Phew. All that from a couple of scatterings of cowrie shells. I consider a number of possible responses, most of them negative, such as: "What the hell are you talking about?" But I don't have time to sort out what I think, because the young man is asking me: "Any other question?"

There *is* one more thing. I take out of my pocket the slip of paper on which I wrote the name of the mãe de santo from the museum. I read it out loud, as a question: "Mãe Iara Pereira dos Santos Silva?"

Dona Janaina beams, points to her ample bosom, saying: "*Mãe! Minha mãe!*" "My mother!" She speaks excitedly to the translator.

"Dona Janaina says, her mother told her about you. Her mother said you would come here because only Dona Janaina can tell what you need to know."

Puzzling. "How does her mother know me?" Have I actually met the woman at some point? Is that why she seemed so familiar? "Where does she live? Does she live here?"

"Mãe Iara died many years ago. But she stays very close to her daughter."

Oh, okay. Well, if that's what they believe. Now I,

personally, can't make a pronouncement as to whether or not there is life after death, and if so, what form it might take. Reincarnation doesn't seem much more unlikely than the alternative, but I have to be a little suspicious here since the departed's function seems to be that of a publicist for her channeler. Hmm.

Well, it looks like the session is over. Dona Janaina and Doidinho are having a chat. Should I stand up? Am I supposed to pay for the consultation? Will it be insulting if I offer? Do I tip the translator? There was nothing on religious etiquette in my guidebook; it only provides a brief description of the major candomblé ceremonies.

Doidinho gets to his feet and takes the mãe de santo's hand, bending over it reverentially and saying a few words; now it's my turn. I offer my thanks as best I can, trying to make up in enthusiasm for what I lack in volubility, because I *am* grateful: the experience was incredibly interesting and regardless of what I may believe about the information provided, it's obvious that these people are good-hearted. I also thank the young man.

Once Doidinho and I are outside I take some money from my pocket and ask him, in sign language, if I should pay Dona Janaina. His response, also nonverbal, seems to be: "Yeah, maybe — that's not a bad idea."

"*Quanto?*" I ask him. How much? He shrugs. I remove a few bills and give them to him.

He goes back in and when he returns gives me a big smile and a thumbs up. We take turns in the little bathhouse changing out of our white clothes, then we're on our way once more.

The trip back seems much shorter. I barely notice the landscape or the other passengers in the bus; I'm busy reviewing the experience at the terreiro, trying to come to a conclusion. Some of what Dona Janaina told me was just plain wrong, didn't apply to my life at all. She probably wasn't being metaphoric when she said that bit about living with the shadow of my husband. Also, the business about the romantic triangle: if there *was* another woman, I certainly didn't know about it, and I'm in no position to hunt her down now and "fix" the relationship. The thought makes me laugh, through a haze of pain: doubt as to Jorge's faithfulness stings like vinegar dripped in a wound. Up to this moment, the most horrible aspect of our breakup was his pleading out on pretext of pure boredom; he swore up and down that there was no other romantic interest involved. I had tried to argue that we could fan the spark back to life, but he insisted it was impossible — did his stubbornness mask desperation, was he prying me off so he could give himself up to another? Bitterness courses through me. But then, I have to remind myself, this supposedly clairvoyant pronouncement was probably made up. After all, the mãe de santo seemed to also think I'd been horseback riding — I've never done such a thing in my life. And the other things she said — that I'm intelligent but emotionally troubled, basically, and that I should pay more attention to my needs than to those of others — that's the stuff of horoscope blurbs, anybody could take it personally. The business about the orixás I can't argue with because I don't know enough. It was kind of impressive that she picked Iemanja for me — but I can't be sure she wasn't tipped off beforehand. All in all, as far as gleaning information about myself went, the whole thing was a washout. And yet, I have to admit that the part about identifying what it is I really need *did* strike a chord; something inside me says, "Yes, it's true," no matter how generic the advice might be.

I lean back in my seat and close my eyes. What *is* it I really need? If I'm honest with myself, I have to acknowledge my doubts concerning the validity of my research project, this task I've poured several years' worth of effort and money into. Not that there's a question as to the importance of the contribution it will make to the field, but is it really what *I* need to be doing? Why did I embark upon it — was it intellectual passion that drew me to it, or other, less noble motives? I remember when I hit on the topic as the perfect way to combine the different strands of inquiry I'd been pursuing. I knew that once the study was published it would enhance my status at the college and might even increase my chances of being hired elsewhere. I was sick and tired of playing second fiddle to Jorge. Tired of being the drab little woman on his arm at faculty teas at the university. Tired of witnessing the effort it took his tenured professor friends to feign polite interest in my activities. It seemed that a part-time lecturer at the rinky-dink community college such as myself, while theoretically entitled to a place in enlightened society, could never hope to scale its heights. My research idea, however, provided a toehold. I launched into the study with great energy and was immediately rewarded by the questions my work generated, by the envy and admiration people expressed at the prospect of all the globetrotting I would have to do. Eventually, though, the novelty wore off, and as I went about the slow, painstaking process of gathering material with nothing to show for my efforts, it turned into: "You know, Josephine's African religion thing." Some people even doubted I would ever finish it — that was the gossip reported back to me.

And then I was thrown for a loop when Jorge told me our life together was over. At that point I had to shelve the project for a while and just try to keep myself together, concentrate on getting to and from the college every day. Once I was back on my feet, though, I threw myself into the research with a vengeance — that was when I decided to come to Salvador. My experiences here have been so fascinating that the project will have served a vital purpose whether I complete it or not, but I really should decide whether I'm going to bring it to term, not diddle along wasting my time on something I'll never finish. I might have to give up the comfort I've taken from having a clear direction, a concise statement of purpose at the ready — the idea of being deprived of that makes me feel shaky.

And since I'm on this train of thought, I need to look at my activities with the Outernet clan. Is *that* what I need to be doing? Have I just gotten swept away by other people's enthusiasm and praise, offering, in exchange, to assist them with *their* needs in whatever way I can? A shudder of dismay passes through me as I contemplate this portrait of myself as gullible victim — yet the feeling dispels with a glance at Doidinho dozing in the seat next to me, head lolling on his shoulder, mouth gaping open. Here's someone who had never met me before and took a whole afternoon out of his life to bring me where I wanted to go, without getting anything in return — not even conversation! Unless of course his reward is the simple satisfaction of helping another. Perhaps I could view my own situation in that light, and recognize that acting as an Outernet guinea pig allows me to express my altruistic tendencies — or, to put it in a more unkind light, satisfies the requirements of an ego that prides itself on generosity.

Well, I'm not reaching any conclusions that would cause a sudden swerve from the path I've been traveling to date, but I vow to be alert from now on, as honest as I can be in analyzing my choices. I'm still left with a queasy feeling of doubt as far as the research is concerned; all I can do is resolve to reach a decision on this in the near future.

The bus is pulling into the central station from which we left. I shake Doidinho awake, and, once we're on the platform, I take leave of him with a big hug that I hope conveys the depth of my gratitude.

Now, where to? Night has already fallen, but I'm not tired. My steps are taking me automatically back toward Rua do Travesso. I had vowed to leave the Outernet crowd alone for a good while, but musing on my past appears to have altered my perspective. Time seems short; a life is soon over. I need certainty, assurance as to who I am, what I'm doing. If I'm going to continue with the Outernet project, I have to understand why Bruno and Veronica treated me the way they did, determine whether they are in fact "safe" for me to be around, or whether there's a risk of getting hurt again. These are things I can't figure out without first talking to them. If I go there now I can get a definitive answer right away — assuming one of them is home.

As if to hasten the speedy resolution I crave, the door at 239 Rua do Travesso is opened by Veronica herself. She registers momentary surprise and then, oddly, relief. Her eyes search mine. "Come," she says, pulling me in by the wrist and shutting the door. "Would you like a coffee? Tea? Have you had dinner?" Her friendliness seems genuine, though she does not smile. The solemn face bespeaks intimacy: she needn't resort to false cheer for my benefit. I don't resent her anymore: my anger after the scene in the rooftop house, my contempt when she snubbed me at the meeting — that's all gone. There may be a trace of huffiness left, but mainly I'm just wary. I'd prefer to refuse her offer of food but realize I'm ravenously hungry, so we go to the kitchen together.

After she's gotten me some leftover salad and bread, we sit across from each other at the kitchen table. No small talk.

"First of all," she says, "I need to apologize to you, Jo. I was very upset with you yesterday but it really had nothing to do with you." She pauses, and I wonder whether that's all the explanation she intends to give. That would be irritating. But she rubs her eyes and continues: "I didn't sleep all night. I was trying to understand what happened to me, to sort it out. I must tell you, when I found you and Bruno together again, with him giving you a treatment, I went absolutely mad with jealousy. I've never felt such rage, such pure rage before. I was so angry I couldn't see straight. And then when it came time to surrender to the Outernet, I simply couldn't do it. I tried as hard as I could to put my emotions aside, to forget, and I actually did: I managed not to think about you and

Bruno at all. Even so, it didn't work. For the first time since I started logging on to the Outernet, I failed. And that's a disaster, especially now. Now is when we need to get more people on, as fast as we possibly can. I was our only reliable connection, and I was making headway in learning how to help others gain access. But now . . . now we're seriously set back."

She finally stops for breath, and I jump in: "As far as the Bruno thing is concerned," I say, "I can assure you there's nothing for you to be jealous of. I'm not interested in him in *that* way at all. But you must have realized that yourself — at least, you don't *seem* angry anymore, so isn't the problem solved?"

She shakes her head. "I thought so, this morning. And then I tried to log on and couldn't do it. I've been trying all day, every way I know how. Nothing. It's very distressing."

"It must be only temporary, Veronica. Try not to be so worried about it. That probably doesn't help." I'm parroting what she and Bruno have told me several times already.

"You're right, you're right. But it's hard. This is happening at the worst possible time, just when the pressure is on us to really make progress. I don't know if you're aware of what's happening politically. Nothing is being said to the public, but across the country a clear pattern is taking shape of certain types of people being moved into positions of responsibility. It doesn't matter what the political affiliation of the individuals is on paper, whether more to the left or more to the right — what matters is where their loyalties *really* lie, and what they would do if it came to a crunch."

"A crunch? What do you mean?"

"I mean if, for instance, in the worst-case scenario, there were a coup. If power is taken over at gunpoint, then everyone has an excuse for submitting to it. Then it doesn't matter if you're a socialist or a communist or whatever, your subsequent actions can be justified by saying you were coerced."

"But aren't you? I mean, wouldn't you be?"

"Certainly, but the more integrity you had, let us say, the more genuine your dedication to a pluralistic system, the more likely you would be to try to put up some resistance. Whereas if the authorities are already pawns in the service of those taking over, there won't be a need to strong-arm them or turn them all loose and replace them with inexperienced people. The newcomers' power will be all the more firmly cemented in place."

"I see." I remember Banger, the newspaper. "You know that policeman, the one who destroyed your computer—"

"Exactly!" she interrupts. "He's one of them. He just got promoted to *tenente* — I suppose that would be something like a sergeant, in English. To get to that level, you normally have to undergo training, then tests. It's fiercely competitive. Knowing that man's intellectual capacity, there's no way he could've passed the course fairly. But if the judges have their instructions, there isn't really a problem, is there? No one else in the course would dare complain too loudly. So, there he is. Now he has far greater power to vent his pent-up anger on whomever he chooses. Before this he had to be careful; now there's very little to hold him back."

"Are you worried that he might interfere with you, with the work here?"

"He hates us, there's no doubt about that. It goes back a long way; things happened that I won't go into — too long of a story. But he hates Bruno particularly, with a passion. And he has other reasons to try to interfere with us: if he could effectively terminate our activities, he'd get just the kind of 'good doggy' pat on the back he wants. If he played it right, it could even earn him another promotion. And wouldn't he love that!"

We stay silent for a minute. I'd been eating while Veronica was talking; now I bring the dishes to the sink, wipe the table, and sit back down. She appears lost in thought. I watch her for a moment before starting up the conversation again. "About Bruno," I venture. "You know there's really nothing between us, don't you? I hope he told you: he was just helping me release some tension. I'd had a very strange experience earlier in the—"

"I know," she says, "he mentioned it. The thing is, it doesn't really matter what you did or didn't do, whether you had sex or not—"

"But we didn't!" I protest.

Her eyes have been fixed on some distant point all this time; now she looks straight at me, giving me a weary smile. "I'm trying to tell you: it doesn't matter to me if you *didn't* have sex. What made me jealous is your connection to each other, the warmth. Something entirely natural, marvelous even, because Bruno doesn't usually let himself get that close to people. I appreciate that he's found a friend; I'm happy for him, and for you. It's just that every time I think about it, or see you two together, I get this horrid feeling in the pit of my stomach, a sort of corrosive acid eating away at me and causing the worst sort of pain."

I'm shocked — I'd had no idea. At least until yesterday evening. "Has it been this way all along?"

"No. I liked you well enough from the start, but you didn't seem, if you'll forgive my saying so, *really* special. Only when I noticed how well you were getting along with Bruno did I start to pay attention, to get a sense of what an interesting and adventurous person you are, and at the same time humble, receptive."

I greet this with a self-deprecating grimace of which she takes no note.

"I enjoyed our conversations very much," she continues. "Do you remember that time we talked about our personal lives, the relationships we've been in?"

"Sure," I reply. "That was right after that first time you

found me sleeping next to Bruno. I was so afraid then that you might be angry or jealous, but you convinced me that you weren't."

"I convinced myself," Veronica says. "Or maybe I really wasn't. I think because I hadn't gotten to know you so well by that point. In any case, it was after that that you and I really started talking. I discovered I felt safe with you. Some of the things I told you I've never told anyone else, not even Bruno. It felt so good to share them; it was a relief, like sharing a burden. It also made me feel very vulnerable and afraid at first, and I had to withdraw for a little while just after; I don't know if you noticed that."

I frown, trying to think back. "Can't say as I did."

"Good!" She laughs. "I didn't *want* you to notice. I just pretended I was very busy, and once or twice I slipped upstairs when I heard you coming. That didn't last long, though, because I *did* trust you, essentially, and I wanted your friendship. So I got over myself, and we spent some more time together, and it made me happy, and I realized I didn't have to be afraid. I loved your willingness to try different approaches to the Outernet, to open up channels that might help you connect. I was playing the role of the teacher and guide, but our interactions taught *me* every time, taught me things I can't describe but am grateful for. I had to laugh to myself, you were so different from what I took you for at first."

Ouch, that smarts. "And what was it that you took me for at first?" I try to keep my tone light.

"Oh, you know; well, just an academic, really. Sort of washed out, or afraid of being a failure; trying to ride on the back of someone else's culture in order to produce something interesting — you get a lot of those here. Brains and not much else."

Damn, she really skewered me. If it didn't hit home, it wouldn't hurt. Bad enough to give that impression — worse is that on some level it *does* mesh with my self-image, with my fears about myself. Even if she claims that's not how she sees me on better acquaintance. I'm hurt and can't hide it; now I'm the one looking off into the distance, toward a point on the other side of the kitchen wall, a mile or so away.

"Oh, Jo," Veronica says. "I'm sorry." She leans forward and puts her elbows on the table and her face in her hands, gazing at me. I see that only in my peripheral vision, because something childish in me refuses to meet her eye. "I admitted that to you because it's so much *not* who you are, but it was thoughtless. I'm sorry."

"That's okay," I say tightly. "Go on. So after a while you noticed that I was more than a brain on legs, that I had ears, too, and was a good receptacle for pouring your true confessions into — did I get that right?"

She looks pained. "You seem to be deliberately ignoring a large part of what I just told you. Or maybe it's easier to latch onto criticism? Hard for you to hear good things about yourself?"

"What good things? How I'm so adventurous, just because I'm willing to help you all with your project?"

Now it's Veronica's turn to be offended. I can see her expression change from hurt to annoyed, and I must say it feels like safer ground.

"You don't make it easy, do you?" she complains. "I'm trying to tell you what I like about you, and you pick this moment to act like a real snot."

"Oh-ho!" I exclaim, enjoying myself now. "It's a snot I am, is it?"

Exasperation has turned to amusement on both sides; she narrows her eyes, appraising me. "Yes, it most certainly is a snot."

We both smile, then a half-frown comes onto her face as she continues to study me. "Truly, Miss Josephine, you are one of the most frustrating people I've ever met," she says.

"You open up, little by little; you offer a glimpse of your fantastic depths, and then bam! Snapped shut again, drawbridge raised, curtains drawn, lights out."

"Fantastic depths, eh?"

"YES!" She practically shouts the word, startling me. "You're amazing! All those weird psychic talents you have — how you've managed to stuff them under and how you're slowly accepting them back. How your attempts to fit in always failed, so you gave up and struck out into unknown territory all on your own. You devised this extravagant idea for a research topic, pretending to yourself that you arrived at it in a purely logical fashion, when in reality you were following much more obscure, inchoate impulses within yourself that demanded your allegiance . . ."

"Wow," I say. "That's a pretty impressive analysis!"

"Don't be fooled by the vocabulary," she shoots back. "And I'm not done. That's one part of what amazes me about you. Another part is your presence: you have a quality of being very present to whatever situation you find yourself in; you both observe and participate, and for all your *fantastic depths*, you emanate a kind of simplicity that is very soothing."

"It's an illusion, I can assure you."

"Hush! And then there's the adventurous part. Traveling to distant countries is one thing, but more admirable still is the willingness to explore the inner landscapes, to investigate techniques meant to enhance self-knowledge. I admire you for that, *not* because you've been doing it in order to help out with the Outernet, but because it takes bravery. Especially in your case, since it means reaching into areas you've tried so hard to stay out of up till now."

"Yes, but—"

"And lastly," she interrupts loudly, "you're caring, interested in others. Genuinely so. That's terrifically important. You've made a great difference in *my* life already, helped me figure things out about myself without even knowing you were doing it. Just being who you are allows us to converse on a certain level, which provides me with new insights. I'm grateful to you."

She's done it: her relentless onslaught has left me unable to fall back on my usual sarcasm. I'm at a loss for words, trying to find fault with the portrait she's painted, but there's nothing I can contradict without the risk of her going into still more embarrassing detail. "Well, thank you, I guess," I say awkwardly. "Thank you for telling me all that. But *I* don't think I'm all that wonderful, and as far as your being jealous is concerned, I'm sure Bruno doesn't either. And I know he's devoted to you. I'm sure I get a lot more out of him than he gets from me; it's kind of unbalanced that way. For instance, that treatment, or whatever it was, that he was giving me: there wasn't anything sexual about it, but it just felt, oh gosh — I don't know how to describe it, you must know."

"I *do* know, and that's what I can't stand! I wish *I* could do something like that for you, give you something you really need, pay you back somehow for what you've done for *me*!"

I'm stunned. The world has suddenly turned upside down. Is she saying what I think she's saying? That it's not me she's jealous of for taking a place in Bruno's affections, but him, for being in mine? I can't let myself believe that, and I'm too shy to ask her outright if that's what she means. "Wait a minute, Veronica. You *know* you've given me a lot, too! I benefited from our conversations a great deal as well! And you've spent so much time helping me to plan what exercises and experiments to try — I couldn't have done half as much without you!"

"Yes, but that's not what I mean. I wish we were easy enough with each other so that we could spend that kind of time you spend with Bruno, *not* talking, *not* planning, just relaxing, being together. I think you don't trust me enough, or something, to let your guard down in that way."

What can I say to that? She's right. When I try to imagine wordless camaraderie with her, I simply can't. The very idea makes me tense. Is it because I've been in such awe of her from the start? I've always felt slightly anxious in our interactions, as though I might prove a disappointment. I do like her, though, very much, and now that she's told me all of this she seems more vulnerable, more human. I feel sorry for her, sorry she's been wanting us to be closer and I was clueless. I had imagined her to be content and self-sufficient, floating above us all in a bubble of wisdom. How can I reach out, convey my genuine fondness for her?

"Veronica, you and Bruno are the two people I've met whom I admire most in the world. I mean it. You're both fascinating individuals, so powerful in mind and spirit. Just look what you've done together: you've created this center, a place for expanding creativity, a safe haven. It's unique. Your garden is tremendous. Your Outernet project is revolutionary and, from what I can tell, will benefit a huge number of people. The two of you care for each other, work well together, do practically everything together. You have a daughter who, for all her problems, sounds like a genius. I'm the one who's been jealous, standing outside the circle of the Perfect Couple, looking in, seeing what a real marriage can be like. The last thing I'd want to do, even if I could, would be to drive a wedge between the two of you. You two are an inspiration; I can only hope that I might still find *my* other half someday, and experience even a fraction of what you have together."

She laughs. She actually laughs at me. "Go on," she says, shaking her head. She stands up: I realize that she is, literally, telling me to leave. There's merriment on her face but it's private, she's not expecting to share it. I stay in my seat, confused.

"You're too much, Jo! You're too cute. 'The Perfect Couple'! If you only knew. Well, I can see I shouldn't have burdened you with all of this. Go on, never mind about me,

I'll be all right. We'll muddle through somehow. It's late, isn't it?" She looks at the clock on the wall. "Oh, indeed! Let's get some sleep — I need it, at any rate, I didn't get any last night. I do feel better though, now I've explained to you why I acted so ghastly, and I'll do my best not to let it happen again."

I'm miffed: there's condescension in her tone; she's distanced herself. Covered up the emptiness she just revealed. Part of me wants to stay and pry her back open, yet even if I succeeded I would have nothing further to offer, no promises or guarantees. I can barely admit my fear that she might be after more than friendship, that she might have an actual crush on me — it was sounding like that for a moment there, but the thought is horrifying. I have nothing against homosexuality in theory, or in other people, but I'm certainly not prepared to embark on a voyage of discovery, and if she were to proposition me it would be terribly uncomfortable for us both. Best not to push the whole thing too far.

I rise, give her a smile and an awkward pat on the shoulder, and advance toward the door. "I *am* tired, too," I say. "I'm glad you told me all of this: I feel much better now that I understand what's going on" — a half-truth. "Get a good night's rest, and I'll come see how you're doing tomorrow."

The way back to the hotel is dark and, tonight, sinister. I keep imagining lurkers in the shadows, not muggers but trigger-happy cops. I'm relieved to reach the hotel, but after a few minutes in my little room its dead air starts to suffocate me and I vow once again to look for a different place. A few days ago I'd been on the verge of asking Bruno and Veronica if I could rent their rooftop room; now that doesn't seem like such a good idea.

I get ready for bed, and when I close my eyes I see the hypnotic movement of the mãe de santo's hands casting the shells and picking them up, casting and picking up, over and over, until I fall asleep.

Next day I awake in time for the hotel breakfast — not exactly a reward for rising early. After wiping the last greasy crumbs from my lips I wonder what to do: I don't feel like going back to my room, wandering the streets, or visiting the folks at Rua do Travesso. Suddenly it strikes me that this would be a fine day to enact my plan of heading up the coast to look for a more decent hotel. It should be easy: after yesterday's excursion I know how to get to the bus station and even which bus to take. I go up to my room to gather the few things I'll need, and set out.

Few stores are open yet but the streets are full of people heading to work or school. There's standing room only in the bus, which makes for a long, uncomfortable ride. Once or twice some of the other passengers point at my backpack, attempting to tell or ask me something. At first I think they must be complimenting me on it, although it's quite ordinary. Maybe they like the color — mauve? I smile and nod in response. Eventually, observation shows me my error: it's standard practice for seated passengers to relieve those standing up of their bags or parcels for the duration of the ride. Strangers helping one another out! I hope my incomprehension wasn't interpreted as mistrust.

When the bus turns and heads inland, I get off and walk back to the beach, intending to postpone hotel hunting; for now, I can concentrate on finding a place to take a swim, contemplate the ocean, and think about things. It would have to be a shady spot, but these are in short supply: the palm trees are all the way up by the road, near the traffic. Closer to the water, the only shade to be found is at the umbrella-sheltered tables of small eateries called *barracas*, and I can't bear the thought of sticking myself to a plastic chair. Luckily it's still early enough that the sun is merely unfriendly, not downright punishing.

It's a weekday, so there's hardly anyone else out here. As I walk along the cool damp sand, an occasional wave washing over my feet, I feel happier than I've been in a while.

Soon, outcrops of black rock start to break up the surface of the beach; tide pools quiver among them. I step onto a wide stone platform surrounded by water and lie on my stomach to peer down over the edge. At my approach, tiny fish scatter like drops of colored light; crabs pause, wary, then scuttle along the sides of the basin, stuffing their mouths as fast as they can with alternate pincers. After a while, a kind of brown finger wriggles out from the shadows. Another one emerges, then two more, and finally the bulbous body of an octopus comes into view. It skims along until the water is too shallow then starts to walk, using its tentacles as legs. When the water gets deeper it pushes off against the sandy bottom to glide, once more, just beneath the surface. It circles round and round my platform.

My back begins to prickle, and I realize I'll be burnt to a crisp if I don't find shelter pretty soon – the ocean breeze masks the sun's virulence.

Standing up makes me momentarily dizzy. The tide has gone out, uncovering rocks studded with barnacles or slick with thick green hair. I head back toward the flat sand and continue walking, looking for a place to rest. I've just about resigned myself to the idea of a plastic chair, when I spot a barraca that's not open for business. The beach in front of it is empty, the small structure shuttered; its thatched roof casts a nice, wide stripe of shade onto the sand. Gratefully, I set up camp, taking out the water and crackers I brought, spreading out my towel to sit on, and leaning against the barraca wall with the empty backpack in between for cushioning. A sigh of relief.

The ocean is now more white than blue. At the horizon, a wavering smudge might be a cruise ship or an oil rig. The great mass of water is barely disturbed by shifting waves, fretful and sluggish like a dog settling down to sleep. There's an occasional bloom of white spray when a wave breaks against rock; wisps of cloud trail across the sky. I yawn, lie down on the towel, and close my eyes.

Now the landscape is reduced to the rustle of wind in the palm thatch, the faint piping of a distant bird, and the dull roar of the ocean. I stretch my arms and let them flop back down. Rolling my head slowly from side to side to loosen the tension in my neck, I notice that this movement causes the pitch of the ocean to vary ever so slightly. Intrigued, I try it a few more times, just to make sure.

There's a lesson in that, I reflect: reality changes according to your viewpoint. I roll my head once more from side to side then lie still again, listening to the tiny, ceaseless fluctuations within the monotone.

An insect lands on my foot – without opening my eyes I flex my toe to chase it away, and realize that the gesture produced an infinitesimal shift in the ocean sound. Bizarre! I can understand the position of my head influencing what I hear, but the position of my toe?

I clench my right hand into a fist: that, too, makes a difference. More astonishing still is the fact that it affects the sound in my *left* ear, the one further from the shore. By concentrating hard, I can now hear the rumble of the ocean on one side and its transposition on the other. There's also a third noise that flutters below the first two and seems connected to them, though I can't tell where it's coming from.

Recalling the conversation with Velma, I wonder if this experiment will have any effect on my brain waves. Focusing on all three sounds simultaneously is difficult; I decide it's not worth the effort. They're probably feeding into my brain whether I'm actively listening or not – who knows, they might make something interesting happen. I let myself relax again – except for the fist.

With relaxation comes awareness of a number of other sensations: the pulsating redness of my eyelids, the lumpy sand beneath me, the caress of a passing breeze, drowsiness. Disconnected visions begin to play out in my mind: I'm drifting off.

And then, it happens. I'm whisked away at great speed in a direction that feels like up, though there are no visual reference points – higher and higher and higher, until it seems that the Earth must be thousands of miles below. At the same time I'm being subjected to a suffocating pressure, as though I were a liquid undergoing distillation. My brain is being squeezed, hard; the vertiginous ascent and contraction stretch it like taffy: thin, thinner – to my horror, I realize my mind's about to snap. It's impossible to withstand the pressure: in a matter of moments I'll be either dead or insane.

Suddenly something wrenches me off course; it feels like the controls are being handed over. There's a lurch, and I stop speeding toward annihilation.

A space opens up. Where I am now, I can't guess, but I'm extraordinarily relieved to be here – anywhere. And it is still me, though apparently I've become pure consciousness: I can see, but I don't have a body. I'm entirely surrounded by a light-gray fuzzy texture bristling with minute, almost invisible spikes, like snail antennae, shooting out and back in. It's odd, seemingly devoid of any kind of information – a bit repulsive. Fear begins to mount in me once more, fear that I'll be stuck in this alien, unpleasant environment forever. I try to conceive of some way to escape, but there's nothing on which to gain purchase. Desperate, I send out a silent plea for help to no one in particular: "Get me out of here!"

Instantly, my surroundings reconfigure themselves. I'm hovering above a semitransparent structure consisting of vaults and corridors. I'm too far away to be able to tell what the spaces contain; I wonder if I can wish myself closer, just as I wished myself out of the bristly gray texture. The thought operates like a remote control, and I immediately "zoom in" to one of the units. It turns out to be nothing more than a cell, a box subdivided by dozens of vertical lines. When I zoom in further, each of the straight lines thickens into the semblance of a manila folder; each folder has a small tab with a label on it.

I pick one at random: its label is printed with today's date, and a time, 08:30. The adjacent folders on the left bear the same date, with the time progressing incrementally from one to the next, from left to right: 08:27, 08:28, 08:29. On the other side: 08:31, 08:32, etc. I turn my attention back to the first folder and will it to open.

A vivid three-dimensional scene unfolds. The small brown octopus glides through the water; I catch the pungent scent of decayed fish and hear the smack of waves nearby. The only sense missing seems to be that of touch: I see my hands on the rock but can't feel its rough surface.

I attempt a zoom out, and I lift off, viewing myself from above, only I'm not controlling my speed very well: within moments I've risen so high that miles of coastline stretch out below me. It's spectacular, exhilarating – until the sudden concern that I might stay lost above Salvador or come down in an unfamiliar place yanks me out of that scenario and back in front of the closed folder.

I contemplate the endless archives. At the thought that each one might represent a single minute of my life, a mixture of glee and dread begins to bubble in me. Seeking confirmation, I move a few compartments over to the left and choose a folder whose date corresponds to yesterday evening, 19:00. Sure enough, it opens onto Veronica's earnest face, repeating her speech to me last night in the kitchen. As she starts in listing my positive attributes I become queasy, and command the folder to close.

Now that there's no doubt about the mechanism, I have to satisfy my curiosity and find out whether my *future* is also recorded here. Scanning the folders to the right of where I first started, several compartments over, I find tomorrow's date. I pick a random time: 02:20.

Inside the folder is . . . another face, in extreme close-up and slow motion. Bruno. Although the image is very dark I can make out the pores of the skin, the flecks of dandruff at the hairline, the liquid curve of a wide-open eye. Why is his face moving in that odd way? Slow zoom out — and a shock that takes my virtual breath away. Bruno and I are kissing, voluptuously absorbed in each other, writhing on top of a bed in a sparsely furnished room I've never seen before. Adding to the strangeness of the scene is the complete absence of tactile sensation. Aghast, I recoil as if I'd stumbled, literally stumbled, upon strangers in the throes of passion. The scene vanishes quickly, replaced once more by the endless rows of files.

Although I don't have a body in this place, my mind and emotions seem to function much as they usually do. Confusion takes hold, embarrassment, desire. Was the kiss real, or will it be? Or do the archives also display elements of fantasy, of mere possibility? Intuitively I feel that what I've seen will come to pass, but the thrill of having that unexpected bit of my future disclosed is quickly buried in an avalanche of questions. Is this entire structure filled with moments from my life? Can I watch my own death? Is everyone's life on file? By spying on the future, would I change it? Could I bet on the races, play the winning lottery number, become a millionaire? The situation echoes so many sci-fi scenarios whose outcomes I've forgotten. If this place *does* register the lives of other people, then it must be something like the akashic records of Hindu mythology, a kind of cosmic warehouse of information on everything that ever did and will exist in the world.

A twinge of fear interrupts my speculations: Where is my body? Is it still where I left it? How is it faring without me? I know I should try to get back, but I don't want to leave before finding out whether this place is just a storage area, or if there's more. How can I get an overview of the whole thing? An analogy comes to mind. "Home page," I command silently. "Site map."

With a sigh, the space around me begins to simultaneously contract and recede. Before, the rows of vaults stretched endlessly away on all sides; now, outer boundaries come into view, set against a lilac-colored background. The archives continue to shrink until they're about the size of a postage stamp. Letters wink on above the small square: RECORDS. More squares slide in and distribute themselves on the background. Their labels read: GROUPS, CHAT, ENCYCLOPEDIA, PROJECTS, CONTACTS.

Suddenly the whole purple field takes on a gelatinous consistency, shivers, and bursts into a crowd scene so realistic I'm not sure whether these are actual people surging toward me or holographic animations. The six labeled squares remain visible, almost eclipsed by the swirl of clothes and limbs and faces of the rapidly approaching multitude. Oddly, there's no sound accompanying the scene, although the people, of all sizes and shapes and ethnic descriptions, appear to be talking and laughing.

As they approach I feel the urge to back away, even though I can tell now they're not real — I'm relieved when they come to a stop. They watch me with friendly, mischievous expressions; then all at once they close their eyes tightly. Some of them put extra dramatic effort into scrunching up their faces and lifting their shoulders toward their ears to heighten the effect. Without warning, though their mouths remain closed, the silence is shattered by a roar, dozens of voices joining in a single word: "OU-TER-NET!"

All the eyes reopen. The people give each other high fives, smile and nod and wave at me. Then they turn, start back in the direction from which they came, and evaporate on the way. Only the six little squares are left, sitting calmly on their purple background.

So this is it! I've managed to log on to the Outernet! If I were in my body, I'd do a little dance. Which reminds me: it's definitely time to go. Let's hope the wishing method works. I formulate the thought clearly: Return To My Body.

Instantly the bristling gray field encloses me again, as well as a high, piercing sound, a thin whine; then there's a jolt and the sensation of falling. The whine becomes a buzz, the buzz slowly dissociates into blips, billions of blips that bounce up into the buzz and back down. With every bounce they lose momentum, finally coagulating and forming larger lumps of sound. The spaces between these lumps grow increasingly small until they disappear altogether and the now-continuous soundscape becomes recognizable as the ambient noise of the beach, the muted roar of the ocean dotted with occasional birdcalls. The spiky gray texture has burned off to the effervescent orange of sunshine playing on my closed eyelids.

Barely do I have time to be reassured by the familiar sensations, however, before I become aware of one that is strange, disagreeable. Something is hemming me in, a great suffocating weight pressing me from all sides. Adrenaline floods in at the horrifying thought that someone might be lying on top of me. Should I keep my eyes closed? Could there be an advantage to pretending I haven't woken up?

I open one eye just the tiniest bit — imperceptibly, I hope. To my astonishment — and enormous relief — I find there's nothing at all on me. I can see the sand, a piece of sea, the line of my own shoulder. Yet I still feel like I'm being crushed.

Then I understand: the pressure is coming from my own body. It's the aftereffect of having been a free-floating consciousness, then plunging down into the density of flesh. Turning my attention to my breathing helps me regain a sense of spaciousness, and after a few in and out breaths the discomfort mostly disappears.

The sun is now almost directly overhead and the patch of shade I was lying in has shrunken away from me. I'm not sure how long I've been here. I sit up, take a swallow of warm water from my bottle, pack away my possessions, and stiffly get to my feet. I'm worried I might be seriously sunburned and my impulse is to get off the beach as fast as possible. Even those plastic umbrellas don't seem as if they could provide more than an illusion of shade.

Before setting off I spend a few moments looking at the ocean through the shimmering heat, a little sad that I've hardly made contact with it. A quick dip would be just the thing to get me reinvigorated for the trip home, I decide. Since I'm wearing my bathing suit under my clothes I just strip off my T-shirt and shorts and walk down to the shore.

Swimming is out of the question: the waves are powerful here, and jagged rocks poke through the surface. I find a small sandy inlet and stand knee-deep in the water. There's a reef a few yards out against which the waves break, spending most of their fury before rushing toward me; I lower my head into the charging foam and get a scalpful of sand. The froth leaves clusters of bubbles on my skin, a tiny convex rainbow in each one. As the waves retreat they carve out hollows beneath my feet, fusing me to the beach. My head empties of everything but the rhythm of the waves, the caress of foam and water, the taste of salt, the swell of larger breakers farther out to sea, and the tranquil horizon beyond.

Eventually, though, the fear of sunburn becomes insistent and I know I must leave. How long has it been — ten minutes, twenty? Such a brief time, yet I'm at ease in my body again. I start back down the beach with my towel draped over my shoulders, humming a tune. Feeling a little strange, as well, since I'm purposely not thinking about my voyage to the Outernet: the entire stunning, complex experience remains huddled just at the edge of awareness, waiting to be summoned. Instinct ordains that I let my mind rest for a while, at least as long as it takes to get back downtown. Hotel hunting will have to wait for another day.

So I retrace my steps, get on a bus, find a seat, and space out. I'm staring vacantly at the passing scenery, when there's a screech and the bus swerves and comes to a sudden halt.

We're not at a designated stop but on the grassy shoulder of a major six-lane thoroughfare. The doors open and two police officers board, dressed in the standard brown and tan uniform with berets, bulletproof vests, and thigh-holsters. Their guns are drawn. Immediately my heart starts to race, but as I look around I see that no one else is startled; in fact, they all seem to know what to do even before the officers issue instructions. All the men, young and old, get off the bus. The women reach for their purses or bags, put them on their laps or the closest seat, and open them up. I follow their example. One policeman has stayed on the bus and makes his way down the aisle, giving most of the handbags and bags a cursory look, searching others thoroughly. Meanwhile, I see out the window that the men have been made to line up and place their hands high up on one side of the bus, spreading their legs wide. They're being patted down by one officer while the other stands watch with his gun at the ready. The men waiting their turn have their hands clasped behind their backs. Will anyone make a dash for it? Will anyone get shot? My attention is diverted by the officer approaching to inspect my backpack: he hefts it, glances at me, then moves on. The men climb back on the bus, take their seats; when everyone has returned and the officer has left, the bus resumes its route. I remain chilled by images I'd only seen in movies and on TV shows, by the indisputable authority of a gun, the message that those in charge may do anything they please.

Tired, when we finally pull up at the bus terminal, and hungry, I buy a fried chicken patty and a juice. I'll go to the hotel, take a shower and change clothes, then go over to Bruno and Veronica's place. I'm anxious to tell them about my experience.

The sour-faced clerk slides my key over the counter in the shadowy reception area, and as I climb the stairs I find myself daydreaming once again about moving out of here — with the difference that now I have an actual destination in mind. How wonderful it will be to live near that beach, to visit the tide pools every day, observing the changing colors of sea and sky at dawn and dusk! Lost in these images, it takes me a moment to register the fact that the door to my room is ajar. Did I leave it open? Highly unlikely, though I can't be positive. A maid, perhaps? But there's never been any sign of anyone coming in to clean before now. I push the door open the rest of the way and flick on the light.

The bed has been upended, the contents of my suitcase strewn about; in the tiny bathroom my few toiletries have been destroyed, the lotions smeared on every available surface along with something that looks suspiciously like feces. All the papers I had seem to have been either torn, wadded up, or stuffed into the toilet. My handbag is lying on the bureau, empty, the items that were in it scattered on the floor, including travelers' checks and a substantial number of U.S. dollar bills.

Where's my passport? It had been in the handbag. My heart sinks. I search feverishly and finally spot it peeking out from under the bed frame. Relief gives way to dismay once I pick it up and find that it's been mutilated: the pages are torn, the picture heavily scratched and half gouged out.

I run downstairs, skid to a halt in front of the clerk, signal frantically for him to follow me. At the door to the room he stands surveying the disaster, his reaction phlegmatic. Crossing his arms, he pulls his mouth down at the corners and nods his head slowly up and down, up and down. I wait for him to say something, but he just turns and makes as if to shuffle off down the hall.

I explode. "Hey!" I shout. "Where the hell do you think you're going?" I grab his polyester sleeve and drag him back, pulling him into the room with me. Still holding onto him, I reach for my dictionary on the floor. Then I realize I need both hands in order to use the book, so I plant myself in the doorway to prevent him from taking off. Leafing frantically through the pages, I locate the words I lack and shout them at him as I find them. "You! *Você! Você é* . . . responsible! *Responsável! Aqui! Você . . . você deve . . . visto . . . ouvido alguém!*" "You must have seen someone, heard someone!" His solemn stare infuriates me all the more. "*Você vai pagar!*" "You will pay!" I shriek, waving my tattered passport in front of his face. Then I have to resort to the dictionary again. "*Chama! Chama polícia!*"

That's the best I can manage. I'm panting, mired in frustration. I want to see him cringe before the vehemence of my rage, stammer an apology or spring into action, but all he does is ask: "Polícia?" A slight frown, the cocking of the head to one side, lips pressed together, eyes vague as though contemplating the possibilities: his expression clearly conveys, "I don't think I'd do that if I were you."

His lack of prompt compliance almost gets me shouting again, but then I stop to think. He's right. Do I really want to involve myself in interrogations and investigations with renegade cops like Stiff and Banger? I'm in their precinct, so it's quite likely I'd be dealing with them. And something else dawns on me: perhaps this seemingly witless fellow is trying to give me a hint. Perhaps he was aware of what was happening, but was unable to intervene — if the perpetrators were the police, this would make sense. It would also explain why the money was left ostentatiously lying around: this was not an ordinary break-in and robbery but a deliberate assault against *me*, a message. But why?

I look up how to say "not yet" in the dictionary, and tell the man: "Polícia, *ainda não*." I step away from the door to let him exit and stand there pondering the matter, trying to decide on a course of action. I was going to go see Bruno and Veronica anyway — it would be best to ask their opinion before doing anything.

A skinny girl with a broom and a bucket appears and starts to unblock the toilet. I'm anxious to get going, so once she's finished in the bathroom I tell her to leave the rest to me;

I take a shower, get dressed, gather up the money and put it in my backpack along with what's left of my passport. The mangled papers and jumbled clothing I'll deal with later.

On the way to Rua do Travesso I pass an Internet place; spontaneously, I decide to backtrack and go in. I'm in no mood to check e-mail but I figure there must be a site for the American Consulate that will provide directions and information on replacing my passport, so I can start to work on that as soon as possible.

I haven't been to this particular "café" before and head toward the counter to find out if I can just get online or have to pay first. The attendant, a woman in her twenties with squarish, black-framed glasses, is in the middle of a heated argument with a customer. It sounds like she's explaining the same thing over and over again; the man is growing increasingly irate. Eventually she starts to lose her patience, too, and they end up having an all-out shouting match. I'm about to give up and leave, when the customer storms out. The young woman turns to me with a sigh.

"Internet?" I ask her. *"Pago depois?"* "Do I pay afterward?"

She sighs again. *"Tem permissão?"*

Faced with my confused stare, and having caught my accent, she translates: "Have permission?"

"Permission?" I repeat. "To use the Internet? I mean, *para usar internete?*"

The woman rolls her eyes and comes out from behind the counter, motioning for me to sit down at one of the computers. Leaning over me, she types in a password, then a few words in a browser. Within seconds an English-language news page opens up before me with the headline: "Internet Access Worldwide Restricted to Bearers of Government Clearance Card."

What the . . . ? Disbelief and outrage course through me as I scan the article: "stringent security measures," "thwarting terrorist hackers," "centralized list," "upon presentation of government-issued Clearance Card."

The woman has been standing back watching my reaction as I read — it must be obvious that I'm not in possession of a Clearance Card. The article is extremely brief and I want to know a lot of other things, like would she be able to get more information about this for me, and how do I apply for a card, and is this situation permanent? The idea of carrying on the conversation in pidgin English and Portuguese exhausts me, however, and I think, once again, that Veronica and Bruno will be able to enlighten me more swiftly and efficiently. In my haste to be on my way again, I forget all about the American Consulate and the passport question.

Walking quickly, I reach Rua do Travesso in under ten minutes. From a distance I see someone loitering near the door of number 239; coming closer, I realize to my dismay that it's the policeman Stiff, observing my approach. I don't quite have the gall to pass him without breaking stride, so I pause with my hand on the door frame and affect a pleasant smile. *"Boa tarde,"* I say — "Good afternoon."

Stiff does not return the smile. "Miss," he says, "did I not suggest you to stay away from here?"

I screw up my face as though I were either trying to remember his warning or admitting my mistake. Thereupon, I attempt to proceed into the building, but he stops me: "Just one minute please. May I see your identification?"

My ruined passport. If I show it to him there will be questions that may lead to a more lengthy interaction. Tourists are told to have proper ID on them at all times; I wonder if I'll get in trouble if I pretend not to have any.

"Oh," I exclaim sorrowfully. "I believe I left my passport at the hotel."

He scowls. "Miss, you must carry your identification with you always. I suggest you to return to your hotel and collect your document."

Now I'm impatient. Maybe if I assume the stereotypical North American attitude of entitlement, treating what he's saying as kindly advice rather than the command it's intended as, I can get by him.

"Thank you so much!" I bestow a large grin upon him, taking advantage of his momentary astonishment to breeze past and disappear up the stairs. An angry shout — *"Ei!"* — but no footsteps pursue me. I imagine he's planning to deal with me on my way out.

The door to the apartment is open. I enter cautiously, half-expecting a scene of destruction similar to the one at the hotel, but the large front room looks much as it usually does. If anything, it seems a little emptier. Muffled sounds reach my ears; I follow them to one of the bedrooms off the hall. Veronica is kneeling on the floor, hurriedly transferring items of clothing from a bureau into a suitcase. When she notices me she stops for a moment and gives me a worried half-smile.

"What are you doing? Are you going somewhere?" I ask.

She resumes packing and starts to talk as she does so. "I'm so glad you're here. We didn't know when we would see you again. We hadn't planned to leave, but now something has come up."

"Is it anything to do with that policeman downstairs?"

"Oh, is one still there, then? Oh dear. Yes, he's definitely here because of us. As a matter of fact there should be more of them coming along shortly. We managed to convince them — but just barely — that they would be better off with a search warrant, so they went to dig up something."

"And you're going away when?"

"Before they come back, we hope," answers Bruno, who has materialized noiselessly behind me, his arms piled high with papers. He dumps them into the suitcase then gives me a big hug. "So good to see you. We have not seen you in so long! I am sorry we do not have any time to talk right now."

241

Veronica snaps the suitcase shut, stands up. "You have the food, yes?" she asks him.

"In the small bag, by the door. Everything is ready."

"But I have to talk to you two!" I cry out. "Where are you going? When will you be back?"

They seem surprised by the urgency in my voice. Veronica comes toward me, holding the suitcase. "I'm sorry, we can't tell you the answers to either of those questions. We don't know when we'll be back, and as far as where we're going, I'm afraid it's not safe to tell you."

"You don't trust me?" I'm hurt.

"It is not a question of that, Jo," Bruno says soothingly. "There are circumstances under which anyone can be forced to tell what they know."

"Let's go, Bruno." Veronica's voice is tense. "Josephine, I do so wish we had more time, but if we don't go now we might not make it. They'll be back at any moment."

"But I got on the Outernet! And my hotel room was wrecked and my passport was destroyed! And I want to know why the Internet is restricted!"

They both freeze, staring at me.

"You got on the Outernet?" Bruno asks. His mouth stays open after he speaks.

"Bruno, we have to go *now*." Veronica is desperate.

"Come with us," Bruno says, lifting a hand to my shoulder.

We hear noise coming from the direction of the front door. Veronica shoves past me, lugging the suitcase, and hurries down the hall toward the kitchen. Bruno moves to follow her but tightens his grip on my shoulder. "Come," he repeats, tugging at me.

We hasten after Veronica, who has passed through the kitchen and disappeared down the back stairwell. Bruno locks the kitchen door after we pass through. "This will stop them for a second," he mutters.

We clatter down the worn wooden steps. I'm wondering how far we'll get — surely the cops know there's a back entrance. Instead of exiting to the street, however, we descend into what must be a basement. There's no light, only the sound of Veronica's swiftly retreating footsteps ahead of us.

"Hold on to my shirt," Bruno says, and I grasp the soft cotton of his T-shirt. The cloth has enough give that I can stay right behind him without stepping on his heels. I don't understand how Veronica and he manage to move so quickly in the pitch-darkness, speeding down the long tunnels, around corners, and up and down short staircases without bumping into a single thing.

"We practiced," Bruno says, as if reading my mind.

Far, far behind us we hear shouts, banging, sharp cracks of what might be gunshot. To my immense relief, the farther we go the fainter these become, until the only sounds accompanying us are those of our own footsteps. My eyes have become accustomed to the darkness enough so that I can make out edges and contours and feel less dependent on Bruno's shirt to avoid wiping out. Some of the corridors are lined with shelves or stacks of boxes; others are just empty tunnels of hard-packed earth. Occasionally we pass a series of closed doors, a staircase or another passage branching off. The adrenaline is wearing off and I'm starting to feel tired but I don't dare slow down or interrupt our progress by asking questions.

Finally, we climb a long flight of steps toward a horizontal strip of light. Veronica reaches the door first and opens it.

We're released into the soft air and slanting sunlight of late afternoon, in a nondescript dead-end alley; a pigeon eyes us nervously while demolishing a crust of bread. Bruno gives me an encouraging smile and pats me on the back a couple of times. Veronica purses her lips then looks toward the end of the alleyway where it intersects with another street. The sound of a motor approaches; a car rolls into view. Before I can even get a glimpse of the driver, Veronica whips around in a panic. She says something to Bruno very fast in Portuguese and he grabs me and presses my face up against his chest, almost smothering me.

"Hey!" I protest, struggling.

His other arm encircles me tightly but gently; he whispers: "Wait, please, we will explain everything in a minute."

Having managed to free my nose and mouth so that I can at least breathe, I let myself relax into his embrace, which is, after all, what it is. I'd never felt the entire length of his body against mine; it's warm, delicious. Is it possible that slight hardness down there is an erection? A pleasurable shiver runs through me as I remember the kiss and wonder whether it will really come to pass.

Meanwhile, it sounds as if Veronica has unlatched the suitcase and is rummaging through it. The car engine has shut off and I can't hear anything more from that direction. Of course, one of my ears is smashed up against Bruno's ribs and the sound of his heart, beating rather quickly, is louder than anything else.

I sense Veronica near us now; Bruno's hold loosens a bit, there's some mumbling, then a piece of cloth is fitted over my eyes and tied behind my head by Veronica's cool, deft fingers. She steps away and Bruno lets go of me, though he keeps a hand on my waist.

"It's for your protection as well as ours," Veronica says. "We're going to take a car ride and it will be better for you not to know where we're going."

I don't reply. I've understood that I'm now a part of something much more serious than I'd previously realized; I feel like a child, limp in Bruno and Veronica's hands, submitting to their greater wisdom. We walk to the car. I get put in the back seat next to Veronica, wondering if she engineered it this way so I won't be next to Bruno. The two of them exchange friendly greetings in Portuguese with the driver, a woman; she starts the engine and we move off amid a torrent of talk too rapid for me to follow. I can tell that stories are being exchanged, opinions offered — all in a tone I find strangely lighthearted under the circumstances. They sound as if they're enjoying the adventure.

I, on the other hand, am becoming increasingly apathetic; the improvised hood is causing me to sink into a kind of torpor. Or perhaps it's a combination of the sun I absorbed on the beach, the dizzying journey to the Outernet, the shock of my wrecked possessions, and the adrenaline of the long subterranean flight. I doze off, awaken briefly to realize I've drooled a little on the musty plush of the seat back, then sink into a deep sleep.

When I come to, the car has stopped and the blindfold is being loosened. A few strands of my hair get yanked in the process. "Ow!" I exclaim.

"Sorry," answers Veronica softly, continuing to pick at the knot. "There," she says, pulling the thing off.

I take a second before opening my eyes, then find myself looking into her face. Her expression is half-rueful, half-mischievous. She's clearly a whole lot more relaxed, which is a relief. In one hand she holds a salmon-colored scrap of synthetic cloth with tentacular things coming out of it.

"What *is* that?" I ask. "Is that what was on my face?"

She laughs and stretches the fabric out so I can see it's one of those women's tops they sell a lot of here: the tentacles are really straps made to cross over a bare back. Ruffles, rhinestones, and a fake zipper adorn the front.

"Do you *wear* that?" I arch my eyebrows to accentuate the mock horror in my voice.

"Not as well as you, dear," she replies, and we both

laugh.

The car is parked amid trees. Both of the back doors are open and a gentle breeze wafts through, carrying in gurgles of birdsong, the hum and chitter of busy insects, the sifting of wind among palm fronds. I can't see the sky from here but dusk is thickening the air.

"Where are we?"

In response, Veronica gets out of the car and starts walking. "Come see," she calls.

The terrain we're on is flat, sandy soil thinly overlaid with grass. Tall bushes growing among the trees prevent me from seeing into the distance, but it feels as if the surrounding wilderness stretches for miles in every direction. Tranquility seeps into me; I feel aerated, lighter. I wish I could stay right here, just sit down and breathe it in for a long, long time.

"Let's go!" says Veronica briskly.

We follow the shallow ruts left by the car; they make a wide curve that ends at a narrow dirt road. Set back from the road by a front yard hacked out of the surrounding brush is a sizable house, two stories high, with a wide veranda running round it. Déjà vu strikes me: momentary confusion, that certainty of a memory I know can't exist. Then the front door swings open, Bruno comes out to stand at the top of the steps, and the sensation dissipates. Smiling a little, he watches us walk toward him.

"Have you told her anything?" he asks Veronica.

"No," she replies. "Let's sit down here" — meaning the veranda, where a few foam-rubber cushions with no covers are piled next to an old sagging sofa. She takes one of the cushions, slides another toward me, tosses a third to Bruno. I place mine at the base of the wall and lean my back against the house. Bruno and Veronica position themselves so that we suggest an almost perfect equilateral triangle.

"Who goes first?" Bruno asks.

Veronica looks at me inquiringly, but I demur. "I'm not

quite ready to launch into my story yet," I say. "This has all been really disorienting. Why don't you first tell me where we are, and why, and until when, just so I can get my bearings?"

"Of course," answers Bruno. "Well, kidnapping you was not in our plans, but here you are. We prefer that you do not know the name of this place, but that is not so important, is it? The most important thing for you to know now is that we are at the house of some very good friends. For how long? We do not know, but there was no doubt that we had to get out of our apartment, out of the city. Approximately one hour before you arrived we had a bad encounter with the police, who made a surprise visit, ready to take us in to the *delegacia*, the police station. They did not even have an excuse, but they have wanted to shut us down for a long time. It appears that at last the conditions are right for them to do what they like. There have been power shifts in the police department; it seems we are now — what do you call it? Fair game."

"How did you manage to stall for time? Why would they need a search warrant to come in?"

"They do not, of course — they came in without one, like always. As I said, it was a bad scene." He touches his temple reflexively and for the first time I notice the flush of a bruise above the ear. "But they agreed to go away and come back with a warrant because, I think, this time what they intend for us is different from anything they planned in the past, it is something that might end up in the newspapers, on TV, and in the courts. They would like to make an example of us, you see. And for this reason, although it was a great annoyance to them, I made them realize they would need to prove that they acted according to law — initially, at least. After that, of course, anything is possible: we can be said to have fired the first shots . . . or hung ourselves in the jail cell . . . we would not be around to contradict them."

"So they went off to get the warrant and just left one man downstairs guarding the door? How could they be so stupid?"

"They did leave another one at the back entrance, too, but yes, it was stupid. It is because *they* think *we* are stupid. They never imagined we would run away. You see, this scene has been repeated many times in the past ten years. Like that cartoon with the cat and the mouse. We always took a hit, ducked the next one, and continued with our business. Where would we run to? Our whole life, our work is in that building, they know that. What they did not realize was that we knew *this* time was different, that this time they were determined to put an end to us for good, and might have succeeded."

"So now what?"

"Now we disappear for a while. In a way, it is playing into their hands, because many of our companions will believe that we have *been* disappeared, and that will produce the same kind of terror and discouragement as if we really had been eliminated. This will be a setback, because Outernet access requires the greatest possible degree of equanimity, of positive thinking, of feeling at one with humanity. Fear is a great obstacle. Even so, the work will go on – if we stay positive we can view this as the push we needed. Apparently you know about the Internet crackdown: this adds to the urgency of our situation, to the need for a reliable alternative communication network. I am so happy to hear that you reached the Outernet!" Bruno stops for a moment to beam at me. "Now, if Veronica and you – and maybe even I – can get on the Outernet as often as possible, we should be able to make much progress in organizing, contacting those who can log on and passing messages through them to the others, continuing to assist as many people as possible to get access. Will you help?"

"Of course I'd be more than glad to; but I only got on one time, there's no guarantee I'll be able to get back."

"True, but without that first time, a second time is impossible. After Veronica found her way in, even though at first she could not access every time she wanted to, she got better and better at it; at least until, well . . ." He stops, embarrassed.

Veronica looks annoyed. "It's not exactly a secret, Bruno," she says curtly. "I already told Jo why I couldn't get back on."

"But surely," I begin, looking from Veronica's grim face to Bruno's sheepish one and back, "surely the, uh, problem is fixed now? You've been able to get on, right?"

"No," she answers, keeping her eyes on the tiny pieces of foam she's picking from her cushion and piling on the ground. Ouch.

"Tell us what it was like for you, how you got there," Bruno urges me.

Without much enthusiasm, conscious of Veronica's sullen attention, I describe my adventure, starting with the creation of a separate tone in each ear and ending with the return to my body. I leave out the part about the kiss.

When I've finished there's a silence — Bruno is nodding, just nodding thoughtfully, but his face wears a poetic expression, as though he were an expert wine taster savoring the bouquet of a particularly exquisite vintage.

"I wanted to ask you, Veronica," I say, "if my experience was at all similar to yours; if what you see when you go there is at all like what I saw."

She lifts her head and smiles, and to my great relief I see that she does not in fact dislike or resent me. I need to stop taking everything so personally: if she's upset, it's probably just distress over her inability to return to the Outernet.

"It is rather as you describe it," she replies in her melodious Guyanese accent, "only less computerish. My version of the Outernet tends to take on the appearance of those cities that certain Native tribes built into cliffs in your country. I don't know why it should look like that, but it does. But the main areas are the same: Projects, Records, Chat, Groups, Encyclopedia . . . and what's the other one? Contacts. Of course. And the logo. The logo is always the same, and always pops up at some point during one's visit." She pauses. "I'm glad you got on, Jo, I really am. Good for you."

"Good for all of us," Bruno adds. "I was thinking: if Jo can get back on we could ask her to do some research, see if we can solve the problem of *your* access, maybe get some help on that, some advice."

Veronica seems taken aback. "I suppose," she says slowly.

Just then the front door creaks open and all three of us look around. Twilight had slowly deepened into evening as I told my story, though I had been barely conscious of the surroundings. I did notice bats swooping in circles over the clearing a while ago, and an occasional mosquito caused me abstracted annoyance, but I hadn't given a thought to the house or its occupants. The silhouette in the doorway gives us a little wave, hesitates, then turns back inside, leaving the door ajar.

"Your friend?" I ask.

"One of them." Bruno is nervous suddenly, fidgety. "Maybe we should have first explained to you what will take place here this evening."

His nervousness is contagious. "What?"

"It's just the timing that's a bit of a problem," says Veronica. "If you think Jo should try to access the Outernet, she would probably want to do it before the meeting, even if she doesn't choose to participate."

"You're having an Outernet meeting here?"

"No, no," says Bruno. "It is . . . well, our friends who live here are part of a . . . type of religion. And tonight is when they hold their monthly meeting. So, very soon now people will start to arrive, and we will have the choice of either joining them or going into a room and staying there while the meeting lasts. Vero, you are right. We have to hurry then."

"What do you mean *we*?" she challenges him. "It'll be only Josephine logging on, won't it?"

"But we always want to have someone nearby, right?"

"But she did it all alone before, right?" They glare at each other. "What if there isn't enough time?"

"I'm sure you can leave me by myself," I put in hastily. "I'm guessing that you two want to attend this meeting."

"My point," Bruno says, "is that we can all do both. It just got dark; it must be around six-thirty. The meeting will not start until nine o'clock, and that is if everyone gets here on time. You are right: Veronica and I would prefer to attend the meeting. Eliane and Hoochie . . ." He stops, aghast, and claps his hand over his mouth.

"Who?"

Veronica is glaring at him. "Now she knows their names." She makes a disgusted face.

"Oh well," says Bruno, recovering himself. "The damage is done. Let us assume that everything will go smoothly and no one will be trying to squeeze any information out of Jo." He clears his throat, and continues. "Eliane and Hoochie, as I was saying, have been inviting us to come to one of their meetings for years, and we have always had some excuse not to go. Now we have had to ask them to shelter us, and by chance it is on the night of a meeting – it would be very impolite not to attend. But I imagine it would be an interesting experience for you, too, and I think we can do both if we get moving now."

"All right, but as I said, if the two of you want to leave me by myself at any point I don't mind at all. Can you tell me a little more about this meeting, this religion, or whatever it is?"

Veronica stands up. "I'm going to go in and talk to Hoochie. When you're ready, just come get me."

I hadn't realized the extent of the pall cast by her presence, but as soon as she disappears, the barometric pressure seems to lighten by a few degrees. My mood shifts from anxious to relaxed: I'm pleased to be sitting with a companion in the soft air of a country night, sharing a restful moment after so many turbulent events.

"Your friend's name is Hoochie?" I ask. "Is that a man or a woman?"

"A woman."

"Is she from the United States?"

Bruno seems puzzled. "No, why?"

"The name sounds funny to me, like one of our slang words."

"Oh, you would probably not pronounce it the way we do. It is a name from the Bible, spelled R-U-T-H; we say 'hooch,' 'hoochie.' "

"Got it." I laugh. "So what is Hoochie's religion?"

"Have you ever heard of Santo Dymee?"

"Dymee?"

"D-A-I-M-E."

"No, never."

"The truth is, Jo, I am not the best person to explain it to you, and in any case Hoochie and Eliane will be giving us an introductory talk. I can tell you the little I know: Santo Daime is either a portal to another dimension, or a religious cult, or a mystical path involving the ritual use of the drug *ayahuasca,* or else it is a name for ayahuasca itself — I am not certain. You see why I am not the best person to explain this. Do you know what ayahuasca is?"

"Some kind of psychedelic rain forest concoction."

"Correct. A potent hallucinogen made from a vine and a root. Now the mythology, I am not too clear on. Something to do with a man discovering an indigenous woman singing Christian hymns in a clearing in the rain forest."

"What?"

"Look, I told you I am not sure about all of this. Hoochie and Eliane will know. In any case, Santo Daime uses imagery from different traditions: Christianity, candomblé, and animist — if that is what you call worship of the sun and moon and things like that."

"Sounds pretty interesting. So does participation in the meetings involve taking ayahuasca?"

"Well, yes."

"Is it legal?"

"Yes."

"Have you ever done it before?"

"No, I have not."

"Why not?"

"Jo, I will tell you, I think it is because I am already in a condition of near overload all the time. When I was younger I tried LSD and mushrooms and a few other things and liked them, but I was always afraid that I would go too far, be permanently affected. It happened to some people. I was afraid of insanity."

"But you're considering attending the meeting tonight and trying the ayahuasca?"

"Yes, actually."

"When you've just narrowly escaped arrest and are probably being sought by the police?"

"Ah . . . yes."

"Have you never heard of something called 'favorable circumstances'?"

He chuckles. "I have, and I know these certainly are not. But I do not think the effects of this substance can be too overwhelming. Eliane is always telling people about her fourteen-year-old daughter Vanuza who has been taking part in Daime rituals since she was eight. How the first time Vanuza took it she went on a long voyage of discovery into the nature of fungus — funguses?"

"Fungi."

"Fungi. She was shown the most intricate details of how the fungi are made and how they reproduce, right down to the microscopic level."

"That sounds good. But how does Vanuza look now?"

"She looks all right." Bruno laughs. Then his expression turns serious again. "What about you, Jo — have you had any experience with mind-altering substances?"

I hesitate. "It's a long story, and a long time ago. I'd rather not go into it right now. Especially if the plan for this evening is to get briefed by your friends, *and* try to get on the Outernet, *and* participate in this shamanic initiation or whatever it is. But if eight-year-old Vanuza could handle the stuff, I think I'd be able to. So let's get a move on?"

"Jo, you are wonderful. I was hoping that would be your reaction. I cannot think of anyone with whom I would rather try something for the first time."

I'm astonished and delighted. Me? What about Veronica?

"Before we go in, there is something else I wanted to ask you," he says. My heart gives a kick. "What was that about your hotel room and your passport?"

Oh. I quickly describe the scene that greeted me at the hotel, remove the passport from my backpack and show it to him.

"It looks like they have found out about you, Jo," he says somberly. "It was a warning. I think it is good that you got out when you did."

"What do you mean, *found out* about me? What did *I* do?"

"You reached the Outernet. And you have been coming to see us quite often."

"How on earth would they know I was on the Outernet, whoever *they* are?"

"Unfortunately there are spies on the Outernet. We do not know exactly how it works, but there seems to be a way that users can be traced."

"Why didn't you tell me that before?" I'm incredulous. "Shouldn't I have been informed if I was putting myself in danger by cooperating with your project?"

"Oh, Jo." Bruno looks very uncomfortable indeed. "There are things we do not usually tell people before their first time because fear is so counterproductive, and—"

I interrupt him. "I can't believe it! How can you play with people's lives that way? So were you really going to tell me all the scary stuff before launching me off again? Somehow I don't think so!" My voice has risen in anger and Veronica comes out to see what the matter is. I round on her. "Maybe you're better off *not* going on the Outernet, eh, Veronica?"

She frowns and blinks and looks to Bruno for help. Receiving none — he is, for once, at a loss for words — she turns back to me and asks, in a concerned manner: "Whatever is the matter, Josephine?"

At that instant my fury subsides — despite their mistakes, I know they mean well. Sadness surges up in the wake of my outburst, sadness and a wave of fatigue, no longer held at bay by adrenaline. "I'm sorry, I lost my temper; can we go inside and get to work?"

Simultaneously, Veronica and Bruno move toward me and enfold me in an embrace. I close my eyes, allowing myself to relax for just a moment, my senses tuned outward once again instead of wrapped up in my thoughts. The caress of the breeze, the tiny ceaseless thrumming of crickets in the darkness, the solid warmth of my friends' bodies: all these serve to anchor me to this time and place, to reassure me that I belong here, that I'm right to have cast my lot in with that of Bruno and Veronica, for better or for worse.

The inside of the house consists of a number of high-ceilinged rooms, largely devoid of furniture. It doesn't look as though anyone actually lives here full-time. Light and noise are concentrated in the kitchen, where the two women, Eliane and Ruth, are putting the final touches on a meal. They're strong personalities, very friendly. Since they speak almost no

English, our interactions are limited to smiles and sign-language versions of, "Is there anything else I can do to help?" and "Reach me that big bowl over there, if you would be so kind."

Soon we all sit down to eat and, with translation assistance by Bruno and Veronica, the two women give the standard introduction to the evening's Santo Daime ceremony. Ruth is the one who does most of the talking, while Eliane listens attentively and contributes additional details or an occasional correction. Although some of the elements of Bruno's earlier narration are more fully explained — the woman discovered in the forest was actually an apparition of the Virgin Mary, and the man was the movement's founder, Master Raimundo Irineu da Serra — little more is added to my understanding, and I conclude that the ingestion of the sacrament will probably tie it all together for me.

After Ruth finishes telling us about Eliane's daughter Vanuza, she asks if there are any questions. Only Veronica has one: she wants to know how long it will take for the ayahuasca to wear off. The answer: it depends on the individual and the circumstances, anywhere from six to eight hours.

Ruth produces a few sheets of paper: consent forms for us to sign. We must promise to stay with the group for the duration of the ritual and not to hold the organizers liable for any distressing experience that may arise. The three of us sign, then there's a pause: it seems nobody can think of anything more to say on the topic. Bruno compliments our hostesses on the meal we polished off almost without noticing it, Veronica and I chime in, and the conversation has moved on to an exchange of recipes, when suddenly Eliane is struck by a realization, which she imparts to Veronica.

Veronica translates for me: "The sessions follow different formats, on a rotating basis. Tonight's ceremony will be a *bailado* — a dance. She says not to worry, the steps are very easy; they will show them to us right before we start. She also said that they will now prepare for the arrival of their other guests and we should feel free to have a small rest or whatever we like. They'll call us once everyone is here."

The women firmly refuse our offers of help with the cleaning up and shoo us out of the kitchen.

We go upstairs. There are four bedrooms, two on either side of a central corridor with a bathroom at the end. One of the rooms has been assigned to Bruno and Veronica; mine is next to it, with a connecting door. We settle in theirs, which is a little more spacious. Veronica lies down on one of the beds, staring up at the ceiling. She's continued to act morose, and I'm continuing to interpret that as a sign of worry, not hostility. Bruno suggests I take the other bed; he sits against the wall.

"So . . . what?" I ask. "I should try to log on now?"

Veronica doesn't answer. Bruno looks over at her. "If you do get there, will you please try to find out anything you can about . . . about unblocking Veronica?"

"How exactly would I do that?" I can't quite imagine, from what I know of the main categories of the Outernet, where I would navigate to in order to solve that mystery.

Veronica answers me, though she keeps her gaze on the ceiling. She speaks in a dull, flat tone. "You wouldn't be able to find much out about me, directly. There are access restrictions on the contents of the akashic records. It's a privacy issue, understandably."

"So then . . . what? Should I try to find examples of similar cases? Will I be able to enter into contact with others there and ask them?"

"That's possible," she replies. "But my instinct suggests that you investigate yourself."

"What? *I'm* not the one with the problem!" That comes out sounding scornful, which was the last thing I intended.

They both seem shocked, and Veronica turns her head to look at me. "You may not *have* the problem, but you *caused* the problem," she says coldly.

The unfairness of this makes me angry. "Now wait a minute. You said yourself . . . well, I mean, you told me that you felt . . ." It's awkward to say this in front of Bruno, even though he must know. "You can't very well say that any feelings you have about me are *my* fault!"

"Not your *fault,* exactly," she replies, "but consider it from my point of view. Bruno and I have been married for twenty-one years. In that time we've traversed all *kinds* of situations. We've had to face, separately and together, all sorts of attractions that have brought up issues of fidelity and loyalty. But nothing, before this, has ever had the power to prevent me from functioning, from going about my work."

"So I guess I'm pretty special, hunh." I'm trying to lighten it up, but her answer is dead serious.

"I told you that already."

Bruno holds up a hand, as though calling for order. "Ladies!" he exclaims, also making an attempt at levity. "Perhaps this discussion should be held later. As we all know, when it comes to logging on, getting upset is almost as bad as feeling frightened. Jo, do you feel *very* upset right now? Should Veronica leave the room?"

Veronica grimaces. I almost laugh. This must be one of the craziest interpersonal situations I've ever been in. I can't stay mad: it's too absurd. "Please stay, Veronica," I say. "But what are you two going to do — watch me? Because I think I'd be too self-conscious."

"No, we will not watch you. We can turn the lights off, in fact. We are just here in case you need us," Bruno answers.

"Why — any other hidden dangers I might run into?"

"No, but sometimes people become — what is that called? Sleepwalkers. They may need physical help if they are moving around without being fully present in their bodies. You know, you saw Veronica: she gets up, dances, goes from place to place. Other people never move a muscle."

"You mean I might have gotten into serious trouble there on the beach? I could have stumbled into the water and drowned?"

"If you had stumbled into the water you probably would have woken up, but it is true, there was a risk in being all alone in an unfamiliar environment."

"You're sure there's nothing else waiting for me out there, besides maybe some spies? No ghouls, astral parasites, viruses, nothing like that?"

"If there are, I fear we do not know about them," Bruno admits unhappily.

It's not the response I was hoping for, but I won't back down at this point. Besides, if they're not aware of it, it must not be too common a threat.

"Well, I guess I'm ready. How long do we have, anyway? What if I don't come back in time for the Santo Daime thing?"

"Then one of us will stay with you until you do come back, and the other will go to the meeting. It will not start until another hour and a half from now, and that should be enough time. Of course, we do not know how long it will take you to actually get there—"

"*If* I get there," I interject.

"—but we have observed that Outernet sessions have a tendency to be short. The process of collecting information there seems subject to a form of compression: you can absorb much more in a much shorter time than you could on our plane here."

"All right." I stretch out on the bed, then sit up again. "Wait — I'd better go to the bathroom."

When I come back, the room is dark, and both Veronica and Bruno are lying there motionless. I make myself as comfortable as possible on the spongy bed and start by willing all tension out of my body. Instantly, I'm assaulted by a barrage of images from the day's events: the men lined up against the bus, the mad dash through the tunnels, the wrecked hotel room, the cop reprimanding me. My Outernet visit plays out in fast-forward from start to finish. The more I try to suppress these replays, eager to move away from the past and into the unknown, the more vivid the images become, so that I have to surrender and just watch.

Finally the scenes become increasingly jumbled and indistinct, until I'm once more conscious of the room, various muffled noises from beyond its walls, and the silent presence of my two companions. The difference between now and when I first lay down is that the rush of images, having subsided, has left my body fully relaxed. I'm even afraid that I might fall asleep, so I harness my attention to my proposed task. Will the same method work? Is there an ambient sound that might serve as a springboard? Listening intently, I notice that the whisper and shuffle of wind in the trees outside is filtered on its way into the room: the result is a near-continuous tone. Although this sound rises and falls more noticeably than the muted roar of the ocean, I'm able to pick out its backbone, and, deep within, the marrow of the backbone: a tone so low as to be almost inaudible, yet very much present.

I do my best to focus on this tone — though I lose track of it and have to ferret it back out a few times — until I get so that I'm able to stay aware of it while simultaneously thinking of other things. Then I begin flexing different muscles and ascertain that movement affects the pitch of what I hear, just as it did on the beach.

I become so absorbed in this exercise that I actually forget why I'm doing it, until without warning I get jerked up and launched on that rocketing journey through increasingly rarified strata. The effect is quite different this time since the territory is more familiar: I'm able to note details along the way, qualities of transformation, the precise manner in which an entire sphere of existence melts into another, giving rise to a third sphere whose attributes consist of the most essential ones of the first two, this sphere in turn melting into a fourth, and so on. The lightning speed at which all this takes place still terrifies me, threatening to bend my cognitive organ permanently out of shape, but I seek out the unshaken part of myself; as soon as I find it, there's that lurch and I end up once more in the calm gray space. Calm, of course, except for the percolating texture.

"Home Page," I think: at once the lavender field unfolds and the six small icons slip into place. A great excitement seizes me: I'm eager to explore all the areas I haven't yet visited, as well as return to the Records and peruse my past and future in a leisurely fashion. No sooner have I identified these desires than the scene starts to waver: I realize my wishes are about to be fulfilled so I quickly reformulate: "Home Page." As keen as my curiosity may be, my priority right now is to help figure out Veronica's problem.

Contemplating the six categories once more, wondering which one will be most likely to lead to a solution, I remember Veronica telling me that *I* was the problem. "Investigate yourself," she recommended. Ridiculous though her suggestion was, it now makes me gleeful: I'll use her advice as justification to take a little detour through the Records after all.

A shift, and the endless compartments of files fill my field of vision. I decide to pick only one episode, look at it quickly, and then get back to business.

My childhood, I think . . . The compartments scroll swiftly to the right and new ones stop in front of me. But which part of my childhood? It might be most interesting to pick something I can't remember at all, something from very early infancy. Zoom into a section of the files. How about — I continue thinking — how about witnessing my own birth? Another zoom: one folder detaches itself from the rest. The date printed on the tab is my birthday. I pause, to make sure I'm really ready to watch the big event, when suddenly my attention is caught by the folders to the left — the ones that reach still further into the past. They stretch off in endless rows. How can that be? Even if they cover every single moment of my gestation, there wouldn't be *so* many; by now I have an approximate idea of how many compartments of folders it takes to make up a month. Let's check this by going back to conception.

Scroll, zoom in: a folder with a date corresponding to nine-odd months before my birthday. *That* is a folder I *don't* want to see into — I form the thought as quickly and firmly as I can, and the folder remains closed. Yet the mystery remains: there still appears to be an infinite quantity of folders to the left of that one. Pre-conception? I select one of the files and decide to take a look.

The folder opens. What greets me is visually inchoate yet conveys an overwhelming sense of depth that generates an immediate, appalling vertigo. It's as if I were on the very edge of a monstrous precipice, poised to plunge hundreds and hundreds of feet to a certain death — though there are no visual details whatsoever to suggest this; it's pure sensation. Although I'm not, in this space, possessed of a body, I distinctly feel my heart rising up into my throat, nausea threatening to empty my stomach, terror to addle my brain. I rear back.

Shaken, I watch the thin folder slide back in among its fellows. Two things occur to me. One: if there's a chance that all the other folders to the left are anything like that one, I don't want to risk opening any of them, ever. The other consideration is that time is slipping away and I *must* tackle the Veronica problem. One last check, I resolve; one last file. Quickly, before I can change my mind, I ask to be shown a folder from about two hundred years ago. Somewhat illogically, I hope that will put me out of range of the vertigo. Quick scroll: a folder presents itself to me. August 30, 1815, 20:30. A bit hesitantly, I will it to open.

My first impression is that there's been some mistake and

I've gone back in time only half an hour, not two centuries. There we are, Bruno and Veronica and I, climbing the stairs and reaching the corridor with the two doors on each side and the bathroom at one end. But then a child appears, scrambling after us, and as the little group peers into one room then another, I realize that our clothes are different, made of heavy fabric to withstand cold weather and cut in an unfamiliar style. Closer examination still — a zoom in — reveals that these faces do not, after all, look anything like those of Bruno and Veronica and myself. The features are completely different — and yet, for all that, in some profound, unmistakable way it *is* us; the more I contemplate the differences, the more certain I become. It's as if the physical bodies were costumes and the selves actors, dressing their parts.

I watch in amazement as the four figures perform a sort of choreography involving entering and leaving the various rooms and taking turns in the bathroom. I discover that my desire not to miss any part of the action has rendered the walls transparent so that I can follow the movements of all the characters at the same time.

One woman — I *must* call her Veronica, because Veronica's essence projects so clearly from her — exchanges a swift kiss with the man as she leaves the bathroom and he enters it. She goes into a room by herself. There's a door from that room into the adjacent one where the other woman— where *I* am waiting for her. I undress and climb onto the bed; Veronica does the same. Meanwhile, the man had stepped out onto the porch; now he comes back inside, goes to Veronica's room, and, finding it empty, presses his ear up against the connecting door. A moment's hesitation, then he yanks open the door, and the three of us are frozen for a few seconds in a tableau that seems to last an eternity.

I stare in fascination at the three faces, the three bodies that are at the same time thoroughly foreign and thoroughly familiar. I watch myself within that voluptuous figure, behind the watchful green eyes. The woman's limbs are elongated almost to the point of distortion, her skin gleams — she seems unreal, like a sculpture or a painting, though she radiates vitality, quiet strength. My own looks, in real life, are perfectly ordinary: my complexion and hair are different shades of brown, where hers are ivory and black, and I'm quite sure I do not radiate anything in particular — yet the woman is me. How to explain this certainty? But then, how do I recognize myself in my present body when I wake up in the morning, before I open my eyes, utter a sound, or move a muscle? I don't need to touch, hear, smell, or see myself to know it is I.

When I was a child, I knew that human beings are not confined to the boundaries of their skin. I soon learned that it was best to shut up about the emanations I perceived, though at first I would respond as immediately and naturally as if I'd been spoken to. I began struggling to block out the information that was unwittingly imparted to me — not only because it was private, but because it was usually painful as well. Most times, what people truly thought about a situation or a person, what they kept to themselves — or thought they did — was a condemnation of some sort. This was devastating to learn of when it applied to me, and even when other people were the targets of unkind judgments or feelings of revulsion, it was peculiarly awful to witness the interplay between the hypocrisy of a pleasant manner and the underlying dislike.

Up until I reached puberty, I kept to myself as much as possible in order to avoid the information overload inherent in interactions with other people. When I then resolved to forge some social connections, the effect at first was the opposite of what I hoped for, because my behavior was so strange. My attempts to tune out psychic communication often resulted in the exclusion of auditory and visual input as well — it was difficult to separate out one sense from another — which caused people to think that I was either not paying attention to them or suffering from some form of mental illness. My frantic attempts at reassurance didn't help much. I spent my entire adolescence without a single close friend, although there were a few girls who would agree to go to the mall with me and talk about clothes and boys. Still, it was clear they weren't too comfortable in my presence and didn't invite me along to sleepovers or rock concerts. In a way this hurt, but on the other hand I was just as glad, since I wasn't all that fond of the girls either and hated engaging in the same hypocrisy that hurt so much to witness.

By the time I got to college I had succeeded in shutting out nonverbal information almost completely, even though I might have gone a bit too far: boyfriends complained that I wasn't sensitive enough to their needs; professors tried to awaken me to the wealth of nuance just under the surface of literary works. I had all but won the arduous battle. Now and then a telepathic beam would break through my painstakingly constructed shell, but I had developed a clever mechanism, almost like a seek-and-destroy missile, that pulverized psychic information as soon as it was identified, before my conscious mind could register its content. And so I made it through college and went on to graduate school, pleased to be above average academically, and otherwise pretty much like everyone else.

Now, after almost a decade, my adventures in Salvador seem to have provided the opportunity for those other dimensions of myself, so effectively repressed, to start to expand. It's definitely an extrasensory faculty that allows me to recognize traces of a familiar struggle in the eyes of that dark-haired woman from long ago: I can tell that she's powerful but isolated; that her true nature is invisible to her two companions, and that she's given up on being known for who she really is. I also understand that she's letting the other woman approach her but that it's only a calculated experiment, a game she's playing in order to either hurt the man or recapture his affection. I see all this and am disturbed and deeply sad for these three troubled souls. The only reason I would want to keep watching is for a chance to glimpse the boy once more. I'm not sure if he was my child or theirs, but his fleeting appearance communicated such a strong sense of joy to me that I can't bear the thought of not seeing him again. In that case, perhaps what I need to do is seek him out another time, in a different context: these other characters are just too depressing.

Immediately the scene dissolves and I behold the rows of folders once again, the simplicity of their clean lines soothing after the welter of emotions in which I'd been immersed.

I consider. Before this, when asked if I believed in life after death, I always said I didn't know, not having proof one way or the other, but that the possibility didn't seem any more bizarre than that of total annihilation. Now there's no doubt in my mind: Veronica and Bruno and I have a shared history that extends back much further than I had realized; perhaps even further than this glimpse I just had. The complexity of our involvement may throw some light onto Veronica's feelings about me in this life, the exaggerated jealousy. Does *she* know about this, our past connection? Could that be why she suggested I "investigate" myself? I'm tempted to leave, to go straight to her with these questions, to find out what she and Bruno think of all this. And yet — there's nothing clear or conclusive about my discovery, in terms of solving the problem of her access. If this vision were to be helpful in any way, it would require a review of that whole past life. I'm doubtful. Time is ticking by. Maybe there's another stratagem that would yield clearer results. Maybe there's something else I can try, just quickly, before I conclude this session. I wish myself back to Home Page.

RECORDS, CHAT, ENCYCLOPEDIA, CONTACTS, GROUPS, PROJECTS. Chat, I think, might have something like a discussion forum where I could put out the question of Veronica's jealousy and how to get around it.

As soon as I decide on this, the six squares on their

lavender background give way to a vast, multicolored mosaic, its individual fragments wavering slightly and irregularly. "Pretty," I think. I wait for the next step, words or something to show me my options. Nothing happens and I start to wonder if there's been a glitch or if the system froze. But maybe it's that I've gotten used to the near-instantaneousness with which processes have been happening here, and this one just requires a few more seconds.

I stare absently at the glimmering pattern, then something catches my attention and I request a zoom. To my surprise, the individual cells of the pattern turn out to be human faces, hundreds and hundreds of faces, every single one of them staring at me expectantly. I can't truthfully say that they're staring at *me,* since my body doesn't accompany me into this dimension, but they certainly appear to register my presence. I test this by shifting my point of view, right and left and back again: hundreds of eyeballs track my movements. Okay, so . . . ? I think — then realize that that is exactly what the expressions on these faces seem to be asking.

"How does this work?" I address them.

"You requested assistance from a forum," a voice says in my head — or rather, in what would be my head if I had one. The sound quality is both distinct and immaterial, like an inner voice. "Once you place a topic or question before the forum it is processed by all users currently logged on to the forum. The Outernet itself in real time registers and compiles all thoughts generated in response to the question formulated. It effects computations that group similar thoughts, takes incomplete ideas to their logical conclusions, uses some thoughts to complete and illustrate others, and eliminates irrelevant information. After these operations have been performed, the questioner receives the most succinct response possible, taking maximum advantage of what the contributors have offered."

Wow. All right — let's see, how to phrase it? Should I make mention of the past-life experience? Better keep it simple. How about this: What is jealousy, how exactly does it interfere with accessing the Outernet, and how can it be overcome?

"You have set forth three questions," states the voice. I can't tell whether it's male or female — it's probably been crafted to achieve precisely this effect. It certainly sounds human, though, not artificial: warm, calm, and matter-of-fact. "Please wait for your answers. Question one: What is jealousy?"

A number of the little faces in the mosaic grow larger, as though they'd been brought forward to a second, transparent plane. There are only a few dozen of them: I assume these are the people who are responding to the question. They've assumed a variety of thoughtful expressions. Two or three seconds pass.

"No answer," the voice states. "Question two — "

"Wait a minute! How can there be no answer to number one? Does that mean that no one knew anything?"

"In this case, 'no answer' means the responses obtained were inconclusive. Question two — "

"But wait! What if I want to know what the responses were, so I can make up my own mind?"

"Request: 'Question one: list.' Question number two — "

"Question one: list!"

"Listing question one. A: Jealousy is a biologically determined response to a threat of deprivation of any resource that ensures survival or enhances quality of life; it is present in infancy and in animals of every species and does not depend on intellectual concepts or social norms. B: Jealousy only arises as the result of social constructs: its causes and the intensity with which it is experienced depend on expectations and vary from culture to culture. C: Jealousy is a composite of two of the six basic emotions, anger and fear, and like the other emotions is ruled by the right hemisphere of the brain. D: Jealousy and the other emotions are not confined to the right hemisphere but are dependent on centers of the brain involving cognition. E: Jealousy is one symptom of a virus unleashed on our planet by beings from another star system wishing to hasten the human species' self-destruction. F: Jealousy is a sign of excess Pitta, one of the three Ayurvedic *doshas*. G: Jealousy is a side effect of gallbladder dysfunction. H: Jealousy indicates imbalance in the second *chakra* called Manipura, associated with the solar plexus. I: Jealousy is nothing more than a spiritual opportunity for growth and self-fulfillment in disguise. J: Jealousy — "

"Okay! Stop! Stop list!" I cry out mentally. There's a momentary silence.

"Question two," the voice resumes. "How does jealousy interfere with Outernet access?"

Some of the faces from the larger set return to the background, some smaller ones come to the fore. A brief pause before the voice delivers the reply.

"It is not strictly necessary for the emotion of jealousy to inhibit Outernet access. When it appears to, this may be a side effect of the physiological manifestations that usually accompany the emotional experience, such as increased heart rate and heightened muscular tension and catecholamine levels. These reactions are inimical to the state of relaxed concentration favorable to Outernet access. On another level, connection to the Outernet is by definition an experience of the interconnection of all humanity, requiring an attitude of openness and permeability, whereas jealousy is seen to either arise from or result in a stance of isolation and exclusion."

"That's it?"

"That's it. Question three: How can jealousy be overcome?"

The pattern of faces reorganizes once again.

"A variety of approaches to the problem of reducing or eliminating the emotion of jealousy exist. It may be noted that the rational mind has little purchase on the matter, and a person may suffer from jealousy while maintaining a firm conviction that they should and need not suffer from it."

Hmm. That would seem to support the theory of a biological basis for jealousy.

"However," continues the voice, "the rational mind is the tool used to dismantle the chain of reactions known as jealousy. Although a number of techniques can be suggested, in all cases the best chances of success exist when willpower is strong and one's sights are not set on eradicating jealousy, but on achieving sufficient self-control so that the emotion does not determine one's behavior."

"Could you please list some of the techniques you referred to?"

"As follows. A: Physiologically Monitored Implosion Therapy. The subject's blood pressure is monitored while he or she relates a jealousy-causing incident, recorded on tape. A rise in blood pressure indicates a particularly distressing event within the narrative. The subject listens to the narration repeatedly until it no longer triggers the rise in blood pressure. B: Persistent jealousy may be due to underlying trauma stored in the *living matrix,* the body's connective tissue. Resolving this trauma allows present occurrences to be unclouded by past events, and can involve the assistance of an intuitive therapist and manipulations of points along the acupuncture meridians. C: Partner-based approaches—"

"Please, that's enough! There's no way I can remember all of that — is there any way I can store that information?"

"By referring to today's date and the starting time of your session, which was 20:13 at your geographical point of origin, you may return to the session at any time by consulting the archives. As you review the session you may interrupt it at any point to request more detail, using the List command."

"Thank you," I say. "Thank you very much, everyone. I hope to come back someday and offer any help I can."

Suddenly there's a crowd of people before me, advancing rapidly in my direction, talking to each other and laughing, though there's no sound. Are these the people who belong to the many little faces? Just as they come to a stop, I remember what it is. Sure enough: they all close their eyes, and in that moment I hear the roar of many voices: "Outernet!"

I wait for the scene to finish playing itself out; it's going to be a little annoying if, as Veronica said, I have to watch this every single time I come here. I guess it beats commercial advertising — then I wonder if commercial advertising ever *will* be allowed here. Perish the thought.

"Return!" I form the silent command.

The familiar gray texture materializes, then comes the swift descent; the physical world coalesces around me and I'm enclosed once more in flesh. I open my eyes after a moment: the room is still and dark. Veronica and Bruno seem not to have moved. I wonder if they're asleep; I have no idea how long I've been gone.

I sit up slowly — and both of them sit up, too. Bruno smiles and leans toward me. I have the feeling that if Veronica weren't in the room he would come over and give me a hug.

"Well?" he asks.

"Well," I begin, and launch into the story. As I speak, Bruno's attention is rapt, emotions succeeding one another on his face: fascination when I tell of the folders preceding my birth, amazement at the description of the past-life scenario, vivid curiosity about the jealousy investigation. Veronica, on the other hand, listens to the whole thing with an expression of serious concentration.

"Incredible," Bruno exclaims, when I've concluded. I wait, hoping for something a bit more profound, but neither of them offers anything more.

"So, Veronica," I say impatiently — I'm getting tired of her sulking, or whatever it is. I've just undertaken a startling interdimensional journey, essentially on her behalf, and she's been taking in my report as dispassionately as if I were a talking head on television. "Did you know anything about this past-life stuff?"

She looks uneasy: her gaze travels around the room before coming back to meet mine. "I did, actually . . . know something about it. I wasn't sure how relevant it was."

"Relevant?" Bruno bursts out. "But of course it is relevant! It is completely relevant! How could you not tell me?"

"Listen, Bruno," Veronica replies huffily, "I didn't say it wasn't relevant, I said I wasn't sure *how* relevant it was, and I'm still not sure. It's certainly very interesting, and colorful and dramatic and all of that, but I don't know if this is the best time to get caught up in something that happened centuries ago, when we need to put all our effort into working our way out of the very tight spot we happen to be in right *now*."

That shuts him up: his head does a little sideways waggle as though he were working himself up to make a retort, but apparently none occurs to him.

"I *thought*," I say very deliberately, with a pretense of calm, "that the point was to figure out why my presence makes you so upset that you're not able to use the Outernet, which would be a help in working your way out of the aforementioned tight spot. Correct?"

Veronica glares at me. "Yes, dear," she answers. The words are delivered with such a sharp edge that they seem to slice through the air. "The fact remains that whether I was jealous two hundred years ago or two thousand years ago or two weeks ago, I don't feel jealous anymore, so why should any of that have to do with my getting to the Outernet?"

"Now wait a minute. You two just sent me out there on a mission to figure out why you don't have Outernet access anymore—"

"*I* sent you? I most certainly did not send you!"

It's true, Bruno was the one who instigated this. He's

been following our exchange like a spectator at a tennis match; now, seeing me frown at him, he shrinks back — and at that moment I catch myself wishing he were more of a grown-up, better equipped to stand up to the likes of Veronica.

"If you thought it was a misguided pursuit," I say with asperity, turning back to her, "you would've done well to have spoken up. I understood you to say just now that you have no time to waste on extraneous efforts . . . ?"

She looks back at me with hostility, but her expression holds just the tiniest suggestion of amusement — a glint in the narrowed eyes, the corner of her mouth curving upward ever so slightly.

Bruno holds up both his hands like a referee — he seems to have recovered his wits. "I think we are letting our emotions cloud our perception of the progress we have made here," he announces. "Veronica, you have said you do not feel jealous anymore. But the information Jo returned with, the part she remembered, suggests that jealousy can continue to have an effect even after the original stimulus has vanished. And who knows, but supposing the problem originates far back beyond this lifetime, the consequences may take even longer to wear off. I, for one, think this is very good news. It means that even though Veronica has not been able to get back on yet, she may be able to at any minute, and we do not need to be so worried, so confused about it. I have to say I am extremely curious about the story of our past together, but we can examine that at some future point. Right now, my friends, we are expected downstairs; I heard someone tap at the door about ten minutes ago — that is, if you have the energy, Jo."

Energy? I think I'd rather do just about anything besides launch on another adventure: sleep would be nice, or losing myself in an interesting novel or movie. Not that the latter are actual options, but at this point it seems like it would be more restful to be involved in anybody else's life rather than my own. Maybe I just need sleep. And yet, how many opportunities will I have to participate in an authentic local ritual involving psychoactive substances? "It's just that I'm so tired right now," I say. "I'm afraid I might not last very long, and the paper we signed says that we would have to stay with the group until the end of the ceremony. Do you know why that is, by the way? I somehow didn't think to ask Ruth and Eliane."

Veronica answers. "They've talked about that before; remember, Bruno? It has to do with the unity of the group, an energy they say is created among those present. If someone leaves, it throws the whole thing a bit off center, creates a sort of tugging away from the rest of the group — at least, that's how I imagine it. Was that your impression too, Bru?"

I don't think I've ever heard her call him "Bru" before; but then again, I've spent far more time with them separately than together. The nickname, plus the reference to a shared history, suddenly throws their intimacy into clear relief, as though they were conversing by a campfire and I were standing just beyond the ring of light in the surrounding shadows.

"I believe that is it," Bruno replies thoughtfully, "but if Jo really wants to join us I am sure we can find a compromise. Maybe you could lie down on the sofa if you become too tired? Hoochie and Eliane are quite relaxed people — I am sure they would understand. But really, if you do not want to join us, please do not feel bad. Veronica and I are participating only because we are already here."

As I hesitate, a rustle in the hallway is followed by a knock at the door, and a low voice says something in Portuguese. Veronica answers *"Já vamos!"* — we're coming! — and stands up. Bruno moves to her side, putting a hand on her waist; they await my decision with an identical questioning look. After a few seconds they appear to reach the conclusion that I will not be joining them: Bruno's countenance takes on a wistful cast, but the trace of smugness on Veronica's face might be my own imagination.

"I'm coming," I say, and am rewarded by their startled expressions. Bruno's changes to one of pleasure, Veronica's to mild amusement.

They wait for me to get off the bed and join them, then Veronica opens the door. Eliane is standing on the other side of it; she waves Bruno toward the staircase and herds Veronica and me into a room across the hall, where two women are busy changing clothes. They smile as we enter but make no attempt to speak to us. Eliane hastens to a bureau standing in the corner and rummages through it, extracting two skirts which she hands to Veronica before starting to attend to her own outfit.

Veronica holds the skirts up against her waist one at a time and passes me the larger one. They're navy blue, pleated, falling to midcalf; mine is a tiny bit loose on me, which is barely noticeable once I tuck my T-shirt into the waistband. The three other women are wearing the same type of skirts, and crisply ironed, short-sleeved white shirts with some sort of embroidered insignia over the breast pocket and navy blue bow ties. Once they're all suited up they look like my idea of British boarding-school girls, though only one of them would be the right age for that; the other two seem old enough to be her mother and grandmother. Hey — maybe this *is* Eliane's daughter, the famous Vanuza; and, who knows, the older one could be her mother: all three of them have a similar doughy nose. I watch in mild shock as they put the final touches on their outfits, straightening hems, dabbing on makeup: I never imagined that this kind of uniform could be associated with hallucinogen use. In my experience — largely secondhand — acidheads and the like did unquestionably dress in uniform, but there was enough variation in the prints and cuts of the clothing to obscure the fact that rigid standards were being observed. Here, the clean lines of navy-blue-on-white allow for no pretense of individuality, and I feel a little uncomfortable in my baggy purple T-shirt, although I'm certain that's just what you'd expect from a newcomer. I suppose they didn't have any extra shirts; and what *do* those letters embroidered on the pockets mean? I touch Veronica's arm, trying to point discreetly, but Eliane notices and we have to go through the rigmarole of translation, back and forth, until it's made clear that C.R.F. means either *Commando da Rainha da Floresta,* Commando of the Queen of the Forest — or *Circulo de Regeneração e Fé,* Circle of Regeneration and Faith, an early organization to which the founder of the movement belonged.

When everyone is ready, we troop downstairs. I find I'm having flashbacks to that other life, that other house I saw — it must be that the layout of the rooms is so similar. Now and then I half-glimpse shapes that aren't really there, less definite than ghosts but more vivid than memories: a dining table in a space that's actually empty, a wisp of an old man disappearing around a corner.

In a large, barely furnished room adjacent to the kitchen, Bruno and five other men are waiting, all smart and neat in dark pants and white shirts with ties — all except Bruno, that is: his shirt is rumpled and his tie is strangely shaped and colored, looking more like a distended piece of liver stuck to his chest. I feel a bit sorry for him. Introductions are made all around: I learn that the younger woman is Eliane's daughter, as I'd suspected, and the older one is her mother, Doralice; the men's names I immediately forget.

We move right into the ceremony. A dour, bearded gentleman stations himself by an iron cauldron in a corner; the rest of us line up in front of him. He dips a ladle into the pot, serving each of us in turn a small plastic cup of the sacred substance. It's thick, with a woody taste — not unpleasant. Eliane passes among us with a garbage bag to collect the empty cups, then we line up in two rows, men and women facing each other.

Now Ruth takes over. She moves to the center of the room, makes eye contact with Veronica, Bruno, and myself, as if to say, "This is for you; watch carefully," then begins to demonstrate the dance. The patterns are simple: two steps to one side, back to center, two steps to the other side, with a few variations. It's a relief to know that that part won't be any trouble: it's more like shuffling than dancing.

Little books are then distributed, one apiece: a sort of hymnal. Ruth leans over and opens mine to the right page. Without further ado, the more experienced members of the group raise their voices in song, simultaneously launching into the shuffling dance. One of them punctuates the verses with a small shakerlike instrument. It takes me a minute to get my feet synchronized and follow along with the words, but once the footwork has become automatic and I've realized that the melodies are kind of arbitrary, wavering around a central tone, I feel I'm doing everything I'm supposed to and some of my nervousness dissipates. One part of my brain is hard at work analyzing the words of the hymns, marveling at the juxtaposition of imagery from different faiths, and wondering if any of this can fit into my study on the migration of African religions. Another part of my brain is on the lookout for strange sensations, for any signs that the Daime is having an effect on my system — nothing is showing up on the radar so far. That concern then lapses into the background, and my attention jumps back and forth between the lyrics, the effort to guess which way the melody is supposed to go at any given point, and the mesmerizing image of our group's twenty-four feet moving in unison.

Hymn follows hymn; we're progressing linearly through the book and I start to wonder whether we have to make it all the way to the last page of the small but stocky hymnal. Surely not, I tell myself hopefully. Every so often we change to another variation on the dance, which provides a brief diversion until the new steps become automatic.

I try again to detect some alteration of my consciousness. Am I falling into a trance due to the hypnotic repetition of the steps and the solemn melodies? Can I let the humble fervor and cosmically charged lyrics — invocations of Sun, Moon, and Stars, Blessed Mother, Heavenly Father, Brotherly Love, candomblé divinities — lift me into a state of heightened awareness? Perhaps the hallucinogenic substance will simply creep up on me and knock me down, putting an end to this whole dancing thing. The only thing I can be certain of, however, is the pain in my feet. It's a dullish ache — not unbearable, certainly, but enough to be worrisome given that we've only traversed about an eighth of the songbook with no sign of stopping.

And then, finally, once I've just about given up and settled into a mind frame of grim endurance, I *do* start to feel something unusual. It's a slight shift in my visual field: a mottling, as if what I see were superimposed upon a textured plane, molded to it, following the outlines of an invisible substratum in subtle fluctuations. Something like that, anyway — I'm busy trying to fit words to the phenomenon while mechanically following along with the dancing and singing, but I'm also bracing myself for what might come next. I recognize this quality of fluid vision from the psychedelic experiments I engaged in as a young adult. It only took a few investigations before I resolved to shun hallucinogens, since their main function seemed to be to unlock the very doors I'd worked so hard to shut, but I was sorry to have to forgo those interesting perceptual distortions: intricate moving figures overlaying every surface, forming patterns devoid of exact repetition; landscapes torn apart like paper to reveal the black void underneath; intelligences shifting questioningly in the grain of wood or linoleum; one's own face in the mirror twisting into that of a stranger. Such phenomena would always be heralded by this same swimming quality, the first sign that the familiar was dissolving and Who Knew What would come next.

So it's with pleasurable though fearful anticipation that I wait to see where the Daime is going to lead me. I forget my feet, the words my mouth is shaping, and concentrate on the letters on the page, some of them bobbing toward me and some of them away, but ever so subtly.

A distraction: something is happening to Veronica. She's stopped moving — the other dancers are adjusting their paths to avoid bumping into her. I can't get a good look at her, *and* follow the lyrics, *and* do the steps, but she seems to be staring into space, or at something only she can see, with a big grin on her face.

Next thing I know, she's been escorted to the side of the room and is sitting on the floor with her legs sticking straight out in front of her, still grinning and, it looks like, mumbling to herself and nodding. Hmm. Will I be next? I wait . . . and wait and wait, but nothing extraordinary happens to me. We switch to another variation on the dance step. The discomfort in my feet has changed to outright pain. It would certainly be a relief to sit down — do I dare, even though I'm not visibly "out of it"? We never did discuss the possibility of special dispensations with our hostesses after all. The paper we signed vowing to remain with the group comes to mind: although it didn't specify "and engage in the same activities as everyone else," there's a tacit understanding that that's the correct thing to do. I decide to take a bathroom break — no one can argue with that.

In the bathroom, I peer at my face in the mirror. My pupils are distended. My vision is still wavering, but that's about it. I would love to stay here, close my eyes, and relax; I suspect that the whole experience would really unfold for me if I did that. It's frustrating to have been introduced to this substance under circumstances that make it impossible for us to really get acquainted. I have to admit it's my own choice to bow to others' expectations: I'm too cowardly to stay in the bathroom or go outside to lose myself in the wind and the stars, to say, "I've had enough dancing, thanks." My weakness depresses me. I make my way slowly back to the others, trying to cheer myself up with the thought that the session can't last too much longer.

As a matter of fact, though, it does. The worst of it is not the steadily building pain in my feet, traveling up my legs to my lower back, nor the annoying sight of Veronica sitting comfortably on the floor, given over to her private visions — it's the knowledge that my discomfort is self-induced, or at least self-sustained.

When, at long last, we reach the end of the hymnal and the session is concluded, I'm thoroughly miserable and it's all I can do to respond to the others' expressions of enthusiasm with a reasonably pleasant smile. I'm hoping to make an unobtrusive exit, creep upstairs, and collapse into bed without having to talk to anyone, but Bruno, kneeling beside Veronica, catches my eye and beckons to me. I can't just ignore him. Slowly, I go over to stand beside them.

"Here she is," Bruno says to Veronica. He looks just about as tired as I feel. Exasperated, too. "She's here!" he repeats more forcefully.

Veronica turns her face up toward me and smiles warmly. Her gaze, though directed my way, isn't actually focused on me. It seems she's registering something other than my physical presence. I even wonder if she knows who I am, but then she says "Josephine" in a wondering tone and reaches a hand up, waiting for me to take it. I do so, reluctantly. She's kind of creeping me out. I'm never comfortable interacting with people who are in artificially altered states of consciousness when I myself have both feet planted on the prosaic ground, and as far as I can tell the ayahuasca has done nothing for me besides produce that little wavery special effect.

Veronica's grip is surprisingly strong, and so is her voice when she says, "Pull me up." Bruno moves to help, but she pushes him away. I help her get to her feet.

"Upstairs," she commands.

A few of the others crowd around with offers of food and companionship, but Bruno politely heads them off, and Eliane helps deter those who are a bit slow on the uptake.

So we find ourselves upstairs once more, in the room with two beds. Veronica stretches out on one of them. I'm not going to stick around to shoot the breeze; it's been a long, long, long, long, *long* day.

"Anyone feel like talking about it?" Bruno offers. I shake my head but Veronica stirs.

"One," she says, and stops.

I start making my way toward the door that connects our two rooms, as casually as possible. "Good night!" I give Bruno a little wave; Veronica is lying on her back and can't see me.

"Wait," she orders.

Shit. Why should I let anyone stand in the way of what *I* want to do? I told them good night; why don't I just head on out the door like I was about to? But I can't. I pause with my hand on the doorknob.

"One," she repeats, more forcefully. "We are all one."

She pronounces the words deliberately and lets the sentence hang there, as if it were so profound it required a great deal of careful consideration. This is what I was waiting for? This lustrous pearl of ancient wisdom, recycled into a platitude of 1960s counterculture?

I turn the knob.

"I am you and you are me," she continues. A direct quote from the Beatles — I was dead on! She's talking to herself, I think, summing up the revelations of her trip. I definitely do *not* need to hear this. I open the door, prepare to slip through it.

"It's true, Jo," she says, stopping me in my tracks. "You and I have a lot more in common than we knew. And I haven't really been fair to you . . . or to you, my dear, dear friend," she adds, stroking Bruno's arm — he's sitting beside her on the bed. "I lied to you. I told you I couldn't get on the Outernet, but it wasn't true. I've actually logged on once or twice in the past week, when you weren't home."

Bruno backs away from the bed, shock and disgust on his face. I'm indignant as well, but also curiously amused. And, to tell the truth, relieved. As firmly as I'd told myself that I wasn't responsible for Veronica's blockage, it seemed undeniable that the coincidence of our meeting had ended up creating a big problem for their group.

"How could you lie like that?" Bruno demands.

"Humans do get so easily upset, don't they," she muses, her voice dreamy. "If we could just drop the illusion of separateness once and for all, what a different world it would be!"

Bruno's response is a string of sentences in rapid-fire Portuguese too quick for me to make sense of, but the fury in his voice is clear enough. Veronica doesn't seem to be much troubled by it; she answers him in English, in the same dreamy tone.

"But I *was* jealous, and I wanted to make her feel she'd done something wrong. I wanted her to decide on her own to go away, and I wanted you to agree it was for the best. Isn't it crazy? It was like those rejected boyfriends who gun down their beloved, saying, 'If I can't have her, no one can.' " She laughs — presumably at the folly of this, because I sure can't see any humor in it. "But then I started to think I'd go mad if she left now, so I pretended I wasn't jealous anymore. But I still wanted to make trouble. I was confused, I admit it."

"Just a minute," says Bruno. "Were you jealous of her, or of me? I want to be certain I understand this."

"Of you, sweetie! She knows; I told her. She knows what she means to me. And now she's found out that we've been playing cat and mouse for a long time — for centuries! Haven't we, darling?"

"Then I will let you two sort it out," Bruno says roughly. He pushes past me through the door to the other bedroom, pulling it shut behind him.

Dumbfounded by this latest development, I also find

myself somewhat titillated. I feel on a par with Veronica in a way I never did before. No longer is she the remote and venerable wise woman I once took her for: she freely admits to indulging in some of the least savory human behaviors: lying and manipulating others to get her way. She's also reiterated my power over her, yet now that I understand that this is older than either of us, I find I'm more comfortable with it — unapologetic, as if it were a mantle I'd inherited, without any presumption of merit. In fact, I now imagine us as costarring actresses, interacting with each other in different roles on the set but going home together at the end of the day, gossiping companionably about our work.

"Now you've done it!" I tell her.

"Oh, don't worry about him," she says lightly. "He's been through this before. With us, I mean. I keep forgetting you don't know the whole story yet. Well, thank God or what have you for this Daime thing, I tell you. It was just what I needed to loosen up and get back on track. Did you enjoy it, by the way?"

"Not at all," I reply. "Maybe it was the dose, or the circumstances . . ."

"Quite right," she says. "Those little bow ties are a trip, aren't they? I think the people use them to keep their heads attached to their bodies. Seriously, though, I know what you mean. I had to make a huge effort to break out of that spell they were weaving with all that singing and dancing. If I hadn't sat down on the floor and just let myself experience whatever came up, I'm sure I wouldn't have gotten half as much out of it. It's always tricky business when humans take something sacred and try to mold it in their own image."

Once again she's earned my admiration: I wish *I* had had the courage to break away. It smarts to be reminded that even if we *are* sisters, I'm definitely the younger and more inexperienced one. Yet it's also reassuring to know that my wiser sister cherishes me — it makes me feel safe. My thoughts return to poor Bruno.

"Shouldn't you go see about Bruno?" I ask Veronica.

"Funny you should say that." She laughs. My puzzled expression turns her serious again. "It's not really funny," she concedes. "But I don't think *I'm* the one who should, as you say, see about him."

"Well, it's just that I think he has the wrong idea. About me, I mean. And you. I mean, *you* know that I don't . . ." I feel myself coloring slightly and am glad she's not looking at me. I try to keep my tone level. "That I can't . . ." I'm realizing that I never *did*, in fact, tell her it was impossible for me to reciprocate her feelings, at least if there's any sexual component to them. But the image of myself waiting for her, naked, on a bed, flashes before me — even though at the time I didn't look like me or she like herself — and the thought that she must know about that episode, and heavens knows what else that happened between us, makes me stumble hopelessly over my words. "Veronica, I never . . . well, maybe not *never*, but never as far as I knew, until this evening . . . well, anyway . . ." I also don't want to make it sound as though she's propositioned me, because she never actually has. Finally, it all comes out in a rush: "I'm totally heterosexual, is what I mean to say, and I don't want to give anyone the wrong idea, which is what I think Bruno has."

There. My face is burning. I expect her to respond with amusement, possibly even scorn or sarcasm, but her voice, when it comes, is gentle.

"I know, Josephine. And I'm sorry if I've made you uncomfortable — I couldn't help telling you how I feel about you, even though I knew I should probably have kept my mouth shut. And now Bruno knows, too, and you're right, he might have 'the wrong idea,' which is why I think you're the person to set things straight."

"I'll do that, then."

I'm relieved that she isn't offended, and glad to have a

task to deal with; I much prefer to address the matter of Bruno's feelings than dwell on the ones Veronica has for me. As I turn to open the connecting door, however, I'm struck by a thought. "Veronica," I ask, "do you know what time it is?"

"I put my watch on the bureau over there."

"Thanks." I go over to check it. "Wow," I exclaim involuntarily.

"What?"

"Two in the morning. I didn't know it was so late." But the real reason I'm taken aback is because if what I saw in the Records yesterday was true, there are only twenty minutes left until I'm to find myself locked in a hungry, searing kiss with Bruno. My rational mind tells me this is highly improbable, but my body responds to the idea with a flush of warmth.

"See you later, Veronica."

"Peace."

The light is off in the room next door, but I can make out Bruno lying facedown across the bed. After quietly closing the door behind me, I wait for my eyes to grow accustomed to the darkness, then walk over to him. Weak moonlight seeps in through the window and gives a soft glow to the edges of his recumbent form. Is he asleep?

"Bruno?" I ask softly.

The answer is a grunt, muffled by the mattress. Not a half-asleep grunt, though — more like the sound of someone who's wounded and reluctant to open themselves up to the possibility of being hurt again. I realize that's a lot to read into a simple grunt, but my interpretation is largely informed by what I'm picking up from the psychic bandwidth. Bruno's distress resonates within me; all I want is to put an end to this suffering — both for his sake and for my own. My instinct is to touch him, soothe him, let him know he has nothing to be afraid of, make it plain that nothing is threatening him besides the demons in his own mind.

I sit down beside him and slowly, shyly, reach out a hand to stroke his inert back. As I do so, I remember how he caressed me, last time — not my flesh but the air around my body, as if in some mysterious way it were an extension of myself. I'll try doing the same thing to him, I think, and divert my fingers as if I were trailing them along the surface of a pond, following the contour of his back without touching it. To my surprise he shudders, even though my hand is not quite close enough for him to be able to feel its heat and I'm carefully keeping everything but my arm immobile.

Abruptly, he raises himself up on one elbow to look at me. The movement causes his body to come into contact with my hand — I don't pull away. We stare at each other for at least a full minute. It's too dark for me to make out the expression on his face but his eyes shine as if lit from within. I don't know what he's thinking — it seems as though he's trying to read *me*. It's very awkward to have my hand stuck to him like this: I don't want to remove it, but I feel too shy, with him looking at me, to caress him. So I just let the hand rest there, until thankfully, after a little while, Bruno drops back into a facedown position.

A shift has occurred, however: less tension emanates from him. It's as if he were saying, "All right, I'm entrusting myself to you; I know you've come as a friend." I consider proceeding with the virtual massage, as I'd intended, but now a strange sensation takes over: my flesh seems welded to his through the cloth of his T-shirt; my fingers appear to be sinking more and more deeply into his body. Of course this must be an illusion, because if they *were* really going that far they'd have come right out the other side by now. Actually, it feels like there *is* no other side — that Bruno is a bottomless well into which my fingers are disappearing. I actually have to look at my hand to make sure it's still there.

The air around us now takes on a peculiar density; there's a slow fluctuation in it, too languid to be caused by a draft. A shimmering form appears to be emerging from Bruno, and, as

I watch, from my own arm — from my whole body, in fact. The shapes peel away from us, translucent doubles of ourselves, and float up toward the ceiling. There, they rapidly become entwined, indistinguishable, moving together like billowing smoke.

Is this the Daime finally taking hold, I wonder? My flesh-and-blood self remains seated, spellbound, one hand buried somewhere deep inside Bruno's back, staring at the ghosts or whatever they are. Slowly, very slowly, they start to disentangle themselves. Their movements have an odd quality, giving me the impression that I'm watching time run backward, as if it were a film. Soon the two outlines become distinct, hovering in the air. They've assumed exactly the same positions Bruno and I are in right now: one in a sitting posture, reaching out to touch the second, prostrate one. They stay like that for about a minute, then fade away.

Bruno has been watching, too. Soon after the whole performance started, just after the two figures merged in the air, he happened to roll onto his back. I instinctively snatched my hand away to keep it from getting crushed underneath him; then, also unthinkingly, laid it on his arm, my eyes never moving from the contortions of the wraithlike beings. Now they've evaporated, and my earlier awkwardness is gone, too, replaced by excitement at what just took place.

"Did you *see* them?" I ask Bruno, shaking him a little, as if to wake him up. Neither the question nor the shaking are necessary of course; they just release some of the tension that's been building inside me, the disbelief.

"I saw *us*," he replies. His voice has something strange in it. Still lying on his back, watching me closely, he places one hand over mine. Then he sits up. "Instant replay," he says hoarsely, and pulls me to him. My face is buried in his neck — it reminds me of the way he held me in the street, but this time he's trembling. Being grabbed like that is flattering, in a way, but not so very exciting. I've never been particularly turned on by the caveman approach.

"Ow," I say, my voice muffled.

"Sorry," he mumbles, giving me a bit more breathing room. He doesn't let go, though; he's trying to tell me something he can't say in words or even gestures — mutely beseeching me to understand him, unwilling or unable to let go of me until I do. I'm reminded of Jacob wrestling with the angel: "I will not let thee go but thou bless me." It's as if his very soul hung in the balance, as if he were striving for redemption: this is not a stranglehold of desire, but of desperation. It occurs to me that his trembling, which at first I thought was arousal, is actually fear. Why, he's terrified! Because he's declared his feelings, and there's the chance I might reject him; to make things worse, he's acted like a fool and almost suffocated me; now all he can do is wait for some word or sign from me that it's all right, that I'm not repelled, that I do want him.

Tenderness wells up in me — the affection I've had for him from the first — and sympathy: he's so exposed, so raw. I encircle him in an answering hug, a strong one, to let him know that I *do* care for him, very much.

He doesn't react right away but the trembling gradually dies down. Then he pulls back, just enough so that we can look into each other's eyes. The moment is approaching, the one I saw in the archives, the one enacted in reverse by our etheric doubles a few minutes ago. The inevitability of what is about to happen allows me to stay calm, my body receptive. I'm glad he doesn't make any further move: it gives me time to feel the gathering heat, to remember all the things I love about him and be thrilled that someone so fine should want me, too.

I can't stand it anymore: I lean forward to close the distance between us, brushing his lips with my own. It's the signal he's been waiting for and he responds passionately.

Before giving myself completely over to the experience I open an eye and confirm that what I'm seeing is identical to what I witnessed on the Outernet. Yet the preview had not rendered the dimension of tactile sensation — the visual image barely hinted at that which roiled under its surface. It would seem to the observer that very little is happening here: a soulful kiss, nothing more. But my breath is taken away — literally, at times — by Bruno's mastery at leading this dance. He leads, not out of machismo, but because he's infinitely knowledgeable, infinitely skillful. I understand that I'm in the hands of a genius. There's nothing mechanical about his actions; if there's any "technique" to speak of, it must consist in his becoming so completely aware of his partner, of the expressivity of the tiniest twitch or shudder, that his own body responds in the most satisfying way possible, whether by pressing forward or pulling back or making no movement at all and letting the tension build, the energies surge from deep within and mingle in the minuscule space between our skins.

As I identify what he's doing, I understand that in order to stay with him I have to push my mind away, to let my body speak unhindered by thought. Telepathy is a swifter form of communication than speech — swifter and more eloquent, since it's not limited by words. This, however, is more immediate even than telepathy: it's the language of ions, electrons, lightning-swift currents; sparks, pools and eddies of heat, conflagrations. I'm catching on quickly and Bruno's delight is apparent, but just as fast as I learn this new language he introduces new subtleties, new complexities, which lift me from one level of understanding — and almost unbearable pleasure — to a whole new one.

Soon the room becomes light, the sun quite high in the sky; we lie back in each other's arms exhausted, satiated — and neither of us has removed or loosened a single item of clothing, undone a button or zipper. Sleep hits us both at once, knocking us out for the next few hours.

ESPEL VALLEY

FLORIAN

Sometimes it is night, sometimes day; I only know by how the light cuts at my eyes or slips across them. Zar is here, anyway, no matter what the hour. I don't know how she does it, and in the intervals when I can muster some semblance of speech I ask her. She smiles and tells me not to worry: she is not going anywhere. Today I open my eyes just as she enters the room. I am about to say: "So, you *do* leave!" but her announcement knocks the thought right out of my head.

"I've summoned Emily!" she says, too excited by her news to even ask how I am. I motion toward the vial of medicine.

"I'm sorry." She reaches for it, takes up the spoon, measures out a dose. "I expected you'd be pleased."

The familiar bitterness slides down my throat. Just in time. Now the pain will be held at bay for a little while. It will lurk till the remedy weakens and then it will shove back in and shred me to bits.

"What do I care for Emily?" I challenge. "Where has *she* been all these years? What does *she* matter?" Zar opens her mouth. "Don't answer," I say. "There are much more important considerations." I am never at peace these days:

whenever the agony subsides enough to let me think, I straightaway must face the terror of approaching death. The end is nigh, no matter that I utterly refuse it. "My life, for instance. My entire life — a waste! And now, all but gone!" I clutch at her arm, bony fingers indenting the soft skin. "Please help me, Zar, there must be something. I need another chance. Let me not be destroyed, snuffed out!"

Zar's eyes are tender. We may have had this conversation several times before. "Oh, Florian," she says.

I sink back in the pillow. Zar's compassion soothes me, while also rendering me uneasy. I turned my back on her for many years, yet when the illness struck, she took up nursing duties with no trace of resentment. Although I wish her sacrifice stemmed from something deeper than sheer duty, I know how fortunate I am and do my best not to complain. But now and then the illness causes a thick hatred to boil up, choking me with a putrid miasma — at those times I find no relief except in turning on her.

"You are despicable," I wheeze; she leans in close to hear. "Unnatural. A witch. You pretend charity but only want to watch me twist and turn. You know that I am dying — why prolong it? If not for your ministrations, I should have been freed by now."

A smile. Malice in it, or so I think. "You won't be freed, you know. It doesn't work that way. I keep telling you—"

"Freed from the pain! The pain, damn you!" It eases me somewhat to shout, to let some of the poison out, but a coughing fit comes on and I cannot breathe for several frightening seconds. Unspeakably exasperating, her philosophies. She tells me our souls have eternal life, that she knows it not only from books but from her own experience. All those years of study and contemplation having revealed to her the indisputable and so on and so forth. What do I care, I say, what becomes of my soul — it is my flesh in hellish torment! But only let the potions carry out their mercy, and here I go, pressing her for details. "How do you know?" I ask. "How can you truly know? Tell me again — how you met them. Can you be sure you were not dreaming?"

"Are you dreaming now?" she answers.

"No."

"How do you know? You see? Shall I adjust the covers?"

"No! Just tell the story!"

"You mustn't get so wrought up, Florian. It's bad for you. Well, then. The first one I met was me. A version of myself. She lives in a time to come. I was slow to recognize her, for I did not know she could exist. But once she succeeded in reaching me, she taught me many things. She showed me still other versions of myself — "

"And me!" I interrupt. The pain is starting up already, a distant thunder rumbling deep within. "You saw *me*!"

"I did." Zar reaches down to stroke my brow. "And I still do."

I make as if to push away her hand but lack the strength. "Tell me," I repeat, more faintly now.

"Oh how I wish that you could see him, too!" Her gaze leaves my face; she drops her voice: "I wonder . . ." She shuts her eyes, bows her head, and remains like that, her being humming like a taut string. She has turned into the old Zar, the one from our beginnings, white hair and sunken cheeks eclipsed by the radiance of purpose. Then: "Bruno!" she calls. Not an appeal, but a cry of recognition. I look about the room, as best I can. Zar laughs, triumphant. "He's here!"

"Oh, fiddlesticks," I say. "Then what is he doing?"

She laughs again. "The same as you. Not much."

"I pray you not to make a jest of me," I grumble. "Why, if he is here, do I not see him?"

"You can't," she says, "foremost because you don't believe in him."

The pain is pressing harder against the barrier of the medicine. "I *want* to believe," I say.

"I know," she answers soothingly. "It takes a while, that's all. Preparation. Just think — here I've been studying all my life, and only now have I been able . . ."

"Then be our go-between. Tell me what he has to say. And I will answer through you."

"It's an idea," she says. That spark of curiosity: again the Zar of old. "I'll try." She cocks her head. " 'Don't be afraid,' he says."

"Of what?" I reply, testily.

"You always were, of everything. And so was he. But now — "

"Now what?" I try to keep the irritation from my voice. The fire has been kindled in my lungs; soon they will be ablaze. This conversation is pure foolishness, but if I cling to it awhile, it may bear me on its tide, postpone the anguish a few moments more.

" —now you are helping him to see he needn't be afraid."

A brittle laugh escapes me. "My example is inspiring?"

Zar listens, then: "He knows that you are he, and so it proves to him there is no death; he need not fear — how did you put it, Bruno? — extinguishment."

"There are worse things than that, my friend," I croak. Each fiber of my lungs is now a blade; the relentless slicing begins.

Zar watches me with concern. "It's worn off so soon," she says. "Would you like a few more drops?"

"No, no." One of these days the remedy will have no effect at all — I struggle to banish the thought, to pick up the thread of our talk. "Bruno," I say. "There are indeed worse things than death."

Suddenly Zar's expression changes. She leans in eagerly. "Listen!" she exclaims. "He says: here, too, you've helped him see: the pain is worth it!"

"Worth it!" I fling out an arm: the water glass flies off the bedside table, shatters on the floor. Zar stares open-mouthed.

"The idiot!" I cry. "What does he know? Has he experienced anything like this?" I slump back from the half-sitting position to which my vehemence propelled me. The shouting has ripped open a hole in my chest, a smoking cavern. Was it worth it? I fix Zar with my best approximation of a glare; unfortunately, I am panting like a dog, which impairs my dignity. I expect a gesture of consolation from her, contrition; it would be seemly of her to dismiss this halfwit future self of mine or give up the pretense — clearly the dialogue is not doing me much good. But Zar pays no attention to my offended posture.

"He says . . . he knows . . . he hasn't been through anything like this . . . except as you." She chooses to ignore my contemptuous snort. "But if, he says, you come out on the other side—"

"If," I interject.

"And if you learn something from it . . ."

It's starting to submerge me once again: my ability to think devoured by the insatiable agony. No time for this prattle. I make one last effort. "I learn nothing from the pain. Only, had I known that things would end this way, I would have lived a fuller life. I would have thumbed my nose at caution, not held myself apart; I would have risked some suffering and sought enjoyment when and where I could — to counterbalance. A life of pain is no life at all."

"He wants to know," Zar says, "why you haven't ended your life, under these circumstances."

"Good question," I manage. "Sensible fellow. I would have, long ago, but . . . "

I stare at Zar; she returns my gaze steadily. My face softens into a smile. "I would not trade this time with you for all the world." Noting with some satisfaction the moisture brimming in her eyes, I add: "Well worth it, as the fellow said."

Then an obliterating wave of pain pulls me under and

holds me there and it is some time, I know not how long, before I resurface. Zar's worried countenance emerges from the fog but suddenly breaks apart, as a reflection on a pool is shattered by a stone. It was a sound that did it, sharp and loud, from quite nearby. A voice. It comes again; this time I catch the words:

"Tough luck, eh, Florian?"

Emily! So long I have not heard that voice, yet I would know it anywhere.

"Not Emily," comes the response. Had I spoken aloud? "But you can call me that. What's in a name? Never mind. I can't stay long, but I wanted to stop in. Might not see you again, not like this."

She seems to expect an answer. I can't think of one. It looks like the pieces of Zar's face are trying to swim together. "Wh— where's Bruno?" I ask.

"Can't keep track of him," not-Emily replies briskly. "Comes and goes. I'm sure you'll see him again. Anyway, I'll be moving on as well. Good luck on the way through . . . looks like you won't have long to wait."

"Wait!" The sound does not leave my mouth. The pieces of Zar's face cannot meet up. I had wondered where the pain was — now I realize it has taken over so completely that there's barely enough of me left to notice it. It leaves no room, is squeezing me out; as I relinquish my hold, a delicious lightness sweeps me up.

"Another chance," I think.

SALVADOR

JOSEPHINE

When I come to, struggling up out of dreams, it is in response to an insistent noise, not loud but repetitive. Some sort of tapping coming from close by. A number of other sensations crowd in: cotton-mouth, full bladder, the weight of an arm flung over my chest. I recall the epic journey preceding sleep and, smiling, open my eyes.

The source of the tapping is Veronica — her fingernail, to be precise, on a small wooden table at the head of the bed. "Ah," she says, seeing that I'm back. Her expression is neutral; it seems as if her mind is elsewhere, even though her purpose is, very definitely, to wake us.

I want to tell her so many things: that I've just understood a secret she must have been in on for ages; that although Bruno has completely ravished me it was in some curious way impersonal: he was the key, the door, the revelation of a world I never knew existed. I know now, really know what she meant about the illusion of separateness, and I can imagine the three of us living, working, and growing infinitely richer through sharing ourselves with one another. If you do value me, I feel like saying, then I will trust that I have something to offer you: recognition, admiration, gratitude, and whatever else that's good that you see in me — I'm sure it's more than I can see myself, but I offer it all up to you. All these and other thoughts and feelings hurtle to the forefront of my mind, jostling one another, clamoring to be spoken; meanwhile, I realize I'm just gaping at her in a way that suggests I can't remember my own name, much less hers.

"I didn't want to wake you too abruptly," she says, frowning a little, as if my witless appearance suggested she had. "However. We must get moving. The police are looking for us — we won't be able to stay here too long. Ruth and Eliane have had a phone call from someone who didn't identify herself, saying she needed to get in touch with us. We can't be certain if it was friend or foe, but nobody was supposed to know that we're here. Ruth answered the phone and thankfully didn't give anything away, but the two of them are quite nervous now. Are you following what I'm saying?"

"Sure," I say, sitting up a little straighter. "Sure am. Gotta get a move on."

"Right. The next step is to go into town and make a few phone calls to get more details on the situation. If we ring from the house phone or our cell phones, the calls can get traced back to us too easily. Even after we use the public phone we'll have to get out of here rather quickly, but it gives us a bit more time."

I remember the call I have to make. "I need to contact the U.S. Consulate," I tell her. "I have to see about getting another passport."

"You can come along with me, then. We don't know if there are alerts out on us, but people are more likely to be on the lookout for a woman and a man than two women. Why don't you get ready — get dressed, do whatever you have to do — and we'll go."

"What about Bruno?" I ask. He's lying with his head sunken into the pillow — it's a wonder he can breathe.

"Wake him up," she says peremptorily. "So he knows what's going on. But he'll wait for us here."

"Bruno." I tousle his hair. "Hey. Wake up. Wake up,

Bruno."

He stirs then turns over, clearly disoriented. His eyes meet mine and the confusion in them gives way to tenderness; I hope my own look conveys the depth of my feeling for him. I'm aware of Veronica observing this silent dialogue.

"Bruno," she says, and he jerks in the direction of her voice. "Are you all right? Time to get up. I was explaining to Jo that we need to make some phone calls from the village. She has to call the consulate, and as it wouldn't be wise for the three of us to go together, I suggest you stay here."

"You will call Paula and Doce, right? And Velma, and Florisvaldo, and who else?"

"Those are the main ones."

"Find out what you can, but don't tell them anything, okay?"

She gives him a scornful look. "Of course."

His gaze rests on me once again and he squeezes my hand. "Hurry back," he says.

After changing out of the slept-in pleated skirt and splashing some water on my face, I meet Veronica down in the kitchen, where a drawn and anxious Eliane offers me coffee and buttered bread. Veronica paces the length of the kitchen floor while I have breakfast. As soon as I drain my cup she seizes the car keys from the table; I decide not to ask for more coffee and follow her out.

It turns out that the town is not very far from Ruth and Eliane's house. The red dirt road turns into pitted asphalt; on both sides matted grass and bushes lead the eye to distant green hills. As we drive, signs of civilization multiply: grazing horses, wire fencing, shacks, then more and more of the roughly put-together red brick houses, many of them unfinished but clearly lived in.

The center of town consists of a church and a handful of stores. Not much going on: a woman waddles along carrying a pail with one hand and dragging a small child with the other; some older boys sit on a doorstep; a man astride a donkey chats with one on the sidewalk. Veronica pulls up to the curb and parks next to two payphones, back to back, each semi-enclosed in a blue polystyrene shell meant to provide shade and noise reduction.

"You take that one," she directs, disappearing beneath one of the shells. She reappears almost instantly and produces a small card that she sticks into the slot of my phone. Cradling the receiver with her shoulder, she jabs impatiently at a few numbers, joggles the hook up and down a few times, hangs up, takes out the card, puts it back in, and repeats the sequence before finally giving up.

"Broken," she declares. "Well, do you mind waiting until I'm done?"

"Not at all, not at all," I answer.

She darts back to the working phone. I lean up against the nearest storefront — the door is locked — and try to appear nonchalant. I'm acutely aware of my sloppy *gringa* appearance, and I have the feeling that Veronica and I are under close scrutiny, even though the men are keeping up their conversation and the boys their desultory scuffling and shifting on the step. The woman with the child and the bucket disappears around a corner, having picked up speed by placing the bucket on her head and the child under her arm. She balances her loads with marvelous ease. I'm wondering what I can choose to look at next, conscious of the covert stares boring into me, when my attention is diverted by Veronica's conversation. She's getting angry at someone.

"Uma amiga! Uma amiga! Não! Por quê? Quem é você?" She slams down the receiver. Am I imagining heightened interest among our audience members? I go over to her.

"What happened? What's wrong?" I lower my voice. "It might be good if you could calm down a little. I think the people over there are kind of curious."

"Of course," Veronica says, adjusting her sunglasses. "It's

just that when I called Paula and Doce's place, this bitch answered and insisted I tell her my name. I tried to be friendly at first, but when she made it clear she wouldn't pass the phone to them unless I told her who I was, I lost my temper."

"Do you think they were really even there?"

"What? Oh, I suppose you're right, maybe they weren't. If they had instructed someone to screen their calls, I can't imagine they would have chosen such an unfriendly bitch. I don't think they even know anyone like that. Anyway, I'll try Velma now."

I watch her face as she dials: her eyes are hidden behind the dark glasses but the set of her mouth and deep furrows in her brow reveal her anxiety.

"Hello," she says at last, "Velma? Oh Velma, I'm so glad I could reach you. What? What do you mean, wrong number? Velma, it's me! Me!" Her voice is rising almost to a shout; I signal for her to keep it down. "Wait!" she cries into the phone, ignoring me, then: "Damn!"

She jams the receiver back on the hook and crosses her arms in the attitude of one too exasperated to even speak. The boys on the other side of the street are now staring openly, and even the men have ceased their conversation, though they're looking at us sideways instead of head-on.

"I think we'd better go now," I tell Veronica.

"What about your phone call?" she asks irritably.

"Oh, right! But how do I find out the number of the consulate?"

"I'll have to ask directory assistance," she snaps, and picks up the telephone again. Once she's gotten the number and dialed it, she hands me the phone and stands back. After a few rings, an American voice answers.

"Hello," I say. "I was wondering if you could help me. I'm staying here in Salvador but my passport has been destroyed, and I'd like to know—"

"Destroyed!" The man sounds horrified, as though we were talking about a human being, not a document. "Well, how in God's name did *that* happen?"

"Uh, I'd left it in my hotel room," I start to explain, before realizing that I need to cut this as short as possible. "It's kind of a long story. Anyway—"

"My dear lady," the man breaks in, "we do advise American citizens to carry their passports with them at all times; were you not aware of that? Some travelers feel they can ignore our recommendations, but this is an example of what can happen, and—"

"Yes, yes," I interrupt him in turn. "What I need to know is what the procedure is for obtaining a new one, how long it will take, and so forth. Could you just tell me that, please?"

The man stays silent a moment — in order, I suppose, to mark his indignation at my disregard for his lecture. But since it's his job to supply me with the information, he can't hold out too long. "Under the circumstances, you understand, we will waive the standard three-day waiting period; you will just need to come to our office with two three-by-four-centimeter identity photographs and the fee, which is sixty-five *reais*. If you come in before we close, you'll have the passport in time to get on one of this evening's flights."

"But I'm not traveling," I say.

Veronica is starting to make impatient signs at me and wants confirmation that I understand them. "Okay!" I mouth at her.

"What do you mean?" The man is shocked. "I hope you realize that in some situations a citizen may ignore our recommendations at his or her own risk. In other instances, however, to do so may compromise national security, and the individual is *not* at liberty to jeopardize the safety of the wider community!"

"What *are* you talking about?" I ask, dumbfounded.

"Have you really been totally isolated from the news

since yesterday afternoon? You missed the urgent call for repatriation of all U.S. citizens? Please, miss, I suspect you are feigning ignorance in order to prolong your holiday, but I assure you, this is a matter of the gravest importance. Do not delay in coming in to see us — we will provide you with a new passport and a voucher for one of this evening's free flights to Miami. Should you happen not to be a resident of Miami, the cost of a ticket to your final destination is your responsibility of course, but there will be no more U.S.-government-sponsored flights out of here after tonight. *And*," he pauses for emphasis, "it's entirely possible that the airport may close down in the next few days — you can't tell me you would welcome being stranded in a foreign country in the middle of civil unrest! A fine holiday *that* would be!"

Veronica has now removed her sunglasses the better to roll her eyes at me. I roll mine back at her and turn away. "I really didn't know any of this, sir, I'm sorry. But what on earth has happened?"

"Politics, miss. I can't say I understand the ins and outs of it all myself, but what it comes down to is that our government has deemed the Brazilian situation to be extremely unstable at this juncture and is recalling our citizens for their own good. And of course, we don't want any hostages taken or anything like that, do we?"

"No, of course not. Well, this is all very unexpected . . ."

"I see now that it is." His tone is kinder. "When you come in, we'll make everything easy for you. Do you know how to get to our office from where you are? Where *are* you located right now, may I ask?"

"I, uh, I'm not sure."

"Excuse me?" I can almost hear his eyebrows lifting; then he decides on his own interpretation. "You mean you're not sure you know how to get here."

"That's right."

"Well, just tell me where you're located, Miss . . . Miss . . .

I'm sorry, did you tell me your name?"

"Uh, no, I didn't."

"Well, let me have your name, last name first, and I'll just ask you a few more questions so we can get the paperwork rolling before you come in."

"Thank you very much!" I say in a rush, and hang up the phone. My heart is beating fast. I look around for Veronica: she's already in the car, drumming her fingers on the steering wheel. I get in and before I even have time to close the door she's pulling away from the curb.

"Took you long enough," she says shortly. Out the window I see our audience's heads swivel to watch us go.

"Sorry. I couldn't help it. The guy told me that all American citizens have to leave the country."

"Are you joking?" Her mood lightens suddenly. She turns to look at me: she can see the answer on my face. "But why?"

" 'Politics,' the man said." It strikes me as kind of funny, and I chuckle. "He didn't seem to be able to explain any better than that."

"So it's really getting serious," Veronica says, her eyes on the road but her thoughts far away. "The U.S. often has a hand in the big power shifts, so they'd be among the first to know." She's silent a few moments, then asks: "So, are you going?"

"Me?" I stall. "Uh . . . I don't think so . . . I mean, it's just so unexpected . . . do you really think there's going to be . . . what? What might happen?"

"Oh," she replies airily, "you might get kidnapped, held for political ransom because of your nationality, or simply be subject along with the rest of us to food shortages, curfews, street warfare, or any number of inconveniences. Although I really think that the greatest danger to you right now is your association with us." She glances in the rearview mirror, then over at me. "So when do they want you out of here?"

"Tonight, actually."

She seems impressed. "Serious indeed. Well, you have a little while to think it over. We'll have to leave here later today anyway; you can get a ride back to the city with us and then head to the consulate and the airport or whatever the scheme is, or you can stay on and take your chances."

I wish her assessment of my options weren't so matter-of-fact — I would've welcomed some evidence of concern ("Gosh, Jo, this must be hard for you"), dismay ("I can't believe you might leave us so soon!"), or attachment ("Please don't go — we need you!"). Not forthcoming. Maybe she's trying to make it easier for me, and it almost worked: my immediate thought was: "Okay, thanks, just drop me off at the airport then, *bitch*." I'm especially hurt by her apparent equanimity since just an hour ago I was on the verge of pledging myself to her and Bruno for life.

I decide to match her casual tone. "I'm not too sure what I'm going to do. I'll let you know." And then, to emphasize that it doesn't matter to me too much one way or the other, I change the subject. "What happened when you called Velma?"

Her face clouds over. This, now, is a topic of worry for her. "She pretended she didn't know who I was. At first I couldn't understand it, but as soon as she hung up I realized that there must have been someone else there and she didn't want to reveal who the caller was. But she sounded awfully stressed and afraid. Not at all her usual self."

I remain silent, pondering the implications. We're already back on the red dirt road; after another minute we turn off into the entrance of Ruth and Eliane's property.

Bruno is sitting at the kitchen table with an old man I recognize from the Santo Daime session. He looks scruffy but clean, like a coat that wasn't meant to go into the washing machine and came out wrinkled and shrunken in places. Bruno and he are deep in conversation, which they break off when we enter.

"Well?" Bruno asks, rising to his feet, but Veronica motions with her chin toward the man who is sitting with his back to us and turning around very slowly. Bruno gets the point and contains himself, though he can tell from our expressions that the news isn't good. He sits down again, speaking in Portuguese to his companion, who has now revolved in his chair sufficiently to be able to fix Veronica and me with bright eyes. Introductions are made — I don't really register his name, perhaps because I'm fascinated by the pure kindness that shines out from the worn-looking face.

"Sentam-se," he requests, indicating the empty chairs.

Veronica declines emphatically, saying something to the effect that we don't have much time. Bruno concurs regretfully, and stands up again. The older man returns stiffly to his initial position: clearly the effort of staying twisted around was too much for him. I'm tempted to go over to the other side of the table so I can keep watching his face, but Bruno and Veronica are herding me back out the kitchen door.

"Senhor Antônio has offered us a ride to Salvador," Bruno says, as the three of us go up to the second floor. "He is a very interesting man, a doctor, an astrologer, and a philosopher. He has been an *espírita* for about twenty years, and was just telling me some things about his experiences."

"What's an espírita?" I ask.

"A follower of the religion called Espiritismo. A mixture of Christianity with reincarnation — extremely popular in this country."

We've reached the bedroom. I flop down on one of the beds, Veronica chooses the other, and Bruno, after the slightest hesitation, sits down next to her.

"I think I've heard of that religion," I say. "Don't they have sessions where disembodied spirits deliver messages to the living?"

"Right," he answers. "I was asking if he—," but Veronica cuts him off:

"Então, liguei primeiro pra casa de Paula e Doce, mas . . ."

Bruno frowns at her and gestures toward me. She grimaces and continues in English, describing her two phone calls. "So you know what that means," she concludes. Bruno looks glum and doesn't bother to reply.

"What does it mean?" I ask, after a short silence.

"It means that our friends are in trouble," Bruno answers, "most probably because of us. It means we must surrender, so that they are not pressured for information about us. We know the police will stop at nothing to try to extract information, and until we are found, they will make our friends suffer. But I do not understand why this is all happening so fast."

Turn themselves in? I'm appalled. Is there no other solution?

"Tell him about the consulate," says Veronica. I comply; when I'm through, he nods slowly.

"Well," he says, "Senhor Antônio has offered not only to give us a ride back to the city, but to let us stay overnight at his house. He knows that we are in some kind of trouble, but does not want to know too much, which is wise. I have tried to tell him that sheltering us will put him at risk, but he does not seem worried about that. Unlike Ruth and Eliane, who, without saying so, have made it very clear they would like us to leave as soon as possible. So, Jo," and now his eyes focus on me, "have you made up your mind?"

"No." I wish I could let him know how churned-up I am inside. I want to tell him everything that's passing through my head: the vision I had of allying my destiny with theirs; my hurt at Veronica's lack of concern; my panic at the idea of being suddenly cut off from him, from a degree of intimacy I had never experienced and might never again. I also want to acknowledge my fear, and my impulse to follow the U.S.

government's orders like a good little sheep. But this seems a time for action, not confession; though my choice is not made, I don't want to muddy up their situation any more than necessary.

"When you decide, you will tell us," Bruno states. "You will come back to the city with us in any case. And Veronica and I must think about what we are going to do, too — right, Vero?"

"We've discussed this eventuality before," she replies. "I think we agree that we have to turn ourselves in. The question is when — today? Tomorrow? Are there some things we can do before then that would be useful — preparations? We should definitely try to fit in an Outernet session to contact any friends we can, get some information about the wider situation, and strategize."

"Let us do that now, then," says Bruno. "Senhor Antônio says he is flexible in terms of departure times, but he wants to leave before nighttime. So we have a little window."

Go on the Outernet again? This is beginning to remind me of that amusement park ride with the giant teacups that nearly jerk you out of your skin as they hurtle this way and that. Except in this case the ride has malfunctioned and I've been trapped on it for days. Don't I get a chance to rest? Then again, there's nothing that says *I* have to go back on the Outernet. Veronica phrased it ambiguously: *"We* should definitely try to fit in an Outernet session." Let's just assume she meant Bruno and herself. I could wander out to the beat-up couch on the veranda, settle down to a profitable nap — though would the mosquitoes pester me? The breeze might keep them away — then I realize the two of them are watching me expectantly.

"What?" I ask, a bit harshly. In my mind's eye I was already lying down on the couch, having adjusted my position to accommodate a renegade spring; a breeze was playing about my face and the hypnotic weft of cricket sounds was lulling me away from consciousness.

"Shall we?" Veronica asks, all business.

"What do you want me to do?" I know I sound grudging, but I can't help it.

Veronica is unruffled. "You and I will try to go on at the same time," she says. "If it works, it'll be doubly efficient. I'll take care of one set of tasks and you'll handle another, and we can check in with each other before we leave, to make sure we covered everything."

Despite myself, I'm interested. "What are the tasks?"

"Finding out what's really going on out there, that's the first thing. What the governments are doing, how the people are responding. First we get some input. Then we *give* any input we can: there are always planning sessions going on, and right now there must be a few that deal specifically with the recent developments."

I speak up quickly. "I'm not going to be able to give any input, I can tell you right now. I hate to admit it, but I know very little about politics, conflict resolution, and that kind of stuff. Even my knowledge of history and geography is patchy. You'd better assign me to the information gathering part of this mission."

"I do not think it can be divided up like that," Bruno puts in. "Veronica will not be able to contribute meaningfully to the planning if she does not know what the most recent developments are. In my opinion, the two of you will have to go around together; the benefits of being two instead of one will come afterward, in the process of reflecting on what has been said and done."

"Perhaps." Veronica looks thoughtful. "There might in fact be some advantage to dividing up the work. We'll decide when we get there. Time is short, though, so let's go!"

"Will you need any assistance — you know, in that first part where your helper spirit or whatever it is comes through?"

"Don't worry about it. Bruno can handle anything that comes up. You just make your own way there."

"What if I can't do it this time?" I ask.

"That'll be too bad," she replies.

"What if I do get there — how will I find you?"

"By wishing to."

"All right."

Bruno settles himself in a corner of the room, on the floor. Veronica and I each stretch out on a bed. I'm worried that I won't be able to relax, but I find that my state of general fatigue overcomes my agitation and quickly brings me down: I have to struggle not to fall asleep outright. This time I have a hunch that I needn't use sound to launch myself off. Instead, I start to re-create the route as clearly as I can in my mind's eye, starting with the suffocation of the first stage. Suddenly the sensation bursts out of the dimension of memory and envelops me, and the journey unfolds as before.

Once I'm back in front of the purple field with the six portals, I get set to summon Veronica. The thought of her instantly awakens a host of resentful feelings: I remember the deception she practiced, pretending she couldn't log on; her lack of concern at the prospect of my imminent departure; the impatience she often displays when dealing with me, as if I were a burden. She certainly wasn't enthusiastic when Bruno suggested we stay together this time — as if I were a little sister she had to drag around. Maybe the fondness she claims to feel for me, the admiration — maybe all that isn't even genuine, but is part of some complicated deception. It's actually easier for me to give credence to that hypothesis than to the compliments she's heaped on me.

I'll show them, I think. I will *not* try and find her, at least right away; after all, there was no guarantee I would even make it here. I'll have a look around by myself and see what I can figure out.

Once more, I survey the six rectangles: Groups, Chat,

Encyclopedia, Records, Projects, Contacts. What would be the best place to go for world news? The rectangle labeled Encyclopedia begins to slide toward me — or I toward it. When its four straight edges are directly above, below, and to either side of me, light infuses the framed space, revealing the presence of written words: it's as if I'd been looking at the page of a book in complete darkness, and then someone came along and shone a flashlight on it. This is, in fact, a facsimile of a page. The slightly old-fashioned typeset is crammed onto it as though space were at a premium, kind of like, well, a page from an encyclopedia. WORLD HISTORY is the heading. All of a sudden, the cramped text beneath it thins out and expands, and a subheading appears: "Week of . . ." followed by last Monday's date. Below that, some paragraphs of text:

> This week was marked by a significant shift in international relations, after a mammoth power structure whose existence had been tactically obscured was revealed to the public. Five multinational corporations, forming an alliance known as Top Five, declared their effective ownership of 97% of the planet's resources. In a press conference held by Top Five representatives on Monday afternoon, the alliance's lawyers outlined the process, initiated several decades ago, which has resulted in their client's incontestable ownership of these resources.
>
> Leaders of the most influential nations have stepped forward to declare their support of Top Five, which includes placing their countries' armed forces under Top Five command. Top Five representatives do not allow the use of the term 'takeover' to be applied to their maneuver, insisting that the 'gradual consolidation of power' has occurred with the full compliance of the leading governments. Police forces in every country were clearly prepared to take swift action against protesters, imposing a choice

between silence and assent. Media sources in a number of countries were shut down or placed under the direction of Top Five representatives with cooperation of the local authorities.

Top Five will reveal its comprehensive plan for the global economy by month's end. Until such time, businesses are to run as usual, the only difference being in the distribution of the profits, which will be allocated according to the determination of Top Five agents, bearing in mind that Top Five is the de facto proprietor of said businesses.

Following this chunk of text comes a table with the heading FOR FURTHER STUDY, with subheadings: "By Country," "Stock Market Reaction," "Full Text of Top Five Press Statement," "Tracing the Evolution of Top Five," and "Analysts Say."

I think I've taken in as much as I can digest for now. The news is so fantastic it's hard to believe, especially in the context of this surreal virtual environment. I wonder if the whole thing is just an elaborate, skillfully constructed hoax. And yet — I remind myself of the very real attack on my possessions, the restrictions on Internet use, the cop posted outside Bruno and Veronica's door, the U.S. Consulate's warning. There's no reason not to trust the information given here — it's not so fantastical as all that, only the logical outcome that none of us really thought we would live to see.

Now what? There are too many implications to even begin to ponder, but I think I remember everything well enough to bring back a faithful report. Wait — there was another part I was supposed to find out — what was it Veronica said? Oh yes: "What the governments are doing; how the people are responding." From what I've read, there was a suggestion of dissent, but how widespread is it? Should I look into one of those other categories, maybe "Analysts Say"? There might be too much to sift through there; if I leave the Encyclopedia area and go to Chat, that should allow me to get an instantaneous answer.

No sooner desired than done; I wonder in passing what it would be like if the rest of the world worked that way, outside of here: a frightening thought. I find myself once more before the mosaic of tiny human faces and zoom in until I can see all their little eyes watching me, waiting.

I try to be as succinct as possible. "What has the popular reaction to the Top Five takeover been?" I deliberately use the word "takeover" out of a childish sense of defiance.

The smooth neutral voice repeats my question and a number of faces slide forward.

"Reactions run the gamut from enthusiastic acceptance to emphatic rejection," answers the voice after a few seconds, "with the bulk of public opinion falling in the latter category. Violent confrontations continue to take place between those with opposing views on the matter. The police, when called on to break up physical fights between individuals and skirmishes between larger groups, have usually been observed to take the side of Top Five supporters. Those in favor of Top Five rule accuse its detractors of sheer stupidity, pointing out that nothing has changed, except that the true owners of the planet have now made themselves known. They argue that this new transparency will greatly enhance the efficiency of global trade: all rules and restrictions based on political considerations have become unnecessary. The pretense of competitiveness can be dropped – all industries are interdependent, serving the interests of a single owner: Top Five. The sum total of the time and materials that went into reinforcing the antiquated economic systems can be diverted to more profitable and enjoyable ends, one of which will be an increase in leisure time per capita, as emphasized in the Top Five model presented under the title 'A New Today.' Protection and preservation of the natural environment is also on the list of Top Five priorities.

"The group's opponents, on the other hand, resist the idea of a monolithic planetary government. When presented with the argument that the system has been in place for some time, they state their categorical rejection of this setup and call for the matter to be put to a planetwide vote. Typically, Top Five opponents take a stance rooted in so-called spiritual and humanistic values as opposed to materialistic ones, demonstrating a faith that these values will triumph over the military and economic resources concentrated in the hands of Top Five.

"Activists are rushing to strengthen their networks and reach consensus on plans for resistance."

What can they possibly do about it, I wonder — then realize that the line here between talking to oneself and talking to others is so fine I've crossed it by mistake. The voice repeats my question, and the squares of faces rearrange themselves. To my surprise, however, instead of delivering an answer after a few seconds, the voice says, "Question," and this time a single face detaches itself from the rest and comes to the fore. It's a woman with a long face that looks Ethiopian. She gazes at me earnestly, and the voice asks:

"What are *you* going to do about it?"

For a moment I think there's been some kind of crosstalk, a technical glitch — someone else's question has mistakenly preempted mine and I've just got to wait for the different strands to get sorted out before getting my answer. But then, as nothing further happens and the serious gal continues to stare at me, pursing her mouth slightly, I become uncomfortably certain that the question is directed at me.

That's when I remember that the area I'm in is called Chat — why didn't I just stick with Encyclopedia? With a little patience I would surely have been able to cull the information I wanted, but I came here in search of a quick fix, instantaneous feedback from real live people. Only I hadn't thought that the real live people might also ask something of me, and now I'm on the spot. Not answering isn't much of an option: the lady's expression is taking on a slightly stubborn cast. I could say, "I don't know," but that seems so weak.

Finally, unable to think of any acceptable out, I start to ponder the question. What *will* I do about Top Five declaring ownership of the planet? So what if the food I eat, the water I drink, the building I live in, the roads I drive on, and the school I work for all belong to one entity? They never belonged to me in the first place, so whether I have to pay my dues to the butcher, the baker, and the candlestick maker, or whether all of them have been subsumed into one big company store, what difference will it really make? My thoughts are divided exactly along the lines of those ascribed to "popular reaction": on one hand the acknowledgment that this shouldn't really change anything, on the other an instinctive rejection of such total domination — not so much a thought as a set of feelings composed of nausea, repulsion, loathing, and a desire to shrink away. It's this deep, incontrovertible refusal that informs me of the general direction my actions must take.

The first thing is to find out if there is in fact any weakness at all in the seemingly omnipotent monster, "Top Five." And wasn't that precisely the information I was trying to find before having been quizzed myself? Then that's my answer to the woman watching me: I'm going to find out if there's any way at all to oppose this thing, and if there is, I'm going to help. There.

A slight smile flickers on the woman's lips, then they open, form a word, and close again. The neutral voice relays the message: "Hurry."

The little square with the woman's face in it recedes. For a moment I want to call her back, to thank her, to ask her about herself, where she lives, what she does — but under the circumstances such a conversation would appear frivolous. "Hurry," she said. I decide to rephrase my earlier question. "How can we stop Top Five?"

The pattern of face cells shifts a bit, then the voice delivers its nugget of crunched and digested information: "The only proposals that would ensure elimination of Top Five involve physical destruction of the greater part of humanity and of the planet and are thus considered unacceptable by the majority of Top Five opponents. The bulk of activist effort is right now concentrated on a plan for a global strike whose efficacy would depend on the number of adherents in all sectors of the economy. This plan is seen as being highly risky and having only a very small chance of success, yet it is the only plan that offers any such chance."

I wait, thinking there must be more, but there isn't. Then the voice says "Question" again. This time I feel pleasurable anticipation as I watch one of the cells detach itself and zip toward me. I wonder who it is who wants to know my thoughts; I feel less insecure this time.

But once the little square comes close enough so that I can see the face clearly, I get a hell of a shock: it's Veronica! She greets me with a wry smile as the voice explains: "This person has requested an interview with you in a private chat room. Do you accept?"

"Uh . . . sure," I say, or think, as my surroundings reconfigure into an impression of a smaller space defined by lines that suggest walls and corners. Veronica is here, or rather, her image is, looking just as it did before we logged on, though strangely inert. Her eyes stare straight ahead; it's like facing a zombie. I wonder what I look like to her.

"Well, this was one way to do it," she says, though her mouth doesn't move. "It's actually a good choice, meeting here, but I didn't have time to create a sophisticated avatar. If you'd tried to find me as soon as you got here, the process would've been a little more complicated, but at least we could've gotten mobile parts."

Resentment surges up in me, as if she'd come to curb my independence, like a mom calling her kid in from the street.

"Did you have a question for me or not?" I ask, peevishly.

Her image hangs for a moment in silence. The little smile was a good choice, I think. All-purpose. I know her well enough by now to be certain that my show of rudeness amused her. "As a matter of fact, I do." Her tone is teasing. She pauses for a few seconds: my guess is that she wants to milk that smile for all it's worth. "I was listening in on that exchange about anti-Top Five strategies. Do you intend to work with us on that — with Bruno and me?"

"Were you already aware of all of this?" Momentarily confused, I don't remember exactly what we were talking about before this Outernet session.

"No, we weren't. But we've been preparing — trying to prepare — for something *like* this, for a long time. And I repeat my question: Are you going to work with us?"

"What if I say yes?"

"Then we'll go back as soon as possible to share the news with Bruno. I've collected enough information so that we can take the next steps, and from what I overheard of your chat, you've gotten some background, too. Where did you go — Encyclopedia?" She doesn't wait for an answer. "If you do *not* care to work with us, then I would urge you to stay here a bit longer, do some more investigation or anything else, but it's important for me, at least, to get back to Bruno and let him know what's happening. Securing our physical situation, shelter and so forth, will have to be our next priority."

I think of the airplanes that will fill up with United States citizens this evening: a crowd of my compatriots, excited, outraged, babbling, swapping hypotheses in their loud, flat voices. I picture the whole trip: the dinner, the movies, the little map showing the icon of the plane advancing toward its destination. Then Miami airport and the hustle of trying to get a standby flight, maybe having to spend hours on one of those hard slippery chairs and then finally, blearily, making it home.

Home. The word causes a fresh cascade of images. My apartment. Potted ferns on the windowsill. The cat's ritual greeting, butt in the air and front legs stretched out. Neighborhood stores: coffee shops full of pierced, tattoo-covered youngsters; the friendly balding bookseller; Mrs. Kwan from the corner market. All owned by Top Five? Guess so. Golden Gate Park: the Tea Garden. The community college: wide halls and ornate columns straining toward grandeur, my little cluttered office, a disheveled student across the desk from me. Home. Will I still fit in? I imagine myself sliding through these decors as if on casters.

"Actually," Veronica resumes, "it's probably best if you come back with me now anyway." She sounds impatient: I guess she had been waiting for my answer. "What if we want to get a ride with that old man right away? It's going to be a bit difficult if you stay on the Outernet and we have to lug your body around."

That doesn't sound too good to me either. "Let's go, then," I say. I'm about to ask whether we can leave from here or have to pass back through the Home Page area, when I'm distracted by the appearance of a group of people, still a long way off, but clearly making their way toward us. They seem to have materialized out of thin air.

"Who's that?" I ask. "Isn't this supposed to be a private chat room?" Veronica's effigy pivots toward the intruders but before she can even answer, I recognize them. It's the Outernet trademark posse. I cringe. "Do we have to wait for them to go through the whole thing?" I ask her.

"No way around it." The lively group is already upon us; though their banter and laughter is soundless, Veronica raises her voice: "As soon as they turn their backs we can leave!"

I marvel at how incredible the resolution of the scene is, taking in the grain of skin, the different textures of cloth, the details of shape and volume that distinguish one human face, one human body from another. Yet there's the unmistakable sensation that they're in fact multiple extrusions of a single being, that all their differences amount to no more than a cunning disguise. They are not, I somehow realize, mere holographic animations: they represent actual people, people logged on to the Outernet right now.

The moment comes when they shut their eyes and mouths. Knowing they're about to mentally form the word "Outernet" in unison, I suddenly decide that this time I'll join in the collective voicing; instead of waiting, bored, for them to get it over with, I find myself anticipating the exact split second when the chorus will intone its part. Only then do I become conscious of the skill involved in this apparently simple utterance: how the hell are the dozens of people able to synchronize themselves in this way — and with their eyes closed? The significance of the instant is that it is so perfectly shared.

My thoughts have distracted me: before I know it, the one-word roar has come and gone and I missed my chance. "Next time," I think, marveling that this repetitive device, this "logo," struck me as a tiresome gimmick just seconds ago. Now I can't wait to repeat the experience.

I gaze abstractedly at the crowd disappearing into the distance, until Veronica's voice startles me. "Come on," she urges.

I turn toward the puppetlike figure just in time to see it evaporate. This produces a surge of anxiety — I don't want to be left behind. Quickly I imagine the country house, Bruno. The briefest recollection of his embrace exerts a magnetic pull that jerks me back to my body immediately: unlike my previous experiences, there's no time to take in the successive strata, only a blur and a sudden sickening feeling, and I'm back on the bed.

Bruno and Veronica are watching me from the other bed.

"All right?" Veronica asks. I nod and sit up.

Bruno comes over and sits next to me, placing an arm

ever so gently around my shoulders, drawing me to him. "You come, too," he tells Veronica, at which the wry smile resurfaces.

"No time for funny stuff," she says curtly.

"It is not 'funny stuff,' Vee," he answers. "While you two were gone I felt so much alone. It was like a wake, like having to stand guard over the corpses of my most favorite people. It was horrible."

"Poor thing," she responds. It's sarcastic, but something in her manner has softened.

"Come over here, Vee," he insists.

"All right, all right!" She plunks herself down on his other side, and he pulls her close. I stare straight ahead.

"So, then. Tell me," Bruno says.

I let Veronica do the talking: she's found out essentially the same things about Top Five that I have, though the elements of the story are arranged a little differently, and she makes references to facts familiar to both of them but unknown to me.

Bruno is fascinated. "Incredible," he sputters, "fantastic! *Puta que pariu!*" Only when Veronica has told all she has to tell does his excitement seem to abate — I imagine that the implications are starting to sink in, that he's considering what this means for the two of them. He turns to me. "What about you, Jo? What was your trip like?"

Veronica had made it clear that we weren't together for most of the time, mentioning that we met up in a chat room before coming back. What my trip was like? For some reason my mood is glum; no spark of enthusiasm, no wish to relate any of it. "What she said," I reply, and resist his entreaties to elaborate.

He's puzzled, a little hurt. If we were alone I'm sure he would try a different language, not so much to extract information about the Outernet but to penetrate into the mystery of my discomfort, which is so plain to see. Perhaps he'd be able to explain me to myself. As it is, however, we have neither space nor time for such communion. Veronica is doing her best to keep her mouth shut, but she's jiggling one foot furiously. After about two minutes of watching Bruno trying to draw me out of my shell she can't stand it anymore.

"Let's decide what to do next, shall we?" She tries to keep her tone light, free of the impatience her foot gives away. Bruno looks regretful, but as he turns from me I see his expression of solicitousness change back to one of lively interest.

"We agree, then, that our first priority must be to participate in the strike?" he asks.

They agree? Veronica had only mentioned the strike in passing. There must be some kind of telepathic communication particular to married couples at work here. Feeling left out doesn't help my mood. "You two don't even have real jobs, do you?" I challenge. "How can you strike?"

Bruno doesn't seem to notice the unpleasantness in my voice. "We have been preparing for something like this for a long time. For the past four years we have acted as recruiters and organizers, signing up those who are willing to participate in an alternative economy."

"Meaning?"

"The only chance we have of sustaining a strike is if there is a network in place of people willing to trade the goods they produce or the services they offer. For example, if Farmer João in Porto Seguro has some sacks of beans he is willing to trade for a few yards of cloth from Salvador, and Maria who has a car is willing to do the pickup and delivery in exchange for a share of the beans . . . you see what I mean?"

"A few yards of cloth? But what if larger quantities are needed? Does anyone you know own a textile mill? And what about the gas for Maria's car? Are you telling me you have oil company executives who sympathize with your views?"

"You are very perceptive, as usual. But you would be

surprised to know who is on our side. It is true that conditions are not perfect for establishing the kind of general barter system that could function long-term. Ideally, society as a whole should dedicate itself to the goal of making such a system work. For now, our operations must be as covert as possible. Guerilla tactics, and so on. Limited resources."

He's staring into the distance, into the future, as he says this. A gleam is in his eye — in his voice the noble determination evinced by movie superheroes before they fly off in pursuit of a dastardly villain. I feel sorry for him, for them. Top Five is much too powerful an enemy to be toppled by such a half-baked scheme — the little I know has made that clear. It's depressing: the vision he's described can't be realized, but stubborn attempts to do so will probably have nastier consequences than those of abject submission. I'm not going to convince them of that, though: they say they've been setting this up for years. "It's a good idea," I say, dispiritedly. I don't add: "But it will never work."

I stand up and cross to the other side of the room, stationing myself by the window and looking at the yard below. Shadows stretch across the scrubby grass: the day is coming to an end. Leaves on the ground move ever so slightly in the breeze that has come to relieve the afternoon heat. A laundry line is stretched between two trees, white shirts pegged to it. Clouds drift in a brilliant sky. It's peaceful here, so peaceful — if only there weren't this undercurrent of urgency.

I turn my attention back to Bruno and Veronica. After looking out into the sunlight it takes my eyes a few seconds to adjust: the room swims in shadow, the couple on the bed seems smaller, like paper cutouts.

"I checked in with the few people we know who were logged in," Veronica is telling Bruno. "I explained why I couldn't stay and said I'd be back as soon as possible to do some more concrete planning. Now that our regular lines of communication are down, people understand that they have to try to be present as often as possible."

"Good, good." Bruno nods.

"Now our real problem is how to get *you* onto the Outernet, Bruno. Isn't there some way—"

Struck by a thought, I interrupt. "How many times have you been on the Outernet, Bruno?"

"Well, once . . . or twice . . ."

"What do you mean, once or twice? Is it once or twice? How can you not know?" I don't mean to be so aggressive — I think I'm taking this as an excuse to let my unfocused feelings of frustration and dismay erupt.

"Once, for certain . . . the second time I did not manage to really stay on."

He looks so sheepish that I regret my outburst. "But why? Why not?"

No answer. Veronica's foot starts jiggling again.

"I mean, you know so much! Not just intellectually — I mean, you *really* know!"

I feel myself coloring and steal a glance at Veronica: the sardonic smile is back. "It wasn't so distressing before, since I was almost always able to be the link," she says. "It's very unfortunate now, however, since we'll probably be separated shortly. It's all too clear that we should've worked on this problem until we solved it; I was trying to push for that. We did think we'd have more advance warning — we were expecting to have maybe another few years before things got this bad. But now . . ." She leaves the sentence unfinished.

Bruno has gone pale. "Separated?"

Veronica's bottled-up impatience explodes. "You never really believed this, did you? That this would happen? That they would take it this far? You were always the romantic, you liked the ideas, the adventure, the excitement — it was like a game to you, wasn't it? How many times did I tell you, Bruno: it's *real*! Even now you seem to think we're just moving up to the next level of difficulty in some 3D video game, but it's more complicated than that, sweetie!" She's standing now, hands on her hips. "Let me remind you of a few things. Our friends are in trouble. What do we do? Run away? You know what we agreed to do: we're going to turn ourselves in, so they don't have to suffer any more than necessary. Right? Right! And you know what that means, don't you? You don't need me to spell it out, do you? All right."

She turns to me. "Do you know what choice the police offered their prisoners, the enemies of the government, during the nineteen-thirties? They said: 'What would you prefer: the *beliscão* — the big pinch — or the electric shock?' Most people would pick the pinch, of course, but what they didn't realize until it was too late was that it meant their navels would be ripped out with a pair of pliers and they would bleed to death. That was just one variation on a theme. Things haven't changed much since then. There are many methods, many stories: we've seen the scars, the limps. And those are the ones who came back. The use of torture on political prisoners is almost an institution. It's not just in our country, of course, but this is where *we* see it."

She turns back to Bruno. "This is really it, Bruno. This is where you figure out how to log on, because they're not going to put us in the same cell, and if they have us spend any time together it will probably be to have one of us look on while the other gets battered to a pulp. And if you can't log on, we might never see each other again."

Here she pauses for Bruno's response, but he gives none. His face has gone sullen during her diatribe: my guess is that he's imagining the inevitable ordeal, that it frightens the hell out of him and he realizes there's nowhere to turn for comfort. I feel foolish, extraneous: I somehow missed it, how serious their situation is, I see that now. Running from the police seemed like a game of cops and robbers, maybe because the cops lost the last round. Now Bruno and Veronica are actually going to serve themselves up and they're not going to get any Brownie points for it, either. But torture? The big pinch? The cops might want to punish them for resisting arrest, they might want information out of them, but how far would they really go?

"What do you mean, you might never see each other again?" I blurt it out, breaking the grim silence encasing us: they look at me in surprise, as though they'd forgotten I was in the room.

Veronica explains it to me patiently. She seems exhausted now, drained by her outburst. The tinge of scorn so often present in her tone over the past few days is gone. "They kill people, Jo," she says. "They really do. If it makes things smoother for them, they'll do it. If there's no one they're afraid of in their way, they'll do it. There's no question that who we are, what we stand for, and what we do are a real inconvenience to them. It's easier to eliminate us than figure out any other possible solution to the problem we present. Because as long as we're here, anywhere, we won't shut up. We might not have a chance in hell of bringing them down but we'll do our best to try. They know that. It's annoying to them, at best. It insults them. It makes them waste time and money, energy. And so, they want to scare us, to warn us, to convince us to stop — or just *make* us stop, for once and for all."

"But you told Bruno, you said: 'If you don't log on, we might never see each other again.' Do you mean they could give you life sentences in separate jails and the only way you'd be able to see each other would be on the Outernet?"

"No — what I meant was that if, *if* they choose to terminate one or both of us, there is the possibility that we *could* continue to meet on the Outernet." She looks toward the window; it seems as if she's calculating something in her head. "Now," she says, "I think one of us should go downstairs and—"

"Wait," I plead. I need to understand. "Are you really

saying that you can meet on the Outernet even if you're *dead*?"

The impatience is back: it manifests in a slight twist of her mouth. "Yes, Jo. To some extent. There are a few problems with it. It's kind of like cryogenics: it's not really clear how you get the person *back*. Still, preserving them in the meantime is a step."

"But if I can't log on—," Bruno interjects mournfully.

"Indeed," replies Veronica, her voice tight. She stands up. "As I started to say, I think it's time to check with . . . what's his name?"

"Senhor Antônio," supplies Bruno.

"Senhor Antônio. See when he wants to go. Have a word with Ruth and Eliane before we do. They've been superhelpful to us, at considerable personal risk. Shall I go down, then? Or shall we all?"

I would prefer to sit here and digest the information I've just been given — perhaps try and wake myself up, hoping this is a bad dream. The fate in store for those two is ominous, but the path laid out for them is clear. My own next steps are disturbingly uncertain. Do I choose the easy way out and hop on the flight to Miami? Or do I stay here, stand by; surely there's something I can do to help? Bring them food, if they're kept in jail? Act as a messenger; ferry information between them and the outside world? Surely that will be less risky for all concerned than giving one of their Brazilian friends that job? I have to have some faith in my relatively protected status as a U.S. citizen.

If I go back home, it's hard to imagine being able to make much of a difference. Writing letters to my congressional representative, contacting human rights organizations: I can do all that here, too. I can see myself in a little office, kind of like my office at school, but in a ramshackle colonial Portuguese mansion in downtown Salvador, running my own one-woman Free Bruno and Veronica operation. They would never ask me to do something like that, of course — they would probably think I wasn't even capable of it. "Too soft," they'd assume, even if it did occur to them to ask me for help.

By the time the three of us have trooped downstairs, my mind is almost made up. It seems indisputable that they need me, even if they don't realize it.

Senhor Antônio is no longer in the kitchen: he's sitting on the front steps, smoking a cigarette. He turns around at our approach; the warmth of his expression breaks through the icy apprehension that has settled over me. He's genuinely pleased to see us; I return his smile and so does Veronica, perfunctorily, but Bruno does not. As the elder man studies Bruno more closely, a look of puzzlement comes over his face, changing to concern. *"O que foi que aconteceu com ele?"* he asks. His speech is slow and clear and I understand the question: "What happened to him?" I also understand why he doesn't address Bruno directly: Bruno's eyes are blank, as if an invisible shutter had been pulled down over them. I can imagine, and I'm sure Veronica can, too, something of what might be passing through his mind, but Senhor Antônio, of course, cannot.

In one surprisingly swift movement, the old man rises, throws down his cigarette butt and crushes it underfoot, and takes Bruno's hands in his.

Bruno glances at him briefly, then his gaze goes glassy again.

"Venha!" Senhor Antônio says, leading him over to the broken-down couch and pushing him gently onto it. He turns to Veronica and me, repeating his question with greater urgency, looking back and forth between the two of us. I have no idea to what extent secrecy needs to be preserved so I leave the initiative to Veronica, but she, too, remains silent.

"Vamos sentar," he says, and the three of us sit on the veranda floor in a kind of circle in front of the couch. Senhor Antônio is still waiting for his answer.

I wish I were free to speak — I think that even with my limited Portuguese I could convey the essential. But Bruno's story is Veronica's, too: she's the one who must decide how much to tell this man, this stranger — or will she fabricate a lie? Since she's hesitating, thinking, I know she must be considering the truth: it wouldn't take her this long to come up with an evasion. I'm startled, though, when she opens her mouth and practically the whole story comes out. I can't follow along word for word, but I can tell she's explaining about the Outernet and their group, and Top Five, and the fact that Bruno can't access the Outernet at will, and what that means now that their lives are in danger.

Senhor Antônio listens without interrupting, taking it all in. At last, when she's through, he nods sadly. Then he looks at me. *"E esta menina?"* he asks. He wants to know how I fit into this — he's referred to me as a girl, which I suppose is what I must seem like to someone as old as he. Veronica says that they met me in Salvador and that I, too, have been able to travel to the Outernet.

Senhor Antônio appears confused, as though he still doesn't understand the reason for my presence: he's asking for more. *"Sim, e . . . ?"* — "Yes, and . . . ?" he prods.

Veronica is a bit taken aback. It seems that she can't think of anything else about me that's relevant, and as a matter of fact, neither can I. Except . . . apparently she and I have the same thought, because she starts to tell him about the past-life connection that we both glimpsed on the Outernet.

A strange kind of excitement seems to take hold of Senhor Antônio as she speaks: his eyes widen, his nostrils flare, his mouth drops open a little; the slumped shoulders straighten and he leans toward her, hanging on to every word. The keen curiosity makes him look suddenly boyish, as if he'd shed decades in just a minute's time. He's interrogating Veronica: he wants her to go into detail, and she does.

First she describes the scene I witnessed in the odd house that looked so much like Ruth and Eliane's; then, as he pressures her, she tells more and more. She's giving the background to that scene; I had no idea she knew so much — why didn't I think to ask her? It's fascinating and I wish I could understand everything but her speech is rapid, the words blur together. She's telling it as though it really were *our* story, referring to one of the women as "I," and the other as "she," meaning me; she makes this clear by looking at me reflexively when she says it.

I can't stand not being able to understand the details. I'll make her tell it all to me later, in English. Maybe during the car ride back to the city? I start to feel uneasy about the lateness of the hour and remind myself that I'm pretty much set on staying in Salvador — I don't need to worry about getting on that plane. But should we be spending so much time here — is it really necessary to satisfy Senhor Antônio's curiosity so thoroughly?

The afternoon light now has that deep golden quality that comes just before dusk. I watch Veronica talking to the older man, using her hands to make her descriptions still more vivid, looking to Senhor Antônio for confirmation that he hears, that he understands; he nods yes, yes, again and again. I suppose she must have needed a confidante, a confessor. It might not feel safe to unburden herself to Bruno or me; there are emotional mines lying around. A perfect stranger, on the other hand, will slip back into the unknown from whence he came, carrying her little repository of secrets, and she'll be lighter for it, freer. But still, I think, resentfully — it's not just her story, it's ours, too . . .

I look over at Bruno, still zombified on the couch, and feel a wave of pity. A quick inner battle between instincts and the stronger one wins: I get up and go sit next to him. I grasp his hand — it's inert, but warm. I press it firmly, not relaxing my grip, hoping to communicate: "I'm here for you, I won't leave you."

It's a great relief to realize he's not actually catatonic: his sad eyes focus on me; he seems to understand what I'm trying to convey and also to reply — and I'm not sure if my interpretation is based on telepathy, nonverbal language, or imagination — something like, "Thanks, Jo, you're so sweet, but there's nothing you can do. Don't worry about me."

I continue to press his hand, willing the gesture to transmit the conviction that even when things look their darkest, unexpected succor may come: an entreaty to stay positive, since despair may blind one to opportunities. My insistence is such that he finally seems a bit amused by it: he gives me the briefest smile and tugs against my grip as if to say, "Okay, okay, you're right, now stop already" — at least that's how I read it.

After that, his eyes go vague again and he leaves his hand limp in mine, but I'm certain I detect more activity behind the zombie mask, the beginnings of speculations, ideas, as he allows himself to believe that there may, just may be a way out after all.

I've been so caught up in this exchange that I barely registered the change in dynamics a few feet away from me: at some point Veronica stopped talking and Senhor Antônio took over. Now they're silent, watching Bruno and me, Veronica with a dazed expression on her face and Senhor Antônio with the most tender smile imaginable. I almost let go of Bruno's hand but manage not to. If she doesn't care enough to comfort him, why shouldn't I?

Next thing I know, Senhor Antônio is coming over to us, moving in hypnotic slow motion, as if he were a cat about to pounce on a bird. He stops, hunched toward Bruno and me, hands on his knees, face a few inches away from ours. Clearly he wants to say something, but he's shivering — whatever it is is so big, so tremendous that he can't quite get it out. Despite this inner struggle he's kept his smile, which is wiggling this way and that; the pure delight it emanates washes over me like a warm liquid. I really don't mind having to wait for whatever he has to say.

Finally it bursts from him: *"Vocês são os meus pais!"* He kneels down and reaches out to enclose Bruno and me in a wide embrace — our legs, that is. He rests his head somewhat awkwardly on the edge of the sofa between us.

I look to Veronica for help. I didn't understand what he said — this time he spoke all in a rush. I got the words "vocês são," which is the plural "you are," and "pai" I know means father, but what . . . ?

Veronica is still wearing her bemused frown. "He says you're his parents."

I stare down at the gray-white head nestled against my thigh. For a moment I don't know what to say. Then I ask Veronica in sign language if the man is crazy, making circles with my index finger near my temple. She shakes her head no.

"Well then," I say out loud, "can you explain this to me?"

"I told him about our past life," she says. She speaks slowly, as if she's not only reconstructing the exchange but also evaluating its significance. "The one you saw a part of, with us in the house. I told him everything I knew about those characters. He kept asking me more and more. I told him what you saw, and something of the history leading up to that, and the little I knew about what followed it. He's convinced that in that life you and Bruno were married, except your names were Zar and Florian. The two of you had a son named Ara, and that's who he was. Or is, I'm not quite sure how he sees it. And I was a kind of stepmother to him."

My son? Amazing! I flash back to the Outernet session in which I saw the three adults in the old man's house and the child who was with them. I only beheld the boy for a few instants, but it was enough to provoke a strong feeling of warmth toward him, of longing. Now I understand that Senhor Antônio embodies the qualities that emanated from the boy: kindness, candor, generosity. I feel a deep sense of gratitude that life has allowed me to reconnect with someone so dear to me, someone whose absence lay at my core, without my knowing it. My child! At the same time, the irony of the situation is not lost on me: for so many years I've wanted to conceive but have held back, not sure whether I'd be able to take care of a child properly, not sure whether it's fair to bring another soul into such a troubled world. And now here's one claiming me as a mother: fully grown, able to take care of himself!

I laugh, more like a snort; Senhor Antônio gazes up at me questioningly. In response, without the slightest premeditation, I lift my free hand and begin to stroke the top of his head, ever so lightly. His hair is fine — ruffled, like feathers. He closes his eyes, submitting to my caress, but then opens them again and releases us, rocking back to sit on his heels. My gesture has reassured him. He doesn't make eye contact now: he understands that this is a lot to digest for me, for us; that it may take time to weigh the information, to decide whether we believe it or not.

I look over at Bruno. He seems to be present, though I can't tell what he's thinking, whether he got the whole Senhor Antônio story; in any case it's a relief to see him looking more like his normal self. He clears his throat, addresses Senhor Antônio: "*Vamos lá?*"

Senhor Antônio beams, nods.

Veronica asks me: "Are you ready to go?"

"Yes," I reply. "I just have to get my stuff from upstairs."

"And we need to say goodbye to Ruth and Eliane. Bruno, you stay here, Okay? We'll be right back."

As I follow Veronica into the house, Senhor Antônio settles himself next to Bruno in a companionable silence.

It takes us a while to get out of there, in the end: first we tidy up the rooms we've slept in, then the farewells with our hostesses drag on — they insist on rummaging through their fridge and cupboards to load us up with snacks for our trip back and various canned and dry goods to prepare once we arrive. The two women follow us out onto the porch to say goodbye to Bruno and Senhor Antônio; night has already fallen. After another round of effusive thanks and hugs, we're off.

The drive back is long. I didn't realize how far we'd come; I guess I must've slept pretty much the whole way there. Most of the time we stay on a major road, a highway parallel to the coast: even though there's just a sliver of moon you can see the palm trees lining the distant shore, and the dark band of the sea. We're driving with the windows rolled down, buffeted by warm wind. We don't talk.

At one point I hear the roar of an airplane and look up to see the soaring dots of red light. I imagine my ride to Miami, the bright cabin, the tiny bubbles in the plastic cups of cola. After that, I pretty much stop thinking and just pay attention to details of the landscape rushing by.

Gradually the city rises up around us until we're in the thick of it. Then we turn off the main road and go down one small side street after another until finally Senhor Antônio stops the car in front of his house. I'm happy at the prospect of a bed, a few hours of oblivion, happy that we'll be staying with Senhor Antônio. I feel comfortable with him, safe.

The house is small. The floor area is about the size of Ruth and Eliane's kitchen: there's a living room, bathroom and small spare room on the first floor and a low-ceilinged bedroom cum study upstairs. On the wall of the tiny staircase hangs a framed black-and-white photograph of Senhor Antônio as a younger man in a white coat shaking the hand of someone who must've been famous. A corridor lined with kitchen appliances leads to a sort of yard, in the middle of which stands an old tree. In one corner of the yard there's a shower and in another a plastic table and chairs. The tour lasts all of two minutes.

After that, we all sit around the table sharing the food we brought back. There's no visible moon and we can barely see what's on our plates; we pass the items to one another with great caution. Senhor Antônio is a lively host, curious about everything: what each of us is eating, how we like it, what other foods we like, and so forth. Sometimes he laughs at his own enthusiasm; the rest of us laugh with him. Bruno and Veronica seem more relaxed, which fills me with unexpected optimism: there's an ordeal ahead of them, to be sure, but they'll get through it, they have to. My help will be invaluable; they don't yet know what a staunch supporter they have in me, but I'll show them.

The meal is coming to an end. Fatigue settles over us but I imagine the others share my reluctance to go inside: after we've spent so long in the soft night air, the small house will be stuffy, the electric light harsh. I'm resting my elbows on the table and my head on one hand, thinking about what I have to do tomorrow — deal with the passport issue, change hotels — when a shift in tone draws my attention back to the conversation.

"*Me diga por que não pode,*" Senhor Antônio is demanding of Bruno. I have consistently been able to understand his Portuguese better than any I've heard to date; I'm not sure whether the precise enunciation alone is responsible for this. He wants to know why Bruno "can't" — can't what? My guess is he's talking about the Outernet. Bruno starts to shrug and shake his head but Senhor Antônio is insistent: "*Você tem medo de que?*" — "What are you afraid of?"

The question cuts short Bruno's pantomime of ignorance. He stares at the older man in shock.

Senhor Antônio leans back, visibly pleased by the reaction. "*Eu te conheço,*" he says — "I know you" — and leaves a pause for his words to sink in. That business about being our son: that must be what he means. I think it's true; though my cynical mind is quick to put forth objections, the affection he elicits from me, as well as his obvious purity of character, allow me to believe the outlandish hypothesis.

I listen with great interest as he launches into a sort of character sketch of Bruno that is supposedly based on this past-life coexistence. I don't really know Bruno well enough to be able to judge how accurate the evaluation is: the level of detail is remarkable, and it's all coherent; I just wonder, as one always does in the case of psychic readings and fortune-tellings, whether the portrait was merely pieced together from a combination of nonverbal signals, casually dropped remarks, and circumstantial evidence or even telepathic information.

According to Senhor Antônio, what Bruno fears most of all is losing his individuality. On some deep level, the Outernet terrifies him, being an amorphous environment in which consciousness is seen to be permeable: it's extremely threatening to his sense of self. Surprising, Senhor Antônio points out, since Bruno does have an exceptional ability to merge with others on a sensual level. (Was the old man peeping through our keyhole last night? I suppose not.) But because Bruno believes that the flesh is of lesser value than the spirit, he downplays the importance of physical interactions. If his *mind* were to merge with those of others, however, then he, as he defines himself, would cease to exist — and *that* is the unconscious belief that makes it hard for him to access the Outernet.

Senhor Antônio spreads both his hands palms upward, as if to say, "There you have it." Bruno is impressed; Veronica, too. They both spend a few seconds nodding silently, like dashboard dogs.

"But how do you know this?" Bruno asks.

Senhor Antônio repeats, with a certain amount of bashful hemming and hawing, his certainty that Bruno and I were his mother and father in a past life. He explains that in that life, Bruno was in the unusual position of loving and living with two women at the same time: Veronica, who went by the name of Emily, and myself. The situation was harder for him to deal with, ironically, than for us, challenging as it did his convictions about the nature of intimacy and jealousy. He had just been getting accustomed to this new perspective, however, when something put it to a severe test: he came across what he thought was evidence that Veronica and I had been secretly conducting an intimate relationship. This, he was unable to accept. His belief in the impossibility of loving two people at the same time turned out to be so deeply ingrained that losing that belief would have meant losing himself. Bruno didn't know all this consciously, didn't think along these lines, but he instinctively withdrew and isolated himself completely. Ultimately, his isolation was fruitful, setting him off on a journey that lasted the rest of his life, a journey of self-exploration and investigation of natural and spiritual forces; yet he never again, so long as he lived, considered studying the mysteries that arise between two human souls. After his initial shock wore off, he inched out of his shell and could be amiable, even gregarious — but only up to a point. He continued to live in the same house as his wife — me — for most of his remaining years, and was as good a parent as he could be, while keeping a part of himself permanently inaccessible.

Here Senhor Antônio stops: it appears the story is over. He looks from one face to the next, apparently surprised that we're staring at him, waiting for more. He upturns his palms again with a rueful smile.

The three of us snap out of our state of suspended animation at the same moment, all talking at once. Bruno doesn't understand how the knowledge of who he was in a past life can help him now. Veronica wants to know what happened to her, Emily. And since Senhor Antônio is an Espiritist, I ask what his views are on life after death. Or rather, life after life.

Senhor Antônio laughs at the sudden babble of our three voices. "*Já é tarde; amanhã preciso trabalhar,*" he says: it's late, tomorrow he has to work. He's already told us that he makes the rounds every day at the clinic he founded, though he's long been officially retired. *"Mas vou tentar responder às suas perguntas"* — but he'll try to answer our questions. It seems he's registered them all, even though we were talking simultaneously.

Covering my hand with one of his and gazing earnestly into my eyes, he explains that after we die our spirits neither vanish nor lose their individuality. They do merge into a greater whole, but only in the sense of returning to the community of their fellows. The period between lives allows the spirit to mull over the lessons it has learned, to evaluate its successes and failures and plan its next incarnation, determining which circumstances will further its growth. The point of reincarnation is, in fact, for the spirit to be able to better itself: it may evolve or stagnate, but it will never regress. According to the Espiritists, planet Earth is just one of many worlds in which one may incarnate, different worlds being conducive to different types of learning experiences.

"But how do you know this?" I can't help asking.

Senhor Antônio replies, without hesitation, that all these facts have been made known by the spirits themselves, speaking through human mediums; the seminal work of Espiritismo is a transcription of question-and-answer sessions with disembodied spirits. Unfortunately, we don't really have time to go into it further, he concludes, but if I'm interested, he'll be glad to suggest some titles for me. Do I read Portuguese? Not so well? No matter, the most important books have been translated into many languages. With an apologetic smile, he pats my hand and turns his chair slightly to face Bruno.

In his past life as Florian, the elder man explains, Bruno was confronted with one of the greatest challenges that exist: that of overcoming a strong personal belief. Spirits are often given this kind of challenge, Senhor Antônio elaborates, so that they may experience the difference between their thoughts and their true nature: most people are so heavily identified with their ideas — the bulk of these received from

341

others — that they have but the weakest idea of who or what they really are. Florian was struggling with the illusion of separateness, a construct that underlies much of human suffering. Spiritual development demands that every soul succeed in dismantling this pernicious illusion, and it usually takes many lifetimes to accomplish; Florian did cover some ground, in that his experience living with Zar and Emily destroyed many of his assumptions about the human capacity to love and share. In the end, however, his convictions were stronger than he: they forced him to isolate himself rather than amputate what felt like an integral part of himself: his belief.

Now Bruno is here to take up where Florian left off. And it seems that success is even more critical in his case, since his physical survival may now depend on his willingness to open himself up and experience interconnection with all beings.

Senhor Antônio pauses. He looks tired. The faint moonlight carves deep shadows under his eyes and hollows out his cheeks, evoking the skull beneath the papery skin.

On an impulse I address the other two, in English. "Let's let him get to bed, shall we?" They're startled at my intrusion. Bruno's expression says it's a reasonable request, while Veronica looks sour: she wants to hear more about *her* past life.

Senhor Antônio speaks up, surprising us all. "You would still treat me as a small boy!" His English pushes its way through a heavy German accent; he laughs at our startled faces. "My mother was German, and I have learned most of my English when I was in the medical school in Germany. But you are American?" He smiles at me. "I knew that you were not from here, but you speak very well Portuguese!"

"Thank you," I manage, smarting from embarrassment: what arrogance to assume he wouldn't understand English!

He frowns briefly and shakes his head, smiling all the while, as if to tell me not to worry about it — or is he saying he's surprised at my uncouthness? "Perhaps you are right," he continues. "Perhaps an old man must go to bed. But you will be my guests, yes? For as long as you wish? Then we will have much time to talk. *Vamos.*" He stands up stiffly.

We gather up the remains of the meal as best we can and put everything away in accordance with his instructions. Then we follow him into the living room. It is indeed hot and stuffy inside, but I'm sure I'll drop asleep within minutes and won't regain consciousness until morning. He gives us a few thin, worn-looking mattresses, a double and a single, to spread on the floor. A couple of pillows and a couple of sheets, and after fond good nights all around our host takes himself off to his quarters upstairs.

Veronica and Bruno and I wait, sitting on the mattresses, listening to the floorboards overhead creaking; then silence reigns. I've realized I can't expect to go to sleep immediately, after all: there's too much to think about. The Espiritist tangent was fascinating, but Bruno's problem remains. I wonder if Bruno and Veronica have any idea how much it preoccupies me: they don't know I've pledged myself to their cause. A few times I almost blurt out my intentions but can't decide on the best phrasing, so I decide to wait until a natural lead-in comes up.

Bruno is first to speak, voicing the question on all of our minds: "How am I going to do this?"

Good for him: he still has hope. Veronica just shakes her head.

"I have an idea!" I exclaim, surprising even myself: the having and the announcing of the thought happened almost in the same instant. "We'll take you there. Veronica and I will bring you."

They both look at me as though I'm crazy.

"You can't *bring* someone onto the Outernet," Veronica scoffs — like: "Didn't you understand *anything*?" She elaborates, with as much patience as she can summon up: "If that were possible, we wouldn't have had to spend so much time helping people figure out what method will work for them individually."

"Yes, but maybe in Bruno's case what will work is having someone bring him!" I'm undaunted by her scorn, excited by my insight. "That may be exactly what he needs!"

"Okay, how?" She folds her arms, cocks her head to one side.

Bruno is staring at me. He's got that look people have when they're trying to recapture a thought that has wafted through their minds and disappeared.

"Well, he has to be sure he wants to, that's the first step. I mean, *really* wants to. Wants to enough so that it overpowers the not-wanting to, the fear, the resistance Senhor Antônio was talking about."

"Do you think that now that my life is in danger I will be motivated enough to overcome those things?" Bruno asks.

"What do *you* think?" I retort.

He nods.

"Sure, you're more motivated — that will help a lot. The next step is for the three of us to synchronize ourselves so that when Veronica and I are ready to go, we kind of, well, bring you along."

Veronica's squint of disbelief corrugates her face most unattractively. "Synchronize?"

"Let us do it." Bruno stands up decisively. He sits down again. "How do we start?"

To tell the truth, I'm not too sure how it should all go, but if I stop to think I'm afraid the current of inspiration might beach me, so I just say the first thing that comes into my head: "Both of you come over here."

They obey.

"Lie down" is my next instruction: our bodies need to be as relaxed as possible. I feign confidence in issuing the commands: this is crucial in order to ensure *their* confidence in me. Skepticism and suspicion are the equivalents of friction on the physical plane: they'll create a drag, make my job harder. Because, although I've said that Veronica and I are going to bring Bruno to the Outernet, I suspect I'm the one who will be doing most of the work. "Try to relax," I say.

The two of them are stretched out stiffly side-by-side; at my suggestion they soften up a little, rearrange their limbs. Now I have to lie down on Bruno's other side.

This is far more difficult than it sounds. Up until now I've shied away from making physical contact with Bruno when Veronica's been around. The few times she came across us together were pretty uncomfortable; I would have avoided them if I'd been able to. The only time I actually reached out to him in her presence was when I took his hand on Ruth and Eliane's front porch, and that was only because he seemed desperately in need of comfort. My challenge now is to snuggle up to him with her watching me: the idea of touching Bruno in the chill of her blank gaze makes me feel sick. It's a fear that grips my innards and squeezes but I can't back down, I have to forge ahead, along the path my instinct is leading me step by step. The fear, I know, is not instinct: it's a conditioned response built on notions of possession, proper conduct, punishment, revenge. Backwash from Moses and newspaper articles about jealous husbands blasting their rivals with sawed-off shotguns. Or jealous wives.

It can't be helped. To insulate myself from her stare, I say: "Bruno, lie on your side. Veronica, can you kind of scoot up to him, as close as you can? There. Put your arms around him — that's good."

They're in each other's arms now, and as I fit myself against his back, at least her eyes are not on what I'm doing even if her mind is. Attraction surges between Bruno's body and mine but we struggle to curb it — this is as difficult as keeping opposite poles of two magnets in proximity without letting them join.

"It's hard, I know," I murmur, deliberately leaving the words open to multiple interpretations. Then I realize I'm going to have to let go, let my body merge with his. Drawing back takes too much energy, too much attention; the main thing is not to get swept up in the sensations, to just notice them while keeping my mind alert for the next part of the process.

It takes just an instant to slip my etheric body inside of Bruno's and receive his inside of me. As soon as we interpenetrate, I realize that Veronica's energy is already enmeshed with his: it's disconcerting, like stepping into a supposedly unoccupied room and finding someone there. She perceives me, too, I can tell; there's a reaction: I think of the soft antennae of snails bumping and retreating and bumping together once more. But is she truly conscious of what she's feeling? That's the important question.

Although I grew up with the irrefutable evidence of telepathy, I was determined to extract myself from its sphere and thus never deliberately used it. The Outernet was the first place I had the experience of "talking" in my head and being clearly understood; if Veronica is receptive, it will make everything much easier. I put out the first question that occurs to me, dumb though it is: "Are you there?"

A quiver of surprise, then a second later comes Veronica's reply, a faint but distinct assent. Bruno's response is more along the lines of snail antennae talk: no sense that he's registered my question as such, just that he's felt a kind of movement in the plasma of our commingling. Too bad, I think. It would be much easier if he were also tuned in — but I suppose the whole problem lies in his refusal to fully accept this plane of reality.

Tuned in . . . the phrase catches at me. Maybe that's how we do it. Not through words. Exhortations to trust, to surrender, must be conveyed in a language like music, though the substance shaped will not be air but the elusive fluid of consciousness. Physics. The more powerful of two vibrations will bring the weaker one into synchrony with itself, if they are similar enough in frequency. It's how the opera singer shatters the glass, how wind can cause a bridge to collapse. It's how, I think, I can gather Bruno up with me and transport him wherever I go. It's worth a try.

I still don't know how exactly to do this, though; I'll have to feel my way into it. And Veronica? She's smart enough; if she can't tag along she'll get there by herself. It's important to have her physical body right up against Bruno's, as a comfort for him, a base. I'm the one who'll take care of the actual journey.

Within a few seconds I've explained my intentions to Veronica — not out loud, and not exactly verbally. Telepathy allows for the transference of ideas that would slip through a net of words: it's extremely practical that way. To know what one means is enough: it gets communicated to the other person. Phrasing, nuance, interpretation: none of these affect the message. Veronica gets it and conveys that she'll stand by and see how I do. She'll help if she can. And she wishes us good luck.

What comes next I can't describe, not even to myself. I've never done anything like this before and don't know how I'm doing it. Something is guiding me — whether it's outside or inside myself I can't tell. Another form of consciousness takes over. All I can say is that a series of intricate alchemical manipulations results in Bruno being bound to me as one molecule binds to another. At a certain moment I understand that this has been accomplished and it's time for the next step, getting us to the Outernet. I know from my last trip that I don't have to go through the whole process of finding an external frequency to use as a point of departure: my psychic abilities are limbered up and it's enough now for me to feel my way directly to the sensations that precede the ascent.

Zoom. We're off — and the next second we're there.

I'm looking at the now familiar Home Page, but with the

difference that my perception is slightly modified, my vision heavy. It is, I realize, because of Bruno being mixed in with me. During the process of transubstantiation I was barely aware of his conscious self — it wasn't relevant. Now I wonder how we're to sort ourselves back out again. It will be necessary for us to come apart in order for him to function in this dimension. And besides, this state of things is quite unpleasant: this heaviness, this confusion muffling my senses. I realize I don't know how to get a grip on it, to pry it off, peel it away. A panic starts to come over me, and then I become aware that a voice is trying to get my attention. Veronica.

"Relax," she says. The telepathic medium allows her to convey, with the one word, that I need to calm down in order to get out of my predicament, and that it's ironic that I was the one exhorting people to relax a few minutes ago. The slightly humorous aspect of this helps me loosen up; the loosening, in turn, helps me identify and differentiate myself from Bruno, and now I can start to slip out of the knot we're in. It takes a curious blend of surrender and great concentration, and I'm aware that I've just about done it, when something abruptly stops me short. If I keep going, I sense, I'll plunge into the void: it's as though I need something else to take hold of in order to finally pull myself free of him, something to gain purchase upon — and there's nothing there.

I hesitate, at a loss, not willing to retreat into the sticky mass I've partially emerged from, or give myself up to what feels like annihilation.

Veronica's voice again: "Hold on to me."

I didn't know where she was in this virtual space, but now I detect traces of her in the part of me that's still commingled with Bruno. This makes sense: she had fused with him to some extent before we traveled, but I hadn't needed to take that into account. It's as if I'd picked him up and slung him over my shoulder, without noticing that his stomach was full.

"Hold on," she repeats; I home in on the source of the command. A yank from her side, and I'm separate from Bruno: she's pulled me through him and out, that's my impression, though I can't actually understand any of it. No idea how she managed it, but here I am, unencumbered and grateful. I thank her effusively.

"Bruno will wake up in a moment," she says. "Shall we fashion avatars for ourselves? Just a quick-and-dirty job, but it should make it easier for him to get his bearings."

Her image materializes in front of me, that same marionette-like one with the wry smile.

"How do you do it?" I ask her.

"Same as anything else," she replies. "Intend it."

I'm surprised at how difficult it is to visualize my own face. I end up thinking of my passport photograph, hoping the imprecision of memory will make the result more attractive than the actual photo.

"There you are," Veronica says.

"So wait a minute. Then how could you see me before this? When you found me in the Chat section?"

"There's a generic cut-out shape the Outernet uses to represent people who don't make avatars for themselves. The way I found you, though, wasn't by searching visually, but by wishing to locate *you*, my friend Josephine, the United States academic."

"That's my address on the Outernet, hunh."

"For me it is."

"And now, how can we see Bruno? I'm worried about him. He seemed pretty inert. What happens if he passes out here? Will he wake up there? Or —"

"You want to see him?" Veronica interrupts.

"Yes."

"Then look."

To my right a silhouette takes shape, wavering slightly. A

human shadow, no features or details of any sort on its flat, translucent surface.

"He's coming round," she says. How does she know? Are they still interconnected, then?

"No, we're not," Veronica answers. This territory is tricky to navigate; I suppose one learns, eventually, how to create the desired boundaries between one's thoughts and another's.

"You're right," she says, and this time we share a laugh. "As for being connected to Bruno, I'm not, not in that way anymore. I had to pull away fast, to help you come apart. Do you understand?"

"No."

"It doesn't matter. Anyway, right now I know he's regaining consciousness because I can hear him. Listen." It's amazing how quickly she's turned back into the one in control. For a while I'd been feeling smug to know they were depending on me, but I guess we're back on her territory. After all, she's known about the Outernet a lot longer than I have. "Listen," she said: all I notice is a small trickling somewhere in the background.

"That's him," she says.

"What?"

By way of reply she keeps quiet so I can listen to the trickling: its tinny edges smooth out into silence, an absence of sound that brims, nonetheless, with presence — Bruno's presence. His avatar remains indistinct, the same watery shadow, but the sense of Bruno himself grows more and more defined. Until finally, after about a minute, he addresses us. "Hey, ladies," he says in a gallant attempt at humor; he's tired, you can tell, not quite himself yet.

I send a smile his way, or hope I do: I imagine the sensation of a smile and will my avatar to transmit it. It takes an effort — I can appreciate the usefulness of Veronica's permanent smirk, a good fit with almost everything she says . . . or doesn't.

"Before I forget, Bruno . . ." The smirk suggests that what's coming next might not be entirely pleasant.

"What?"

"I don't know how conscious you were of the process of getting here . . . ," she begins.

"Not very," he admits.

"Well, the last step involved Jo leaping into my arms, figuratively speaking. If it hadn't been for that, you wouldn't be a freestanding consciousness right now."

"Is that what I am? Well, I am glad, but why are you telling me this?"

"I just wanted to make a point."

Bruno takes a moment to think this over and as he does, it occurs to me that her justification is only half true: she also wants to exercise his intellect, bring him into a bit sharper focus.

"Okay, I understand you," he says. "So now what? We are on the Outernet, I imagine, but where exactly?"

"What do you see, Bruno?" I ask.

"I see you — that is, a kind of picture of you, and a picture of Veronica, as though you were both standing in a bowl of soup that someone was stirring, except I cannot see a spoon. There are other things floating in this soup, I do not know what they are."

"A bowl of soup!" I'm shocked. I knew people's perceptions of the physical layout of the Outernet could be different — but *that* different?

"Look more closely at those 'things,' " Veronica instructs. "Tell me what you see."

"Ah . . . like small . . . what would you call them in English — squiggles? Wait. Writing? Yes: writing. One of them — they are going around fast, it is hard to read — one of them . . . Oh! It just stopped! It says 'Groups.' And another one . . . Here we go . . . 'Chat.' Oh, I know, this is that Home Page place, right?"

"I thought you said you'd been here before," I can't help remarking.

"I have," he replied, "but it was confusing. Like walking around with the wrong kind of glasses on, too strong or too weak, changing between the two. Veronica was with me, though; she helped me."

"What are *you* seeing right now, Veronica?" I ask.

"The face of a cliff," she replies promptly, "very high, with a strip of brilliant blue sky above. Staircases are carved into the rock and the entrances to several caves are visible at different heights. Each cave has a pictogram etched just outside its entrance. They used to be regular words, but I changed them to the kind of pictograms the Pueblo people might have used to represent equivalent concepts."

"You created the whole thing?"

"No — it's more or less how it presented itself to me the first time I came, for reasons I won't go into now. I just changed some of the details. You can change yours, too, you know."

I glance over my lackluster purple backdrop with the six squares arranged in a neat grid, glad that neither of them can see it. "I might do that," I say.

"What will happen now?" Bruno interjects anxiously.

"Happen?" Veronica answers. "There are a couple of things that could happen. We could get in on a resistance strategy session, or see if we can obtain any information that could help you log on by yourself."

Bruno hesitates. "Maybe it is best to check on the others first. Is there a way to do that quickly?"

"The Chat section might be the quickest," I volunteer. "Instead of reading a whole bunch of stuff, we can just ask what the latest news is."

"Agreed," says Veronica. She turns to Bruno. "You want to go to Chat?"

"I do," he replies, and disappears, whisked away by his

affirmation.

"Let's go," Veronica says.

I find myself contemplating the mosaic of faces, Bruno and Veronica at my side.

"Ask," she commands him.

Bruno is leaning forward, as if trying to make out what is in front of him. "Ask whom? Ask what?"

Veronica makes an impatient noise. "You ask, then, Jo."

Why doesn't she do it herself? I hope she doesn't pick up on my peevishness: the situation is urgent; maturity is called for. Focusing on the mosaic, I say: "Please tell us what the most current plans are for resistance to Top Five, and how we can help."

The shuffling goes on longer than usual. Finally the smooth voice states: "There is at present no agreed-upon plan for resistance to Top Five rule."

I feel as if I'd been jabbed in the pit of the stomach. "What happened to the strike idea?"

Reshuffling. "The strike stratagem was determined to be not viable. The majority of dissidents admitted they would not be capable of adhering to a strike if they and their families were threatened by physical harm, which would undoubtedly be Top Five's first line of recourse."

Veronica and I stare at each other, dismayed; I can tell Bruno feels the same way.

The voice resumes, startling me: "As for the second part of your question: the only way you can assist is by generating a proposal for resistance that will garner the Outernet community's approval by consensus."

What!? Come up with a plan to overthrow a global power that presently controls the sum total of the planet's resources — a plan convincing enough to win unanimous approval? Fat chance.

I turn away, face my companions. "Well?" I ask, hopelessly.

For the first time, Veronica's smirk looks more like a grimace of pain. "No idea," she answers.

Bruno seems confused. "What did they say?"

I'm starting to understand that the blockage that made it so hard for him to log on to the Outernet hasn't been dismantled just because we got him here. He's still resisting the interpenetration that characterizes communication on this plane. He's still controlled by the brainwashing that would have us believe we're independent entities, forced to assert our needs over those of others. This conviction is absorbed by infants along with their mother's milk, rooted in so deeply that it becomes almost impossible to identify, let alone excise. In his incarnation as Florian, Bruno never wanted to let jealousy overcome his better self; now, he would like nothing better than to participate fully in the greatest adventure of the century. What if he could understand — not intellectually but on a deeper, visceral level — that he has nothing to lose by sharing himself completely? What if he and all those others fighting to retain what they consider theirs and theirs alone could see through the illusion and peacefully give up the struggle? Those Top Five magnates, for instance, they must be wealthy men — mostly men, at any rate — living in high style and able to guarantee the same for generations of their descendants. Why isn't that enough for them? Is it because the fear of scarcity subsists well beyond its usefulness? Because of the fundamental belief that humanity consists of individuals in competition? It would never have occurred to me that Bruno and the gloating capitalists could have much in common, but I see now that they share a significant similarity.

I look over at Bruno's avatar, wavering disconsolately as Veronica explains the outcome of the chat session to him. Painful though it is to see how poorly he functions in this environment, the important thing is that we got him here. His resistance was vanquished, at least temporarily — then might it be possible to affect the Top Five contingent in a similar fashion? Of course, there's only one of him and who knows how many of them: that alone makes it seem impossible. And yet, maybe the same principle *could* be brought to bear.

I cast my mind back to our lift-off from Senhor Antônio's living room. It all started with the idea of entrainment, of forcing Bruno's brain waves to synch up with ones that would carry him in the desired direction. If we could use the same technique to literally change the minds of those in charge of Top Five, would that do the trick?

"Bruno! Veronica!" They appear astonished by the urgency of my tone. "What if . . ." I hesitate. It's just a hunch, I have no idea how we'd do it — but then again, that's how it started with Bruno. I'm afraid of their reactions: my spark of excitement could easily be snuffed by pessimism.

On impulse, I turn back toward the dormant Chat mosaic. "I have an idea!" I state. "For resisting Top Five. At least . . . the beginning of an idea. How does this work? Do I tell you all now?"

The squares go into motion. I can sense Veronica and Bruno gaping at me. "Your idea must be presented in the appropriate forum," replies the voice. "Go to the Groups section and address the Top Five Resistance Group."

Groups. I remember seeing that icon on my purple field, and immediately I'm standing before it. Veronica and Bruno materialize beside me; it seems like she's half-supporting him, although the weight can't be physical.

"What is it?" she asks, pushing herself up in my face. "What's your big idea? Aren't you going to tell us first?"

I recoil slightly. "No point in wasting time explaining it twice," I say, surprising myself with this improvised bit of logic. I fix my eyes on the square labeled "Groups" and think: "Top Five Resistance Group."

Thwack! I snap into an empty space. More like water than air, it presses softly against one part of my body after another. Just as I'm starting to get the creeps, Veronica and Bruno hurtle in.

"I'm glad to see you!" I exclaim. "This place—"

"Well, have you spoken to it?" Veronica interrupts.

"It?"

She looks up, around. "I think it's waiting."

"Waiting? I was the one who was waiting. And what do you mean, *it*?"

"The group, silly. Since you came looking for it, you're the one who's expected to make the first move." She reaches out a hand, experimentally patting the space. "If you don't, I will."

"Go ahead." I move closer to Bruno, trying to imagine my arm around his shoulders, hoping the sensation communicates itself. "How are you doing?" I ask him. "Are you okay?"

Bruno's thoughts — or voice, I can't really tell which — come out with an effort. "I am tired, Jo. It is wonderful, to be here, but difficult for me. I am almost blind: there are shadows everywhere. My hearing does not work right either. But I *am* glad I can see even some of it, and I am glad" — a smile comes into his voice — "to be with you."

"Hello!" Veronica calls out, staring into the emptiness. "We've come to propose a plan for overthrowing Top Five!"

The answer is immediate: "Welcome!" Unlike the neutral Chat representative, this is a vibrant composite of voices, male and female, widely differing tonalities and accents pressing together to form the single word.

Veronica yanks me away from Bruno and pushes me forward, as if to place me under an imaginary spotlight. "Go ahead!" she says in a stage whisper.

"Uh . . . hello," I begin.

"Hello!" responds the voice in a friendly tone.

I do the best I can to explain my idea, defining "entrainment," talking about the frequencies that allowed me to get to the Outernet initially, and explaining how we got Bruno here through similar means. When I've gone over all of that, I pause, trying to formulate a brilliant conclusion, to suggest some method for using this principle against Top Five — but nothing comes to me. "And so," I wind up, "I thought maybe something like that could work on a larger scale. If Top Five has control of all the food and the firepower and all of that, it seems impossible to fight against them on the material level. But if we could change their minds . . ."

The silence following my words stretches out for ten seconds, twenty, then is shattered by a great, fragmented roar. Veronica cowers; Bruno turns his head this way and that. Only when the noise dies down do I recognize it as the sound of applause. It trails off completely, and the composite voice speaks again.

"Thank you," it says.

How do they *do* that, I wonder: talk all at the same time? Or is it thinking? But why be surprised — there isn't much around here that obeys any of the physical laws I was taught to believe.

"Your idea falls in with some of the suggestions we have already examined," the voice pursues. "But all our research to date has centered around ways to bring members of Top Five onto the Outernet. We hoped that a direct experience of the communal nature of existence would change their perspective, making it incompatible with a greed-based one. But this has not appeared to be possible, at least in significant enough numbers, owing to the basic incompatibility between their mental attitudes and ours."

"So Jo's idea" — Veronica pipes up — "could provide a way to get them all onto the Outernet!"

"No," the voice replies. "The entrainment only worked for her because she was already endowed with the necessary qualities of willingness and psychic aptitude. It functioned to a degree with your friend, here, but not well enough to allow him to be fully present. What Jo's idea has made us realize is that there's a chance of getting at the people we wish to target, not by bringing them here, but by a concerted effort on this plane that will affect each and every one of them, wherever they happen to be."

"But how?" I ask.

"According to the principle you have mentioned, if all of us here synchronize our thought patterns, forming one gigantic tidal brain wave, it could bring countless scattered, weaker brain waves into resonance with it. This is the initial certainty. Already, some of the members of our group, specialists in different areas, have begun studying various possible outcomes of this scenario. In a matter of minutes we may have a proposal that we can test on a limited scale; if the test is successful, we submit the plan to the entire Outernet community. Would you and your friends like to join our group?"

"Yes!" I say. "That is . . ." I realize Veronica has disappeared.

"Where did she go?" Bruno asks, sounding forlorn.

"She joined the group, I think. They invited us. Is that something you'd be up for?"

No answer.

"This has all been a bit much for you, hasn't it?" I say gently. "Would you like to go back to your body now? I would come with you, of course, to make sure — "

Bruno interrupts with a violent "No!" A pause follows, after which he adds, in a subdued tone: "Not . . . that. No."

Veronica pops back out of nowhere. Her features haven't changed, but she radiates excitement and purpose.

"Guess what!" she exclaims, before I can speak. "It's absolutely fantastic! We're going to try something out! They're letting everybody know right now! And it's all because of your idea! Isn't that great?"

"I guess," I answer. I'd like to let it go at that, but of course I can't. "So what is it?"

"There's a Top Five press conference scheduled to start in

about five minutes. Something major, a global simulcast. The biggest chiefs are going to give a briefing. There are twelve of them; they call themselves the First Fraction, isn't that ridiculous? Anyway, they're the figureheads, and they're going to outline the procedures that each country is supposed to implement right away to adhere to Top Five policy. And we're going to get at the First Fraction and knock their conference off course. Isn't it exciting?" She goes on, without waiting for a reply: "And once we see how that goes, we'll be able to tell just how effective the tactic is, and maybe put them out of commission once and for all!"

"Ambitious," I say curtly, though I feel a mounting delight. "So what exactly do we have to do?"

"Well, we can be anywhere on the Outernet," she begins.

I interrupt her. "Then let's get out of here. Something I can't see is nudging my leg and I don't like it."

"Why don't we go back to Home Page? There will be a signal, and we'll all concentrate as hard as we can on shifting the First Fraction's sense of purpose."

"That's it? Those are the only instructions?"

"Essentially. And there will be a kind of feed in from the conference that we can use as a focal point."

"Okay."

"Bruno!" she says sharply. "Are you still there?"

He flickers, sighs.

"All right then. Let's go!"

Back to my purple field with the six little squares. I like it better now, after that other place: it might be dull, but at least it's spacious — nothing pokes at you. Veronica and Bruno are beside me. "Look!" Veronica points. It's a window. Small figures appear to be moving purposefully about on the other side of it; I squint, and the image rushes toward me.

In an auditorium filled to capacity, a phalanx of suited, smooth-faced men and women gazes out over our heads. They hold themselves perfectly still, until one man gets to his feet, stands for a moment with his shoulders thrown back, then calmly makes his way down the aisle. Several rows away, another figure does the same, and then another, until a handful of people, men and women, have collected on a kind of dais at the very bottom edge of the scene. They stand facing the multitude with their backs to us, in a very straight line; there are twelve of them.

"First Fraction," Veronica whispers.

Just then, I'm overcome by a feeling that seems to have nothing to do with the scene I'm witnessing. It's as if a warm liquid were being poured into the top of my head, a glorious sensation that spreads through every inch of me. The glow is so delicious that I just want to bask in it, without troubling about what might have brought it on. But Veronica nudges me, a jab no less painful for being immaterial. "The signal!" she cries. "Concentrate!"

I scramble to gather my wits. Concentrate on what? Surely there must be other instructions! "Veronica, tell me what to do!"

No response. Veronica has already retreated behind the hermetic surface of her avatar. Already the comforting warmth has started to drain from me. There's nothing for it, then — I'll have to improvise.

I close my eyes — that is, I wipe out my visual field and plunge into a mottled twilight. I suspect I can tune in more accurately if I think of the First Fraction folks rather than watch them. I try to put myself in their place, to *feel* the pride so eloquently expressed by their posture. As the select representatives of the most powerful organization on Earth, they're inflated by self-importance. "Me! Me!" they repeat to themselves, silently, ceaselessly, each repetition of the magical pronoun bringing a fresh shiver of delight.

"Mine! Mine!" derives naturally from "Me! Me!" as First Fraction members survey the world from their elevated standpoint. The triumph lies in having wrested something from another's grasp: victory at last. Echoes of a struggle long ago: I hear the cry again, but plaintive now, the pleading of a hopeless child. "Me!" it mewls. "Give it to *me!* Take *me* with you! Love *me!*" The vicious loathing welling up against the chosen. The determined, painful effort to claw one's way into the inner ranks.

I'm so absorbed in these cramped, nasty feelings that it comes as a surprise when I regain consciousness of the wider world. What brought me back? I still can't see anything but the twilight I created as insulation, but I can tell there's something else here now. Something huge. Bearing down on me. No time for thought: it's either plunge straight in or be crushed. I plunge.

Relief: I wasn't annihilated, on the contrary. Now there are a million of me, millions, a billion or more. We rush on, gathering more along the way, still no time to think, nothing but velocity and quantity and a sense of purpose: we're speeding toward a goal. We're going so fast that we reach it in an instant; to my surprise it turns out to be the very thing I had just been contemplating, the worm of hatred twisting in the core of the First Fraction. How could I have traveled so far to reach the place I left only a moment ago? But now I am many, and our purpose is to sway this parasite, which, though tiny in comparison to us, is unimaginably strong. It can't be ripped apart or pulverized. Can it be softened? Would it melt? All we can do is fling ourselves upon it, our vast body enfolding, embracing, caressing the angry filament. And something gives. Something almost imperceptible: outwardly the worm appears the same, defiant, indestructible. But something. Jubilation inundates my boundless self.

"Look! Look!" An intrusion from a different plane: I rise through layers, as if from sleep to wakefulness. Charcoal gray turns to purple: a shapeless lump resolves into Veronica's avatar at my side. "We did it! Look!" She means the conference screen. It takes me a few seconds to understand what I'm seeing. The image's stark lines have broken up: no longer are the dozen chieftains in their rigid pose. Most of them stand slackly, stunned. Two support a third whose legs appear to have given out; a man is sitting on the floor, his face buried in his hands; another staggers toward the onlookers with arms outstretched; a woman faces us, puzzled, searching.

A cloud of sound detaches itself from the scene and floats over: moans, confusion, muffled imprecations. The audience members are pushing into the aisles; someone is trying to gain control of the microphone but their voice gets mangled by bursts of static and the intolerable screech of feedback.

Mercifully, the cloud passes on, leaving silence in its wake; the images jerk fitfully on the screen. Veronica's no longer next to me, I realize, though Bruno is close by; I'm about to address him when she shows up again. "I've just been to check in with the group," she informs us. "The test was a success! Top Five doesn't know what hit them! Everybody saw what happened but no official explanation is being given out — they're going to need at least a couple of minutes to find a spin to put on it. The others in the group are really excited. They're saying we're going to need a few days to study exactly what happened and how we can dismantle the whole thing once and for all, then we'll marshal all the people we can for one huge effort. It can't be done immediately but it has to happen as soon as possible because you can be sure Top Five is going to be working just as hard to try and figure out what happened and prevent it from happening again." She pauses. "Whew! Incredible. And all thanks to you, Jo."

"Oh, come on," I reply. "Millions of people made it happen. But I *am* really glad I could help. So," I say, turning back to Bruno, "are we done here?"

"I do not *want* to go back!" Bruno blurts out.

"Now, Bruno," Veronica chides. "We've had a strenuous couple of days, and while we're here our bodies don't get the kind of sleep they need, even though we're not technically 'conscious.' Next time we come—"

"Next time?" He sounds desperate. "There might not *be* a next time!"

"You got here this time, didn't you?" Veronica's tone is that of an adult trying to make a child see reason. "That's a good sign, isn't it? And it looks like this whole Top Five horror might be over sooner than we thought, so maybe we don't have to worry so much."

"But we cannot be sure of that, and you said it will take them a few days to decide on the next move! Meanwhile, the police are still looking for us, and if we do not give ourselves up tomorrow our friends will pay! And once we are in police custody, we will be separated from Jo, and you and I will be separated for who knows how long, and who knows what they will do to us, and . . ."

He seems to be nearing hysterics, wanting someone to contradict him, to tell him it's just a nightmare and he'll wake up soon, but Veronica and I both know there's no point in offering false comfort.

"Let's just assume we *will* figure out a way for you to log on by yourself," she says.

"I have been trying for so long!" His anguish is almost tangible. "Even if we find an idea, now, tonight, there is no certainty that I will be able to make it work!"

Veronica seems to have no further encouragement to offer. Should I tell them of my plan to remain close by, to start a support organization, to assist in whatever way I can? "You know, I'm going to stay in Salvador," I say. I'm about to add, "just so I can help you out," but I hold back. "I'll come visit you whenever I can. Maybe we can find a way to bring you back to the Outernet even if they keep you in police custody. Who knows? Maybe they'll allow an unsupervised visit; maybe—"

Veronica laughs bitterly. "It seems our friend here still

underestimates the diligence of our worthy law enforcers!"

The jibe hurts. She's left my kindly intentions unacknowledged and chosen to emphasize my ignorance. I'm about to retort, when Bruno suddenly wails:

"Kill me!"

A few seconds of shocked silence, then Veronica chides him. "Don't be ridiculous. We have enough drama as it is. Whatever do you mean?"

"I mean: kill me!" he pleads. "It is clear to me that if you do not do it, they will."

Veronica is impatient. "There's no guarantee of that!"

"And no guarantee to the contrary! I am not being dramatic. There would be nothing dramatic about them killing us. Getting people out of the way is ordinary work for them. You know that. Especially now. So I want *you* to kill me instead. You or Jo."

I feel strangely flattered by his inclusion of me, as if the willing surrender of one's life to another were one of the greatest possible intimacies. Embarrassed by my reaction, I hope fervently that it hasn't been communicated to the other two.

"Let's reconsider our plan, then, shall we?" Veronica offers. "Go into hiding instead of turning ourselves in? They'll probably end up going after our friends no matter what we do. Maybe we take a bus back out of the city tonight; by tomorrow we could be in Fortaleza, then we make our way up to Guyana—"

"Absolutely not!" Bruno replies, horrified. His voice is thick with disgust. "How can you say this now? Of course some of our friends will be targeted, but the violence directed at them will be much more severe if you and I are on the loose. There is no doubt about that, no doubt at all. If you want to go back on your word, if you want to run away, go ahead!"

Veronica's manner becomes gentler. "Come on, Bru," she

says. "Don't be silly. The three of us are going to look around here, see what we can find out to help you log on by yourself, and then we'll go back and get the best sleep we can on Senhor Antônio's flea-ridden mattresses. In the morning you'll feel better, you will."

"I will *not!*" Bruno's anger seems to be giving him a newfound strength. "In the morning I want to be dead. If you cannot do this for me, Veronica, Jo will. Right, Jo?"

This is preposterous. I'm speechless.

"I have thought it through," he continues. "This is not an emotional decision."

"But look at you, you're so upset," Veronica protests. "Why don't we wait and see how you feel after—"

"I am upset because I cannot do this on my own, and if you refuse to help me I am lost! It has to be done now, so I know I will stay here even if my body dies! There is no way to be certain I can ever get back once I leave!"

I remember the analogy between the Outernet and cryogenics. "Are you really sure you stay conscious here if your body is dead?"

"Jo," he replies, "I think it is true, that is all I can say. From the people I have spoken to and everything I have heard. And frankly, even if it is not true, there is a lot of evidence for continuity of the spirit in one form or another. I only want to play it safe. I am as far from irrational as one can be, at this moment."

In the silence that follows, I find myself wishing I could be as convinced as he is that death is not the great End to everything. Maybe he's *not* crazy, and it *does* make more sense for him to sever the connection with his physical body while he's still on the Outernet, but can he really expect me to help carry out his decision?

"You're right," states Veronica. "It's the safest thing to do. I'll come with you."

Now Bruno is the one who is taken aback. "Come with

. . . ?"

"Come, or go . . . I'll die too, and then we'll be sure to be together."

"Now wait a minute, you two," I interject, visualizing myself being led off to jail for double homicide. "Are you sure you don't want to think this over? As Veronica suggested, after some sleep . . . if you want, we can most likely come back here in the morning."

"No!" Judging from her tone there's no doubt whatsoever in her mind. "I've just thought of how to do it. You go back and talk to Senhor Antônio. Explain our decision to him. He's a doctor; he'll know what to do. I'm sure he'll help us."

"I'm supposed to wake Senhor Antônio up in the middle of the night and ask him to kill two people he's just met?"

"You could wait until morning, I guess. Go and get some rest yourself — you'll need it."

All of a sudden it overcomes me: total exhaustion. Not of the body but of the mind, the soul perhaps. This has all been too much. I don't want to argue, I don't even want to think about any of this anymore. The easiest would be to just get out of here, sleep — she's right. Anything else can be figured out afterward. "Okay," I say. "Bye."

Bruno surges toward me. The presence behind his flimsy avatar is much thicker and richer than the one that can be seen — a swirl of thoughts and emotions. Worry is predominant. "You *will* ask him to do it?"

I just want to leave; I can't bear any more discussion. "Bye," I repeat.

A quick getaway is prevented, however, by the irruption of the Outernet Gang, as I've come to think of them. I sigh in exasperation, willing the display to come to an end as soon as possible, but my impatience has no effect on their leisurely approach, their silent laughter and conversation. Resentfully, I watch them shut their eyes; then, anticipating the moment when they'll all roar in unison, I say the word to myself, as if to hasten them along. Surprisingly, my utterance coincides with theirs, and the result is not only a sound but also a powerful sensation, as if I were rushing forward on the crest of a wave, borne up by an incalculable number of loving presences. Warmth floods through me, and exhilaration. Just as the wave is about to fold in on itself, the scene changes and I find myself in the midst of the brightly colored multitude I'm used to watching from a distance. We're sharing in the afterglow of the collective ride: fond farewells are exchanged, people embrace me and I hug them back, hard. These strangers feel like family; only the prospect of a future reunion can attenuate the sorrow of separation. Then they vanish and I'm back with Bruno and Veronica.

Before either of them can speak to me, I put all my energy into visualizing my body with myself in it.

Presto. I'm getting good at this. The half-suffocated sensation of being encased in flesh lets me know I've arrived.

I have a bit of trouble opening my eyes; there seems to be some kind of interference; something's not working right; there's a pressure. A jolt of panic — then I manage to focus one eye and realize that there's a finger stuck in the other. I jerk back and the finger pops out, revealing the surprised face of Senhor Antônio only inches away.

"Ah!" he exclaims. "I was starting to worry!"

He unfolds himself awkwardly from his crouched position, turns a bit, and stoops over Veronica's supine form. Reaching down, he pushes up one of her eyelids to reveal the white beneath; frowns. "But what is wrong with them? This is not *sleep!*"

In the harsh overhead light, dismay seems etched on his face in lines of black ink. Tufts of hair stick up from his head; his skinny torso protrudes from a pair of threadbare pajama pants. I hasten to reassure him. "It's the Outernet, Senhor Antônio: we were all there together and I decided to come back. But they're fine, really they are."

"Strange," he mutters. Then, straightening out once again, he asks: "The ring of the telephone, did you hear?"

"No, not at all."

"No? So unusual, when almost nobody has my number, and they only called and then put down the telephone and called again. So I thought, it must be a wrong number, or maybe a call for one of you, and I came to see if you were awake. At first I thought you all slept, but the breathing was not right, and I became worried." His sudden smile reveals the boy behind the mask of aging flesh. "I am happy that you are all right. It seems a funny thing this Outernet, no? But what is with them? Do they come back now, too?"

He's poised to leave the room, already reassured as to his guests' well-being. I almost let him go: he's clearly worn out; so am I. Yet the very difficulty of what I have to tell him compels me to get it over with: I let the words spill out before I can change my mind. "They don't want to come back, Senhor Antônio," I say. "They're afraid of what might happen to them here. They asked me to ask you to . . . to help them stay there. If you could find a way."

"I am sorry?" He frowns, at a loss. "To help them? I would help when I could, but how?"

There's nothing for it. "If you could help them die. They said only their bodies would die but their minds, or . . . or whatever, will stay on the Outernet."

Senhor Antônio's eyes go wide at this. While he takes it in, I think how glad I am to have delivered the message; now we can both shake our heads over it and then go on to sleep.

But I've misjudged the man. His expression has turned vague, his lower lip is pulled up into a thoughtful pout; he nods his head very slowly and solemnly, up and down, up and down, as if ticking off items on a list with each nod. "It can be done, yes," he finally decrees. Returning his attention to me, he takes note of my silent distress and gives me a compassionate smile. "Do not have any fear. They will not feel a thing."

"But . . ." I can't help voicing some form of protest — this is all so sudden and bizarre. I'm not sure what exactly to say: it's the whole thing that seems fundamentally preposterous. All of a sudden I wonder whether Senhor Antônio is really trustworthy — might he not be a government pawn, introduced in order to win our confidence, knowing somehow that things would develop along these lines, primed to deliver the fatal injection?

Something of what I'm thinking must be evident on my face; certainly the man can tell I'm not convinced. He frowns slightly and asks: "Are you very sure that your friends wanted to do this?"

"Yes — well, I'm sure Bruno did . . . and Veronica *said* she did . . ."

"She seemed to me a very determined lady, and if she said something so serious as that, I would believe it. What troubles you, then?" He doesn't wait for my reply and pursues: "I know, I know. To die — how do you say it? Death?" He overemphasizes the unaccustomed *th* sound, thrusting the tip of his tongue through his teeth. "Death is an idea what frightens most people. But really, really it should not. And this you must know, because you and your friends have the excellent fortune of getting to this place, Outernet, that shows to you your life before. I would be very interested to see this myself. This information what you have, it is something what in most cases people receive only *after* death; for this reason you are lucky you benefit from it while you are still living. And this of course is why your friends have no fear to take such a step. It seems so . . . so radical, but really only speeds up a little bit the process."

I can't share Senhor Antônio's faith, but I'm too tired to counter it with my reasonable skepticism. This whole thing has gotten way out of hand and it seems to me I have only two options: to refuse to have anything more to do with it all, or to go along with my friends' wishes, no matter what I may think of them.

I ponder this choice while Senhor Antônio awaits my response, leaning forward and gazing at me with kindly concern.

"So . . . what can I do?" I finally ask.

He relaxes his posture, visibly relieved. "I do not know exactly how this must be done: we two can make a plan. The easiest part is taking away the life; it is more difficult to handle the bodies so we have no trouble with the police."

I think it over. "But the police have to know that they're dead, otherwise they'll keep looking for them and arresting their friends and so forth."

"Aha, I see," Senhor Antônio says, and considers this for a moment. "So we must deliver the bodies to them."

"And yet," I reflect, "maybe other people need to know, too. In case the police pretend they *haven't* found them and continue to use that as an excuse to harass others."

"Very good thinking, young lady! I understand already why the universe puts us together in this mission. You have the quick thinking, I have the experience. I could not do it alone, and you also could not. So now, let us see. The police are already looking for these two, yes?"

"Yes."

"And do you know if there is a . . . a warning? In the television, the newspapers?"

"I don't know."

"Unfortunately I do not give as much attention to these things as I should. But let us suppose I make a telephone call to the most important television station, and say that I have found two dead people on my doorstep? Then they would make it public, the police would be notified, and everybody else."

"But why would they appear on your doorstep? Wouldn't you be taken in for questioning? What if there's an autopsy?"

"Ah," Senhor Antônio smiles, "again the quick thinking. But I have no fear of questions from the police. There are times it is convenient to be an old man. Younger men usually think we are quite stupid, so it is easier to fool them. And also, you may not know this, but I am a respected person. Famous, you might say. I have my own clinic what has been operating for many years. My name is already known as an expert who speaks about public health, sometimes on the radio, sometimes on the television, so nobody will be very surprised to hear me say something in connection with this case. And if there is an autopsy, well, it does not matter what has been done if there is no proof who did it."

"You sound very sure of yourself."

"Yes, I am," he nods. "Not in all things, but in this. I know my chemistry. And now, I think, if you wish to sleep, it is better to feel rested before our big task." He shuffles off toward the stairs. "Do you need something? A little water?"

"No, thank you. But — Senhor Antônio?"

"Yes?"

"Uh . . . nothing. Good night."

I had wanted to appeal to him for a bit of comfort, to confide that my alarm persists, despite his reassurance. I wanted to tell him what it was like to be in a strange country, swept up in a fierce tide of events and discoveries I could never have imagined. I would have liked to ask if I could bring my mattress up to his room and sleep on the floor next to him, rather than with the two almost lifeless bodies. But shyness stills my tongue.

He waits a few moments to see if I have anything more to say, then wishes me good night and leaves the room. I lie down and pass out instantly.

Several hours later, Senhor Antônio is shaking my shoulder gently. It feels as if I've just been asleep for a few minutes, but daylight is streaming into the room along with the twittering of a particularly enthusiastic bird.

I sit up groggily and the old man puts a mug of coffee into my hand. "It makes me sorry, I have no milk," he says. "Also, I would like to let you sleep longer, but we must move forward with our project."

I glance at Bruno and Veronica. Their positions haven't changed since they first lay down.

"What are you going to do?"

He reaches into the pocket of his thin blue slacks and produces a hypodermic needle and a rubber cord. I take a hasty gulp of coffee to fortify myself against what's coming, but it scalds my mouth. Half-distracted by the unpleasant texture of burnt skin on my tongue, I watch as Senhor Antônio lowers himself into a crouching position by Bruno's side. He hands me the cord and indicates that I'm to tighten it around Bruno's upper arm. Holding the syringe up to the light, he taps it a few times, then with a physician's deftness inserts the needle.

It seems to be taking my mind some time to catch up with the fact that I'm witnessing actual euthanasia; by the time it's sunk in, Bruno is already reacting to the shot. His body begins to tremble; larger convulsions take hold, the back arcs upward, the hands clench, open, appear to be hunting for something to grab on to.

Senhor Antônio looks over at me apologetically. "I am sorry," he says, "perhaps you did not need to see this. I must now go to prepare the next injection for the lady, but I will be back quickly." He leaves the room.

Thankfully, Bruno's seizures are becoming less violent and his fingers have stopped their crablike searching: the worst seems to be over. A waxy pallor infuses his face. As I settle down next to him I reflect on my feeling of detachment:

I think I'm probably in shock. Recalling elementary-school briefings, I wonder whether I'm supposed to place my feet above the level of my heart, or whether that's only for victims of physical, not emotional shock.

My thoughts are interrupted by movement from an unexpected source: Veronica is stirring. I stare in disbelief as she rolls her head slowly from side to side, stretches her arms above her head, and opens her eyes.

Just then Senhor Antônio returns. Catching sight of Veronica, he stops abruptly; the hand holding the syringe falls to his side. She notices the gesture: her gaze travels to the syringe, back up to his face, over to me, and finally comes to rest on Bruno's twitching body. All three of us watch as the jerky movements diminish in intensity, until finally he is still.

Only then does Senhor Antônio break out of his pose and come forward, kneeling with his ear against Bruno's chest, then checking his pulse. He frowns. "He is alive."

A long, drawn-out, raspy breath issues from Bruno. Is it the death rattle? Senhor Antônio slaps the motionless figure a few times and puts his fingers back on the pulse, leaving them there for a long time. "The metabolism has stabilized," he pronounces at last. He looks extremely worried. Bruno lets out another rattling sigh. "Some kind of a coma. This was not supposed to happen."

Veronica gets to her feet. She swiftly crosses over to where Senhor Antônio is standing and I see him cringe as if expecting her to lash out at him, physically or verbally, for what has happened to her husband. Instead she bends down to retrieve her bag, which she had left on the floor; standing back up, she throws us a cryptic look and disappears through the doorway. We hear her unlatch the front door, close it behind her, and walk quickly down the steps and away.

"Is she going to come back?" I ask after a moment, stupidly.

Senhor Antônio shakes his head slowly. All of a sudden

he looks much older, as though he should be taken out of circulation and forced to stay in bed for the remainder of his days. "I do not think she will be back, but I have fear that she may send the police."

The idea is appalling. "She wouldn't do that!" I exclaim. "I mean, I don't understand why she came back and then left without saying anything, but—"

"That is the problem: we do not understand what she did, so we do not understand what she may do. With even the small possibility that we will be discovered here, we are in great danger."

A stertorous sigh from Bruno punctuates the doctor's pronouncement.

"Do I try to finish the job?" Senhor Antônio continues. "If she testifies against me, this will surely be worse."

"Testifies," I think. "Accomplice to murder." I see the walls of a grim jail cell materialize around me, a bucket in a corner, a jeering cellmate.

"On the other hand, if we let the police take him in this way, we cannot know what may happen. He may one day awake — or not. If he does, we cannot know what brain function he will have."

Senhor Antônio motions for me to sit down on one of the two straight-backed chairs against the wall, and he lets himself down onto the other. The silence is broken only by the intermittent ostinato of an exuberant songbird. I realize my attention is tightly stretched, as though sounds now inaudible could erupt at any moment: a police siren, heavy boots on the front steps, rough voices.

"You could leave now," Senhor Antônio suggests gently, as if reading my thoughts.

Relief fills me at these unexpected words, though I fight against it. "I can't leave you alone like this," I answer reluctantly, hoping he'll contradict me.

"There is nothing you can do to help," he says. "I think it

is right to bring him to the hospital, and suggest to them that they notify the police. Otherwise we have accomplished nothing. What then happens, we will see. When there is any problem, I will take responsibility. When it comes to the worst, and Veronica accuses us, I will insist you did not know anything about it, that you were sleeping."

Now I feel much less threatened, lighter — and thereby stronger and more courageous. "I was planning to stay here in the city," I say. "I thought the two of them would be in jail and I might be able to help, to try to get them out, or at least to visit them. Even if it's only Bruno, I can still do that. I can visit him in the hospital. If he comes out of the coma—"

"I think you should go away, Josephine," Senhor Antônio interrupts. It's the first time he's called me by name. "Go back to your own country. You need to think about yourself."

This takes me by surprise, and is slightly irritating. "I think about myself plenty, Senhor Antônio," I retort. "In this case, I think my duty is to help my friends . . . or friend." I become conscious once more of Bruno's labored breathing: it had lapsed from my attention. My body begins to prickle with anxiety once more. "Shouldn't we be going?" I ask.

But Senhor Antônio is off on another train of thought. "Do not forget I know many things about you," he says. "Maybe not so much about who you are now, but I know who you were, and what I see tells me you have not changed so very much."

"What do you mean?"

"You were my mother, in another life. Even if you do not believe this, for me it is the truth, and I must still think of you as my mother even when you have another face, another history. My mother was a very special person, very unusual. In some ways she was strong, and in other ways she could not insist on what she needed. As a young girl she was lonely, and my father was the first man who could truly appreciate her qualities. But their marriage was a mistake in many ways"

— he laughs — "although of course I cannot complain, since I was a result! But they were very different one from the other, and she stayed very lonely still. She did not know how to get more of what she needed. When my father started a relationship with another woman, my mother reached for a friendship with this woman, but after a time it was clear that the woman . . . how to say it . . . was not interested in the same things as my mother. It may seem strange: although they had a strong bond, they did not have very much in common. And this relationship also damaged my father, so that he became even more distant from my mother than before. So both my parents lived for the rest of their lives in a kind of isolation; they had many interests, they stayed busy, but they never developed close relationships with anyone. They might have continued to grow, to expand, in other circumstances, with other people, but they were not willing to go too far from each other."

"Why not?"

"Afraid. Afraid to cause pain; a kind of loyalty. But also afraid of the unknown, afraid they could not stand on their own."

"That sounds sad. But you see, me — even if I *was* your mother, I'm a very different person now. After all, I've come all the way to Brazil by myself; and in my country I live alone—"

"Because you want to?" Senhor Antônio interrupts.

"No, but—"

"Every new incarnation is chosen," he interrupts again, "to provide opportunities for us to evolve in new ways. You are an adventurous spirit, as my mother was, and you are giving yourself room to grow in the ways your spirit requires. This is the reason why I say to you: go. You do not owe anything to this man. Friendship is beautiful, strong: true connection lasts through many lifetimes, as yours with my father, with my stepmother. As important as these may be, the responsibility to yourself is more important still. And sometimes we receive a test: to choose between what is important and what is *most* important. Often a difficult choice." Senhor Antônio stands up. "Now I think we must leave here," he says. "First, you can help me to lift him into the car. I will bring you where you like — to your hotel, maybe? Then I will take him to the hospital. I am certain that they will allow me to make recommendations for his treatment, and I will be prepared to stand by as long as he is in there. If necessary, I will even be able to attempt again what we have failed to do here. We will stay in touch, you and I. And you, now? Do you have a ticket to go back to your country?"

Before I can answer, his eyes widen in alarm. "Hush!" he commands. My heart leaps to my mouth and I feel the blood pounding in my veins. He cocks his head to one side, listening intently, eyes roaming around the room. I strain to hear whatever he is hearing, but there's nothing. And then I realize. Nothing! The low rasp of Bruno's breathing is gone.

Senhor Antônio hoists himself off the arm of the chair on which he was perched. He hurries to Bruno, hunches over him, and searches for his pulse, while I wait, frozen in place. At last he straightens up and comes toward me, a bit unsteadily, a wistful smile on his face. "He is gone."

The old man opens his arms to me and I let myself fall into them. For a long time I weep on his bony shoulder. Finally, when the violence of grief starts to abate and self-consciousness takes over, I pull back a little against his surprisingly strong embrace, and he releases me.

"Let us go," he says.

I've never seen a dead body up close before and am startled by the swiftness with which it ceases to resemble the living person. This is helpful, as it makes carrying the rubbery corpse more like hefting a strange object than a dear friend. We support it between us, one of its arms around each of our shoulders, the feet dragging against the ground as we maneuver it down the steps and fold it awkwardly into the back seat of Senhor Antônio's car.

Mercifully, no one appears until just after we've accomplished this; then a person turns the corner and comes down the sidewalk toward us. I press myself up against the car, pretending to be fumbling for something in my pocket while shielding the rear window as much as possible, until they're out of sight.

As we drive through the unfamiliar streets, my mind is blank, as though I'd been stunned by a heavy object. The city is waking up, the early-morning traffic just beginning to circulate. After a few minutes Senhor Antônio speaks up: "What is your work, Josephine?"

I'm shocked by the banality of the question; it seems so irrelevant. I'm tempted to simply shrug, but I try to provide a coherent answer.

"My work. Well, I'm a teacher, I suppose. An academic. I came to Salvador to work on a dissertation. Really, I hoped I could publish it as a book. But now I'm not so sure. It's an interesting topic, I'm just not sure it's interesting enough. Given everything I've experienced here, it's started to seem like a very narrow focus. But if I don't keep on with that, then I don't know what I'll do. So I'm confused. At least if I stayed here to help Bruno — and Veronica, if it turns out she needs help — then I'd know I was doing something worthwhile. Otherwise, I don't know. I can't imagine going back, really, to any of it. Not the dissertation, and not the teaching either."

I hadn't even known those were my feelings. They're thoughts that have been nibbling at the edges of my mind over the past few days but I'd never gathered them up and put them all together, contemplated the picture they make. It's startling, and kind of scary, but liberating, too. As I say it I feel how true it is: I can't go back to that.

Senhor Antônio is watching the road, but a small smile

plays on his lips. "It is what I thought, although I knew no details of your past. It was clear to me that you are at a beginning, a new start in life. And I am convinced, this new life will not be what you have described for me, this vision of waiting to be of help, devoting yourself to friends in trouble, even if they are important to you, even if they have been your companions over many lifetimes. No, your task now is to discover what you must do for *your* self, for the parts of you that are still sleeping. You must forget the limits of what you *think* you can do, and discover what you are passionate about, for that is where you must lead your life. And when you find that, I think I am right to say you will end up assisting many people, many more people than one or two here in Salvador."

I have to laugh. "You sound just like a book," I say, "a self-help book."

His puzzled look tells me he's not familiar with the expression. He waits politely for me to explain.

"It's not important," I say. "What's important is that you're right. It means a lot to me that you see all this, because it echoes what I was already guessing, only I didn't quite want to admit it because it's scary."

"The unknown often makes one afraid," Senhor Antônio puts in.

"So I guess I *should* go back home, and figure out what to do next."

"I think this will be easier to do in a place where you have a house or apartment, where you know more people, and speak the language."

"I suppose. I don't know how the political situation will change things, but I do have a place to start out from. And I'll be visiting the Outernet as often as I can."

The streets outside the window are beginning to look familiar: I realize we're only a few blocks away from my hotel. Senhor Antônio and I will soon be parted, perhaps forever. I scramble for something to say, some way to convey

379

how grateful I am to him, how painful it is to leave, my fervent hope things will go well and he'll acquit himself of his final task without incurring suspicion. Instead, a question surfaces, something I'd forgotten in the rush of events of the past twenty-four hours. "What makes you think we all shared the same past life?" I blurt it out then realize how rude it sounded. "I mean: How did you know?"

"There was a *médiun* — how do you say it? Medium? A medium I met through my church, Dona Isolde. She gave messages to people after the church service, messages from family or friends who had disincarnated. She and I became friends, and I had many private sessions with her. She was very generous with her gifts."

"And that's how you found out about that past life? But if we had another life and then disincarnated, or died or whatever, and now are in *this* life, how could we send you messages?"

Senhor Antônio laughs. "*You* did not send me messages. But a spirit came forth, through the intermediary of Isolde, and this spirit acted as a guide for me. He told me many things about my life, my past, things to help me understand my present circumstances. He told me much about the incarnation where you and Bruno were my parents, many details that Veronica confirmed. To tell the truth, I was expecting to meet the three of you one day — almost, I was watching for you. Spirits who have such strong connections usually meet again, even when they play very different roles from the time before."

He pulls over in front of the hotel and stops the engine. We're double-parked; if another car comes from either direction he'll have to move. I become keenly aware once more of the blanket-covered lump in the back seat and the need to ask any further questions as quickly as possible. "What about Veronica, Senhor Antônio? What happened to her in that past life?"

"I do not know. A very fine soul, very brightly burning, like a star. But unstable. What I have seen of her this time shows me, in many ways she has not changed. She disappeared from my parents' lives as quickly as she came, and after that I have no information about her. But she loved them both, I know she did — only she loved herself more." He pauses. "As it should be."

I reach down and pick up my backpack, slip an arm through one of the straps. It's hard to look at him, to say goodbye. I force my eyes to meet his and no sooner have I done so than I feel the tears welling up.

He puts one hand out and touches my face ever so delicately. In that moment, the connection between our eyes is so intense it's almost solid, as though they were linked by transparent tubes. Everything else becomes insubstantial: our faces, our bodies, the interior of the car, the street beyond. What exists between us is indestructible. Circumstances and personalities may shift and rearrange themselves, but this bond, however long it may be obscured, will never vanish.

The impression fades in an instant, but the insight was profoundly reassuring. My sadness has metamorphosed into gratitude. Behind us, a horn honks. Senhor Antônio glances at the rearview mirror.

"What does it all mean?" I ask him.

"That I do not know," he answers. Then he laughs. "Find out, please, and tell me!"

He opens the glove compartment, pulls out a business card, and hands it over. The edges look a little frayed, as if something had gnawed it, but his name, address, and telephone number are legible.

The other car honks again. I slide toward him on the seat and we hug each other tightly.

"Give my warm greetings to Bruno!" he says, as I push open the car door.

I get out and head toward the hotel, the consulate, the

airport. I'll find a flight somehow and make it back to San Francisco, though it won't be the same city: the world I knew before has lost its shape and gained another. It's all inside my head and I'm inside of it, the boundaries blurry and the paths uncertain. There's just one thought that comforts me, and I strive to keep it in mind as I pack my bag, hand in my key, and hail a taxi: I may be setting off for the unknown, but someone there is awaiting me anxiously. Someone strong, dependable, and kind, who wants me as a friend although we don't quite know each other yet: myself.

ABOUT THE AUTHOR

Alisa Clements was born in Detroit, Michigan, and grew up in Paris, France. She received her undergraduate degree in Visual and Environmental studies from Harvard University and her MFA from the Massachusetts College of Art's Studio for Interrelated Media program. Her experiences as a teacher, performer and composer of electronic music and other experimental art forms enter into this first novel, *All at Once*. Currently, Alisa spends much of her time in northeastern Brazil, where she co-founded the nonprofit organization *Diáspora Solidária*. She teaches English and French, practices Capoeira, and studies life in general and her two children in particular.

ACKNOWLEDGMENTS

Heartfelt thanks to all who inspired and encouraged me to write this book, including: Tico Camaleão, the Clements family, Ann Dugan, Laurence Egret, Fabio/Mandingo and the *Quilombo Cecília* crew, Christen Goguen, Joycie Hollingsworth, Molly Hunt, Ochazania Klarich, Charlotte Kraemer, Dave Leggatt, Suzanne Linton, Ian MacKinnon, Pauline Oliveros, Rebecca Ostriker, Harriotte Ranvig, Yá Marlene Rodrigues and the Terreiro Vintém de Prata, Reese Scott, Susan Sheffield, Julia Soyer, Ivan Tcherepnin, Stephen Upjohn, Diana Warwin, Neil Willcox, and Rosemarie and Orian Worden.

Many thanks also for the support of members of the Harvard Fiction Workshop and the invaluable clear-sightedness of proofreader Susannah Noel.

Other novels published by

Harvard Square Editions

The Conjurer's Boy, Michael Raleigh

Gates of Eden, Charles Degelman

Patchwork, Dan Loughry

A Weapon to End War, Jonathan Ross

Spiders and Flies, Scott Adlerberg

Trading Dreams, J. L. Morin

CPSIA information can be obtained at www.ICGtesting.com
Printed in the USA
BVOW081133181112

305848BV00002B/5/P